Coyote's Revenge
DEFENDING AMERICA SERIES
BOOK ONE

VANNETTA CHAPMAN

COYOTE'S REVENGE

Copyright © 2017 by Vannetta Chapman. This title is also available as an e-book and print book. Visit www.vannettachapman.com.

Requests for information should be addressed to:

VannettaChapman (at) gmail (dot) com

Any Internet addresses (websites, blogs, etc.) and telephone numbers in this book are offered as a resource. They are not intended in any way to be or imply an endorsement by the author, nor does the author vouch for the content of these sites and numbers for the life of this book.

ALL RIGHTS RESERVED. No part of this publication may be reproduced, stored in a retrieval system, or transmitted in any form or by any means— electronic, mechanical, photocopy, recording, or any other—except for brief quotations in printed reviews, without the prior permission of the publisher.

Note: This novel is a work of fiction. Names, characters, places, and incidents are either products of the author's imagination or used fictitiously. All characters are fictional, and any similarity to people living or dead is purely coincidental.

Cover design: Ken Raney

Interior design: Caitlin Greer

Printed in the United States of America First printing, 2017
ASIN: B076KQQJBY

❦ Created with Vellum

For Pam and Carol,
Who first introduced me to Glacier

Chapter One

Aiden Lewis stared across the crowded airport waiting area at Gate 14 and considered disobeying a direct order.

He had an international terrorist in his sight.

He had a clean shot.

He had a loaded firearm.

What he didn't have was permission to take the shot.

"Tell me why I'm staring at the number five man on our watch list." Aiden Lewis kept his voice low and his hands at his sides. "How did he get inside the security barrier?"

Someone had screwed up. He would find out who.

"New passport. Coyote's traveling under the name Sergio Mancini." Commander Martin's voice in his earpiece did not ease the knot in Aiden's gut. "No one dropped the ball this time, Lewis. We're lucky the Jeremiah facial recognition program caught him. It's now 93 percent accurate."

Aiden grunted. "It's an operating system, not a person. Who decided to name it after an Old Testament prophet?"

"Operating systems are named alphabetically—like hurricanes," Martin said. "Jeremiah replaced Isaac. You'd do well to

1

respect computers with this level of sophistication. He beat Dexter at chess three out of five games last night."

"He can have my job and the unit's chess board if he'll identify Coyote's handlers. We end this here tonight, with or without Jeremiah's help."

"We're cross-referencing passenger lists with previous flight logs from when Coyote traveled as Ramzi Allawi and Taha Haddad," Martin said.

"Any handlers would be using different aliases as well."

"Jeremiah will scan all identification photos and security tapes. If Coyote is using any of the same people from the last three years, we'll know it."

Aiden had been briefed again on the way to the airport—though he didn't need it. He was aware what was at risk. US Citizenship and Immigration Services (USCIS) would apprehend Coyote this night, but they preferred to capture him alive. As third man to Abu Yassin, he had masterminded five bombings in Europe and South America. Taken alive, he could provide information capable of preventing future carnage.

"He's standing with a Jane Doe. Sending her picture now." Aiden touched a button on the earpiece he wore, simultaneously taking and transmitting the photo. Aiden surveyed the scene as he waited further orders. He passed through Dallas/Fort Worth International Airport often. Tonight rain pelted the long row of windows and lightning split the evening sky.

His heart rate was only slightly accelerated—enough to pump the adrenaline to his extremities should the need arise. He continued to scan the waiting area even as his mind focused completely on the madman standing forty feet across from him.

Coyote shouldered his backpack, picked up the woman's carry-on, and motioned her toward seats near the windows.

"Picture received. Processing now," Martin said. "Records indicate Coyote used a woman accomplice in two of the last five bombings."

"They were both European," Aiden pointed out. "He prefers tall, black hair, and long legs."

Aiden fumed silently and waited for the identification of Jane Doe. She was beautiful, probably in her twenties, with long brown hair, and approximately five and a half feet tall. She looked American. Dressed in casual jeans, a Nike top proclaiming Just Do It, and sneakers that had seen better days, she might have been a college kid at the end of summer break. But college kids didn't usually sit with international terrorists.

"Jeremiah has found no matches for previous handlers in the passenger logs," Martin said.

"And the girl?" Aiden asked.

"Jane Doe does not appear in our database."

"We're not losing him again this time," Aiden swore. He kept both Coyote and the girl in his line of vision as he picked up a copy of the *Wall Street Journal*, walked to the kiosk's counter, and purchased it.

"She might have no connection at all," Martin reasoned.

"That's what we thought in Costa Rica."

"No one would have expected a grandmother."

"Well I should have. Perimeter teams, keep your distance," Aiden said. "Let's make him comfortable. We need him to enter the jetway."

"Perimeter teams are at two and eight and holding their position," Martin confirmed.

Aiden knew this included Servensky and Jones—both men he had worked with before.

"We have men stationed at the cockpit door. Lewis, you'll precede him into the jetway. Dreiser and Jones will follow. We'll clear everyone from the gate area as soon as we have your signal."

"Copy that," Aiden said.

The communications device from USCIS looked like any other wireless set. It allowed Aiden to be in contact with every man on his team simultaneously, as well as those providing surveillance information from headquarters. More technologically advanced than anything on the consumer market, he could speak at a whisper and still be heard by his entire team.

Sensitive electronics weren't an advantage when you wanted to release a string of oaths at maximum volume. Despite his desire to shoot Coyote earlier, Aiden realized he needed him to enter the jetway, and he did not want him dragging an innocent woman in his wake. Taking the man in the middle of the terminal would be a nightmare.

Aiden had also been lead man at LAX and Grand Central Station in Manhattan. Both times Coyote had managed to elude them. He would not allow the man to slip away tonight.

"Stats indicate passenger numbers are down a third," Martin reported.

"Thank God for August thunderstorms," Dreiser said. "We could take him down right here with minimal collateral damage."

Dean Dreiser sat at the bar across from Gate 14. The best point man Aiden had worked with, he always remained calm and cool. Aiden had taken to calling him the Falcon because of his eyesight and his speed. He missed nothing and was a crack shot.

"That will be our backup plan if he balks at the jetway, but I'd rather have him in a confined area," Aiden said.

"It's the jetway or not at all," Martin said.

"You said we wouldn't be overruled by offsite anymore." Aiden fought to keep the whine out of his voice. "Who made that decision?"

"The wise men in Washington," Martin said. "Who else?"

"The men in Washington are fools."

"Nonetheless."

"We are not letting this man walk. If he doesn't enter the jetway, we'll take him here. I zipped fifty-three bodies into bags in Germany. I will not let him escape again."

"You have your orders, Lewis. If you can't follow them, stand down and we'll put in a man who can."

Complete silence filled the comm unit while Aiden struggled for control. As always in Aiden's life, control won. "You heard the boss, Dean. Perimeter teams hold your position." He folded his paper, walked to the gate counter, and offered the airline worker his best smile.

"Good evening, Mr. Lewis." The beautiful redhead couldn't have been over twenty-two. She greeted him by name before looking at the ticket. "I'll need to see your identification."

"You always go by the book, don't you, Ms. Stephens?"

"Rules are rules, Mr. Lewis. Even for our first-class Frequent Flyers."

"I appreciate that, as does the supervisor watching over your shoulder." Aiden gave the man standing toward the back a small wave, then winked at Ms. Stephens. "Let me see where I put my identification."

Aiden pulled out his wallet, thumbed through several credit cards, found his license and handed it across the counter. "Here it is. Not my best photo though."

Ms. Stephens took the license and tapped his information into the computer.

"Doesn't look like a full flight," Aiden said.

"It's lighter than usual. Microsoft had a large group connecting through to Salt Lake, but they pulled out because of the weather." She shook her head, tossing red curls, and handed back his license along with a boarding ticket. "It won't be a problem though. Our pilots are more than used to these Texas thunderstorms."

"If you say it's good to go, I'm going." Aiden smiled as he returned his wallet to his pocket. The role of millionaire playboy came naturally to him, probably because it wasn't much of a role —he'd grown up gnawing on the proverbial silver spoon.

Ms. Stephens blushed slightly and motioned for the next customer.

Picking up his single carry-on, Aiden moved to the far corner of Gate 14. He passed so close to Coyote, he could smell the man's musky aftershave. It took all of Aiden's strength not to reach out and kill the lunatic on the spot. One blow to his larynx and the world would be a better place, but orders were orders. He'd wait until they were in the jetway.

Chapter Two

Madison Hart stared at her carry-on suitcase and wondered again why she'd insisted on packing so much.

"Thank you again for helping me." She shifted the strap of her backpack to her other shoulder and offered her hand to the European gentleman who had rescued her.

He was in his fifties and clean-shaven with olive skin, and he had picked up the bag as if it weighed nothing. Carrying a tweed sports coat and backpack over his other arm, he reminded her of an English professor she'd had.

"It is no problem. It was obvious that you were struggling under its weight." He shook her hand, but released it quickly.

Madison looked toward the windows where the rain continued to fall in sheets. She pushed back the memories of that other flight and tried to smile. "Hopefully it isn't an omen of things to come."

"Do you believe in harbingers?" He looked from her to the windows and back again.

Madison felt his gaze settle on her hand, which continued to shake as she rested it on the top of her suitcase.

"Perhaps you should sit down," he said.

Madison sank into the nearest chair, one where she could keep an eye on the weather.

"Do not worry about the storm. I can assure you it is perfectly safe to travel, or they would cancel our flight."

"The last plane I was on crashed." The confession surprised her. That flight wasn't something she normally spoke of. She looked around to see if anyone else had heard, but folks continued about their business at Gateway 14. No stampede. No panic. She managed not to scream *run for your lives.*

"My name is Sergio Mancini." He sat down beside her, placed his backpack on the floor and his jacket over his pack.

"I'm Madison Hart. I don't know why I told you that."

"It takes courage to fly again after a crash. However, the statistical odds of being on two flights in a row that experience any type of mechanical problem are quite low."

"I had travelled to Peru on vacation. There was a storm like this." The wind rattled against the windows as if to lend credence to her story. "The pilot circled as long as he could, and finally attempted to land on a highway. Thirty-seven people died."

Madison closed her eyes and fought the images that threatened to overwhelm her, struggled to remain in the present. After several deep breaths, she opened her eyes and looked at the stranger sitting next to her. "I couldn't bring myself to fly home. I took a cruise ship back."

"And yet you survived."

"Yes." The word was barely a whisper. "My mother always said I was a survivor."

"Your mother is a very wise woman."

"Was."

Sergio didn't respond to that, and Madison turned her attention to the rain. Around them passengers continued to make their way into the gate area.

"Did she perish in the plane crash?"

Madison pulled her gaze from the storm, though its intensity called to her. Its dark promises somehow mesmerized her. She shook her head, then snapped her chin up a fraction. "No. Cancer. My mother died of cancer. I believe a crash is a more merciful way to go."

Sergio seemed to weigh her words. Finally he inclined his head slightly. "God's ways are not our ways."

"And His love is refining, so Mama said." Madison checked for the silver necklace. It was there, of course, since she never took it off. It had slipped under the neck of her shirt. Still, rubbing the small angel pendant brought her a measure of peace.

"I am only connecting at Salt Lake City," he said. "Is that your final destination?"

"I'll travel on to Montana from there. It seems odd to go west and then back east, but that's the way Delta does it."

She looked out the window at the lightning and rain, and she nearly drowned in the old familiar panic. She could not get a break. First her car had been totaled, then her vice principal had called informing her she had to report to work a week early for training. She'd been left with no option but to fly and buy a car once she reached her new home.

Madison tucked her hair behind her ear, then pulled her book out of her backpack. Sergio reached for his own magazine. As he did, Madison saw him glance at the boarding pass that she had pulled from her book.

Madison looked down at the pass, let her fingers run over the words and the row number. Forty-two. Her mother's age. Perhaps it was a sign—her mother's smile of approval. She still couldn't believe she was moving to Montana. The insurance money had barely been enough to settle their debts and give her mother a decent burial. She couldn't afford the house they'd always rented on her teacher's salary. Then there was the deathbed promise she'd made to look for her father. She didn't care about finding a man she'd never met, even if he was her only living relative. But she had given her word.

"I did not have time to pre-print my boarding ticket." Sergio stood and shouldered his backpack. "It has been a pleasure meeting you. I wish you a safe and prosperous journey to Montana."

"And I wish you the same in Salt Lake. Thank you again for helping me with this." Madison gave the bag a firm kick at the same time thunder shook the windows.

Sergio bowed slightly, then turned and walked toward the ticket counter.

Madison stared after him as he walked away. There had been much in the news about profiling Europeans in airports. Sergio was a prime example of the absurdity of such tactics. The man was a perfect gentleman, and if it weren't for him, she'd still be dragging her overloaded carry-on from the security gate.

Another streak of lightning tore across the sky, revealing a bit of prairie not concreted by airport runways. It was immediately cloaked again in darkness, a blackness so complete it reminded Madison of her mother's eyes. They had seemed so serene those final days, but also distant. As if she had already gone to a place Madison couldn't reach.

Now Madison remained stuck in between. She couldn't follow her mother, but she couldn't find her way back either. She understood it from the outside as a part of the grieving process. From inside it felt like an endless midnight. Staring into the storm, the bleakness seemed a mirror image of her heart.

Chapter Three

Sergio scanned the waiting area as he made his way to the ticket counter. Two USCIS agents stood near the jetway, and the air marshal in the Hawaiian shirt sat near the windows. Then of course there were the usual airport security personnel. Once he switched his seat, he would text their description to Yassin.

As he waited in line, he allowed his mind to slide over the details of Yassin's plan. It was a work of art, as surely as Picasso's *Maisons sur la colline*. Sergio had long ago traded his Spanish heritage for his Muslim faith, but there remained in him an appreciation for the things of his youth. He couldn't help comparing the beauty of their current plan to the near perfect lines of Picasso's early work.

No doubt the Americans' computer program was even now establishing his identity and connecting it to his previous aliases. Choosing to use his real name was one more stroke in the painting they were creating. The agents would no doubt search Ms. Hart's luggage, wasting more precious time. By creating a rapport with her, he would draw less attention to himself. It was important the other passengers expect nothing. He wanted them to remain guileless sheep. All the better when the story was leaked to their media that he had slipped among them—a coyote in their midst. What good had their precious security measures done them? None.

Meanwhile, another trap was being set thirteen-hundred miles to the east. Both were misdirections, but useful in their own way. Misdirection increased fear, and fear reduced conceit. Moving forward in the line, Sergio watched the waiting area continue to fill with families and their unruly children.

Then there were the wealthy businessmen, whose arrogance made his blood boil. The man in the corner was a prime example. With his Armani suit and Ferragamo shoes, his air of superiority did much to fuel Sergio's anger. While his own people suffered in poverty, the hedonistic Americans spent money as if it were of no consequence at all. The cost of the man's briefcase alone could have fed a family for a year in his country, or financed one mission. Sergio smiled at the thought.

In fifty-eight days we will see what is left of their arrogance. When their cities lie in ruin they will no longer smile so smugly nor enjoy their richness with such disregard for the rest of the world.

Perhaps, before the night ended, he would steal the man's briefcase. It would be an easy thing to do while the capitalist pig flirted with the ticket agent or enjoyed the luxuries of first-class. The thought pleased him, as did the memory of Ms. Hart waiting so innocently a few feet away.

"Can I help you?" The ticket agent smiled brightly, her red hair falling immodestly around her shoulders. The provocative scent of her perfume carried across the counter to him.

Sergio handed her his boarding pass and identification. He averted his eyes from her low-cut blouse, praying to Allah for forgiveness as he did so. "I noticed my seat is located next to the emergency exit. I'd rather have a different one if I may."

"No problem at all, Sir." She keyed his information into her computer. "We have several open seats due to the weather. Is there a particular row you would prefer?"

"I'd rather sit toward the back of the plane. Do you have anything in row 42?"

Chapter Four

Aiden stared intently at the *Wall Street Journal*. He hadn't digested a single word from the front page. Every ounce of his being was focused across the gateway, though he forced himself not to look in that direction.

"Coyote has left the ticket counter and is sitting again in the vicinity of Jane Doe," Dean said.

"What did he do at the counter?" Aiden asked.

"Delta authorities have confirmed he changed his boarding ticket," Martin said. "It appears he likes being close to our Jane."

Every hair on the back of Aiden's neck stood up.

There were two possible scenarios, neither of them good. Either she was his accomplice and they were playing it very cool, or she was an innocent he'd picked up for cover. Either situation would complicate matters.

"Background is in on Jane Doe," Martin continued. "Name is Madison Hart, twenty-five years old, born here in Texas. She's flying to Salt Lake, connecting to Kalispell where she has reserved a car to drive to Edgewood. Looks like you're going to have a new neighbor. Hart recently accepted a teaching position in the Edgewood School District."

"If she survives the flight." Aiden rustled the paper loudly as he turned the page. "He's using her for cover. There's something in his backpack he doesn't want noticed."

"Negative," Martin said. "We just reviewed airport security tapes. The backpack is clean of explosives, weapons, or tools."

Martin's news was met with silence.

If Coyote wasn't there to bomb the plane, why was he there?

"She doesn't appear to be in immediate danger," Aiden said.

"I want her boarding delayed. There's a reason he's using her as a distraction."

"There's no better way to avoid detection than place yourself in the company of a lovely woman." Dean's voice teetered between admiration and anger.

"Flight will board in twenty minutes," Martin said. "We're nearly through combing the cabin. Cargo area is clean."

"Any new intel?" Aiden folded the paper and threw it on the seat beside him.

"All reports confirm Coyote plans to leave the country via the Canadian border."

"My gut tells me something else is going on here," Aiden said. "There are less visible ways of traveling to Canada. Why through Dallas? He met someone here, and I think he'll meet someone in Salt Lake. I want double the manpower we currently have scheduled on the ground in Salt Lake."

"Aiden, he'll never make it to Salt Lake," Martin said.

"That's the plan," Aiden muttered, but he knew they were missing something important.

There were many ways Coyote could have moved material through airport screening. He could have bribed a baggage handler or stashed explosives on the plane. Coyote wasn't suicidal. The explosion in Hamburg had occurred after he'd left the plane. Unfortunately, more than two hundred other people hadn't.

Maybe he was playing with them, keeping them on edge. The only certainty was that Coyote had planned every move carefully.

Aiden stood and hazarded a glance across the waiting area just in time to see Madison Hart attempt to pick up her bag.

"We still take him in the jetway," Aiden said. "Let's isolate him from Hart. Martin, pull her ticket. Find something wrong with her luggage. Anything to keep her out of the jetway."

"Copy that. You'll go in first, Lewis. When you signal the pilot, he'll lock the plane door protecting himself and any passengers who have boarded ahead of you. Coyote will board directly after you. No one will be allowed on after he enters the jetway. Dean and Jones will follow and protect the innocents. Hopefully you'll get off a clean shot before anyone's hurt. I'm briefing the pilot now."

Martin clicked off for several seconds, then came back.

"The plane has not been fueled. I repeat. The plane has not been fueled in case any rounds go wild, but let's keep the shots to a minimum."

The call came announcing all first-class passengers to board. Aiden stretched and gratefully moved away from the screaming children he'd had the misfortune of sitting near. Dean remained in position at the bar.

Aiden walked up the ramp and waited until the passenger in front of him had cleared the plane door. He was about to signal the pilot to close the door when Martin broke in.

"Abort operation. I repeat, abort operation. Dean and Jones, do not enter the jetway."

"What's going on?" Aiden asked.

"Lewis, proceed onto the plane. There's been a change in plans."

"But we've got him."

"Claudia's security detail has been breached."

Aiden forced his feet to keep moving, even as his mind tried to process what Martin was saying. "Say again."

"You heard me, Aiden. Keep walking or Coyote's going to bump into you. He should be coming up the jet way now. If he's not allowed to board this plane, Claudia will be killed."

Aiden understood the weight of the First Lady's life rested on his next actions. He somehow managed to smile at the flight attendant, continue into first-class, and find his seat.

The President's wife flatly refused to be called Eagle 2 or Dove or any other name they suggested. Claudia was her middle name and worked fine for her.

"Lewis, are you there?" Martin asked.

"Yes." Aiden sank into the leather seat and busied himself shuffling through his leather satchel as he saw Coyote pass his seat and continue toward the back of the plane.

"We received confirmation the First Lady's security was compromised. Unless Coyote is allowed to board this plane and deplane in Salt Lake, they will kill her."

"That's an unacceptable negotiation." Aiden's throat had gone so dry he could barely push the words out. It was agony to keep his tone normal, to sound like just another businessman connected to a Bluetooth.

"Not our call." Martin brought his voice down a notch with some effort. "No one here likes it either, Aiden. Passengers are continuing to board now, and the flight is currently being fueled."

"You are not going to let him get away again."

"We'll try to follow him, but he pegged two of our men. Dean and Jones are out. He's allowing the air marshal on since people expect that, with the stipulation that he board unarmed. He hasn't tagged you so far."

"Why Salt Lake? What's there? I thought he wanted to cross the Canadian border?"

"We're working it on this end, Aiden."

"What about the girl?"

"Apparently he's using her for cover. She's entering the jetway now. Stand by." Martin clicked off. When he returned Aiden could hear the chaos in the background. "I need you to get the plane to Salt Lake. Your air marshal's name is Stephen Slater. We'll stay with you until transmissions are cut, then you'll be on your own. We were able to pass Slater one of our comm units."

Chapter Five

Madison pulled the carry-on toward the jetway.
It hadn't seemed nearly as heavy when she'd strolled toward the security counter. Stupid bag. What had she been thinking? All she really needed was a few changes of clothes. The rest would arrive via her movers by the weekend.

Madison looked past the other passengers who were ahead of her. Why did her bag have to be checked again? Only three passengers had been pulled out of line to have their bags rechecked. Did she look dangerous?

Rain pelted the windows so heavily she couldn't see the plane. She wiped her hands on her jeans and prayed fervently for the storm to ease. This wasn't Peru. This was Dallas. But her heart had nearly stopped when she'd learned the aircraft was the same—a Boeing 737.

She didn't want to die on an airplane.

Finally her turn came to hand her boarding pass to the ticket agent. She limped down the jetway, pulling the too heavy bag with first her right hand and then her left. As she entered the first-class seating, a passenger stepped into the aisle, blocking her way.

"I'm so sorry. I need to put this with my bag." The cowboy

gave her a winning smile, one he no doubt handed out like candy on Christmas.

She tapped her fingers impatiently against her bag as he turned and opened the overhead bin. His movements were maddeningly slow and deliberate, as if he owned the plane. Madison rested her bag against the seat beside her and watched him. At first she squelched her impatience by enjoying the view. Broad shoulders, tanned skin, good-looking. Without a doubt very rich and self-absorbed.

He was also oblivious. Or maybe he didn't care that he was holding up the entire flight. He removed his Armani jacket, folded it and laid it in the bin. Next he took off the Stetson hat, revealing sandy-blond hair that curled slightly at his neck.

"Not many people wear a cowboy hat with an Armani suit," she said.

Again, the dazzling smile. "We take our western image seriously where I come from."

"We take flight schedules seriously where I come from."

"Sorry," he said.

He brushed up against her as he turned to sit, and Madison felt an electrical jolt course through her.

"I am so sorry. I didn't mean to—" He ran his hand through his hair, messing it up and looking even more cover-boyish in the process.

"No, it's okay, really."

"I've been holding you up though. It was rude of me."

The man looked genuinely embarrassed. Probably a nice guy, just clueless.

"If I could squeeze by."

"Of course, my apologies again."

Forcing down her irritation, Madison made her way to row 42. Using the last ounce of her strength, she attempted to pick the carry-on up and shove it into the too crowded overhead bin. A teenage boy caught the luggage as it began to topple out.

"I think there's room in this one," he said.

"Thank you."

Madison squeezed past the aisle seat, which had a tweed coat placed neatly across it. She collapsed into the window seat and tried to remain calm, but she couldn't draw a good deep breath. No doubt it was the heat and humidity causing her heart to race. She closed her eyes, touched the necklace again, and prayed she wasn't having another panic attack. She hadn't had one since her mother's funeral.

When she opened her eyes, she peeked out the window. The storm seemed worse. Madison's stomach tumbled at the thought. Pushing it from her mind, she stared at the back of the seat in front of her, tried to focus on settling in for the three-hour flight.

"We meet again."

Madison looked up as Sergio settled into the seat next to her. "What a pleasant surprise."

Her smile faded as she realized he had seen her boarding pass when they'd talked earlier. Maybe he was a stalker or one of those creepy older, internet guys who preyed on twenty-something-year-old women too terrified of flying to notice.

"My seat assignment was near the emergency exit doors," Sergio explained. "I do not like the idea of being called on to perform such an important duty, so I requested a different seat. When they asked if I would like to be near anyone else on the flight, I realized I would rather sit near you than the screaming children several rows up."

Madison relaxed a little as the baby let out another howl. She couldn't really blame the guy. "I understand. I like children, but not on airplanes."

"Perhaps it is fate then that we found each other for seatmates," he said.

"I wish fate would ease up on the storm outside." Pulling her hair back with one hand, she wiped the sweat off her neck with the other, then reached for her seatbelt. "It's never too early to buckle up, right?"

"I suppose. The storm seems to have intensified. That could be the reason our flight is taking longer to depart."

Madison adjusted her necklace, touched the pendant, then turned to look out the window. The rain was pouring down even harder. How was that possible? She snapped the cover shut over the small window. Out of sight, out of mind.

But she could still hear the rain beating against the window.

Chapter Six

"She's a feisty one." Dean's admiration came through loud and clear over the comm link.

The banter might be inappropriate, considering the First Lady's life was on the line, but it helped to ease the mounting tension. Aiden realized that the most important thing at this moment was for him to appear relaxed and bored.

"Just your type," Dean added

"I don't think so."

"What's wrong with this one?"

"Too young, too sad, and too skinny."

"Well, Aiden. You can feed 'em you know, and they do age with time. Wealthy guy like you, I'm sure you can find a way to cheer her up."

"Fueling will be complete in another twenty minutes," Martin said. "Are we filling dead time with Lewis' lack of a social life again?"

"We've been trying to hook him up for two years," Dean said.

"The last date you got me had a mustache," Aiden said.

"She was a great agent," Jones piped in.

"We arm wrestled and she won."

"That's a problem?" Dean asked.

"Most days." Aiden continued setting up his laptop, turning on the filters, which would shield his screen from anyone else's eyes. "I have visual."

"You have to admit this one's gorgeous," Dean said. "Coyote's lucky day it seems. I should be sitting back there with her. Want me in the cargo hold, Aiden?"

"Negative," Martin overruled. "For all we know he has handlers on the ground. We will not be taking chances with Claudia's life."

Jones began humming Beautiful, Beautiful Brown Eyes.

"I noticed the eyes," Aiden admitted as he adjusted the angle of his laptop.

"So you are interested."

"I'm not dead, Dean. Just old."

"Thirty-two isn't exactly ancient. We'll give you pointers if you've forgotten how to woo a woman."

"Don't do me any favors." Aiden switched on the transmitter to the surveillance device he had planted on Ms. Hart's sweatshirt.

Any conversation would be relayed to his smart phone instantly. Coyote and Hart would come in his left earpiece. Martin, Dean, and Slater in his right. Some stereo.

He opened his newspaper, then reported, "I have audio."

"Confirmed. Slater should be passing you now." Martin's voice had been replaced by that of a technician.

Aiden saw the Hawaiian shirt out of the corner of his eye.

"Copy. Has he been briefed?" Aiden asked.

"We transferred all data to him ten minutes ago," Martin said. "He'll be sitting two rows up and across the aisle from Coyote. Remember the conditions of his boarding—he's unarmed."

"Then what good is he?" Aiden asked.

Aiden's voice had remained level, but the intensity had notched up. The first-class passenger across the aisle sent a questioning gaze his way.

"Stockbrokers," Aiden offered a dazzling smile and rattled his *Wall Street Journal*. "They should be shot."

"No shooting, Lewis. Remember Coyote is supposed to walk." Martin's tone left no room for discussion. "That is your new directive, whether you like it or not."

Aiden resisted the urge to argue. Some ops go bad, and this one had. They would apprehend Coyote, but it wouldn't be tonight. This had turned into a surveillance mission. He forced his pulse down. At least Coyote hadn't pegged him—yet. If he could ensure Claudia's well-being and see Madison Hart safely off the plane...if he could get them all safely deplaned, the mission would be a success.

A few clicks of the mouse brought row 42 into focus. The camera worked off line-of-sight and could penetrate anything between the transmitter and the receiver. He'd placed the transmitter on the right side of Ms. Hart's sweatshirt. With Coyote in the aisle seat, Aiden could easily watch every move the man made. The audio picked up anything within five feet of the transmitter. All he had to do was sit back, watch, and listen.

Chapter Seven

Madison searched through her backpack for something to distract her from their imminent crash. Her fingers touched the letters from her father. She had sat in the backyard and read them with her mother. Some were twenty-five years old. She touched the packet and tried to draw a bit of courage from them. Sitting on a plane in the middle of a torrential downpour, they didn't offer her much comfort. They only held more mysteries, and her life already had enough question marks in it.

Snatching her book from the bag, she forced the pack under the seat in front of her, much as she forced the memories of her mother to the back of her mind.

Who was she kidding?

Flying wasn't safe.

It went against all the laws of nature. The bodies littered across the highway in Peru had proven that. She should have driven. If her car hadn't died last month she would have. The storm continued to rage outside her tiny window as the plane backed away from the gate—each raindrop like tiny needles piercing her heart.

Finally the plane began accelerating. Madison stole a glance at

Sergio and realized she was trapped. She clutched her book and forced herself to take deep breaths, praying she wouldn't hyperventilate. She looked again at Sergio. He still sat with his eyes closed, oblivious to their mortal danger. Somehow, she found the courage to nudge him.

"Excuse me. Could we change seats?"

He opened both eyes and raised one eyebrow. "Now?"

"I feel airsick. If I could have an aisle seat..."

A look of irritation briefly crossed his face, but it was gone as quickly as a cloud flies before the sun. Or perhaps she had imagined it. He unbuckled quickly, and they changed seats and rebuckled at the exact moment the plane left the ground.

Madison ignored the glare from the flight attendant. Instead she grasped her pendant and tried to think happy thoughts.

Sergio reached for the airsickness bag and passed it to her. "Would you like me to call for assistance?" he asked. "Perhaps a drink of water would help."

"No. This is much better. Thank you."

She would not cry. She was a grown, educated woman. Logically, she knew the chances were nil that her first flight in two years would end in disaster. She clutched her necklace and choked back the tears threatening to escape. Sergio would be mortified if she broke out in sobs. He was acting as if they were in no danger at all and in fact had already closed his eyes again. At least she had a considerate seatmate. Already the pendant was exerting its influence.

Chapter Eight

Aiden resisted the urge to punch his tray top, which was in the upright position. By moving to the aisle, Madison Hart had effectively cut off his view of Coyote. Airsick? The woman was airsick? That's all he needed. As if he didn't have enough complications on this mission.

"I still have him in sight," Slater murmured.

"We're going dark until we achieve altitude." Aiden switched off his audio receiver, but kept the laptop focused on row 42. Now he could only see Madison and the center aisle of the plane.

Until they leveled off, he would have to watch and wait. He forced himself to remain calm, willing the plane to climb quickly so he could resume audio surveillance.

As long as Coyote remained on the plane, chances of an explosion were minimal. The man's profile strongly concluded he was not suicidal.

Great. I'm betting the lives of everyone on this plane, including my own, that some government shrinks did their job well.

There was always the possibility of a hijacking, but no such priors existed in Coyote's file. Why was he going to Salt Lake City? Why tonight? Why on this flight? He could have rented a car if he wanted to visit Utah, and he didn't have to kidnap the President's wife to get there. Whatever was going on here, Aiden knew it was big. Much bigger than Hamburg or Tokyo.

What was near Salt Lake?

Forcing himself to relax into the leather seat, he continued to watch row 42.

If Nate could see me now. But Nate thinks I'm on a golfing trip. My brother will never know I tried to make my life count for something.

USCIS didn't send flags to the families of the deceased. Instead they penned a fictional cover story and released it to the press.

Of course his brother would receive the extra life insurance USCIS funded, but money wasn't exactly scarce in their family.

Aiden adjusted the angle on his laptop.

The brunette remained hidden behind her book.

She wasn't much of a flyer. There would be finger imprints on the book cover from the way she clutched it. She stared down as if riveted by what she read, so he couldn't see her eyes, but chestnut hair spilled down her shoulders.

He continued to watch, thinking about what her hair would feel like between his fingers.

Now where had that come from?

It wasn't like him to be distracted on a mission. Perhaps he should put in for a vacation. Martin had been harassing him to take some time off for months.

"Is there something you need, Mr. Lewis?" The flight attendant's voice was friendly, the smile even more so.

Raven hair, long legs, European accent. All of Aiden's warning bells went off at once. He looked over the top of his laptop. "A cup of ice would be great."

"Sure thing."

"Bourbon would be good too."

"Bourbon and ice. Got it."

"Bring one for yourself while you're at it."

28

The flight attendant flashed a convincing smile, brushed her hip against his seat as she turned, and walked to the front galley.

She was definitely with Coyote. She didn't have his name tattooed on her wrist, but Aiden knew. In five years with USCIS, he'd learned to trust his instincts.

Hopefully the drink and flirting would confirm he was merely another obnoxious first-class passenger.

The plane leveled off, and the captain announced that those purchasing Wi-Fi access could now connect to it via their electronic equipment—of course the access was complimentary in the first-class seats. Aiden had the audio reactivated before the captain finished his announcement. Row 42 remained silent. Slater came in loud and clear.

"No change on 42. Both are still seated. Coyote appears to be napping."

Aiden didn't know much, but he knew Coyote wasn't napping. He wished he had a video of the man, as if an image would allow him to read the man's mind.

"I've got a hostile in first-class," Aiden said.

"Roger. I'll forward the information to the pilot."

"Tell him to remain on Alert Level 4. He's to keep the cabin door locked for the duration of this flight."

"Affirmative. Description?"

"Five feet nine inches. Female. European. Black hair. Flight attendant. Nametag says Maira."

"Copy that."

"Your priority remains row 42."

"Roger."

"There may be more, Slater. Keep your eyes open. I have no idea how many, where he has them, or what he has planned next."

"Hell of a thing they've put us in the middle of."

"That is God's truth."

Why had Coyote put Maira in first-class? How did he get her scheduled on this flight? Had he broken into the airline's secure system? Did he have inside sources in personnel? If he could break into the President's security system, he could break into any system he wanted.

With one eye on the galley, Aiden split the monitor's screen and opened the briefs Martin had downloaded to his computer before their flight took off.

> USCIS has confirmed at least five different persons working under Abu Yassin are planning to cross the U.S.-Canadian border in the next three-seven days. All except Coyote are considered low level operatives and are to be monitored only, not apprehended.

The fact that no contact was to be made explained why Aiden had been pegged to keep tabs on them. USCIS preferred to schedule him on monitor-only missions. They didn't want to expose their wealthiest mole.

Aiden moved easily in and out of Canada's best resorts. He was the perfect candidate for watching and obtaining information since he had all the necessary tools—wealth, background, access. He'd grown up in resorts where rooms regularly cost a thousand dollars a night. He had a reputation as a philanthropist, a millionaire playboy, and an amateur-pro golfer. More importantly, he had the single item they couldn't teach any of their field agents—a pedigree. The term made Aiden feel like a poodle.

> *Sources corroborate Yassin will continue to use luxury Canadian resorts to filter his men and women through. Recent activity suggests operatives will stay between two days and two weeks before attempting to cross the border.*

Aiden made no effort to block his screen as Maira handed him his drink. The filters would only allow viewing if you were sitting directly in front of the monitor. Unless she climbed into his lap, the information remained safe. Popping the seal on the bourbon, he poured it over the ice, handed the bottle back to her, and moved his leather case off the empty seat next to him. "Have a seat," he said.

"We're not allowed."

"What a pity."

"I'll tell the lead attendant you said so."

"Tell her I'm lonely."

"A wealthy, nice-looking man like you? Now that is hard to believe, Mr. Lewis."

"Call me Aiden."

"All right, Aiden." Already she'd dismissed him and begun watching the other first-class passengers. "I'll be back to check on you in a few."

He nodded at the empty bottle in her hand.

"Bring another one of those when you come."

"Absolutely."

He downed the drink as she moved away. Good thing training included building alcohol tolerance. Aiden's assignments often involved beautiful women and drinking, a fact Dean liked to remind him of whenever he had the chance.

Aiden turned his attention back to the monitor. Ms. Hart still clung to her book.

> *Highest priority should be given to intercepting identification records. Forward all information through secure channels only to predisclosed IP address.*

Maira continued working the first-class passengers. Now that Aiden had tagged her, the woman's moves were obvious. Either

Coyote suspected an agent was planted in first-class, or he had a flight attendant in both cabins.

For the next hour row 42 remained quiet, but even with the second bourbon Maira so dutifully served him, Aiden couldn't relax his shoulders. They remained firmly knotted. He continuously tightened and flexed his calves as if he might need to sprint at any moment. They had covered every scenario, but he couldn't lose the nagging suspicion something was about to happen.

If he could see Coyote, he might be able to read the man's body language. Unfortunately his monitor continued to display only the lovely Ms. Hart, who seemed to be napping. Aiden was readjusting the view when the plane hit an air pocket, knocking his laptop off the drop-down table.

"Let me help you, Mr. Lewis."

"I've got it. Thank you, Maira." He smiled as he snapped the laptop shut and placed it back onto the table.

"Are you sure? I'm pretty good with electronics."

"Thank you, but I'm sure it's fine." The clock in Aiden's head continued to tick. Ten seconds. They had been out of his view for ten seconds.

"Let me bring you something to drink. Another bourbon?"

"That would be great." Twenty. He had to get rid of her.

She smiled but seemed in no hurry to move on.

Thirty seconds. Anything could have happened in thirty seconds. Aiden wanted to push her toward the kitchen. Instead he put on his best nonchalant demeanor. He had to be sure she didn't suspect him, so he looked down at the computer and grinned. "It's only stock reports, but my accountant wanted me to go over them before tomorrow."

He glanced again at the seat beside him. "Are you sure you can't take a break?"

Maira smiled indulgently and shook her head. "Let me check on the other passengers, then I'll bring your bourbon."

Aiden put on his best playboy pout. Maira laughed and turned away, started back toward the front of the plane.

He opened the laptop, but the screen had gone blank. The receiving software continued to run, but no visual was displayed. He could still hear Slater's obnoxious seatmate in his right ear, but only silence came through his left. He tapped it lightly. Still nothing. Not only had he lost visual for row 42, but he'd also lost audio. Coyote and the lovely Ms. Hart had effectively disappeared.

Chapter Nine

Madison barely noticed when Sergio left the row. The exhaustion of the previous weeks and months finally claimed her. Caring for her mother in April and enduring the agonizing weeks before her death in late May had bled all of Madison's reserves—emotional and physical. She had braced herself for a long fight against the breast cancer. Losing her mother in such a short time had devastated her.

She allowed the motion of the plane to blur the memories. For a few minutes she fell into a dreamless sleep where she forgot to worry about her new teaching job in Montana, forgot even the father she was somehow supposed to find. When the plane hit an air pocket, she stirred, but refused to waken, clinging to that blissful blanket of darkness.

Some part of her mind registered when Sergio returned to his seat, squeezed past her.

Then there was more turbulence, and he fell against her.

He murmured an apology.

Madison nodded, but kept her eyes closed, willed herself back to sleep. She knew she should be afraid of the flight, vigilant of the emergency procedures, but she couldn't find the energy to care.

Then he grasped her wrist painfully in his hand. "Please do

not yell, Ms. Hart. I might have to do something we would both regret."

He spoke softly, but when Madison opened her eyes and looked into his, the expression on his face was anything but calm. In fact, Madison hardly recognized the man sitting beside her. The gentle face had been replaced with barely controlled anger, and Sergio's eyes had turned into two black coals.

He leaned toward her, still firmly gripping her wrist. "Tell me, Ms. Hart. Where did you get this listening device?"

Madison looked down at her hand. It seemed disconnected from her body. Surely it belonged to someone else. This was not happening to her.

"What are you talking about? You're hurting me."

"You know what I am talking about. Do not play with me."

"I don't—"

"I will hurt you more than you can imagine," Sergio continued softly. "Tell me why you had this listening device on your shirt and who you are listening for."

Madison stared at the tiny device he held in his other hand. It was nearly the color of her sweatshirt, and she had never seen it before in her life.

"I don't know what you're talking about."

"Is this why you insisted we trade seats?" he hissed in her ear. "You will tell me."

"I don't even know what that is."

"I can break your wrist, Ms. Hart. I can also do much worse."

For the second time in her life, Madison knew unmitigated fear—ice in your veins, paralyzing fear. Terror that made her instantly forget her flying phobia. Her heart hammered against her ribs. She glanced around, but couldn't catch anyone's eye.

"They will not notice." Sergio twisted her wrist until she looked back at him again, tears now running down her face. "Most of them are wearing head phones or sleeping. To them it appears we are traveling together, especially since we have been speaking on a first-name basis. Even the air marshal two rows over will not notice for I have an associate who has conveniently placed a beverage cart between our seats. It would be better if you would simply tell me who you are spying for."

"I am not spying." Her denial was the barest of whispers.

"You do not want to anger me."

What an understatement. The man was insane. How could she have mistaken him for a gentleman? And what was the thing he claimed to have pulled from her shirt?

"I don't know what that is," she repeated, whispering in the hope of calming him. "I've never seen it before. Please let go of me."

"In fifteen minutes we will walk together to the back of the plane. You will not look or speak to anyone, or I will kill you immediately. You do realize I don't need a weapon to kill you. All it would take is my hands."

He reached out and touched her face, turning her head, and forcing her to look in his eyes. She'd never seen such madness. Nodding dumbly, forcing the tears to stop, she reached to unbuckle her seatbelt, but her hands were shaking too badly.

"Let me do that for you." His voice remained calm and even, but Madison couldn't stop the shudder as he leaned across her.

"Now we will wait. Fifteen minutes. Then slowly and quietly, we will walk toward the back restrooms. Remember to do exactly as I say."

Chapter Ten

"I've lost audio and visual," Aiden said. "What's going on back there?"

"Nothing," Slater said. "They're both in their seat."

"You can see them?"

"No," Slater admitted. "There's a beverage cart in the way, but they're only two rows over. I would hear if there's a problem. I can see the tops of their heads. Everything is fine."

"Everything's not fine," Aiden hissed. "I can't see or hear a thing. He must have found the bug."

"I don't think so. They're talking, he's helping her unbuckle I think. Hang on, I'm trying to see around this stupid cart. Yeah, that's about it."

"Why would she need help unbuckling?"

"Airsickness? I checked a minute ago, and she was sleeping. I guess she woke up sick again."

"Are they moving?"

"Negative. They're still sitting there. Probably waiting for the cart to move like everyone else."

Aiden quickly considered their options. Slater was seated across the aisle. He could still see and relay any information. Perhaps the bug had simply fallen off or malfunctioned.

"I want to know if he so much as coughs." Aiden said.

The next fifteen minutes were among the longest in Aiden's life. Maira was making a last walk-through of the cabin before their descent when Slater reported back.

"They're both moving to the back of the cabin," Slater said. "Looks like he's helping her to the ladies' room. Should I follow?"

"Do you see a weapon?"

"Negative."

"How does she look?"

"She's pale. My guess is she's going to hurl."

Aiden knew if he moved to the back of the plane, it would raise everyone's curiosity. First-class passengers didn't use the facilities at the back. Maira would tag him for sure. He couldn't risk the exposure unless he knew Hart was in danger.

"Do you still have visual contact?"

"Negative. They've moved behind me."

"Give them exactly five minutes. If they're not back in their seats by then, I want you to make up some excuse to go inside those bathrooms."

Adrenaline rushed through Aiden's veins. Perhaps she was airsick again. Possibly the bug had fallen off. Or maybe Coyote intended to kill her. But why do that and risk being caught in mid-flight?

It didn't make sense. If the man had wanted to highjack the plane, he would have chosen a flight attendant, someone with instant access to the cockpit.

The minutes crawled by as an endless array of possibilities paraded their way through Aiden's brain, each worse than the last.

"They're moving back to their seats," Slater reported. "He's asked the flight attendant for a bottle of water. I think she was sick. She certainly looks awful."

Aiden leaned back and forced his heart rate down. Madison remained less than ten feet from Slater, she was safely in her seat, and they were forty minutes from touchdown.

Chapter Eleven

Madison knew she couldn't think about the way he had touched her in the bathroom—his hands on her arms, her legs, even in her hair. All the time chanting words she didn't understand. She knew, with certainty, if she ever started screaming she wouldn't be able to stop.

He claimed to be looking for additional listening devices. The man was delusional.

Filthy. Her skin crawled with his filth. She needed soap and hot water. She needed a dark room, and she needed it now. How could she ever have accepted his help? This was all her fault. She should never have spoken to him. She knew better than to talk to strangers. She should have stayed at home. She shouldn't have traveled alone.

As he had frisked Madison a sob had escaped from her lips, and his hand clamped down again on her arm.

"Say nothing, make no sounds, and I will not hurt you."

"You're lying," she whispered.

"Your typical American bravado will not serve you well tonight, Ms. Hart. Close your mouth and perhaps you will live to see Montana."

Madison didn't believe him, but she clung to the hope as if it were a life raft in the midst of a vast and deserted sea. She didn't want to die here. She didn't want to die never having met her father, and she realized in that moment she did want to find him.

In the meantime, Sergio or Mr. Mancini, or whomever he was had calmed down somewhat. His face again looked relaxed and gentlemanly. Only his eyes betrayed the depth of his insanity.

"It appears you told the truth. I am sorry, but I had to be sure."

The flight attendant stopped at their row as Sergio motioned toward her.

"Ms. Hart would also like a bottle of water. She's not feeling well."

"Certainly."

The idiotic woman actually smiled at them both, retrieved a bottle of water from the galley and patted Madison on the arm. "We'll be landing soon. You'll both want to buckle up."

As the flight attendant walked away, Sergio reached across Madison to fasten and tighten the seatbelt, pulling it snugly across her lap. When he brushed against her she began to shake uncontrollably. He simply took the blanket she had been using earlier and placed it across her lap.

Then he continued in the same matter-of-fact tone he had used earlier. "You will take this pill. I apologize, for it will give you something of a headache."

Madison put her hand to her mouth and stared at him in horror. Now she would scream. She would unbuckle and run. But even as the thought formed, he put his right hand on the back of her neck, squeezed tightly as if to remind her of his strength.

She picked up the pill from his left hand, put it in her mouth, tried to hold it under her tongue.

Sergio put the bottle to her lips though, insisting she take a long drink.

The plane tilted as it began its descent. She glanced at Sergio who seemed bored and was looking out the window. She tried to ask him why, but then couldn't remember what she wanted to ask. She looked past him, out the window and into the total darkness of the night.

She had been afraid to look out that window. But there was something else she should be afraid of. What was it? Why did she suddenly feel so tired? Why was this man holding her hand?

The last thought Madison had was that she should ask for help.

Then everything went black.

Chapter Twelve

"This is Lewis. We have a hostile exiting the plane now. Five foot eleven. Female. Black hair. Flight attendant. Nametag says Maira. She's pushing a woman in a wheelchair."

"Mike Truss here, Aiden. We see her now."

"I want her photographed and followed," Aiden said. "I'm waiting for Coyote and Hart to exit. Be sure you have at least two men on whoever walks through the gate first."

"We have direct orders. No one is to follow Coyote," Truss said.

"I understand we aren't going to apprehend him, and I—" Aiden lowered his voice as the other first-class passengers began exiting the cabin, "I even understand why, but you cannot tell me we aren't even going to put a tag on him."

"My orders came from the top. Coyote walks," Truss said.

"Mike, you were with me in Hamburg. You know what this man is capable of, and you know we cannot trust him to honor any deals he's made."

"Not our call, Aiden. Our orders come from the President this time. We have a visual on your hostile now. I have two men on her. We've checked the terminal for explosives, and it's clear.

Whatever Coyote is up to, it isn't an attack here. We'll be scanning all exits to confirm he leaves. Beyond that the situation is out of our control. Do you need help with Hart?"

"No, I don't need help with Hart," Aiden said. "I think I can handle a hundred-and-twenty-pound innocent on my own."

"Coyote has exited his aisle," Slater reported. "He's coming toward you now."

"What about Hart?"

"Negative. Ms. Hart is still in her seat."

"Slater, I want you to keep Coyote in sight, but don't move in too close. Make sure he walks into and out of this terminal gate. Apparently our job ends there."

"Copy that."

Aiden forced himself to smile at the remaining flight attendant as the coach passengers began to exit the plane.

"I need to take care of a few emails. If I could exit last, I'd appreciate it."

"Sure thing, Mr. Lewis."

"Thank you."

"No problem." The flight attendant patted his shoulder, then continued straightening rows for the next flight.

Aiden pretended to work on his computer. Since he'd lost audio and visual there was absolutely nothing he could do but wait.

He should have been relieved when Coyote finally passed without even a glance his way, but like everything else about this night it felt wrong. Slater passed two passengers behind Coyote.

"Mike, he's exiting the plane now."

"Three of our agents followed the woman. We have all monitors up and running. We'll confirm Coyote exits the airport as promised."

Aiden powered the laptop off, closed the case and slid it into his father's leather satchel. It was one of a few items he kept close to remind him why he had chosen this life. When the burdens weighed too heavy, and occasionally—like tonight—they did, he would grasp the handle of the satchel, and think of his father's hands. Doing so always reminded Aiden of how he was responsible for stealing that presence from his family.

Technically it had been an accident, but he was mature enough to carry the weight of the responsibility for what he had and hadn't done. His father's death was his fault. He would be a man and accept the blame. Carrying the satchel reminded him he chose to be an agent in order to repay the debt he owed.

As he closed the latch on the satchel, Mike Truss reported back in.

"Transfer confirmed."

Aiden tapped his headset to acknowledge Maira and Coyote were now under Mike's supervision, then he retrieved the rest of his items from the overhead bin. He placed the Stetson hat on his head. He would follow Ms. Hart off the plane, see her safely to her connecting flight, then use the first-class lounge to file his report. Unfortunately that meant he wouldn't make a connecting flight until tomorrow. Lovely. Another night spent in an airport.

Despite the fatigue washing over him, he allowed himself a moment of hope. Maybe Claudia was safe. Coyote hadn't harmed anyone on the plane. Mike would confirm he had left the airport. They would catch him—eventually. Some days that was as close to a successful mission as you got.

The thought had barely crossed his mind when he heard the cry for help from the back of the plane.

Chapter Thirteen

Aiden passed a male flight attendant and elderly woman on his way to Hart's seat. He wanted to push them out of the way. Instead he waited for them to move haltingly down the aisle.

"I thought she was sleeping." An older woman shuffled down the aisle, hands trembling even though she clasped them together. "When I tried to nudge her, she wouldn't wake up. Isn't that strange? She didn't stir at all."

"Yes, ma'am." The flight attendant glanced at Aiden, then back at the old woman who was apparently in his charge. "It is odd, but you did the right thing not to attempt to move her. Could I help you to the lounge and order you some tea?"

"Should I leave though? She might need my help."

"We're calling paramedics now. I'm sure she'll be fine."

"Well, all right then. I suppose tea would be nice."

They finally managed to creep by Aiden. He covered the rest of the plane in a single bound and reached Hart's side at the exact moment the lead flight attendant spoke into her emergency transmitter.

"Captain, we have a situation back here. What are the medics ETA?"

"They're entering the jetway now."

"I have an emergency medical certification. Is there anything I can do?" Aiden tried to sound casually helpful, even as his own pulse skyrocketed.

The truth was that the sight of Ms. Hart unconscious in her seat nearly undid him. It wasn't like he was attracted to her in any way, but it was his job to see her safely off the plane and now Coyote had managed to mess this up too.

Another flight attendant knelt before Ms. Hart, holding her wrist as she gazed at her watch. "I have a pulse. It's slow but steady. I'm not sure why she won't wake up."

Aiden didn't doubt for a minute why she wouldn't wake up. Coyote had drugged her, but with what? And why?

Then he noticed the transmitter he had placed on her sweatshirt was gone. Aiden knelt in front of her and reached for her other wrist. As he monitored her pulse, he also noticed a fresh bruising on her wrist.

He'd kill Coyote himself.

He should have done it three hours ago, and he would do it now.

The steady beat of her heart calmed him only a little. It took every ounce of training he possessed not to scoop up the lovely Ms. Hart and carry her off the plane. One thing was certain, he wasn't leaving her side until he figured out what had happened.

How had Slater missed this?

The captain's voice came back over the flight attendant's transmitter. "Medical help has boarded the plane. Do you need me to come back there?"

As he spoke, Ms. Hart began to stir. The look of total disorientation confirmed to Aiden that Coyote had used either Mexican Valium or Liquid Ecstasy—date rape drugs. Both operated within twenty minutes, with effects lasting up to twenty-four hours depending on the dosage. He'd know soon. Liquid Ecstasy caused nausea—Ms. Hart would be vomiting within a minute of waking up. If he'd used Mexican Valium, she'd have decreased blood pressure and a blinding headache.

Chapter Fourteen

Madison tried to open her eyes, but the pounding in her head was so intense, she couldn't. Someone was holding her arm, and for the life of her she could not remember where she was. Her head was going to explode. She tried to curl onto her side, shield her eyes from the light, but a gentle hand wouldn't let her.

"Miss. Can you open your eyes?" The male voice was soft and low, nearly a caress. The hand on her arm applied a gentle pressure.

With a heavy sigh, then a shaky breath, Madison gathered all her strength. She opened her eyes slowly.

How could light cause so much pain? And who was the cowboy looking at her with such concern?

The pain was too much. She snapped her eyes closed and tried to pull her hand away. She needed to block out the light. A conversation continued around her, but it made no more sense than the man holding her hand.

"Medics are here."

"We've contacted the local hospital. The ambulance's ETA is ten minutes."

The word ambulance caused Madison to force her eyes back

open. She'd been in too many ambulances in the last three months with her mother. She had vowed to never ride in another one. "I don't need a hospital."

She struggled to stand up, but again the intensity of the light stopped her and she collapsed back into her seat. Strangely, the cowboy placed his hat onto her head.

"Here. This might help."

The Stetson at least blocked the glare of the overhead lights, bringing a small measure of relief.

Madison sat up straighter, pulled her hand away from his grasp, and rubbed her face. Looking around, she suddenly realized she was on a plane and terror again filled her soul.

"Did we crash?"

The cowboy moved aside as a medic replaced him, slipping a blood pressure cuff over her arm before she even realized what he was doing.

"No, miss. You're safe and sound on the ground in Salt Lake City. Try to relax while we take care of you."

"I think I'm all right. I have a headache."

"That's what we're here to confirm." The medic set to work, putting a stethoscope to her chest, calling out vitals to his partner who keyed them in to a laptop. "Blood pressure is 85 over 50. Pulse 55. All low—"

"My blood pressure is always low." Madison pulled the blood pressure cuff off and tried again to stand, but her legs buckled. She had to be somewhere, but she couldn't remember where.

"Miss, you should probably remain in your seat for a few minutes. We can reschedule your connecting flight." The medic was an older man with salt and pepper hair. "The last thing you want to do is board another plane feeling this way."

The second medic kept tapping information into his laptop. "Could we have your social security number?"

"I'm not giving you my social security number." Madison looked around as the evening came crashing back with startling clarity.

She was moving to Montana.

She'd boarded her flight.

It was raining.

Just as it had been in Peru. She glanced around again, expecting to see the bodies, the children, the carnage of the dreams that never stopped.

A shiver passed down her spine, but she had no idea why. Something had frightened her. Something worse than Peru?

"I'm fine, really. I'm connecting to Kalispell. If you could point me toward my flight."

The cowboy she'd seen when she first opened her eyes popped back into view. Madison suddenly remembered she was wearing his hat and wondered how ridiculous she looked. She'd have to give it back, but she needed to find her sunglasses first. Why were the lights so bright? And why was a million pounds of pressure crushing her head? She'd had migraines before, but never anything like this.

"I'm connecting to Kalispell as well. I'd be happy to show you what gate the connecting flight departs from."

The last thing she needed was help from a cowboy, but then again standing, let alone walking, was proving a real challenge.

"Easy now." His voice was soft in her ear, his hand protectively holding her elbow. "Take it slow."

The older paramedic gave her a fatherly look that nearly undid her. "Are you sure you don't want to go to the hospital, Miss? An ambulance is in transit."

"That won't be necessary." Madison turned away, reached for her backpack and nearly fell over from the pain when she bent down.

"I've got it." The cowboy shouldered her backpack, a purple and pink canvas thing which did nothing for his expensive suit.

Another spike of pain tore through her vision.

Something was very wrong. Why did she feel this way? She had to reach Kalispell. Check into her hotel room. If she could hold together until she reached the dark room and sink into a night's sleep, she would be fine.

"I have a carry-on too," she murmured.

"Got it."

Before she could say anything else he had reached into the overhead bin and pulled down her bag as if it weighed nothing.

"At least let us show you to the lounge." The medic still blocked the aisle, hesitant to let her pass.

"I can take her there." Again the cowboy's voice, soft and low.

"Airline policies strictly state when a passenger becomes sick upon flying a report must be filed and—"

Aiden cut off the lead attendant who'd joined them. "I'm sure Ms. Hart would be happy to sign any release forms in the lounge. The important thing now is to help her off this plane."

If she could make it to the terminal, she could lose the cowboy. First she had to get rid of these medics. Just like an airline to be worried she was going to sue them, as if they had somehow caused whatever was wrong with her.

"Thank you." Madison tried to smile at the cowboy, but it only made the pain intensify. She shut her eyes briefly, then opened them and offered what she hoped was a brave, healthy smile.

"I'm much better." She turned to the medic, looked him directly in the eye. "I'm sorry to have caused so much trouble."

"Not at all." He shrugged and stepped ahead of her in the aisle, led the way as they started off the plane.

The flight attendant handed the cowboy a leather case. "Here's your bag, Mr. Lewis. We'll have a porter take both of your carry-on bags to the connecting flight."

"You'll go to the lounge?" The cowboy's voice was a whisper, a soft undertone to the chaos surrounding her.

Madison had a distinct feeling if she refused now, she would end up back at the mercy of the medics. "Yes. Thank you."

As the medics led her out, Mr. Lewis kept his hand on her elbow. They made their way out of the plane, down the jetway, and into the terminal, where the lights were even brighter. Madison tried to ignore the pressure behind her eyes, tried to keep walking. The cowboy must have said something else, because the medics finally moved on, the flight attendants nodded and left.

"Let's find you some sunglasses." His voice was for her ears only as he guided her toward a shop across from the gate.

Had she said she needed them? Or had he simply read her mind? She couldn't remember. Sunglasses and a bottle of water, then she would send him on his way.

Chapter Fifteen

Sergio slid into the front seat of the Nissan Acura. He waited until they exited the airport before he removed the woman's headdress. Made of an inexpensive cotton and simply embroidered, it did nothing to attract attention. Next he removed the long brown wig, not that a single hair of it had shown, but one could never be too careful. He knew their cameras to be quite advanced. His men employed in airport security had assured him they captured anomalies in shape, texture, and color—even beneath garments, in a crowd, at a distance.

The guise had been a precaution. He'd been assured by various federal agencies that he wouldn't be followed, and he believed them. They would do much to save their precious First Lady. Still, one could never be too careful.

Sergio placed both carefully on the seat beside him.

"I trust your flight was comfortable?" The driver hazarded a glance, apparently uncertain whether to look at him directly.

"Yes, Mohammed. Thank you for asking." Sergio planted his feet so he could pull up the full-length abaya and remove it. When he had done so, he folded it neatly and placed it on top of the other items.

"The clothes pleased you?"

"They did. I passed through their surveillance devices undetected. There is no need for you to watch your mirror. I made sure we are not being followed."

Sergio's thoughts returned to the woman on the plane. It was a pity he had to drug Ms. Hart, but he could not risk her remembering his face. Of course he could have killed her, his mission was more important than the life of one infidel, but it would have given the government agents one more reason to reconsider their deal. As if they had any bargaining chips.

The voice from the back of the car broke through Sergio's thoughts.

"We have sent the encoded message stating their precious Claudia is safe."

Sergio did not bother to turn around. He would have known Abu Yassin's voice anywhere. He did not have to see the man he had pledged his life to in order to recognize him. As a sheep knows his shepherd—

"You used their code name?" Sergio asked.

"Yes. We want them to know the extent to which we have penetrated their security network."

"They will tremble before the force of our attack is realized."

"Yes, they will. Which was one point of tonight's exercise. They will spend even more of their resources increasing security around their President and First Lady."

"Yet our attack has nothing to do with them."

"Exactly. They will also increase airport security more, further slowing the wheels of their precious commerce and frightening passengers."

"Ms. Hart was quite frightened tonight," Sergio said evenly.

"As they will all be in fifty-eight days. It is what the Americans deserve."

The statement hung in the car as they sped across the desert, the lights of the city fading behind them.

"Tell me about the woman on the plane."

Sergio resisted the urge to wipe the sweat beading on his brow. He knew he had made no errors, and yet he did fear Yassin's anger.

"Her name was—"

"I know her name."

"Of course. She was wearing one of their newest model listening devices."

"Who planted it?"

"I do not know. I do know it was not on her shirt before she boarded the plane."

"You looked at her closely in the lobby then."

Sergio shifted slightly in his seat, resisting the urge to defend himself.

"Yes."

"It is an unfortunate but necessary part of your mission that you must look at their women. Your sins are forgiven. Who could have planted it on her?"

"Someone in the airport perhaps. I don't think it was anyone on the plane and certainly not the air marshal. I watched him the entire time. There was no other agent onboard. We had three associates searching—first-class, mid plane, and in the back galley. No one reported any finds."

"It is important we learn who has been identifying our agents as they cross the Canadian border. Tonight's little drama was meant to frighten the Americans, but it was also to lure out their Iceman. Your people missed something."

Sergio resisted the urge to defend his team. "We will go over the manifest again."

Mohammed spoke for the first time since Yassin had made himself known. "All three members have checked in. They cleared the airport, but are being followed."

"As we expected they would be. It is of no consequence. We will have lost their agents by morning. The passenger lists must be analyzed again. There is someone we missed."

Mohammed pulled the car into a deserted business complex. Driving around to the loading area, he stopped beside a small private plane. The large vacant parking area provided an acceptable airstrip. The only lights in the entire complex came from the aircraft which was powered up and waiting for its single passenger.

"I must leave," Yassin said. "May you both remain strong in your faith, focused on your mission, and firm in your resolve."

Sergio and Mohammed both exited the car, accepted the traditional greeting, then waited as the man few in their organization had ever seen boarded the plane. When darkness again blanketed the parking area, they returned to the car.

"We have a six-hour trip to our destination," Sergio said.

"Yes. I thought you would like to rest, so I reserved you a room outside of town."

"There will be time to rest after our mission is successful." Sergio's voice tightened and the flame of anger surged again within him. He was frustrated he had missed the agent on the plane and embarrassed he had again disappointed Yassin.

"Of course. We will drive there now."

Silence filled the car as they again sped south.

"I would like to see the sun rise from this engineering marvel," Sergio said.

"It will not be a marvel for long," Mohammed said.

"Everything is in place?" Sergio knew all the explosives were set. He had monitored the placements via satellite feeds himself.

"Of course. There was no need for you to visit. Excuse me for saying so. Everything is ready. All we need is for you to give the word. You could have left with Yassin."

"It is important I see it myself," Sergio said. "Not only to confirm the practical details. Some things must be seen to satisfy the heart."

The silence weigh between them for a few minutes. Finally Mohammed said, "You may take a tour if it pleases you."

"Only of the outside."

"No. You can tour most of the interior of the structure as

well, and for only eleven American dollars. You can even walk through the 250 foot tunnels to the generators."

"There are no guards?"

"There are some, but so many people pass through on the tours the guards have become complacent. Antonio was able to acquire a job as a tour guide. That is how we gained access to the restricted areas and were able to plant the explosives near the generators in case the underwater ones malfunction."

"The underwater explosives will not malfunction, Mohammed."

"Of course not."

"You must have faith."

"Yes. I will pray for more faith."

"Fifty-eight days, Mohammed. The world will change even as it did on September 11. You are blessed to have a small part. We have both been favored in the eyes of Allah." Sergio looked out into the night, thought of the woman's softness under his hands, tried to push her from his mind. It was an unholy image, and it angered him that she should cross his mind at such a moment. Perhaps he should have killed her. "I will rest now. Wake me when we reach the Nevada state line."

Chapter Sixteen

It seemed to take every bit of Madison Hart's strength to put one foot in front of the other. Aiden wanted to allow her to sink into the chair at the front of the store, but he wasn't about to let her out of his sight again—not even for a second.

Propelling her to the carousel of sunglasses, he picked up the first pair he saw. They were ridiculous things with fake rhinestones on the sides, but they would do. Turning her toward him, he placed them gently on her face. As he slipped them on her, he stared briefly into the most stunning brown eyes he'd ever seen. The vulnerability and confusion he saw there distracted him, caused him to hesitate, made him want to smooth the pain away with a touch of his hand.

Focus on the mission, Iceman.

The struggle was brief. His training had been the best and within seconds he managed to detach himself from the situation. Accompany her on the plane. Transport her to Edgewood. Find Coyote and kill him. He could be objective.

"You look lovely. Do they help?"

She nodded, but didn't say a word. Aiden noticed a trembling in her chin and hurried her toward the register before she melted completely into tears. After paying, he guided her back out into the corridor.

"The lounge is a little way down. Can you walk that far?"

"Yes." She raised her chin a little, trying to look brave and in control. It didn't work.

"You're not fooling me, Ms. Hart. I can tell how much pain you're in. I'd be happy to pick you up and carry you."

She shook her head slightly, but the tears spilling out beneath the glasses were more than Aiden could stand.

When he picked her up she was lighter than he expected, and he'd expected her to be light. He thought she might resist, but instead she buried her face in his shoulder and sobbed softly.

"Almost there, sweetheart. Hang on."

His anger resembled a bear's awakened from its winter nap as he stomped into the first-class lounge. Why would someone drug a lady like Madison Hart? And why use Mexican Valium? Give her a sleeping pill if you have to, something without the terrible side effects.

The receptionist looked up as he banged through the first-class door. One look at Aiden sent her scurrying around the desk.

"We've been expecting you, Mr. Lewis. Would you like to use the study?"

"Yes, thank you, Diana. If you could make sure we're not disturbed."

"Certainly."

Diana opened the door to what could have been an exquisitely decorated study in any million-dollar mansion—complete with a mahogany Victorian desk, oriental rugs, and shelves from floor to ceiling lined with a collection any librarian would drool over. A matching Laura Ashley loveseat and chair in Cambridge fabric were tucked into the corner. Growing up in the best suites Europe and the US had to offer, Aiden knew quality from fluff. This was quality. No expense had been spared.

Aiden headed toward the sofa. "Please dim the lights, and bring me two bottles of water. Be sure they're unopened."

Aiden wasn't putting anything past Coyote. If he'd managed to drug her on a plane with an air marshal across the aisle, he could have slipped into the first-class lounge as well.

As Diana shut the door, he lowered Ms. Hart to the couch.

Her arms remained clasped around his neck. Aiden gently pulled away, but not before he'd let his hand trail down her arm. Not before her scent had permeated every bit of the ice he was supposedly so famous for maintaining.

Her hands found his, and she clung to them as if he were a lifeboat. He had to lean close to make out her words, which were shaky, tearful, and filled with a pain he could only imagine.

"Please don't leave me. I can't remember why I'm so afraid, but I am."

"I'm not going anywhere, and you can stop being afraid."

Aiden lowered himself to the floor as she curled into a fetal position. He reached forward and removed the Stetson from her head, then couldn't resist tucking her hair behind her ear. It was soft and thick, and it took every ounce of control Aiden possessed not to sink his hands into it, feel the weight of it, bury his face in it.

"You're going to be all right. Hold on."

"I don't understand."

Her tears continued to fall. He wiped them away with his thumbs, held her face in his hands, and willed her to stop crying.

"I know."

By the time Diana brought the water, Ms. Hart was fast asleep.

Aiden found a blanket and covered her with it, then removed the sunglasses. He continued to monitor her vital signs, noting them on a pad he'd retrieved from his satchel. Her breathing had evened out as soon as she'd fallen asleep. Her pulse remained slow but steady. Aiden continued checking both every ten minutes.

When he was finally convinced the immediate danger had passed, he went over to the desk, pulled his laptop out of the leather satchel, and booted up.

Typing in the IP address, he waited for the system to request his thumbprint. When it did, he touched the mouse pad in the center and waited for the beep. His report was cryptic.

Package transferred. Hart injured but stable. Going dark.

He waited for the acknowledgement indicating his message had processed, then promptly did a system shut down. As an afterthought, he switched his phone to silent.

With nothing left to do, he moved the chair closer to the couch and watched Madison. The old ache stirred, and he wondered why he couldn't meet someone like her under different circumstances. Women like Madison Hart had no place in his world though. Of course there were women in ops. Aiden respected their hardness and their intelligence, but they didn't stir him the way the woman lying on the couch did.

In another life, if he met a woman like Madison, he would ask her out. They could see a movie or go out for coffee. They could even saddle up a couple of his horses and ride the range together. A normal life. Something he didn't have now and probably never would, at least not in the foreseeable future. Not as long as men like Coyote roamed free.

Some days he wanted to walk away from it all.

But he wouldn't. Tomorrow he'd crawl out of bed, holster his weapon, and debrief his mission file. Like he'd done today. Like he'd done yesterday.

Best decide what to do when she woke up. He couldn't tell her she'd been drugged. Protocol strictly stated he take her in for debriefing only if and when she remembered what had happened, not before.

So he couldn't tell her the truth. It wouldn't do any good if he did. She wouldn't believe him. It would only frighten her more.

She would sleep off most of the effects of the drug. Hopefully she hadn't been raped. The thought made his mouth go dry and sweat run down his back. He reached for the bottle of water, popped the seal, and drank half of it. Unexplainably his throat remained dry.

Had Coyote raped her?

He could take her to the hospital, but it would raise too many questions. A report would be made and all passengers would be questioned. USCIS wouldn't tolerate that kind of scrutiny. Coyote was on their critical watch list. Lots of questions, that's all a hospital report would generate. Best to avoid the hospital if possible.

They'd probably already missed their connecting flight to Kalispell, which meant they'd catch the red-eye. Somehow, the thought of spending the night in the airport didn't bother him as much as it had before. Watching Madison, Aiden realized he could study that face a long time.

The ice cracked again, and Aiden drew a deep breath. The team would laugh to see him now.

Iceman.

He'd first heard the nickname in a bar in Barcelona. It was the end of a month-long op that had begun in Warsaw, continued through Frankfurt and Munich, and finally ended in Milan with one dead.

The team had gathered in a small pub in southwest Barcelona. By the end of the evening, only he and Dean were left sitting at the bar, nursing beers and trying to silence the ghosts that haunt all agents.

"Who is Iceman?"

"You are, bud." Dean signaled the bartender to bring another round for them both.

Aiden grunted. Everyone was given a name. He supposed there were less accurate ones than Iceman.

"Want to know why?"

"My lack of personality?"

Dean studied him in the mirror over the bar.

"Back there in Milan, when you killed Stretch—"

"Any man in the agency could have made that shot, would have made it."

"Right. With a locked and loaded 357 less than two feet from their own head, any one of us would have still taken the gamble, aimed our weapon, pulled the trigger, made the shot."

"We're trained not to back down."

"We are."

Dean downed half the beer the barkeep set in front of him.

"So why Iceman?" Aiden turned the glass, stared into the amber liquid.

"Because, my friend, any one of us would have made the shot," Dean stood and reached for his wallet. "But the rest of us would have broken into a sweat."

Aiden waved for him to put his wallet away. "It's on me."

Dean nodded and finished the beer in another long gulp. "There were three guys within ten feet of you and Stretch. They all swear you never flinched, just took the shot and walked away."

Dean's eyes met his in the mirror, then he slapped Aiden on the back, said good night, and was gone. Aiden was left alone, staring into his own reflection, the reflection of a man he didn't really know anymore.

He'd killed three men since joining USCIS. Truth be told, he'd never hesitated, never broke a sweat, never had a moment's regret about ending their pitiful existence.

No, the guilt that plagued him was a different sort. When he woke in the middle of the night, sheets wet from the sweat pouring off his body, adrenaline pumping so that he was sure he would have a heart attack, it was never the men he'd killed in the line of duty that haunted him.

The image that tormented him was his father's. Aiden accepted the blame for his father's death as if he had aimed a pistol and shot him dead. The way Aiden saw it, not pulling a trigger could make you as guilty of killing a person as pulling one—in certain situations.

Iceman. Yeah, he felt encased in ice all right. He might as well have the name tattooed on his arm.

Aiden looked over at Madison and wondered why the ice around his emotions threatened to crack now. Why did she awaken feelings in him that hadn't stirred in so long, feelings he thought long dead? He remembered the softness of her hair against his fingertips, brushed his hand over his face, and found her scent lingering in his palm. Above all he wanted to hold her again as he had when he'd carried her into the lounge. Instead he counted her breaths, unconsciously timed her pulse against the clock in his head.

He'd wait, and he'd watch, and if Coyote dared to come near her, he'd break his neck with his bare hands.

Chapter Seventeen

When Madison opened her eyes, her first thought was that the pain was gone. Her second thought was it must have been a dream. Then she sat up and looked around.

She was in a room decorated with designer furniture and soft colors. The lights were dim, making it impossible to tell what time it was. Sitting two feet from her, staring straight at her, was the best-looking cowboy she'd ever seen.

"Where am I?" Her throat was dry, her voice a raspy whisper.

"You're in an airport lounge. Drink this." He handed her a bottle of water.

She tried to open it, but her hands were shaking too badly.

"Let me help you." He lowered himself onto the floor in front of her.

Madison wondered if he always sat on the floor while wearing Armani and a Stetson. The suit looked like one she'd seen in a catalogue she'd poured over with her mother. They had been picking out perfect men, who of course wore perfect suits. The thought of her mother brought back the old pain, and she knew she wasn't dreaming. If this were a dream she'd have the cowboy, maybe the suit, but not the pain in her heart. She automatically reached for her necklace, the comfort of her mother's blessing.

Madison took a long drink. The coldness brought a measure of relief to her throat. She'd chugged half the bottle, when he reached out and took it from her.

"You should go slow with that," he said, moving back to the chair he had pulled up close to the couch.

Madison let him take the bottle and looked around the room in amazement. "I'm not in Kansas anymore."

His laugh was nice—deep and genuine. "I believe you started in Texas."

"Right." The silence went on for a moment as she scanned the room, looking for a clue to help her remember how she'd come to be in this place with this man. "Who are you?"

"Aiden Lewis," He reached up and tipped the Stetson. "Pleased to meet you, Miss Hart."

"Madison, please." It was an automatic response, quickly followed by suspicion. "How do you know my name?"

"We were on the same flight."

"A flight that didn't crash." She pushed that old fear away as she distinctly remembered a paramedic assuring her they had landed safely.

"No, but that seems to be a big concern of yours—"

His explanation was interrupted by a soft tap on the door. An older woman walked into the room. She wore a nametag which said, DIANA, LEAD RECEPTIONIST.

"It's good to see you awake, Miss Hart. Is there anything I can bring you?"

Madison looked at Mr. Lewis.

He shrugged. "They have great food here. Are you hungry?"

"No, but I would like more water."

"I'll bring some more right away," Diana said.

"Thank you." Her voice was still scratchy, and she still couldn't remember what had happened.

Mr. Lewis waited until the door had closed before he continued.

"You don't remember?" He handed her the water, which she quickly finished.

"No. I remember arriving at the Dallas airport, and that's it. Why can't I remember the flight to Utah?"

A look of uncertainty passed over the cowboy's face so quickly Madison wondered if she imagined it.

"You fell asleep during the flight and woke with a terrible headache."

There was more he wasn't telling her, but she had no idea what or why.

"A headache?"

"A blinding headache. Any history of migraines?"

"I have the occasional one, but I've never forgotten an entire evening. It is still evening. Right?"

"Actually it's morning." He looked at his watch. "Three a.m."

Madison nearly jumped off the couch. "I have to catch my plane."

"It's gone already. The next one is in three hours."

Madison sank back into the couch and stared at him, fidgeting again with her angel pendant. She searched her mind for any detail, any clue to the hours she'd lost, but there was nothing.

For some reason, the cowboy looked familiar. Sandy-blond hair, tailored suit, black Stetson. He was trim, muscular, but not overly so, with a tan that indicated he made his living outdoors—something she seriously doubted given the suit. He watched her as she tried to work through her fog, not rushing her, not interrupting, just watching. He didn't stare exactly, but neither did he look away.

She'd looked into those gray eyes before. Hadn't she? It was in there. She could feel it—a memory that she couldn't retrieve.

"I don't mean to sound rude or ungrateful, but who are you, Mr. Lewis? Why are you here, and how did I miss my plane?" Her voice rose as the questions tumbled out and her pulse quickened.

Something wasn't right. She should be in Kalispell, Montana now, tucked into the hotel room she'd reserved for the night. She should be resting up for the morning drive to Edgewood, not sitting in a first-class lounge with a rescuing cowboy.

The door opened again, and Diana returned with two more bottles of water. She handed them both to Mr. Lewis, who popped open the seal and handed one to her.

"Thank you, Diana," Mr. Lewis said.

The woman nodded and left without another word.

Madison thought about following her, but hesitated when she saw the expression on the cowboy's face. He looked tired and somehow vulnerable despite his size.

"I should go, Mr. Lewis."

"Please call me Aiden. I was on the same flight out of Dallas that you were on. When we arrived in Salt Lake, I remained on the plane to check a few emails. I'm usually the last to leave the plane. I see no reason to hurry up and stand in line to exit the contraption just so I can wait somewhere else to board another."

Aiden hesitated, opened his own bottle, and drank the entire thing. Setting it on the Persian rug beside his chair, he rested both his hands on his knees.

"And?" Madison asked.

"And as I was gathering my things to leave, I heard an elderly woman call for help from the back of the plane. I have my emergency medical certification, so I went to see what was wrong."

"And you found me?"

"I found you."

Aiden stared into her eyes, and Madison again struggled against that stirring deep inside. He had the look of a man trapped, and she wondered why.

"Your blood pressure was very low and you had a blinding headache. The flight attendants tried to send you to the hospital, but you refused."

"That sounds like something I would do."

"Why? Most people would want help when they're in extreme pain."

Madison searched for her angel pendant, found it, adjusted it on the chain around her neck so she would have an excuse to touch it. "I don't like doctors."

"Apparently."

"Then what happened?"

"Then I brought you here."

"And here is—"

"First-class lounge."

"I'll say." Madison looked around her, took in the fine furnishings and original oil on canvas paintings. She would never have guessed such a place existed inside an airport. "So, I'm in Salt Lake City."

"Correct."

"And it's three in the morning."

"Correct again."

"And you've been sitting there watching me sleep."

"I couldn't just leave you." He had the grace to blush. "I felt responsible since I brought you here."

"Right."

"And we're both connecting to Kalispell."

"Really?"

"Yes. I live in Edgewood."

Madison chuckled softly. "I'm going to be living in Edgewood as well. I somehow doubt we'll live in the same part of town though."

"You might be surprised. It's a fairly small place."

She stood, gathered her pink and purple backpack and looked around for her carry-on.

"They're holding it at the gate for you."

"First-class service is certainly accommodating."

He had stood as well, and when she walked over to him she had to look up to see into those guarded gray eyes.

"Thank you, Mr. Lewis." She held out her hand, which was immediately lost in his.

"Aiden. I'm on first name basis with all the women I rescue."

Madison looked at his hand still holding hers and wondered how often he did this sort of thing. She was standing so close she caught the light woodsy scent of his cologne and something else as well. Soap and deodorant and something that had her wanting to lean up into his neck. Why did he seem so familiar? She pulled her hand away gently and shouldered her bag.

"Thank you, Aiden. You've been more than kind. I do appreciate it. Now I have a flight to catch."

She turned and walked out of the room. He caught up with her before she'd found the main reception area.

"Where are you going?"

"To the gate." She stopped at the reception desk and spoke to the receptionist. "I'm connecting to Kalispell. Can you tell me which gate that flight departs from?"

"Sure thing, Ms. Hart. You'll be leaving out of Gate 16, Terminal 2." Diana handed her a boarding pass. "Your bag is waiting for you there."

"Thank you so much."

Madison walked out into the corridor and scanned the signs for Terminal Two. It wasn't until the room started to spin and she began to fall that she realized Mr. Lewis was still with her.

Chapter Eighteen

Aiden slipped an arm around Madison as she was about to go down.
"Steady there."
When she looked up he couldn't help smiling into those brown eyes. You'd think he'd saved her from a burning building.
"Mr. Lewis."
"Aiden."
"Aiden, thank you. I'm fine though. Really."
"Collapsing in the middle of the airport isn't what we call fine in Montana, and I doubt it's what they call fine in Salt Lake. I'm sure those paramedics are lurking around somewhere if you want me to call them."
Her eyes went wide, and he knew he'd hit the spot he was aiming for.
"Maybe I did rush it a bit."
"Yeah, I guess you did. Maybe you need something to eat."
He guided her toward his usual stopover spot. He'd have to trust the food was safe, that it at least was out of Coyote's reach. If he'd wanted to poison her, he could have done it on the plane. She really did need to eat something. Food would help push the Valium out of her system.

Dinner would also give him an excuse to stick with her a bit longer. She could have latent reactions to the drugs Coyote had given her—it was rare, but not unheard of.

Then there was Coyote himself. In all likelihood the man had left as he'd claimed he was going to, but Aiden wasn't willing to bet Madison's life on that probability. Of course if Coyote had wanted to kill her, he could have done it on the plane. Homicide on a plane is a messy affair though. It would have been discovered within minutes, and murders tended to shut down airports for several hours.

Why had he drugged her to begin with?

What am I missing here?

Aiden kept his arm around Madison's waist, supporting her as they walked through the airport.

"I can walk on my own," Madison said, attempting to pull away. "I'm fine, really. I was only dizzy for a minute."

"Are you sure?"

"Yes."

Aiden stopped in the middle of the concourse, which was nearly deserted given that it was close to 3:30 in the morning. "If you pass out I'll have to throw you over my shoulder."

"Is this what you normally do in the middle of the night? Walk through airports looking for women to throw over your shoulder?"

Aiden tilted his head back and laughed, then placed his hand under her elbow and continued propelling her toward the only eatery open all night. "You are definitely feeling better."

"I'm beginning to wonder if you were following me."

"We are going to the same connecting flight. Or were you in such a hurry to ditch me you forgot that?"

"It's kind of creepy though. Having this rich guy pop up every time I pass out."

"How do you know I'm rich? And I was raised with better manners than to follow women. I was worried when you rushed out of the lounge like a crazy woman."

"Hmm."

"Is that what you say when you don't want to answer a question?"

"Which question?"

"How do you know I'm rich?"

"Please. The clothes, the haircut, don't ask me to make a list."

"I like lists," he teased.

She shook her head from side to side, causing her lovely brown hair to cascade over her shoulders. "I feel like I know you from somewhere, other than the lounge I mean. I can't remember though." Her frown deepened. "Actually, I seem to have forgotten most of the evening."

"All the more reason you should have a bite to eat. I bet you don't remember whether you've eaten either." He did his best to lighten the mood, desperate to put her at ease.

"I am sort of hungry."

Her smile nearly took his breath away.

Stay cool, Iceman. You're on a mission, not a date.

But regardless how his brain argued, his body and heart responded to this woman.

It took all his control to leave his hand at her elbow and not travel up her back. He wondered again what it would feel like to hold all of that hair, to touch the back of her neck, to kiss her lips. He was so focused on what he shouldn't do and keeping an eye out for Coyote, he walked right past the café. He stopped in the middle of the terminal, trying to get his bearings.

"Where were we going?"

Madison laughed and pointed to the OPEN 24 HOURS sign they had passed. "There?"

"Right." He shook his head and turned them back toward the café. "Food and coffee, which I obviously could use right now."

The bantering relaxed her, but Aiden was oddly disoriented by it, as if he had taken a Valium himself.

He needed to see Madison safely to her destination, debrief, and catch some sleep. But as he led her to his regular table, one near the windows that looked out into the black night, he found himself hoping the service would be slow and the meal long. He wanted to spend more time with her. Coyote would be easy to spot in the empty restaurant.

For the moment, they were safe.

Chapter Nineteen

Madison settled into the chair Aiden pulled out for her. The table offered a breathtaking view of nothing, since all was dark outside. She couldn't make out a thing, which reminded her of the fact that she couldn't remember a thing. The view pretty much mirrored her mental state.

Aiden had barely stowed his leather satchel under the table and sat down when a waitress appeared.

"Good evening, Mr. Lewis. What would you like to order this morning?"

"I'll have some coffee, Jamie. How are you doing?"

"Great. This is my last late shift this week. I'll be home by the time Taylor wakes up."

"He's four, right?"

"Four going on fourteen. The sitter lets him stay up much too late, and then he's a grouch in the mornings. I like being there when he wakes up though."

Madison listened to the exchange in disbelief. Did this guy know every receptionist and waitress in the airport? She studied him as the conversation continued. At first, she thought he was patronizing the young woman, but Madison quickly realized

Aiden really was listening to what the waitress had to say. She was so preoccupied trying to figure him out, she didn't pay any attention to what they were saying.

"You were hungry, right?" he asked.

"Me?" Madison looked back and forth at the two of them as they stared at her, waiting. "Oh. I'll have some coffee."

Jamie pulled out her pad. "Sure thing. Anything to eat?"

"No. Thank you." Madison handed the menu back.

Although she was hungry, she did have a connecting flight to endure. After Peru, then this, she didn't trust herself to eat a thing. Of course coffee on an empty stomach probably wasn't a good idea either.

Aiden didn't even bother to look at the menu. "Why don't you bring us the combination appetizer, and if you could add some fresh veggies on the side that would be great."

"I'll bring the coffee right out, and the sampler will be ready in about fifteen." With a nod of her head Jamie slid the order pad into her apron pocket.

A quick smile, a toss of her ponytail, and she'd moved on to deposit their order in the kitchen.

Madison wondered if there was more to this cowboy than met the eye, not that there was anything wrong with what her eyes were seeing. No ring on his left hand, although Madison was old enough to know that didn't mean a thing.

He was obviously wealthy, and he was a charmer, whether he was talking to a fellow airline passenger or a waitress.

"What? You're looking at me like I've grown a second head." Aiden carefully touched the top of his Stetson, as if he'd find something unexpected up there.

"It's nothing. Really."

Aiden sat back and stretched his legs into the aisle. "In my experience when a woman says it's nothing, it's most definitely something."

Madison took a sip of her water and tried not to return his smile, but her pulse jumped under his gaze.

"You might as well say whatever it is you're thinking," he added.

"It's just that you seem to know every woman you come across."

"Really?"

"Yes, really."

"Like?"

"Like our waitress."

"And?"

"And the receptionist in the lounge."

Aiden smiled even broader, picked up his own water and took a long, slow drink. "Women like a man who pays attention."

Madison tried not to spew water across the table. Instead she managed to swallow an ice chip. She coughed so long Aiden finally reached across the table and patted her back.

"Are you all right? I didn't mean to drown you with my obnoxious comments."

Fortunately, at that moment Jamie returned with their coffee. The interruption gave Madison a chance to regain her composure.

"Women like men who pay attention?" she asked.

"Sure. Usually gets you faster service too."

"So you flirt with women to get faster service?"

"Now you're being harsh. There's a difference between making conversation and flirting."

"Right. Spoken like a real man."

"I'll take that as a compliment."

"Who flirts like a pro."

Aiden didn't bother to argue. With one eyebrow raised, he took a drink of his coffee, studying her the entire time. Setting the cup down, he crossed his arms on the table, leaned to within a few inches of her, and said softly, "I could flirt with you too. Then you wouldn't feel left out."

Madison couldn't help laughing. "Are you always this arrogant?"

"No, but then I don't always have the pleasure of eating with an attractive woman who blushes easily."

Madison realized he was playing her like a yoyo, and she was surprised to find she sort of liked it. She'd been dealing with death for so long she'd forgotten what it was like to live. The heaviness around her heart had lightened just a little, and she couldn't remember the last time she'd smiled so much.

Plus the conversation helped take her mind off the evening, which was disturbing to say the least. She still felt slightly off center, and one part of her mind warned she should be careful with this cowboy.

In the other part, she heard her mother's voice—that sweet, gentle voice she missed so much—coming in loud and clear, reminding her "It's just as easy to fall in love with a rich man as it is to fall in love with a poor one." Not that she had any intention of falling in love. She wouldn't be jumping on the love train for a long time. She was fulfilling her promise to her mother, searching for a father she had little chance of finding, then moving back to Dallas and her old life.

While she was in Montana, she might as well enjoy herself though. The thought made her smile.

As she studied Aiden, the silence between them stretched and practically crackled with their attraction, which was odd. She should be worried about what happened on the flight, but there wasn't much she could do about it now. And somehow she knew she was safe while Aiden was with her.

Her head was starting to clear, and she actually felt good except for the giant hole in her memory. Maybe if she sat talking to him it would come back to her. After all, at this point he was her only link to the flight from Dallas.

Chapter Twenty

Aiden knew he was coming on strong, purely for professional reasons of course. He needed to keep her with him, at least until she boarded the plane to Kalispell. That he was plainly flirting had nothing to do with Madison's beauty or appeal. So her hair was gorgeous and those brown eyes were the loveliest he'd stared into in a long month of Sundays. His cover called for him to act like a millionaire playboy, and he was simply playing the character. Technically, he was a millionaire playboy, but that was beside the point.

Madison reached for her coffee, took a small sip, then placed it carefully back on the coaster. She finally raised her eyes to his.

"I still can't remember the flight," she said.

"You should probably see a doctor when you arrive in Montana. I can give you the names of a few good ones."

Even as he casually scanned the terminal, Aiden kept one eye on Madison. She played with the rim of her cup, absent-mindedly caressing it with the tip of one well-manicured finger, nails painted a dusty rose.

"Actually, my head is fine now. How could something hit me so hard and then disappear?"

"You don't think it was a migraine?"

"This feels different. Usually the migraines last much longer."

"You were lucky this time."

"I guess, but it doesn't feel lucky. For some reason, it feels like a near-miss."

The joking was gone, and when she looked into his eyes she didn't even attempt to hide her vulnerability. In that moment, staring into those brown eyes he could get lost in, he almost told her. He wanted to come clean, then whisk her out of there. Take her somewhere safe and hold up until they'd confirmed Coyote was out of the country. Where was the ice he was so famous for now?

Before he could find a response, she stood up and shouldered her bag. "Any idea which way the ladies' room is?"

Aiden nodded toward the left of the bar. She turned and walked toward the back. Once she was out of sight, he pulled out his phone.

He had missed eight calls, all from Commander Martin.

Chapter Twenty-One

Madison stared at herself in the mirror. She looked the same, so what had changed? Why did she feel so different? And what was she not remembering? Washing her hands slowly she allowed the warmth of the water to calm her, then turned the tap to cold and rubbed some of it on the back of her neck—anything to make her feel fully alert. Anything to help her remember. She reapplied her lipstick, finger-combed her hair, and took several deep breaths. Time to face the mysterious Aiden Lewis again.

Well, send me into the briar patch.

When she exited the ladies' room, she saw Aiden had walked away from the table and was on his cell phone. He was watching for her and offered a little wave.

Jamie arrived with their food—one large plate was covered with potato skins, fried mushrooms, cheese sticks, and chicken wings. Freshly cut celery, carrot sticks, cucumbers, sliced tomatoes, and radishes cut like flowers fanned out around the edges of the second plate. The waitress had placed a small bowl of ranch dressing and another of marinara sauce on the table when the shouting began.

"What do you mean you lost him?"

Madison and Jamie both turned to stare at him, which Aiden didn't seem to realize at first. His face had turned a dark shade of red, and he'd taken the hat off his head and was waving it around as he spoke. When he noticed they were staring, he turned his back to them and talked less than a minute longer before shoving the phone into his pocket. He stood there another minute, then squared his shoulders and walked back toward their table.

"Good luck, girlfriend," Jamie said. "That did not sound like good news to me."

Jamie made a quick escape before he returned.

Aiden sat down at the table, plastered a smile on his face, and said, "Food looks good."

Madison wasn't buying it. "Who did you lose?"

"Excuse me?" Now he was being the innocent cowboy. He reached for a potato skin, plastered it with ranch dressing, and popped it in his mouth.

"It's really none of my business, but apparently you lost someone."

Aiden finished chewing, then took a big drink of water. Either the man was very meticulous about his eating habits or he was stalling.

"Oh, you mean the phone call?" Aiden picked up another potato skin, covered it with more ranch dressing and popped it in, taking his time to chew before answering.

"If you don't want to answer my question, just say so."

"It was a what not a who."

"You very plainly said what do you mean you lost him? That sounds like you lost someone, not something."

Aiden focused on the plate, chose a wing, then shook his head. "A horse—I lost a horse."

"Your horse?"

"Well I wouldn't be upset about losing someone else's."

"Special horse?"

"Very."

"How do you lose a horse?"

"Apparently it's not hard."
"Who lost her?"
"My ranch foreman, and the horse is a him."
"You have a ranch?"
"Of course, did you think the hat was just for looks?"
"I thought the hat was to pick up chicks."

That earned her a smile at least. Madison reached for a carrot stick and wondered again what he wasn't telling her. She had always had good instincts and her instincts told her she could trust Aiden.

But her internal alarm system also was flashing red. Something about this entire situation was not what it seemed to be.

Chapter Twenty-Two

It was all Aiden could do to hold an intelligent conversation with Madison and digest what he'd learned from Martin at the same time. Somehow the cameras had managed to lose Coyote. Even Martin's precious computer program, Jeremiah, hadn't managed to come up with a match of the man leaving the airport. Martin claimed it was no one's fault and the main objective—Claudia's safety—had been met. He reminded Aiden that Coyote's terms insisted he not be followed. But the surveillance cameras should have told them something.

Martin's call meant the possibility of Coyote still hiding in the airport had increased exponentially. A man posing as Coyote had boarded a flight for Seattle. USCIS had sent their agents via other carriers on faster flights to SEA-TAC, but of course it had all been a ruse. By the time they'd figured it out, the only agent left in the Salt Lake Airport was Aiden. None of the security tapes showed Coyote was still in the airport, but neither did they show he'd left. Local agents had been sent to cover rental agencies, bus stations, and the two private airports.

The President's security detail had received word and proof that Claudia was safe. Claudia. They knew her code name. Whatever Coyote was up to, as usual, it was well planned.

Martin didn't believe Coyote had remained in the Salt Lake Airport. In the meantime, Aiden was to provide Madison an armed escort to Montana, but how did he do that without scaring the daylights out of her?

"Sierras is a dappled Palomino quarter horse," Aiden explained. "He's an amazing animal."

"And your foreman lost him?"

"Someone put him in the south pasture but didn't close the gate. When they went to check on him yesterday morning he was gone." Aiden casually scanned the terminal as he spoke.

"So how will you find him?"

"Sierras will come back. He has a wild streak, but he always comes home eventually."

"Do you prefer animals with wild streaks?"

Aiden set his cup down so he wouldn't drop it, pushed his hat back and stared at the woman across from him. "You could say I'm intrigued by the untamed."

"So you can domesticate it?"

"No. Not necessarily," Aiden refused to look away from those beautiful brown eyes.

"Do you two need more coffee?"

Jamie caught the cup Aiden nearly knocked over, and the moment was broken. Mugs were topped off, a few more travelers straggled into the cafe, and Aiden suddenly realized he was starved. He couldn't remember the last time he'd eaten.

Madison continued to watch him as he dove into the food while keeping an eye on the terminal.

"I don't usually eat fried foods at four in the morning," Aiden explained. "But I'm going to make an exception because of the company."

"Because of me?"

"Yes, ma'am. You are going to eat, right?"

Madison tentatively reached for a carrot stick, but simply stared at the fried food. "I'm not sure I should. I sometimes get airsick when I fly."

"You're more likely to be sick if you only eat carrot sticks and celery. Last I checked rabbits don't do well at 30,000 feet."

He reached for a mushroom, dipped it lightly in the ranch dressing, and held it out to her. She screwed her nose up, exactly like a rabbit would, and he couldn't help but laugh. Even after all that had happened this night, and considering the danger she might still be in, he was glad he'd met her, grateful they'd spent this night together.

She touched his hand and pushed the mushroom back toward his mouth. Her hand on his caused the old desire to stir again. Aiden wondered if it might be possible for them to see each other after this was all over. As he was about to suggest it, his phone rang.

Madison pulled her hand back. "Maybe they've found your horse."

"I need to take this. Don't eat all the ranch dressing while I'm gone."

Madison crossed her heart as he pushed away from the table. "Your ranch is safe with me."

Walking away from the table, Aiden wondered if his ranch in Edgewood would be safe with her. It would definitely be more interesting.

Chapter Twenty-Three

Madison salted a radish and played with the tiny petals as Aiden walked away. Most people didn't leave the table when they received a phone call. Maybe it was his girlfriend. Maybe it was his wife. Madison dropped the radish.

Aiden was standing outside the restaurant, his back to her as he continued talking on his phone. She could tell by the set of his shoulders and the way he dropped his head that whatever he was hearing wasn't good news.

She should go. She reached under the table and pulled out her backpack. Rummaging through it, she pushed aside her phone and found her wallet.

She looked for Jamie so she could pay part of the bill. As she waited for her, she reached back into her pack and turned her phone on. Looking at the display, Madison saw she had two messages.

Aiden was still on his phone, and Jamie was taking an order from a table on the other side of the restaurant. Checking her watch, Madison saw she still had plenty of time to make the 6:00 a.m. flight. Tucking her hair behind her ear, she hit the button to play her messages.

Her best friend Renee had called twice. The first time she left a message assuring her the cats were adjusting fine. The second time she pleaded with her to change her mind and come back home.

They'd been through this before. Renee was convinced a promise made on a deathbed didn't count, that Madison's mother would not expect her to give up her job and friends to move to a new state, take a new job, and look for a father she had never met.

But that's exactly what her mother had asked her to do. Renee hadn't been the one to look into her mother's eyes that day in April, sitting in the backyard, and give her word. Madison had.

Her mother didn't weigh quite eighty pounds by that time. She was wrapped in a winter blanket, shivering, but she'd still wanted to sit outside in her garden.

She'd held Madison's hands and made her promise she would go to Montana for one year—to look for her father. This was after they had laughed and cried over his letters. After her mom had tried to describe the passionate romance that had lasted a month, and how John Gibbs had been deployed again in September. Left for a special op he couldn't talk about, even years later when they had begun corresponding again.

Then her mother had explained how the letters had stopped. The next time she heard from him Madison was a year old, and her mom couldn't find the words to tell him of the child. By then her mom understood John had been wounded in more ways than physically.

As they'd sat in the garden that day, Sonya had pleaded with Madison to go to Montana. She admitted she'd always dreamed of them going there together—to look for John, but also to see the way the sun rose over the mountains, to experience the magic of twilight on the trails, to hear the sound of the snowmelt as it rushed down the mountainside in the summer.

As Madison watched Aiden, she wondered what her mother would think of him, what her best friend Renee would think. Mama would laugh and tell her to jump in. Renee would think he was scrumptious.

Madison had only had a few boyfriends, and then her mother had become ill and even the casual relationships had slipped away. Now she knew when she did fall in love, she needed someone who would stick when things became difficult. She wanted a man who would help her through the bad times as well as enjoy the good. Isn't that what love was about? And if such a man was impossible to find, then she wasn't really interested.

As Aiden walked back toward her, Madison stuffed her phone back into her pack as Aiden sat down at the table.

"Someone find Sierras?" she asked.

"No, not yet." He signaled Jamie to bring their ticket. "That was another business call. There were some things I thought could wait until Wednesday, but turns out they can't."

"And they call you in the middle of the night?"

"Yeah, it's sort of an emergency."

Madison thought about asking him what he did for a living, but somehow the teasing mood between them had changed. She wanted to ask if he was married, but it didn't seem to be any of her business.

Aiden handed Jamie two twenties before she could pull out the bill.

"You always pay too much, Mr. Lewis."

"Take care, Jamie. I'll see you on my next connection."

"Sure thing. Be careful."

Aiden and Madison walked slowly toward Gate 24. Madison tried to squelch worries that he might be engaged or married or married with children. She reminded herself this wasn't the beginning of a relationship. It was simply a walk through an airport terminal.

But she couldn't deny the goosebumps running down her spine when Aiden cupped her elbow in his hand. As they approached the ticket counter, his hand moved to her lower back, and a delicious electrical impulse danced up her arms.

"Could we change Miss Hart's ticket to first-class please?"

Madison tried to protest, but the ticket agent was already punching the changes into her computer.

"Of course, Mr. Lewis. We still have thirty minutes before we'll begin boarding."

Aiden thanked her, then turned Madison toward the windows.

"We might as well wait over here."

Madison tried to push down her panic. She moved closer to the window, but she could only see lights shining on the small commuter jet.

Stepping closer to the window, she placed her fingers against the cold glass, tried to see another plane on the ground on a starlit night in Salt Lake City, but she couldn't.

All she could see was the jungle city of Pucallpa, Peru. A flight attendant in her uniform but with her hand severed. The bodies of children. Rain falling in sheets. Which was why she kept slipping as she ran from person to person. Sometimes finding one that was still breathing, or crying horribly. Sometimes bumping into another survivor sliding in the mud, trying like she was to pull bodies away from the wreckage. Away from the flames. As the rain continued to pour down.

Aiden was saying something, but she couldn't hear him over the pounding of her pulse, over the sound of the rain in her ears.

And that was when she realized she was going to be sick.

Chapter Twenty-Four

Aiden's first thought was Coyote had poisoned their food, but then Madison whispered, "I'm not sure I can do this."

He suddenly remembered the image of her clutching the book on their initial flight. Great, add an airsick babe to the mix, as if the night wasn't complicated enough.

He took her hand and attempted to pull her into a seat with her back to the window. From there he could keep an eye on her as well as the terminal.

"Why don't you sit down a minute?" he suggested. "You're not looking so good. Queasiness coming back?"

"I can't get on that plane." She pulled away from him and turned toward the corridor.

"Of course, you can. It's our flight."

"No, Aiden. I can't get on that plane."

He suddenly realized she was more than a little scared, she was terrified and about to bolt. He moved his hands from her arms to her face. "Look at me, Madison."

"I have to go. I can't stay here." Her eyes were dilated and darting from object to object, unable to focus on any one thing—as if she wasn't really seeing what she was looking at but something else entirely. All color had drained from her face. Her breath came in rapid, short gasps as if she'd been running a marathon.

"Madison, you're having a panic attack. I want you to look at me."

All hundred pounds of her had gone rigid, and she tried to pull away from him, but Aiden held firm. He was peripherally aware of the other passengers watching them and the ticket agent picking up the phone, but he remained focused on Madison, kept his voice low and gentle, his hands soft but firm.

"I want you to take three deep breaths. Then if you want to walk away you can. Understand?"

She nodded, though her gaze continued to dart about wildly.

"We'll take them together. Okay? First one, real deep."

He breathed with her, his hands never leaving her shoulders, his thumbs gently rubbing circles even as his fingers lightly massaged.

"Good. Second breath now. As deep as you can." Again, they breathed deeply, like divers about to go down.

He felt her body lose a bit of its tension, saw the security guards enter the gateway, and prayed they would stay back a little longer.

"You're doing great. One more, okay?"

Her eyes never left his face. When the third breath pushed through her body, she collapsed into the chair and buried her face in her hands.

Aiden stood to intercept the security guards. "She's fine. A little panic attack is all."

The Canadian Air representative stepped through the guards and reached for Aiden's hand.

"Mr. Lewis. Good to see you again. Is there a problem here?"

"No. Ms. Hart has had something of a panic attack. She's fine now though. Aren't you?" He gently nudged Madison, who took a shaky breath, pulled herself up straight, and turned toward the airline rep.

"Yes, I'm sorry. It's been a long night."

"You're sure you'll be all right, Miss?"

"Yes, of course."

"If there's anything we can bring either of you, please let the ticket agent know. We'll be boarding in a few minutes."

Madison nodded. Her face was still pale and had taken on a distinctively green tinge. Aiden had seen that same look on the golf kids he coached at Edgewood High School on a volunteer basis, usually before their first tournament. It never forecasted anything good and usually meant the inside of his car would need to be cleaned again.

"Maybe you should put your head down a minute." Aiden rested his hand on her back and gently pushed until Madison's head was between her knees. "Take a few more deep breaths. You'll be fine."

"This is embarrassing," Madison mumbled.

"Twenty-five percent of all flyers experience some degree of nervousness."

"How do you know that?" Madison turned her head sideways, looked up at him through that velvety mass of chestnut hair.

"Magazine," Aiden said softly, reaching out and tucking her hair behind her ear.

Aiden accepted the bottle of water from the ticket agent. "Take a drink, Madison. It will help."

She sat up, pulled her hair back around her shoulder. When she glanced back at the plane, he saw her hands begin to tremble.

"It's a perfectly safe plane."

"That's what they said about the Peruvian airliner I was on." Madison accepted the bottle, opened it, and took a long drink.

Aiden stared at her and tried to make sense of what she'd said.

"What Peruvian airliner?"

"The one that crashed in August of 2005."

"You were on that plane?"

"Yeah. I was on that plane."

Madison leaned forward, elbows propped on her legs, hair

once again obscuring her face. Aiden stood up, moved around in front of her, and knelt down. He pushed that lovely hair back, forced himself to let go of it, but kept his hands on her face. Forced her to meet his gaze.

"I'm sorry that happened to you, but this plane is safe. I am not going to let anything endanger you, Madison. I promise you that. Do you trust me?"

Chapter Twenty-Five

Sergio frowned at the vibration from his phone. Snagging it from his pocket, he punched an icon, entered a passcode, and opened the encrypted message. The caller was identified as *unknown*, but he'd only given the burner phone's number to one person—the man he'd left at the Salt Lake City Airport, the same man who had provided his disguise.

Unkn: Still following MH. Leaving SLC now. Destination Kalispell.

SM: Can you get on the flight?

Unkn: Yes.

SM: Continue surveillance.

Unkn: And then?

SM: Report back once you arrive in Kalispell.

Unkn: Do you want me to kill her?

SM: Not yet.

Sergio placed the phone back into his pocket. Omar was heavyset, balding, and older. He was also new to the cause. He could not be expected to understand the intricacies of what they were trying to accomplish. Sergio had already ascertained that Madison Hart was not a threat, but someone else had used her to try and get to him. That person was the one that he meant to find and destroy.

Chapter Twenty-Six

Aiden kept a hand beneath Madison's elbow. She had looked absolutely terrified crossing the tarmac and boarding the plane. There was one point when he actually thought she might turn around and run.

Aiden had been flying since he was a small child, often on private jets smaller than this. He couldn't personally relate to her fear, but it wasn't hard to see it was very real. After surviving a plane crash in Peru, who could blame her? He'd never been in a plane crash. He'd zipped bodies into bags after the results of one though. He'd seen the carnage firsthand, and so had she. Still, she was sitting beside him, buckled in, calmly watching the sky lighten over the mountains.

His respect for Madison grew the longer he knew her, and he'd known her less than twenty-four hours. Many people never flew again after a crash. It took guts to get on a plane after what she'd been through.

The look of relief on her face when she'd finally dropped into her seat had pierced him to the core. Then she'd reached for the necklace, and he'd wanted to take her in his arms. When she'd messed with her hair again, something he'd noticed she did whenever she was nervous, it was all he could do not to reach out and run his fingers through her long chestnut mane.

He didn't though because this was business.

He had a mission to finish.

He was simply trying to calm her and transport her to Montana, so he could figure out what Coyote was up to next.

But he couldn't deny the rush that threatened to consume him every time he touched her though. Maybe the absence of a social life was messing with his mind. Maybe he was lonelier than he was willing to admit. Whatever the reason, this Texas girl was playing hardball with his mind as well as his heart. And the endearing part was she didn't seem to even realize it.

Although she was staring out the window, she hadn't pulled her hand away. As Aiden continued rubbing her hand with his thumb, he could feel her pulse still racing. Was she terrified of take-off? Or was she feeling the same emotions he was? Probably both. Regardless, he was not letting go of her hand until they were safely leveled off at 30,000 feet.

Reaching with his left hand, he turned off his phone. It had intruded enough for one night. Aiden couldn't remember a dinner he had enjoyed as much until Martin's call.

Coyote still hadn't shown up on their net, but Abu Yassin's other men had moved earlier than USCIS expected. Martin's sources told him they were to arrive in Banff as early as Wednesday, and there was little doubt they would stay at the Fairmont. It was the largest resort in the area, an easy place to hide simply because of its size. Moreover, the Fairmont had a reputation for protecting the anonymity of its guests.

Whether a business CEO from the states sneaking away for a weekend with his family, or movie stars hoping to protect their anonymity and enjoy a quiet vacation, The Fairmont provided privacy. International tourists often chose the hotel because of its cuisine and European-savvy staff. Yassin had processed operatives through there before, successfully. He wasn't one to question success. He would use it again.

Aiden scowled as he accepted the extra pillow and blanket the flight attendant offered.

"Is something wrong, Mr. Lewis?"

"No. Just tired." He set the pillow and blanket in Madison's lap as the attendants prepared the plane to taxi.

"We're taking off already?" Madison's eyes searched his. She was trying to be brave, but the grip she had on the armrest told a different story.

"Tell me why you're going to Edgewood." Aiden reached out with his left hand, tucked her hair behind her ear. He let his hand trail down her neck, amazed how her skin reminded him of silk.

"You're trying to distract me, aren't you?"

"Is it working?"

"No. Yes. When you touch me it does."

The plane's engines vibrated as they backed away from the gate.

"Then I'll keep touching you." Aiden stroked the inside of her arm, watched the goosebumps rise, tried to breathe evenly through his own racing heartbeat. "Tell me why you're going to Edgewood."

"I'm going there to teach."

"Really?" He tried to act surprised. "You don't look like a teacher."

"And what exactly are teachers supposed to look like?"

"Generally, they're large."

"Large?"

"Yes, and they're taller."

The plane picked up speed as it accelerated down the runway, rising in a perfectly smooth ascent.

"I need to be large and tall in order to teach kids?"

Aiden set his Stetson on his lap and drummed his fingers against its rim. "I think so. In fact I'm sure the school board passed mandatory teacher requirements that said as much."

She smiled. "Any other requirements I should know about?"

"Yeah. I'm afraid your hair isn't going to work."

"My hair?" She pulled a strand forward and looked down at it. "What's wrong with my hair?"

"You have to wear it in a bun."

Madison smiled her thousand-watt smile and a giggle escaped her lips—lips Aiden wanted to brush with his own. He was sure he could make her forget her fears, at least for a few moments.

"So you want me to gain weight, grow taller, and corral this mop of hair into a bun."

"Yes, and add some large glasses. No kid is going to be able to learn if they're staring at your beautiful face and your hair."

Madison's eyebrows shot up as she blushed.

"Have you been staring at my face and my hair?"

"No ma'am. We don't stare in Montana. We just notice."

Chapter Twenty-Seven

A soft *bing* pulled Madison out of the conversation. She looked out the window, saw nothing but clear morning sky, a spectacular sunrise, and the Wasatch Mountains. She looked quickly over at Aiden. "Is that an alarm? Is something wrong?"

The pilot answered her question before Aiden could, assuring the passengers they were running on schedule and could now move about the cabin if they needed to.

Aiden let go of her hand so he could accept their coffee and juice from the flight attendant.

"I can't believe we've already leveled off," Madison said.

"That wasn't so bad. Right?"

"You distracted me."

"Exactly."

"Thank you." Madison raised her orange juice to her lips, took a sip, and set it on the tray in front of her. "Thank you for everything."

"You're welcome—for everything."

Madison leaned back in her chair, sighed, and closed her eyes. "These seats are great."

"Air Canada spares no expense to make its passengers comfortable."

"Beats economy." Madison opened one eye and peeked at him. "Not that I remember anything about our last flight."

"Still nothing?"

"Nothing."

"Let's see what I remember. I think I did see an attractive brunette, sitting at the back of the plane, clutching her book so hard I thought she'd leave finger imprints on the outside."

Madison closed both her eyes again. "Now you're mocking me."

"Possibly."

"Tell me what we're flying over."

"Changing the subject?"

"Um-hmm."

"All right. At the moment we're flying over the famous salt flats of Utah..."

Aiden realized he should be sleeping. He would have to pack the minute he arrived home if he hoped to leave for Banff by noon. He should catch some rest while they were in flight.

Instead he spent the next thirty minutes telling Madison about the Great Salt Lake, the largest body of water between the Great Lakes and the Pacific Ocean. As he spoke of Anasazi Indians and the Donner-Reed party, she curled into her seat, feet pulled up, hand tucked under her pillow, blanket across her lap.

"Have you ever crossed it by car?" she asked.

"Once, in the fall of 1990. I was fifteen years old. It was the year I had become cocky and somewhat careless. My father was determined to teach me the power of nature. So instead of flying from Salt Lake City to Kalispell like we normally did, he rented a car and we drove across the salt flats."

Madison reached a hand out from under her blanket and lightly ran her fingers across the back of his hand. Every nerve in his body jumped to attention.

"Did it work?" she asked.

"Did what work?"

"Did you learn to respect nature?"

"It was certainly a humbling experience. Combined with the bear we crossed while hunting that winter." Aiden fought the old ache, tried to bury it as he always had. "Those two events changed my life."

"You crossed a bear?"

"He attacked my father." Aiden drew a deep breath and pulled his hand away.

"What happened?"

"He died." Aiden counted to ten, then pushed the memory back into the place he kept it.

"The bear?"

"No. My father."

"Aiden, I'm sorry. I didn't mean to pry."

"It's not your fault. It's not something I talk about."

Madison continued tracing some invisible pattern on his hand. They had dropped their voices to a whisper, trying not to bother the other two first-class passengers. Aiden had to lean closer to hear what she said next.

"Your childhood must have been very different from what most teenagers experience."

"Not so much. Other than occasional trips, it was pretty normal. My parents wanted my brother and me to grow up independent, able to make it without their money."

"Could you?"

"Make it without their money?"

Madison nodded as she snuggled into the leather seat, trying to get comfortable after a long day of airports and airplanes. Aiden raised the armrest between their seats, and pulled her toward him, placed his arm around her. She hesitated for a moment, but her tiredness won over the resistance that played across her face.

Curling up beside him, she repeated her question. "Could you?"

"Yeah, I could. I've lived both ways though, and believe me, this way is better."

As Madison snuggled into his arms, Aiden lost the last of his reserve. Burying his face into her hair, he took a long deep breath. In that moment he breathed in more than the clean fragrance of her shampoo or the softly sweet scent of her perfume. It was as if he breathed in the essence of who she was.

He wondered if he should slow down, but before the thought was fully formed he kissed her hair, ran his hand again down her arm, lost another piece of his heart.

By tonight he would be in Banff. He'd follow Martin's orders, somehow resist killing Coyote if he did happen to see him. He'd fulfill his duties, the way his father had taught him to, regardless of his opinion of those orders. But for the rest of the flight, he would enjoy the smell and feel of her. For a few moments, he would stop being Aiden Lewis, millionaire agent, and enjoy being a man standing on the edge of a turn-your-gut-inside-out love.

If things were different, he would pursue her. He would pursue her and win her over. For the rest of their short flight, Aiden allowed himself to enjoy the thought. If only things were different.

Chapter Twenty-Eight

The flight attendant's hand on his shoulder jerked Aiden from his sleep. She leaned down to whisper, "There's a call for you up front."

Aiden nodded and tried to remove his arm from Madison without waking her.

"What's wrong?" She sat up with a start, rubbing at her eyes, trying to get her bearings.

"Nothing. I need to go up front for a minute. Go back to sleep."

She leaned her head back against the wall of the plane, set her feet in Aiden's seat, and gave him a sleepy smile. "I'll save your place for you."

"Absolutely. Don't let anyone else sit here."

Following the flight attendant to the front of the plane, he wondered what Martin was up to. No one else could have gotten a call through a private carrier. All calls would have to be patched through the airline and approved by the captain flying the plane. Not a routine thing to do, but then Aiden had learned Martin had friends everywhere.

"The Captain has routed your call to this phone." The flight attendant pointed to a handset near the sink in the fore cabin. She quietly pulled the curtain to give him privacy as she returned to check on the passengers in the first-class cabin.

"Lewis." It came out a little rougher than he intended. As expected, Martin's voice came back across the line.

"Jacob will pick you up at the airport."

"Of course he will." Aiden tried to sound bored, the way he'd been taught. Should anyone be listening, hopefully they would think the airlines were simply bending the rules for another rich playboy.

Replacing the handset, he opened the curtain, smiled his thanks to the flight attendant and made his way to the closet restroom.

Turning the water on, he splashed some on his face, studied himself in the mirror, and wondered what was going on.

"Jacob will pick you up at the airport." That was the extent of Martin's message. Jacob wasn't supposed to pick him up though. He had left his Chevy Avalanche at the airport so he could drive himself. He was supposed to go home, pack, and leave that afternoon. Something had changed. As with everything else on this mission, things were not going according to plan.

Sighing heavily, Aiden reached for a paper towel, dried his face, and made his way back to his seat.

Madison was fully awake and looking worried. "Something's wrong. What is it?"

She moved to make room for him, but Aiden simply picked up her feet, sat down and placed them in his lap. As he tucked the blanket around her toes, he noticed the Snoopy socks.

"Nothing's wrong. I've had a change in transportation plans. My chauffeur is going to pick me up at the airport."

Madison stared at him in disbelief. "That's it?"

Aiden shrugged.

"They called you on a plane to say your chauffeur would pick you up?"

Aiden ran a finger down the bottom of her foot. She tried to pull away, but he was enjoying himself too much to let go. "Do you have a problem with that Ms. Hart?"

"No. I hope they don't have to divert the plane to meet your granny. Or add a stopover for your dry cleaning."

"Now you're mocking me."

"Would I mock you?"

"Absolutely."

"Ok, I'm mocking you."

"By the way, my chauffeur picks up my dry cleaning."

When Madison slapped him on the arm, he grabbed her hand, held it tightly in his and entwined his fingers with hers.

The captain's voice interrupted them, advising all passengers they would be landing within fifteen minutes.

Madison pulled her hand away, refusing to look him in the eye. Aiden watched her as she folded the blanket, smoothed her hair, and retied her running shoes.

Then they were landing. Aiden realized he was going to have to leave her. He'd hoped to drive her to Edgewood himself. Looking out the window, he saw Jacob waiting as promised.

"Madison, I didn't expect to have to leave so suddenly."

"It's not a problem."

She was making a valiant attempt to look like the calm, cosmopolitan traveler she was not. The plane had stopped and the steps were being wheeled up to the door. Aiden grabbed his Stetson and his overnight bag. He paused long enough to reach out and touch her cheek, long enough to promise with a look what he didn't have time to promise with words.

"Edgewood is a small school district. I'll call you as soon as I can."

She nodded, looked down, then glanced back up. For a moment he thought she would lean forward, kiss him softly, touch his face. Then the moment passed, and she began gathering her things together.

The flight attendant confirmed with a look that he was cleared to leave before the other passengers. As Aiden descended the steps he was amused to see Jacob decked out in his chauffeur outfit. Aiden nodded to him, careful not to shake hands, then followed him into the airport.

He stopped once, despite the impatient glare Jacob sent his way. Speaking to the airline rep waiting inside the door, he handed her a hundred-dollar bill, then turned and sprinted through the near empty airport.

He stepped into the Yukon SLT, noting the words Wild Horse Limo printed boldly on the side. He barely managed to buckle his seatbelt before Jacob pulled away from the curb.

Aiden was so distracted thinking of how he would find Madison and cursing himself for not asking for her cell number, that it took a few seconds before he noticed he wasn't alone in the backseat of the limo.

Chapter Twenty-Nine

Madison stepped into the terminal, once again loaded down with baggage. Between her exhaustion, the backpack, and the carry-on, she was lucky to stumble across the tarmac without falling.

Aiden had left so abruptly Madison hadn't been able to process what she was feeling. Abandoned? That was ridiculous. It wasn't like he owed her anything. What had she expected anyway? A ride in his limo? Did she think Aiden would stay around to help her home with her luggage? She didn't even have a home.

In fact, where were her reservation papers? She needed to call the hotel and see if she could receive a refund on the room and then find her rental car. Dumping her bags into the nearest chair, Madison was searching for the reservation information in her backpack when a porter walked up and cleared his throat.

"Ms. Hart?"

Madison looked up, surprised to hear her name in a place where she knew no one.

"I'm Madison Hart." She pulled the reservation sheet from her pack and zipped it back up.

"I'll help you with those, ma'am. If you'll follow me, there's a taxi waiting for you outside."

The boy looked barely old enough to shave. In fact, he probably didn't shave. He also didn't have any trouble picking up both of her bags.

"But I haven't called a taxi yet."

"Mr. Lewis took care of it for you. He also said you'd need help with these." The boy shuffled from foot to foot, apparently uncertain how to convince her to go with him. He was tall and gangly and young.

Madison looked around the empty terminal. All the other passengers had managed to leave while she was looking for her reservation form.

Suddenly the exhaustion won. She couldn't remember the last time she'd been to bed. She considered going to the hotel, checking into her room, pulling the drapes, and sleeping twenty-four hours. Truth was she felt ridiculous going to bed at eight in the morning though. What she needed most was to leave the airport.

"All right. Show me the way."

"Yes, ma'am."

It was a small airport. They were outside within five minutes. She tried to tip the boy, but Aiden had taken care of that as well.

"I need to go to Avis Rental."

"Yes, Ma'am."

The drive to the rental agency revealed little of Kalispell. Madison called the hotel while they traveled past empty parking lots and sleepy neighborhoods. She was upset to learn she would be charged for the room since she never showed up or cancelled it. After talking to a manager, he agreed to comp her account. Wonderful. She had an all-expense paid night in a Holiday Inn Express of her choice.

But Madison didn't want to stay in a Holiday Inn. She wanted to be home, in her little rental house in Dallas, which she couldn't even afford on her teacher's salary. No doubt someone else lived there now. She looked out the window and saw flat land

and in the distance the promise of mountains. It was hard to realize this was home now. At least for the next year it was.

She'd rent her car and be in Edgewood within the hour. Madison's exhaustion was wiped away by a small, sudden thrill of anticipation. She was headed toward her new life, her new apartment, her new job.

The driver insisted on transferring her bags from the taxi to the lobby of the rental car agency. When she tried to pay him for the fare she again heard, "Mr. Lewis already took care of it, ma'am."

She waited in line behind a short, chubby older man who continuously ran his hand over the top of his balding head. When he finished with his reservation, he turned, smiled once, and then exited through the sliding doors to where the rental cars were parked.

In twenty minutes she was on the road to Edgewood. Despite the unbelievably odd beginning to her trip, things were turning out well. The weariness was there, beneath the surface, but she could ignore it for now.

As she drove through the Flathead Valley, the river snaking along one side of the road, the mountains towering around her, Madison felt as though she were driving into a postcard. She had seen the pictures on the Internet, but they did nothing to prepare her for the majesty of the scene before her. The Rocky Mountains literally took her breath away. Was that snow on top of the peaks? In August? The town of Edgewood was nestled at the base of the Big Mountain, and Madison was grateful she didn't have to drive any of the steep roads she saw snaking up its side. In truth, she was terrified of steep roads. She had figured she would overcome that fear when she had to, which was not this morning.

Today she needed to focus on her new apartment, finding furniture with her meager funds, and purchasing supplies. Instead her mind kept going back to a teasing smile, a black Stetson hat, and the feel of Aiden's hand over hers.

Chapter Thirty

Aiden stared at Martin. "I hope you're here to explain to me what happened."

"Coyote insisted he not be followed or Claudia would be killed. We had electronic surveillance on him and still managed to lose him. He's a master of disguise, Aiden. You know that. We also managed to lose Maira. We think there was at least one more operative in coach class, which is how he managed to drug Hart without Slater seeing."

"How is that possible?"

"There's more."

Aiden didn't trust himself to answer. He waited, sure he did not want to hear what Martin was about to say.

"Coyote and ten of Yassin's men have set into motion a plan to blow up ten of the largest dams in North America. We believe it will happen on September 28 when the G8 summit is scheduled to convene." Martin handed his phone to Aiden. "Here are photos of five of the men."

Aiden took a few moments to memorize their facial features and study their dossiers. Returning the phone to Martin, he leaned back into the leather seat and studied the man he had learned to consider his friend as well as his boss.

"Why didn't I know about this earlier?"

"You didn't need to know until now."

"Coyote could have killed her. I would never have allowed Madison to remain on that plane if I'd known Coyote was in the middle of an active operation, and I sure wouldn't have used her for intel."

To his credit, Martin let him vent without reprimanding him.

"You should have told me."

"Hart is fine. Take my advice and forget about her. We need you on this, and we need you at the top of your game. Dambusters has been given top priority from the President and is now an intercept mission. It's critical we move on all ten operatives at the same time. Otherwise the remaining players will go underground until September 28."

"Dambusters? I assume you are not referring to the Call of Duty game."

Martin grunted and relaxed a little. "Caught my grandson playing the game last week. Horrid entertainment. Dambusters refers to attacks made on German dams in 1943 by RAF squadrons known as the Dambusters. Barnes Wallis was the designer of a drum-shaped bomb that could spin backward at over 500 rpm. Dropped at a low altitude and at the right speed, it could bypass dam protection and detonate against the wall of the dam underwater."

"Was it successful?"

"Minimally. Only two dams suffered a major breach, killing less than 1300 people and temporarily reducing water output and electricity production. Recent intel suggests Yassin has purchased smart bombs modified with Wallis's design that can be delivered by much smaller planes."

"Commuter?"

Martin nodded. "Our analysts predict a similar attack on U.S. dams would be cataclysmic. While less than 15 percent of our electricity comes from hydropower, the cities most affected are already experiencing rolling brownouts due to energy shortages."

"Los Angeles."

"Yes, but that is only the most obvious one. I've sent you an encrypted list of the most vulnerable cities which you can review on your way to Alberta."

"How much have we narrowed the field?"

"There's the rub. Of course we're watching the largest dams—Oroville, Hoover, Dworshak. However, they could also create substantial havoc hitting the mid-tier."

"Projected loss of life?"

"If all ten are hit, initial casualties could equal more than ten million. Subsequent deaths due to rolling power outages could double or triple that number."

Martin gave Aiden a minute to let the numbers sink in, then continued in a tired voice. "America and Canada are the largest users of hydropower. Not only would such an attack cripple us economically, but it would create the kind of chaos and fear Yassin has been striving for since the 9-11 attacks."

"What makes you think Yassin will move his men across the border early?"

"Sources tell us a meeting is to take place in LA in three days. We think Coyote was here seeing to last-minute details. He may or may not proceed to Canada to help with the crossing of the other operatives."

"Still no idea as to who the mole passing them through immigration is?"

"We're narrowing it down with each crossing. But no, we don't have a confirmed identity yet."

Martin rubbed his bald head. It was something he did whenever he was frustrated.

"And you're sure these ten will be at the Fairmont?" Aiden asked.

"Not all ten, but at least three. We know Yassin has operatives in place on staff there as well as a few other hotels in Jasper and even Waterton. Agents will be in place at all three resorts. Banff is the largest facility though. It's easier for them to check in and out undetected."

Martin signaled to Jacob, who pulled into a near empty parking lot on the outskirts of Edgewood. Aiden hadn't even noticed they'd passed through Kalispell and into his town.

"We have fifty-seven days to stop this," Martin said. "If we tip them off to the fact that we know their plans, they'll either do it earlier or go to Plan B."

"Which is?"

"You're not authorized to know."

Martin's expression convinced Aiden he was better off not knowing.

"Be careful, my friend." Martin placed his phone into his shirt pocket. "We have no indication Yassin is on to you, but it's always a possibility."

Aiden shook hands with the older man. Martin left the limo without another word, entered a black suburban parked beside the Jack in the Box, and drove off in the direction they had come. As Aiden watched, Jacob lowered the window separating the front seat from the back.

"Next stop Alberta, Canada." Jacob said. "Six hours if we travel straight through. You might want to catch some sleep since you have a 3:00 p.m. tee time."

"Martin is trying to kill me." Aiden didn't quite manage to keep the sarcasm out of his voice.

"Everyone knows millionaire playboys love to play golf."

Aiden studied Jacob's reflection in the rearview mirror. "If I didn't know any better I'd say you're enjoying this."

"I enjoy any chance to stop Yassin and his kind."

Aiden remembered his driver had lost more than one partner to Yassin's network.

"Yassin isn't stupid. He'll know USCIS is on to him. The only question is can his men spot us before we move to intercept."

"Guess I need to catch some rest then, since I didn't get much last night." Aiden tried to keep the smile off his face, but he wasn't quite successful.

"Was she worth it?"

Aiden didn't bother to answer Jacob's teasing. He pulled the pillow out from the bin under his seat and was asleep within minutes. The last reminder he tucked away as he was drifting off wasn't about Yassin's men, it was to call the Edgewood School District office as soon as possible.

Chapter Thirty-One

Madison looked around her classroom. It had taken all week, but she'd managed to make it presentable. Textbooks were stacked neatly by grade level on the shelves of three of the large bookcases. She'd created a reading cove in the corner with a garage sale coffee table and three director's chairs ($9.99 at the local Walmart). What she hoped was an appealing display of current titles ($1 each from Half Price Books) dotted the coffee table and moving crates which sat beside each chair.

When she'd seen her classroom, she'd wondered what she would do with it. For thirty years it had served as the Edgewood High School choir room until it had been deemed too outdated. Last year a new state-of-the-art choir room was built. The cavernous room that should have been demolished or at least remodeled had been bequeathed to the new teacher. No one had wanted this room. It was hard enough to corral teenagers in a small place, let alone a room this size.

On Tuesday, still reeling from her nightmarish trip, Madison had reported to work only to meet the vice principal from the underworld—Ms. Simone Joseph. Madison had hoped Ms.

Joseph was joking when she showed her the room. She soon learned levity wasn't Ms. Joseph's personal strength.

Setting up her classroom, in addition to bringing some sort of order to her new apartment, had exhausted her. At least it had kept her mind off the cowboy who hadn't called, or so she told herself. All week she had snapped to attention every time someone in a black Stetson walked by, which in the town of Edgewood was about one out of every three men.

It was hard to admit she'd let him raise her hopes of a relationship. Not that Aiden had promised her anything, but he had said he'd call. Why was she surprised he hadn't? After all, she barely knew the man. Still there had been something in his eyes, the way he touched her, that had made her think—

"You need to go home and get ready."

She looked up and smiled at her new friend. Pam was identical to Madison in height and weight, a good ten years older, and everything a new teacher could hope for in a mentor. She had smooth chocolate skin and a smile that never quit.

"I really don't want to go. Can't we tell them I'm exhausted? You're my mentor. Help me out here."

Pam shook her head and walked around the room, turning off lamps. "Nope. The Welcome Back Banquet is required for all district employees, and it's fun. Plus everyone is dying to meet the new teacher from Texas."

Madison put her head down on her desk in mock despair. "No. Please, no. Don't make me do it. You'd think Texas was on a different planet the way people go on about my accent."

Pam smiled, retrieved Madison's laptop bag from the closet, and set it on her desk.

"Wait. I know why I can't go," Madison said, hope brightening her face. "I still don't have anything to wear. I know I told you I'd go shopping, but I've been busy scouring garage sales for furniture for this gym you gave me to teach in. I totally forgot about shopping for a dress."

Pam unzipped the laptop bag and gave her the motherly look

that was becoming all too familiar. "Now how did I know you'd say that? I have three dresses in my car that are exactly your size. I'll let you take them all home."

Madison realized arguing was hopeless. In the end she would still lose, and she could be spending the next hour in a hot tub instead of sitting here creating excuses. With a sigh that came from the deepest part of her soul, she slipped the laptop into the bag, shouldered her purse, and followed Pam to the parking lot.

She might have to attend the dance, but she didn't have to stay. She'd go home, enjoy a hot bath to the sounds of Nora Jones, make an appearance, and be in bed by nine.

Chapter Thirty-Two

Aiden slammed the door, tossed his keys on the entry table and collapsed on the couch. He'd had the worst five days in his entire intel career. Too much golf, too many women, and not a single terrorist.

Martin hadn't phoned him again, but he didn't need to. The warning he'd given still rang in Aiden's ears, even in his sleep. They had fifty-four days to find Yassin's men and stop them or several major towns in America would be flooded. The newest projections for loss of life were even higher, considering the panic that was sure to occur. Emergency evacuation plans were being made, but with no idea where the terrorists would strike, they couldn't evacuate every town with a dam.

Aiden knew Martin had the bulk of the department working on it, so he had no excuse for feeling personally responsible. He'd been trained well though, and he did. Never assume the next man will lead in an op—especially an op as critical as Dambusters. Assume it's totally up to you.

The pressure was exhausting.

Add to the mix a six-hour drive both ways and the fact he hadn't slept in his own bed in two weeks and you had a man fit to be tied.

His agitation wasn't helped by the fact that he still hadn't been able to contact Madison. He'd tried every elementary school in Edgewood. They all insisted no Madison Hart was teaching there. He'd even tried the schools in Kalispell, but again came up empty.

Maybe he was remembering her last name wrong.

Maybe he had dreamed up the entire thing.

When he heard his brother's voice in the front hall, it was all he could do not to scream. Instead he sat up and tried to look better than he felt.

"I'm in here, bro."

Nate started shooting questions before he even stepped into the room.

"Where have you been? Did you ever think to call? Do you realize you have obligations to this family and you can't go off on a golfing spree when you feel like a weeklong vacation?"

Aiden's older brother flopped down in the leather armchair, the scowl on his face nearly comical in its intensity.

"Hey, big brother. It's nice to see you too."

"Nice to see me? That's it? That's all you have to say for yourself?"

Aiden raised his hand to stop the barrage. "I could use a drink. Anything for you?"

"I'll take some water. And find yourself something to eat. You look like death warmed over."

The growl remained, and Aiden found himself wishing for the hundredth time he could tell his brother the truth. If nothing else, it might keep him off his backside for a few minutes.

Aiden returned with the drinks, handed the vitamin water to his brother, and collapsed back on the couch. He picked up his glass of tap water and studied his brother. "Didn't Jacob call?"

"Yes, Jacob called. Who is he anyway?"

"Jacob—"

"I know," Nate snapped. "Jacob is your chauffeur. He told me. What do you need a chauffeur for? Last time I checked you were still able to drive yourself, and what was so important in Banff?"

Aiden sighed and held the glass to his head. Since he couldn't tell Nate the truth, he tried for the next best thing—a good lie.

"So if you were single, and a nice-looking blonde invited you up to The Fairmont for a few rounds of golf, you would turn her down?"

Nate set down his bottle, walked to the kitchen, and returned with a can of peanuts.

"I should have known a woman was involved. Good grief, Aiden. When are you going to grow up? And what about Sharon?"

"You sound jealous, big brother."

"You're thirty-two, Aiden. It's time to honor your commitments." Nate's disgust was evident, but instead of continuing the lecture he reached for the remote of the large flat screen TV and turned on ESPN.

Aiden was beginning to doze on the couch when the doorbell rang. He opened one eye but made no attempt to move.

Nate threw him an impatient look and muttered, "Next you'll be hiring a butler." Muting the TV, he walked to the front door.

Aiden had actually dropped back into never-never land when he opened his eyes to find a well-manicured hand shaking his shoulder.

"Aiden. Wake up, Aiden. We're supposed to be at the banquet in forty minutes."

He rubbed his eyes, recognizing the voice, but not quite comprehending what she was saying. "Banquet?"

Sitting up, he took another drink of the ice water, and finally turned to look at Sharon. She was dressed to the nines, her size-six figure tastefully poured into an ivory cashmere dress, stiletto heels adding a good two inches to her five-foot-eight-inch frame. Her blonde hair was pulled back severely to reveal intricate pearl earrings, a perfect match to the pearl necklace adorning her lovely neck.

Nate picked up his bottle, returned both it and the peanuts to the kitchen. "I'll leave you two alone."

He kissed the air beside Sharon's cheek, she murmured something in return, and then he was gone.

"Obviously you've forgotten," Sharon said. She perched on the chair across from Aiden, studying him with real concern in her eyes.

"I'm sorry." Aiden ran his hands through his hair and wondered if this day would ever end. "Do we have to?"

"Yes, Aiden. You're the one who insisted we attend the school banquet, the newspapers will be expecting it, and I'm already dressed. We have to, even if you do look completely hung over."

Aiden gave her his best boyish smile. "You still love me though."

"Yes, I still love you. Now please, shower and dress."

Chapter Thirty-Three

Madison tried to act like she was listening to the two-hundred-and-fifty-pound cowboy who was describing the calf he'd pulled that morning. In reality, she was looking for Pam, determined to find a way out of this party. She'd spotted her near the mayor and was about to excuse herself from Bubba's presence when a hush fell over the room. Turning to see what the commotion—or rather the lack of commotion—was all about, she found herself looking across the expanse of the giant lodge room at the elusive Aiden Lewis.

In a tuxedo and with an even deeper tan than he'd had a week ago, he was much better looking than she remembered. Without the Stetson, Madison could see he'd tried to tame his curly hair but without much success. The exquisite blonde hanging on to his arm completed the picture several photographers were eagerly taking.

Aiden's eyes scanned the room, finding hers so quickly it startled Madison right out of her shock. Even across the expanse of the room, she could feel the intensity of those gray eyes. She wanted to turn away, but couldn't. He held her there with his gaze, leaned toward the blonde and whispered something, but never broke eye contact. It was as if he was afraid she'd disappear.

The blonde touched his arm with a familiarity that spoke volumes and nodded her agreement to whatever he had said. Then he was walking toward her, stopping every few steps to shake hands with someone, but his eyes always quickly returned to hers.

Madison turned her back on him, hoping to disappear into the crowd. The noise level in the room quickly returned to normal, and Bubba was once again talking about his calf. Maybe she could hide behind Bubba. If she could turn him, maybe Aiden wouldn't see her.

She should have known he had a girlfriend. It would explain why he'd never called. Nothing shocking there. He was a nice man who'd helped her through a difficult night and then forgotten about her. It wasn't like he owed her anything. It wasn't like he'd promised to call. Okay, so he had promised. Men made promises and then they broke them.

She'd learned that lesson in Texas. Several guys had promised to be there for her when Mama got sick, but they all had excuses when she'd needed someone to talk to, or a dinner out, or simply a friend to see a movie with. Promises were easily made but rarely kept. She knew that. Why would she expect things to be different in Montana?

She tried to think of a question she could ask Bubba about the calf, but her mind had gone blank.

"Aiden and Sharon make quite a pair," Bubba said.

Madison did her best to look confused. "Who?"

Bubba might be big, but he wasn't stupid. He laughed and took a drink of his beer. "Don't worry about it, little lady. All the women look at Aiden Lewis, but looking is all you want to do."

Madison wanted to run away. She had no desire to hear what Bubba was about to say, but something held her there. Was it mere curiosity? Or the need to drive the knife a little deeper and permanently end the dream that had sprung to life during one very long plane flight to Montana?

"Don't take me wrong," Bubba said. "Aiden's a good guy, and

he does a lot for our town. That one isn't ready to settle down though. Most people think he never will. He's been a wild one since he was a teenager, since the accident with his dad."

Madison was about to inquire more when Pam appeared at her side.

"Bubba, are you hogging Madison? She needs to meet the rest of the school board."

"You can't blame me for that, Pam. She's the prettiest thing around here since the southern belle you all hired from Georgia."

"And we'd like Madison to stay a little longer than Stella did, so quit boring her to death with stories about your calves."

Bubba had the good grace to blush.

"Nice to meet you, Miss Madison. If there's anything you need at all, you have my business card." And with that the big man was gone.

"Come on," Pam said. "I want you to meet Aiden. Did you see him come in with Sharon? They're a picture-perfect couple. We're all expecting a wedding announcement any time."

While Pam talked she'd taken Madison's hand and was pulling her across the room. Madison tried to protest, tried to think of something she could say to interrupt her friend. The week had been too long, she was too tired, and she could not face Mr. Aiden Lewis tonight. Unable to articulate the feelings overwhelming her, she simply stopped moving.

"Are you okay, honey? You don't look so good."

Madison shook her head, still unable to find her voice.

"It is kind of warm in here. Maybe we should go outside. That crazy Bubba had you pinned in the corner for at least twenty minutes. I should have rescued you sooner."

Madison tried again to answer, but she couldn't. All she could do was stare at Aiden, watch him cover the ground between the two of them. Mesmerized by the look on his face, the recognition and surprise in his eyes, she tried to look away. Before she could offer a word of explanation to Pam, he was at their side.

"Madison," Aiden sighed her name more than he said it. "How are you?"

His eyes seemed to cut through hers and settle on her soul. He reached out, touched the side of her arm, let his hand drop when she still didn't say anything.

"Aiden. I didn't know you'd met Madison." Pam looked from one to the other, obviously confused by what was going on.

"I tried to find you," Aiden explained, his words coming faster now. "I called all the elementary schools. They didn't have a Madison Hart."

Madison remained silent, trying to think of what to say, wanting to say a thousand things, saying nothing.

"Madison is our new high school English teacher, Aiden." Pam continued to look bewildered. "Bubba had Madison cornered for the last twenty minutes, and I think he wore her out."

She offered a little laugh, trying to lighten the mood but failing.

For the first time, Aiden seemed to notice Pam was there. "If Bubba cornered her she probably could use some fresh air. I'll show her the patio."

Before either woman could answer, he'd turned Madison toward the patio doors and begun gently nudged her in that direction.

Madison wanted to walk away. She was afraid her heart might literally beat right out of her chest. Was this what a heart attack felt like? Could you have a heart attack at twenty-five? She had a million questions, but she didn't really want the answers to any of them. Had Pam said the words wedding announcement? Where had Aiden been all week? Had he really tried to find her? And who was the blonde he was about to marry?

Chapter Thirty-Four

The tiredness fell off Aiden like a heavy coat he'd left behind. He couldn't believe Madison was here, not only here, but lovelier than he'd remembered. The sapphire blue dress she wore accentuated her figure while somehow still emphasizing her smallness, her femininity. She looked better than she had a week ago, though how that was possible Aiden couldn't say.

The trip from Dallas came rushing back to him, and he suddenly remembered the feel of her in his arms, the smell of her hair, the softness of her hand on his arm. If he didn't get her out of this crowded room soon, he was going to pull her into his arms in front of everyone which would suit him fine.

Keep it cool, Iceman. She was collateral, nothing more, and you are still in the middle of Dambusters.

Aiden didn't even try to listen to the voice of reason that usually ruled his every move. He'd managed to lead them across the room and out onto the patio, a patio that was blessedly empty of people.

Reaching the corner of the terrace, he tried to turn her toward him, but Madison pulled away. Putting several feet between them, she leaned against the cedar railing and looked out at the Montana night. Something in her stance stopped his questions. He had always been good with women and his natural instincts kicked in. She reminded him of a doe about to run. Better to give her space and tread lightly.

Instead of pulling her into his arms, he settled for standing next to her, his arm barely brushing up against hers. He looked out at the scene she seemed mesmerized by, mountains disappearing as darkness fell. A thousand points of light brightening the sky. A slight breeze rustled the trees, intensifying the feelings dancing between them.

"How was your first week?" he asked softly.

She drew a deep breath. "Good." She still didn't look at him, but seemed slightly less ready to bolt.

"Is Pam helping you out?"

"Pam's a godsend."

Aiden turned to look at her, drank in the sight of her. The mass of brown hair was piled on top of her head, revealing a slender neck. The breeze tickled a few strands of hair that had escaped, and Aiden nearly came undone. He wanted to pull it all down, bury his hands in it, nuzzle her neck, feel her in his arms again.

"You don't owe me an explanation, Aiden. You helped me through a difficult night, and I appreciate that. It's okay that you didn't call."

"It's not okay, Madison. I tried to call, but I couldn't find you. It never occurred to me you might be teaching at the high school." Aiden ran his hand through his hair, then turned her gently to look at him. "I would have found you, Madison. I arrived back in town this afternoon. Trust me when I say by Monday I would have found you."

Madison met his gaze. He looked into those brown eyes and fell a little farther, heard the last of the ice around his heart crack away. Without it he felt completely alive and vulnerable, more than he had on any mission.

"It was only one night," she whispered.

"No. It was more than that." The rebuke came out sharper than he'd intended. Unable to stop himself he reached out and touched both her bare arms, ran his hands up and down her soft skin. He needed to feel her, to know she was real, to somehow ground himself in her presence.

"It was more than that," he said more softly. Then he pulled her to him, and he was kissing her—first tenderly, his lips barely brushing hers. He caressed the goosebumps on her arms. Her body perfectly melted into his.

Suddenly she stiffened and pushed him gently away.

The night had turned cool, but Aiden's fingertips burned as if he'd spent long hours in the middle of a Texas summer day. Madison walked away from him. When she turned, she pressed her fingers to her lips and said, "Sharon..."

As if the word had conjured the woman, Sharon appeared at the patio door—blonde, elegant, and confident.

"Aiden?" She hesitated when she noticed Madison, took in the scene, and seemed to understand it in one sweeping look. "Aiden, the mayor would like a few more publicity shots."

"Sure. Thanks." Aiden felt as shaken as Madison seemed. Covering the distance across the patio in three strides, he took Sharon's hand, pulled her over to where Madison still stood.

"Sharon, I'd like you to meet Madison Hart. Madison, this is my friend, Sharon."

"You're new to Edgewood."

"Yes, I just moved here from Texas." Madison shook Sharon's hand.

"I hadn't had a chance to tell you yet," Aiden said. "I met Madison on the flight from Dallas."

"Welcome to Edgewood. I trust if you need anything, you will let the school board know. Now if you'll excuse us..."

"Yes, I will," Madison said. "It was nice to meet you."

Sharon nodded again, then turned back toward the room, never checking to see if Aiden would follow, which he did.

Chapter Thirty-Five

Two hours later Aiden escorted Sharon to her Porsche 911 and grunted when she handed him the keys. The Carrera 4S was a true sports car with four-wheel-drive and a 355-horsepower engine. The car was quite a luxury, but one Sharon could afford given her status as Edgewood's top lawyer.

Aiden worked through the gears silently. He had tried to find Madison again later in the evening, but she had fled. The look on her face when Sharon had shown up still made him feel like a complete jerk. He'd find her tomorrow, and he'd explain. He'd make her understand.

"Do you want to tell me about Miss Hart?" Sharon's voice was quiet, nonjudgmental, even a little amused.

Aiden tried to think of how to explain Madison. He had no idea where to begin.

"You could begin with the flight."

"The flight." Aiden thought about the last week, considered what he could tell Sharon and what he couldn't.

"You flew from Dallas to Edgewood." She settled into the corner of her seat so she could watch him closely, obviously enjoying his discomfort.

"Right." Aiden sighed and ran his hand through his hair. "Madison was sick on the flight, and I took her to the first-class lounge. We both missed our connection, so we had a few hours to kill. Then she saw the puddle jumper."

The memories hit Aiden like a punch to his gut. Madison sitting next to Coyote. Madison unconscious on the plane. Madison wearing those goofball rhinestone sunglasses. Madison in his arms as he carried her through the airport.

"Aiden, maybe you should let me drive."

"Why would you say that?"

"Because you're going eighty, and you seem a little distracted." It was Sharon the lawyer speaking now, and her practicality brought Aiden back to the present with a thud. He slowed down, waving away her offer to drive.

"You're attracted to her."

"It's that obvious, huh?"

"Half of Edgewood is wondering why I put up with you, Aiden." Sharon reached out and touched his arm. "If only they knew, right?"

"Yeah, if only they knew."

Aiden focused on the car, the gears, and the winding road leading up the mountain, the whole time thinking—for probably the hundredth time—how lucky he was to have a friend like Sharon.

"Perhaps they should know." Her voice was soft, testing the waters, daring him.

"I wouldn't do that to you, Sharon. We said we'd stick by each other, and that's a promise I'm not going to break."

"But we knew we'd have to come clean one day."

Aiden pretended to concentrate on navigating the curves up the mountain.

"And I think I'm ready," she said.

Aiden jerked the little car into a pull-out overlooking Edgewood. They had climbed high enough that the lights of the town were a mere twinkle, one building indistinguishable from the next. Each melted into a menagerie offering no beginning and no end, much like the lies he had told. He set the brake and turned to look at her, taking a minute for his eyes to grow accustomed to the darkness, studying her face.

"You're serious," he said.

"Yes, I am."

"I can be more discreet."

"It's not just about you, Aiden. Bix has been pressuring me to be honest with my parents, but I didn't want to abandon you. After all this relationship is your cover story as well as mine."

Aiden leaned against the door, weighing their alternatives, trying to put Sharon's needs ahead of his own galloping emotions. "What about your parents?"

"I have an established clientele now. I didn't have that five years ago when we hatched this crazy plan. I don't think my parents would actually pull my inheritance off the table, but if they did I would survive. Besides, I'm learning there are things more important than money or approval. I want to spend more time with him. I want to go to hear his band. I want to travel with him."

Aiden reached across the gearshift and hugged her. "My family's in for a big surprise."

"I think they'll be relieved. One more lecture from Nate on how I shouldn't tolerate your carousing anymore and I'm going to belt the man."

"He has your best interests at heart."

"Right."

Aiden grinned, started the car, released the brake, and pulled back onto the road. "Bix is lucky to have you."

"He knows."

"I'm lucky to have you too."

"I'm glad you realize that."

"I'm serious, Sharon. If there's anything I've learned in the last five years it's that true friends are hard to come by."

"Thank you, Aiden. But you have more friends than you realize."

"Maybe."

A comfortable silence filled the car as he turned into the golf course community and pulled up to his house. A fraction of the weight he was carrying around had been lifted, and for that Aiden was grateful.

He had set the brake, unbuckled his seatbelt, and reached for the door handle when Sharon put her hand on his arm.

"Tell me about her."

Aiden released the handle, letting the darkness settle around them, wishing again he could tell her everything. If there was one person he could trust to know of his involvement with USCIS, it was Sharon. Unfortunately, too much was at stake. All it would take was a single slip and his cover would be lost. With the clock for Dambusters ticking, Martin needed every agent he had.

Telling Sharon what he really did on his golfing trips was out of the question. He'd have to be satisfied with telling her about Madison.

"I've never met anyone like her."

"Go on."

"She's smart and funny, even when she's—" He almost said *in danger*, but he caught himself and backtracked. "Even when she's scared. If you could have seen the look on her face when she saw our connecting plane."

"They are rather small."

"Yeah. She came to Montana to teach."

"There are teaching jobs in Texas," Sharon said.

"True. I don't know why she decided to teach here." He shook his head in the dark, at the absurdity of it, at the wonder of it. How had she landed in his life?

"You're serious about this one."

"Yeah."

Aiden rubbed his face with both hands. The last week was catching up with him. He needed sleep and time to unwind, but mostly he had to see Madison again. Feel her in his arms. Explain so many things to her.

"Take some advice from an old friend? Go slow. You've known her less than a week."

"Right."

"Not just for yourself, Aiden. Go slow for Madison. Dating you can be rather intimidating. You *are* one of Montana's most eligible bachelors."

Aiden scowled at the reference to an article published last month in several of the state's papers. Even with Sharon as his supposed girlfriend, the press kept hounding him.

"She's probably not used to a lot of public attention," Aiden admitted.

"Probably not."

Sharon got out of the car, walked around to the driver's side, and held her hand out for the keys.

"I'm going to miss driving this car."

"Buy your own."

Aiden laughed and put his arms around her. "I'm going to miss you."

"I'll still be around." Sharon stepped back, then reached forward and raked his hair out of his eyes. "You need rest, Aiden, and a haircut. Then go after Madison."

"Right. Rest. Haircut. Girl."

"Don't screw up the order."

"Rest. Haircut. Girl."

Aiden plodded up the walk, murmuring the words like a mantra. Deactivating his security net, he entered his home and dropped his keys on the table in the entryway. He briefly considered attacking the pile of mail, but he couldn't do it. He could barely drag his exhausted body up the stairs.

As he collapsed onto his bed, he thought of Madison, how she had looked in the blue dress, the softness of her in his arms. If only he could have held on to that vision as sleep overtook him.

Instead he dreamed of Coyote, Dambusters, and the Hungry

Horse Dam located outside of Edgewood. Even as he slept he chased the shadows, determined to protect her, doggedly trying to save them all. Hearing the ticking of the clock firmly in place at the back of his mind. Fifty-four days. He had exactly fifty-four days.

Chapter Thirty-Six

Madison woke to the memory of his kiss, his hands caressing her arms, his voice soft and persuasive. Then she remembered Sharon.

"Move eighteen hundred miles across five states and find another cowboy who makes another worthless promise." Throwing the covers off she stomped into the bathroom, turned the hot water on to the shower, then lectured the reflection in the mirror. "Mama did not raise a fool, and you will not make the same mistake again."

The reflection looked ready to argue with her, so she stripped off her pjs, jerked back the shower curtain and stepped into the water without testing it, earning herself a very cold wakeup.

"Where is my hot water?" Jumping back out she grabbed one of the new yellow towels she'd purchased and wrapped herself in it. After a week in the apartment she knew the shower took a good five minutes to heat up, but she needed to scream at something and the plumbing was handy.

Thirty minutes later she'd finished her shower, made a cup of the strongest coffee she could brew, and was intent on reading through her English curriculum when the doorbell rang.

Only Pam knew where she lived, and Pam had gone to the

Summit Station Lodge for a before-school-starts weekend away with her husband. Madison was tempted to ignore the ringing bell, but her visitor was relentless. He was going to wake up the stuffed bears lining her window seat if he didn't go away.

"I'm not interested," she said in no uncertain terms as she jerked the door open. The bouquet of roses temporarily caught her off guard, as did the teenage boy holding them. He wore a Edgewood Florist cap and seemed at a loss for words.

"Oh. Um. I think you must have the wrong address." She started to close the door, but the boy edged forward and finally found his voice.

"Are you Madison Hart?"

"Yes." Madison had a bad feeling about this.

"Well these are for you then."

"But I don't know anyone here."

"They're from Mr. Lewis. He wanted to send more, but my boss told him a dozen would be plenty."

Madison resisted the urge to grab the flowers and throw them across the parking lot. She wanted to scream. She did not want flowers from an engaged man.

"It just so happens—what is your name?"

"Gabe."

"It just so happens, Gabe, that I'm not accepting flowers today."

The boy looked so confused Madison almost pitied him.

"But you have to accept them."

"No, actually I don't. I can refuse them. And that's what I'm doing, Gabe. I'm refusing them."

The boy looked at the flowers, then back at her, then at the flowers again.

"No one refuses flowers."

"Well I am."

"What am I supposed to do with them?"

"Take them back to the shop."

"I can't do that. My boss will kill me."

"Then take them home to your mother. Or give them to your girlfriend. I don't really care what you do with them, but you are not leaving them here."

Madison slammed the door a little harder than she meant to, but it had the desired effect. When she peeked through her curtains, Gabe was walking slowly across the parking lot toward an old pickup truck, shaking his head and no doubt muttering about the strange ways of women.

Her day went downhill from there.

She tried housework, but there was no satisfaction in it. The place wasn't dirty. She attempted to work on her lesson plans, but her computer was acting up, had been acting up for the last few days—since the internet people came to work on a problem that she didn't have. How they messed that up, she couldn't guess. Now she had a problem, and she'd need to call them back. Only when she contacted her service provider they had no record of anyone having been at her house.

She was put on hold and after twenty minutes gave up and collapsed on her couch. Looking out the window she thought again of the flowers, and Sharon, and Aiden's kiss. She jumped off the couch as if a snake had bit her. She couldn't sit there thinking about him.

If she couldn't clean, she could hike.

Chapter Thirty-Seven

Aiden drove down the mountain at nearly the same speed he'd driven up it. He'd followed Sharon's directions pretty closely, and of course they hadn't worked. His sleep was long enough, but hardly restful given the number of bombs he'd tried to disarm. His hair appointment was scheduled for this afternoon, the earliest opening he could find on a Saturday, though with the Stetson he always wore he couldn't see how hair mattered. The next logical step seemed to be to send flowers.

Aiden's hands gripped the wheel harder as he tightened into the curve ten miles per hour faster than he should have. What kind of woman refuses flowers? They weren't poisonous. If she'd read the note, she'd known he was on his way to explain everything. According to the idiot delivery kid, she wouldn't even look at it. Well she might slam the door on a skinny kid, but she'd listen to him.

Aiden was so focused on how he'd convince her to open the door, he almost missed the rental car pulled over on the shoulder of the road. The driver sat leaning out the door, head between her knees, lovely brown hair brushing the ground.

She didn't look up when he pulled in behind her. Slamming

the door on the Avalanche he walked over to her and stopped inches away. She still didn't look up.

"You seem to favor this position," he said.

"Go away."

"And leave you here on the side of the road?"

"Yes."

"What seems to be the problem?"

"There is no problem."

"Huh."

"Go away."

Aiden wanted to laugh. He longed to pull her into his arms and kiss the stubbornness out of her. Instead he squatted down in front of her and gently parted her hair to get a look at her face.

"What are you doing, Madison?"

She refused to meet his gaze, ducked her head lower instead. Though her misery came through loud and clear, he had to move closer to be able to make out her words.

"I wanted to go hiking."

"You didn't make it to the trails."

"I'm scared of driving mountain roads."

He didn't even try to stop his laughter.

"I thought I could do it," she explained.

"You can do it, Maddie. Look at me."

"Go away."

"If you'd kept my flowers you wouldn't be in this position."

Aiden had wanted a reaction, and Madison gave him one. Her head snapped up and chocolate eyes reminded him of a caged cat, a very unhappy caged cat.

"I don't want your flowers, and I don't need your help." Madison got back in her car, slammed the door, and rolled up the window. She started the car and pulled out onto the road, spraying gravel.

So much for being afraid to drive on mountain roads.

He could follow her, but that would do no good if she wouldn't talk to him.

He could wait at the bottom of the road. She had to come back this way, but what was the point? She'd shown him in no uncertain terms she wanted nothing to do with him.

It didn't help that he'd received no update on Dambusters. Coyote seemed to have disappeared into thin air, and there was no additional activity being reported. The worst part of any op was the down time. If Aiden had been able to spend it with Madison, he wouldn't be as frustrated.

But for now, it seemed as if frustration was his lot in life.

Chapter Thirty-Eight

Monday afternoon Madison walked around her classroom, straightening chairs and stacking books. She needed to work on exit procedures since her students had left the room in complete disarray. Still, she'd managed to survive her first day at Edgewood High School, and that put it in the success column.

The morning began with a class of thirty-five juniors, including none other than delivery boy, Gabe. He was as surprised as she was but recovered faster.

"You're the flower lady."

"And you're the delivery boy."

"Why would Mr. Lewis send you flowers?"

"I'd rather not discuss my personal life, Gabe. I believe your seat is in the first row. Check the seating chart on the board to be sure."

She had hoped it would end there, but of course it didn't. After that she heard whispers in every class. Mostly the boys snickered and the girls stared. Madison ignored it as best she could. What with distributing textbooks and assigning enough work to convince them English III was not going to be a breeze, students didn't have much time for socializing anyway.

Seven hours later, she collapsed at her desk and went to work finishing up her day's paperwork. Entering the last period's attendance, she was surprised to hear her classroom door jerked open by demon principal, Miss Joseph. Either she disliked Texans in general, or she simply hated Madison.

"Is there a reason you're not at your duty, Ms. Hart?"

"Duty?"

"I sent you an email over an hour ago reminding you to be in the gym at 3:15."

"The gym?" Madison realized how stupid she sounded, but she couldn't imagine what she would be doing in a gym. By the look on Miss Joseph's face, the Vice Principal couldn't imagine what she was even doing in the school.

"Surely you know where the gym is."

"Well, yeah. I saw it when I went to lunch."

"Yeah? I would prefer a simple yes or no when you're answering me. How do you expect to teach your students proper English if you can't even provide a decent example?"

Madison stared at the woman. She was in her early fifties and one of the most bitter souls Madison had ever met.

"Now if you would be so kind as to report to your duty–in the gym—I'm sure the golf team would appreciate it." And with that she was gone.

Madison shook her head, opened her laptop, and scanned through the emails she had not had time to read because she had been teaching. Sure enough, there it was.

> *Report to the gym on Monday, Wednesday, and Friday afternoon for your assigned duty—golf club sponsor.*

Golf club? What kind of school had a golf club? And why was she its sponsor? She didn't know anything about golf. She'd never even watched it on TV. And why did she have a duty that met three days a week, including every Friday?

Madison allowed herself a full minute to think wistfully of Texas, where football, basketball, and baseball reigned and they wouldn't allow an English teacher any closer to a team than the stands. Shaking her head, she placed her laptop in the bag and headed to the gym.

Chapter Thirty-Nine

Aiden looked out at his team and relaxed for the first time in weeks—until he thought about the brunette down the hall who still wasn't talking to him. He'd spent all of Sunday trying to charm his way back into her good graces.

He didn't even know what she was mad about. He'd tried flowers again, sent chocolate, even balloons. No go. She'd taken to not answering the door to delivery men. He'd tried calling, but she'd hung up on him.

No doubt the entire town knew Madison was refusing his deliveries. They also knew he and Sharon had "broken up." His brother had already called him twice advising him to reconsider.

"Maybe you should try saying you're sorry, Coach." Chase was the team captain. At six and a half feet, two hundred and thirty pounds, he looked more like a linebacker than a golfer, but the kid had taken them to the state title the year before. He was a born leader, and Aiden would miss him when he graduated this year.

"I do not want to talk about my private life, Chase. Now I've passed out our schedule. As you can see, between varsity and JV we have fifteen tournaments in the next ten weeks, so we have our work cut out for us."

"What did you do to make her so mad?" Kevin asked, pushing up his glasses.

"Yeah, you're always lecturing us about being sensitive." Justin was also a senior and known for his temper. He'd received more than one lecture from Aiden about the importance of considering other's feelings.

"Sounds like you blew it, Coach," Chase said.

"Speaking of blowing it..." Aiden picked up his whistle and blew it shrilly. "Ten laps everyone."

Amidst groans and claims of gimp legs, the boys climbed off the bleachers and started toward the door leading to the track. Aiden was staring down at his summer stats report when the boys suddenly stopped moving and grew strangely quiet. He suddenly realized every boy had his eyes locked on the gym door, and it only took him a second to figure out why.

Aiden's pulse jumped as his eyes met hers.

She looked tired, cranky, and more than a little mad, but to Aiden she was as attractive as ever.

"This is my duty?" she asked. "With you?"

All eyes turned toward him.

"Uhh. Let me see. I'm the volunteer coach, and I guess you are—"

"The team sponsor. Why do I smell a set up here, Mr. Lewis?"

She had stormed her way across the gym, and now stood in front of him—hands firmly planted on her hips, eyes blazing, a stubborn look on her face Aiden was sure he could kiss away if he could lose the dozen boys staring at them.

"Maybe we should talk about this in private, Ms. Hart."

Madison turned to stare at the boys, then turned back to Aiden. "Why would we need to do that? Obviously, they all know about our situation already, since I have had to deflect questions about it in every single class. How small is this town anyway?"

"Pretty small," Chase said.

"Way too small," Justin added.

"It's enough to make you crazy," Gabe piped in.

Aiden's look silenced the boys, but they still didn't move. As a last resort, he grabbed the whistle and started blowing. Either that or the stormy look he sent them worked. They were out the door in record time.

The last week finally caught up with Aiden, and the absurdity of it won. What started as a chuckle ended up as an outright laugh—earning him a look from Madison that might have caused damage if he'd ever stop laughing. Sitting down on the bleachers he set the clipboard beside him and leaned forward, arms resting on his knees, studying her and waiting.

"Aren't you going to storm out?" he finally asked.

"Excuse me?"

"You stormed out of the banquet. You stormed off the mountain. I figured now you'd storm out of the gym."

"This happens to be a part of my job, buster." She walked over to where he sat and stopped within a few inches of him.

She was so mad her brown eyes had turned nearly black, and still he was drawn to her, the attraction so strong it caused an ache in his bones.

"Whether I like the assignments I'm given or not I will do them. So, no, I am not storming out. Though I can't imagine this is a coincidence."

"Oh, it is a coincidence," Aiden said. "Do you think I'd really ask for you to be our sponsor? You have no sense of humor, you're more stubborn than any woman I've ever known, and you probably don't know a thing about golf."

"I do have a sense of humor. I have every right to be angry with you, and it's not my fault I don't know anything about golf. It's not even a real sport."

"Madison, if you'd let me explain." When Aiden stood up she practically jumped back, then moved even farther away as Gabe walked back into the gym.

"I forgot my water bottle. Sorry, Coach."

Madison took a deep breath and watched the boy scuttle away. "They put him up to that."

"Absolutely."

"No doubt he's reporting every word he heard."

"No doubt."

Madison crossed her arms and looked around the gym as if she'd never been in one before.

"They're good kids, Madison. Just curious."

Madison raised an eyebrow, but she didn't argue with him. Aiden wanted to cross the floor and shake the stubbornness out of her, or at least pull her into his arms and hold her until the fight was gone. He resisted the urge, knowing it would only raise her defenses at this point. He wasn't sure who had hurt her in the past, but he suddenly understood this wasn't solely about him.

To his surprise, she walked slowly across the gym floor and stopped mere inches in front of him. "How long is golf season?"

"Ten weeks, twelve if I can arrange an additional tournament in Banff."

"I suppose we could find a way to work together for twelve weeks."

Aiden pretended to think about it, rubbed his chin, and finally shrugged. "I guess we could."

"Entirely on a professional basis."

"Understood."

"And only because I have to. Evil Ms. Joseph set this up. The woman hasn't liked me from day one."

"This is day one."

"Exactly."

"Madison, if you want me to request a different sponsor—"

Her chin went up in what was becoming a familiar look of defiance. "I can do this. Tell me what my responsibilities are."

Aiden pulled the season's schedule from his stack of papers and went over it with her, explaining where the meets were, what the practices consisted of, and what they would need her to do. Madison kept her distance the entire time, but he thought she relaxed a little.

And, suddenly, that was all right. It was enough for now to be near her and to know he would see her on a regular basis. He still didn't understand why she wouldn't give him a chance to explain, but it was a small town. She'd learn he'd broken up with Sharon, and then she'd listen to him.

All he had to do was wait, and he had no doubt Ms. Hart was worth waiting for.

Chapter Forty

Madison climbed into the van and gave Aiden her best you-better-behave teacher look. It worked on the teens, but Aiden's grin only grew wider causing her heart to skip a beat or two.

The man was tenacious. She'd give him that.

There were several times when she had wondered if he'd hired someone to follow her as it seemed that she saw the same two cars in her rearview mirror much too often. But stalking wasn't Aiden's style, and no doubt seeing the same cars over and over in a small town was normal. He'd continued sending gifts to her house every day for a week. She'd refused the roses, tulips, carnations, potted plant, balloons, chocolate, and books.

But when she'd opened her door to a giant bouquet of Texas bluebonnets, she couldn't send them away. She was suddenly more homesick than she'd ever have thought possible. She might be an independent woman, but even independent women miss the green, green grass of home—or in this case the bluebonnets of home.

He followed that with a week of phone calls, exactly what she needed to reestablish a baseline of trust.

"You can stop grinning," she told him.

The noise from twelve boys juggling for seats in the back of the van covered their conversation quite nicely.

"Am I grinning?" he asked.

"You are."

"We're going to our first meet. I have a fantastic golf team and the very best sponsor in Edgewood, who also happens to be the most enchanting woman on staff. Why wouldn't I grin?"

Madison made a face at his obvious flirting and turned to look out the window to hide her own smile.

"You look pretty happy yourself, Ms. Hart."

She swung back around to look at him, brown eyes dancing. "I am happy, actually. The first two weeks of school are over, I have an excused-early pass on a Friday, and I'm going to visit a part of Montana I've never seen before. It should be quite an adventure."

"You're going to love Missoula." Aiden's voice grew serious, tender really, and the look he gave her almost melted Madison in her seat.

She'd been relieved to learn he had broken up with Sharon, although she still didn't know why. He'd tried to explain it to her in one of their nightly phone calls, but she'd insisted she wasn't ready to talk about past relationships yet.

The week she'd spent angry with him had given her a little perspective. The flight from Dallas had been traumatic and thrilling at the same time, but it had sent their relationship careening off in a serious direction much too quickly. Madison knew, instinctively, that she needed to apply the brakes.

She was eager to see more of Montana. She'd had no luck finding her father, but there wasn't a day that passed where she didn't remember her promise to her mother or the conversation they'd had that day in April. It seemed as if this trip would be fulfilling part of that vow. She couldn't help wondering if her mother had followed this same road with her father.

The noise level in the van settled down to a dim roar as the boys became absorbed in their cell phones.

"What will we see?" Madison asked.

"I can take you out and show you the stars tonight."

"I was talking about scenery."

"Oh." Aiden gave her his hurt cowboy look as he pulled out of the school's parking lot. "If it's scenery you want, it's scenery we'll find. You'll be able to see parts of the Bob Marshall Wilderness to the east and the Flathead Indian Reservation to the west."

Madison slipped off her shoes and pulled her feet up into the seat, hugging her knees. "What kind of Indians?"

"Big ones," Jack muttered.

Aiden laughed. "Some of the Kootenai are rather large. There are over 6,800 tribe members in all, including Salish and Pend d'Oreilles."

"How do you know so much about them?" Madison settled into the corner of her seat and watched Aiden as he drove.

"He was one." Gabe shouted from the back.

"They listen to every word we say, don't they?"

"Unless it's instructions." Aiden tried to sound disgruntled, but didn't quite succeed.

"So, there's an Indian reservation. What else?"

"Not just any Indian reservation. The Flathead Indian Reservation is 1.2 million acres. It's a majestic mountainous area. You'll enjoy the drive."

"What was the Bob Marshall thing?"

Chants of "Bob, Bob, Bob, Bob" filled the back of the van.

Aiden gave a short blow on his whistle he wore on a lanyard, and the boys immediately settled down.

"Are they always this crazy on a trip?" Madison asked.

"YES," twelve voices shouted at once.

"They love the Bob Marshall," Aiden explained. "Most of the boys have been going there since they were old enough to hold a paddle or shoot a rifle."

"Shoot?"

"Absolutely. It's one of the best hunting areas in the U.S. Of course, there are restrictions. You can't just go in and start blasting away, but there's plenty of game to be had."

"Yeah, there's lions..."

"And tigers..."

"And BEAR!"

Aiden laughed again. "They're right about the bear. The Bob Marshall is the last habitat south of Canada for the grizzly." Something passed over Aiden's eyes, but he glanced quickly out the side window, and when he looked back at Madison, it was gone.

"What else?" she asked.

"Gray wolves, which are endangered. Elk, deer, lynx..."

"Bobcats."

"Bighorn sheep and black bears."

"Wolverines and cougars."

The boys tripped off the list as if they had memorized it for an exam.

Madison pulled her jacket a little closer and checked her seatbelt.

"They can't open car doors, Miss." Jack reached forward and patted her clumsily on the shoulder. "You're safe with us, and if we have to actually leave the car, we'll protect you in the great outdoors."

That sent the boys into peals of laughter.

"How far did you say it is to Missoula?" Madison asked.

"Nearly a hundred and fifty miles. We have time to tell you about lots of animals." As Jack paused to consider which animal would gross her out the most, Aiden mercifully turned on the radio and slipped in a Kenny Chesney CD.

"Beach music is exactly what I need." And with that Madison scrunched down in her seat and gazed out the window, thankful for the metal and glass between her and the wild.

Chapter Forty-One

It was almost a perfect day. Aiden was pumped about the upcoming meet. The boys' enthusiasm reminded him of all he loved about the game of golf. The weather was perfect, and the woman he most wanted to be with was sitting beside him.

If he could just ignore the text messages from Martin, he could relax. Unfortunately, he couldn't.

> Coyote might be on the move. Awaiting confirmation. Be prepared to move in tonight.

Aiden knew one of two things could happen.

Nothing.

Or their operation could break wide open.

USCIS received false tips all the time. High-tech eavesdropping was a wonderful thing, but it wasn't exactly a secret. As a result, quite a bit of decoy chatter was strategically released with the knowledge USCIS couldn't listen to every transmission.

Aiden was officially on alert, which meant he had to continue with his regular activities as if nothing was going to happen. However, if and when Martin was able to corroborate the information that Coyote was moving operatives across, Aiden would have to be in position.

Aiden slowed down to point out elk near the roadway for Madison. She stared at them with a look of complete wonder.

"What magnificent animals," she said softly, turning and putting her hand on his arm, melting another piece of his heart.

Aiden didn't want to think about how he would be letting down his team if he had to deploy. Then again, he didn't want to cancel the trip if he didn't have to. In fact, for the sake of his cover he had to keep up all appearances.

One part of his mind reasoned that he had received three such messages in the last week, and nothing had come of any of them.

The other part of his mind chaffed, listening to the clock ticking down to the G8 Summit, now only thirty-nine days away. As far as they could tell, Dambusters' plan continued on schedule.

Chapter Forty-Two

The C'mon Inn had an indoor pool, five hot tubs, a game room, jacuzzi suites, kitchenette suites, two-room suites, and an indoor waterfall. No doubt Aiden was hoping it would keep the boys out of trouble, but Madison knew teens. Where there was a will there would be a way, and from the look she'd seen Jack give to Matt, there was definitely a will. They were good boys though, so she was not going to worry about it. She planned on enjoying this evening.

She'd spent the last day and a half watching the boys putt and drive, and it was a sight to behold. Two weeks ago she'd never seen a round of golf, but even she could recognize how they'd come together as a team. They were in second place with one round left to play the next morning.

Checking her eye makeup one more time, Madison spritzed her wrists with a hint of perfume, then raised her hair and dotted some along the back of her neck. Aiden was treating her to dinner at the hotel dining room which just happened to boast a highly acclaimed chef. The boys had opted for a swim in the indoor pool followed by pizza and video games in their rooms. Neither Madison or Aiden dared wander too far from the team, but the hotel dining room seemed a safe distance while still allowing them some privacy.

Madison walked toward the lobby, her mind combing over the highlights of the trip.

"You Texas women do clean up nicely."

Madison stopped, turned around, and found herself face-to-face with Aiden. His voice was teasing, but his eyes were serious. And those gray eyes were something she could drown in if she'd let go for a moment. Falling was such a scary thing though, and Madison still wasn't sure she could trust this cowboy with her heart.

Then he leaned forward, and she thought he would kiss her. Her breath caught in her chest, and she suddenly knew that it was too late, she already had fallen.

Aiden kissed her cheek, put his hands on her arms and gently spun her toward the dining room.

"A day on the course can work up an appetite," he said.

"Is that why I'm so hungry?" Madison tried to match his lighthearted tone, but she could still feel the warmth from his kiss.

"Keeping up with twelve boys is no laughing matter."

The hostess showed them to a table near windows which allowed them to look out across the valley and the Clark Fork River. Aiden pulled out her chair, then scooted it in for her. Ignoring the place set beside her, he walked to the opposite side of the table and sat down.

"Afraid to sit near me?"

Aiden accepted the menu from the waiter and waited until he'd filled their water glasses and informed them of the dinner specials. Once the man was gone, Aiden set the menu aside and leaned forward, elbows on the table, chin propped on his hands. "Actually I wanted to sit across the table, where I could lose myself in those pretty brown eyes."

Madison tilted her head back and laughed. "We are going to need a lot more ice water if you're going to play it that hot, Mr. Lewis."

"I'm playing, am I?"
"Yes, you're playing."
"So you don't think I'm serious?"
"I know you're serious, but I also know you're playing."
"I'm serious, but I'm playing."
"Right."
Aiden shook his head. "That would only make sense to a woman."
"You're playing because you enjoy flirting."
"Guilty."
"But you're serious, because you're hoping it will work."
"And is it working?"
Madison did not have to answer, because the waiter arrived to take their order.

As the dinner progressed, they talked of everything from national news to school gossip. The mountain trout was fabulous and the service impeccable. The sun setting across the valley, the shadows of the mountains, it all seemed like a scene from a romantic movie.

"You look happy." Aiden sipped his coffee as they waited for dessert.

"I am." Madison added cream to her cup, taking her time, enjoying the way the milk stirred into the blackness of the coffee, committing to memory everything about this evening. "It's been a long time since I've been this comfortable with someone, with a man."

Aiden covered her hand with his own, played with her fingers, and then ran his forefinger from her fingertips to her wrist, back and forth.

"I know what you mean," he said.

"But you were comfortable with Sharon. That was obvious."

It wasn't an accusation, simply a fact. Aiden squeezed her hand, let go of it, and relaxed back into his chair.

"I was very comfortable with Sharon. We'd known each other

for so long, and then there was no pressure about whether the relationship would work or not."

Madison had been staring out the window at the shadows and play of light as the sun set. She took a sip of her coffee, then looked directly into his eyes—eyes that seemed bottomless at times.

"I don't understand. Explain to me how you could walk away from such a beautiful, accomplished woman."

Chapter Forty-Three

Aiden folded his arms on the table and looked directly into her eyes. "Sharon is in love with a rock musician— a long haired guy named Bix and someone that her parents strongly disapprove of. That's what I've been trying to tell you since the night of the banquet."

Madison tried not to look shocked, but she knew she didn't quite accomplish it. "Rock musician?"

"Yes, ma'am."

"But she's...she's an adult...a lawyer."

"We all strive for our parents' approval, regardless our age, and for Sharon that also translates into a lot of money. She's finally decided that being with Bix means more than her inheritance."

"Would they really do that? Cut her off?"

"They might."

"But...she's a lawyer." Madison realized she was repeating herself. "I'm sure she makes a good living."

"She does, but the amount she stands to inherit? Well, I'm not actually giving away a secret to say that it's seven figures."

Madison set down her coffee cup, looked at the chocolate velvet cake the waiter slid in front of them, but didn't bother to pick up her fork.

"I'm sorry. I don't understand. You mean you knew Sharon was in love with someone else all that time?"

"I read people pretty well. I knew something was going on with Sharon. There had to be a reason she wasn't dating, and it was more than the fact that she was busy establishing her law practice."

"So you asked her out."

"I did."

"And she refused."

"Right."

"You were intrigued."

It was Aiden's turn to put his head back and laugh. "I'm not so conceited that I can't handle being turned down."

"Right. Like you handled being turned down by me."

"That was different."

Madison merely smiled, waiting for him to go on.

"I'll admit I've had problems with women since my mom and dad died, earlier really—although I didn't realize it at the time. I would think they were interested in me, then one way or another I'd eventually realize it was my money that infatuated them."

"Not your charm?"

Aiden cut a rather large piece of cake with his fork. "Eat this, so your mouth stays busy and I can finish my story."

Madison accepted the warm chocolate, loving the taste and richness of it as much as the smile on Aiden's lips.

"I finally guessed why Sharon had no men hanging around her office door. I waited for her after work one night, took her for coffee, and asked her about it."

"And she confessed."

"At that point she thought her parents would grow out of wanting to control her life. She thought if she waited, things would smooth out and she could tell them about Bix."

"So you two came up with this plan—"

"To provide a cover story for each other. That way she could still have Bix—"

"And you could have?" the question hung in the air as Madison pushed the chocolate toward him.

"Peace and quiet. The chance to pursue my hobbies and my interests."

"But haven't you been lonely?"

"Yes. I was."

The past tense warmed her more than the chocolate or the coffee did. Aiden signaled for the check, signed for the dinner, then guided her through the lobby and out onto the patio where a dazzling array of stars lit the sky. As she watched, a single star fell, streaking its way across the heavens.

"What about you?" Aiden asked.

"Me?"

"The men must have been lining up in Texas. So why does this seem so new to you?"

"I had boyfriends, of course."

"Of course." Aiden took off his jacket, placed it over her shoulders.

"Then mother became sick, and they sort of disappeared. You find out who your friends really are when you need them. I found out I only had one—Renee. She was there for me. None of the guys I knew were."

"What happened to your mom, Madison?"

"Cancer. It was breast cancer. By the time we knew, it was too late. She was really young, only forty-two. We always seemed more like sisters, you know? Suddenly, she was dying, and I had to be the older one."

"That must have been a very hard thing to watch."

Madison swallowed back the pain. "It was, and then she told me about my father. I thought he had died, but turns out he hadn't. He lives here in Montana, or he did. And she made me promise I would come here and try to find him. She said even if I didn't find him I should experience the mountains. I know it sounds crazy, but I promised and in my family when you make a promise you keep it."

"If you hadn't kept your promise, we might have never met." Aiden entwined their arms, took her hand in his.

"I've thought of that," Madison reached for her necklace, touched the angel.

"Do you believe in guardian angels, Maddie?" Aiden whispered.

"Maybe. Maybe I do."

Madison turned to look at him, wanting to catch his reaction, expecting to see even the slightest bit of ridicule in his eyes. All she saw though, and it shocked her to realize it, was adoration.

"I think I do too." He touched her face, put his hands under her hair, pulled her toward him.

And then he was kissing her, like he had the night of the banquet.

She was falling in love with Aiden Lewis, and it didn't scare her nearly as much as it should have.

Chapter Forty-Four

Aiden stormed around his suite, hastily but carefully packing. What he didn't need would be left in a suitcase and checked at the front desk. The rest he stuffed in a smaller bag with his laptop.

The call had come at 3:00 a.m. Not that he'd been asleep. All he'd managed to do was toss and turn, still thinking of Madison and the unexpected feelings she stirred in him.

Twice he had started to call her, and twice he had hung up before the connection had gone through. He'd finally given up on sleeping when his cell phone had rung. He'd leapt on it, knowing it was her, certain she was as miserable as he was.

Instead it had been Commander Martin.

Why did these things always happen in the middle of the night? It was someone's sick plan to keep agents on their toes.

Cursing everyone from the Chief of the CIA to Jacob who was waiting in the parking lot, he checked his Glock—being sure he had the license and two extra magazines for it in his laptop bag. One of the disadvantages of undercover work was being held to the same laws as the average citizen. He would have liked to carry a little heavier firepower tonight. An instinct he'd long ago learned to trust told him he might need it.

If he didn't need it, he could shoot something anyway. It was bound to ease this restlessness that threatened to consume him.

Focus on the mission, Iceman. The mission doesn't come first. The mission comes first, second, and last. The mission is all there is.

He'd drilled that into his teams. Now he needed to follow his own advice.

One last look around the suite, then he picked up his bag, locked the door behind him, and walked down to Madison's room.

He tapped softly on her door, wondering if he should have called. There was no easy way to do this. He listened to her stumble out of bed, turn on a lamp, and then press against the door, no doubt looking through the keyhole like her mama had taught her. Convinced he wasn't the big bad wolf—though he wasn't so sure of that anymore—he heard her remove the security chain.

She opened the door and stood there looking at him, concern and confusion playing over her face. He knew in that moment he did not deserve someone like Madison. He didn't deserve her, but he needed her.

The mission, Iceman.

"Aiden, what's wrong?"

She wore a big fluffy robe and her hair had tangled into a cloud around her head. No makeup. Barely awake. And yet in that moment he was more attracted to her than he had ever been.

"Come in." She pulled her hair back nervously and sat on the edge of the bed. "Why do you have your bag?"

"Something's come up. I have to leave for Banff."

Madison waited for him to explain. When he didn't she searched for the necklace she wore even in her sleep. She stared at the floor a minute, then looked back up at him where he still stood beside the door.

"I don't understand."

"That's really all I can tell you. I'm sorry."

"All you can tell me? You haven't told me anything."

"I'm sorry."

"You said that already." She stood and paced toward the windows, arms crossed, confusion battling with anger. By the time she turned around, he knew the anger had won.

"What about the team? They have to play tomorrow."

"I'm sorry."

"Don't say that again. What is this about, Aiden? Where are you going?"

There was nothing else he could say. He pulled out a sheet of paper and tried to hand it to her. She stepped further away from him, acting as if the paper were a snake that might bite.

"I've taken care of your transportation. I secured a driver to take you all home."

"Is that your answer? You walk out on your team, on me, and you think it's okay because you've found a driver?"

"Samuel will take you to Edgewood and catch a ride back here. You can trust him. He's a good man."

"I don't know Samuel, and I don't need Samuel."

Her chin went up and he realized there was no use arguing with her.

"I can't believe you, Aiden. What happened to the man who puts his team first? Suddenly you get a social call or a business call or whatever kind of call you got and then we're not important anymore." She walked toward the window, stood with her back to him, dismissing him with her disdain.

He knew Jacob was waiting for him, knew he needed to go now, but he couldn't leave her like this. Setting his single bag down, he moved to her side. He put his hands on her arms, but she pulled away and stepped out of his reach.

"You're leaving us. The whole team. Because you need to go to Banff at four in the morning."

He wished she had kept yelling, but instead her voice had grown softer as her disappointment had solidified. When he turned her to face him, the disapproval in her eyes hurt him more than anything she could have said. He pulled her to him, put his arms around her and spoke softly into her hair. Her body was so tense it was like holding a surfboard. Fleetingly, he wondered if she would ever trust him again, but then he realized it didn't really matter.

He had a job to do.

Dambusters was about to break wide open.

"Let the boys play their final round. Tell them an emergency business meeting came up and I had to go."

"Business meeting?" She jerked away and stormed across the room to the door. "You don't even have a job. You're a millionaire who volunteers as a part-time coach, apparently only when it's convenient though."

"Samuel will be here at the hotel after lunch to take you back to Edgewood."

"Why did I think you would be different?" Her voice softened as tears pierced through her anger. "I could have fallen for you."

He barely made out the words. His senses were overpowered with the smell of her, the feel of her, the memory of her. And Jacob was waiting.

"I have to go." He summoned the strength to cover his hurt with the ice he was so famous for.

"Go then. And tell Samuel we don't need him, and we don't want him."

He picked up his bag, hesitated as he brushed past her in the doorway, willed her to look at him, but she stared at the window, refusing to meet his eyes.

He walked out of the hotel without looking back up at her window. He didn't want to know if she was watching. He couldn't bear to think his job might have cost him more than he wanted to give.

Chapter Forty-Five

Sergio sat in the back booth, a woman on each side of him, and wondered why he should wait another thirty-six days. For that matter, the opulence around him proved the town of Banff was as corrupt as any American city.

So why did Yassin refuse to let him act? With sufficient charges in the correct places, he could reduce the exclusive Fairmont Banff Springs to a pile of rubble.

The women didn't speak. They wouldn't unless answering a question. They were props, nothing more. The blonde folded her hands on the table. Her nails were painted a hideous red.

Sergio continued to watch the cowboy standing near the bar. The man was familiar—black Stetson hat, designer clothing, and a hideous amount of money he was throwing around buying drinks for anyone who sat near him.

The girls cozying up to him in the booth had been sent by Yassin. They were a useful cover. True believers always traveled alone or with other men.

He indicated to them that he was ready to go, and they stood quickly, silently waiting to follow him from the bar.

As they walked toward the hotel's main corridor, Sergio again noticed the wealthy American. He had seen him before on the flight from Dallas. That was the flight where he had been tagged, a fact that still infuriated him. It could be a coincidence the American was here tonight, but then Sergio didn't believe in coincidences.

He pretended to stumble, knocking one of the women with him into the American.

"Easy there, ma'am."

The American gave her a lopsided grin and reached out to steady himself.

"A bea-u-tiful la-a-dy like you should be careful." The words slurred and collided even as he sought to regain his balance.

Sergio could smell the alcohol from his breath a good two feet away.

"Perhaps you should watch where you're going." Sergio spoke in a low measured tone, not bothering to mask his contempt.

The American had trouble locating where the threat came from. His eyes lingered on Dolly a moment longer, then with seemingly heroic effort he pulled his gaze away to try and locate Sergio. When he did, it was plain the infidel had consumed more alcohol than he could tolerate. The man sickened him.

"There you are. I knew that voice was coming from somewhere." He tipped the black Stetson hat toward them, dropped it in the process, tried to retrieve it from the floor and nearly fell over.

An elegant black woman picked it up for him. "Let me help you, Aiden." She flashed a smile to the trio, not noticing the hatred in Sergio's eyes.

"We probably stayed at the bar a little too long," she offered quietly. The woman was dressed exquisitely in a long, black dress that was backless. Diamonds adorned her neck and shone from her earlobes. Her hand reached out to steady the cowboy—hands exquisitely adorned with expensive rings, although a wedding ring was not among them. Her manicure was tasteful and expensive. Sergio could tell she hadn't worked a day in her life.

His mind flashed back to his companion's bright red fingernail polish, and he nearly flinched at the indignity of it all. The cowboy deserved these tramps, while he should have the well-bred woman in front of him.

"Let's get you out of here, Aiden. We can go to my suite." She spoke softly, but the cowboy shook her off.

"Car-o-line, we are here to p-arty, and I ain't done yet."

The cowboy rose and stumbled toward the other end of the bar, and Caroline offered them a weak smile, apologized again, and followed him.

The encounter had lasted long enough for Sergio to confirm it was indeed the man he'd seen on the flight from Dallas. If he were an agent—which Sergio seriously doubted—he was a very bad one. Yet the man reminded him of someone else, a woman more beautiful than either of those with him tonight.

He had let Ms. Hart slide from his memory. Omar had followed her for days, but the woman did nothing other than go to work and home. They'd even put surveillance in her apartment, and it had confirmed that she was who she appeared to be—a teacher.

But many people led a double life. Possibly he had not been persistent enough. Allah could have provided this encounter to stir his memory. Tomorrow he would pursue this path.

With a nod to the wait staff, the three left the bar and entered an elevator. Sergio's mind was consumed with the revenge he would exact, whether Yassin decided they would do so in thirty-six days or tomorrow. Sergio was ready to give his life whenever it was required.

Chapter Forty-Six

Aiden settled into the back booth at the Waldhaus Pub. He'd asked Caroline to go to the dining room and speak to the chef. He'd pretended to be starving, and of course the dining room had closed hours ago. Aiden was one of their best customers, and Caroline could be quite influential. He hoped the errand would keep her busy for at least half an hour. He needed time to think.

He'd caught Coyote staring at him an hour ago. There was no doubt he would make the connection to the Dallas flight, so Aiden hadn't even tried to hide his identity. Instead, he did the next best thing, which was to practically stumble into the man's lap. If you can't blend into the background, be a noisy part of the foreground. A single shot of whiskey combined with his drunk and disorderly routine had certainly convinced Caroline he was over his limit. He was sure by the look of disgust on Coyote's face he had bought it as well. No self-respecting agent would get totally plastered on a job, and if he did he would hide in a back booth, not put himself on public display.

The result was Coyote had confirmed his identity, which he would have done anyway, and dismissed him. He was now just another wealthy, obnoxious regular at the Fairmont.

"Coyote has entered his room." Tony's voice came through the earpiece, mirroring Aiden's own disgust when he saw the way Coyote looked at the two women. They might be foolish, but they didn't deserve what the terrorist no doubt had planned.

"Is there any way we can get them out of there?" Aiden strongly disagreed with the decision to not interfere.

"Negative." Martin's answer was cryptic and offered no room for discussion.

They all knew what was at stake—millions of American lives. The women would have to fend for themselves. There were times Aiden really hated his job. His mind drifted to thoughts of Madison, but Caroline appeared and he pulled himself back to the present.

"The chef is sending down your steak."

Aiden slipped back into his drunken role, pulled her down onto the seat beside him, put his arm around her, and smiled. "Aren't you handy to have around? I guess this is just my luck-i-ly night. I could use another drink. Bartender? Another whiskey. Another drink for everyone."

With a broad gesture, he indicated everyone in the room, as if the bartender—who happened to be an agent as well—couldn't figure out everyone included the four people left. Both of the other couples smiled tolerantly and waved at Aiden, who waved back and nearly fell out of his booth in the process.

Caroline reached out a steadying hand, holding on to him a little longer than necessary. She was an attractive woman, and Aiden was surprised that in his very sober state he felt absolutely no attraction.

"You are something, you know it? Just a little less whiskey might be good though." She was trying her best to reprimand him, but Aiden could tell her heart wasn't in it. "After you have something to eat, I think we should call it a night."

Those perfectly manicured fingers touched his cheek and she leaned forward to brush her lips against his. Halfway through the kiss he found himself comparing her to Madison, and for reasons it would take hours to list, he found her wanting.

"Aiden?"

"Hmmm?"

"Would you like to—"

Fortunately for Aiden, at that moment a waiter appeared with his porterhouse steak.

"Feel like I haven't eaten in days. Why don't you go on up to your room, and I'll call you when..." He left the sentence unfinished, knowing that he would not be calling her tonight or any other time.

She took a pen from her purse, and slipped out of the booth. Taking his hand, she wrote her room number on the inside of his palm, then turned and sashayed out of the restaurant.

"That is one beautiful woman." Justin's voice in his earpiece reeked with envy. "When do I get to move from the bar to the booth?"

"When you learn to keep your trap shut on open frequencies." Martin's reprimand silenced the young agent.

Thirty-six days. Just over five weeks.

There were at least two more operatives at the Fairmont, and Aiden had to find them, or in thirty-six days millions of Americans would die.

Aiden put enough money on the table to cover the food he didn't plan to eat. Waiting to be sure he wouldn't bump into Caroline in the elevator, he made his way to his suite. Counting the night he hadn't slept in Missoula, he'd been up for nearly forty hours. The fatigue washed over him in waves.

He surveyed his room to be sure no one had entered it in the last six hours, then removed his earpiece, took off his shoes, and threw his jacket across the Castle and Son desk. Checking his Glock, he placed it on the nightstand next to his bed.

Then he collapsed on top of the comforter and allowed sleep to claim him. As he was nodding off, he remembered Caroline. With a groan, he snatched up the phone and dialed the concierge.

"This is Mr. Lewis in Suite 756. Would you please ring Miss Caroline James and tell her I won't be able to make it tonight?"

He didn't wait for an answer. He hung up the phone and was asleep within seconds. Although the mission clock was still ticking in his head, over it he could hear Madison's voice, see the disappointment written on her face. He might not be able to tell her why he'd left or where he'd gone, but he would find a way to make it up to her.

Madison was more gorgeous than he remembered. When she turned to look at him, the lips he longed to kiss parted and she said something important. But he couldn't make it out. Whatever it was, she was in danger. He started across the room to get to her, but the faster he moved the more the distance between them grew. The hotel room became impossibly long.

He began to run—his heart thundering uncontrollably in his chest, but she was inexplicably farther away than when he started. He still couldn't make out her words, but he could follow her gaze.

She continued to look at him, her eyes pleading for him to get there, and then she looked down at her hands. Her eyes widened, and she started to scream.

He ran faster.

He could now see her hands were covered in blood. Aiden knew if he didn't get to her soon it would be too late. He had to close the gap between them. He had to move faster.

He woke with his heart racing, sheets tangled around his body, which was drenched in sweat. Instinctively, he reached for his gun, but it wasn't on the table where he'd left it.

"You don't want to shoot me." The voice was calm, sure, and Aiden knew he was no longer dreaming.

Chapter Forty-Seven

In the complete darkness of the room he couldn't make out the man's form, but Aiden knew who it was.

"Why not?" he growled. His tone would only provoke his late-night visitor, but he couldn't bring himself to care.

"Because you'd lose your job. And we all know how dedicated you are to your job, Iceman."

Martin had never called him that before. Aiden slung his feet over the side of the bed and tried to coax his heartbeat back to a regular rhythm. How did Martin manage to enter his room? Aiden was sure he'd set the deadbolt and the security chain. He couldn't have broken in, or Aiden would have heard him.

"Some nightmare you were having. Want to talk about it?"

"When did you earn a psych degree?" Aiden knew he was dancing close to insubordination, but he was too tired to worry about it. The clock next to his bed confirmed he'd had less than two hours sleep.

"Coyote escorted the women back to his suite."

"Are they all right?" Aiden's eyes had adjusted enough that he was able to make out Martin's profile in the suite's wingback chair.

"We created a bogus plumbing problem and managed to

insert an agent into his room. Both girls were dazed and disoriented. There were no visible injuries."

Aiden thought of Madison, remembered the dream, and fought an overwhelming urge to break something.

"He drugged them. I told you we should pull those girls out of there." Aiden's voice rose. "You were wrong to let them go with him, and now you have to live with their scars."

"They won't be the first scars I've had to live with or the first sacrificial lambs I've offered up." Martin's voice became all business. "We're looking at a catastrophic loss of life if even one of the dams are breached. You and I both know that has to be our priority."

Aiden walked to the bathroom, splashed water on his face, and tried to gain control of his emotions. By the time he walked back into his room, the ice was firmly back in place. The light from the bathroom illuminated Martin's face, showing lines Aiden was sure hadn't been there a week ago. Thirty-six days, correction thirty-five. They had exactly five weeks, if their intel was accurate.

"What do we do now?"

"You have a tee time at 7:00 a.m."

"Aren't we carrying this cover thing a bit too far? Coyote is sleeping in this hotel, and you want me to play golf? Why don't we bring him in? You know we can make him talk."

"Yes, we could make him talk, but he can only tell us what he knows. In all likelihood he doesn't know the names of the other operatives. What is certain is if we bring him in the operational timeline will accelerate or their goals will change. We can't afford for either to happen. We need the names of the last two operatives."

Aiden gave up fighting Martin's plan. In the end, he would assign a different agent if he had to, but he wasn't going to change his mind. And maybe he was right.

"So I have a tee-time in four hours."

"Three hours and forty-five minutes."

"What are we doing to find the other two?"

"We've run background and travel checks on every male guest of Middle Eastern heritage."

"Expand it to women."

"Tony started on that three hours ago."

"Americans?"

"We're checking any American males, aged seventeen to thirty-five."

"What do you want me to do?"

"Maintain your cover. Coyote doesn't suspect you after last night's drunken debauchery. Looked pretty real, Aiden."

"I had one drink." Aiden rose to the bait, even though he knew better.

"From the sound of your dreams, you should have had one more."

As Aiden tried to think how to respond, Martin disappeared. One minute he was looking at the outline of his boss across the room, and the next he was gone. Turning on the bedside lamp, he found his Glock on the desk next to the wing-back chair.

If he'd slept hard enough for someone to enter his room and take his weapon, you'd think he would at least feel rested.

With a groan he called the front desk and scheduled a wakeup call, fought the urge to call Madison, and finally fell back into a mercifully dreamless sleep.

Chapter Forty-Eight

As he walked toward the eighth hole, the muscles in Aiden's shoulders relaxed as naturally as night followed day. There was something about playing golf on a cool August morning, in the shadow of the Canadian Rockies, with elk grazing just beyond the fairway that improved his mood—even when his game was terrible.

"I hate water shots." Bob was a good ten years older than Aiden, and only a marginal golfer, but his enthusiasm for the game made up for his lack of skill.

Aiden had golfed with him before and could trust him to keep quiet while he lined up his shot. Noreen and the Colonel rounded out their foursome. They were an odd pair, but then how often did you see a normal couple these days? She was in her early forties, athletic, intelligent, and completely smitten with the older man. Colonel Peter E. Bishop was a regular at the Fairmont. Aiden had known the man casually since he was a boy, staying at the hotel with his mom and dad. In his mid-sixties, the Colonel could still play a competitive game of golf. Water shots were his favorite.

"We all know the eighth separates men from boys. No offense, Noreen."

"None taken, Peter."

Everyone else called him the Colonel. Aiden was sure he could remember his own father addressing him that way. A veteran of the Vietnam War, Col. Bishop had come out of retirement to serve in the Gulf War. Rumor had it he'd only retired because he'd sustained an injury from shrapnel and it wouldn't heal quite right. If he couldn't serve in the field, the Colonel wouldn't serve. Though by the way he played golf, Aiden couldn't detect any lasting handicap. He was certainly giving Aiden a run for his money.

"Low trajectory shot to the left, Aiden." Coming from the Colonel it was more an order than a suggestion.

Aiden peered over the green and lined up his shot. Water dominated the middle of the hole, with a small island in the middle of the pond. Last summer a family of beavers had taken up residence on the island and proceeded to build a dam from the island across the left side of the water. Aiden liked the fact The Fairmont had chosen to leave the dam there. It reminded him he was inside Banff National Park, not puttering around on some urban course.

He took two practice swings, stepped closer to the ball, and lobbed it right into the middle of the water.

"I said a low trajectory, not in the middle of the dam. With your swing I'm surprised you didn't bust it wide open."

Every hair on Aiden's neck did an immediate salute. Surely not. It was only a phrase, an odd coincidence. Only Aiden didn't believe in coincidences. Careful of his expression, Aiden turned to face the man.

"My swing isn't that hard, Colonel. I doubt I could even dislodge a twig on the dam."

"You hit the ball like a baseball." The Colonel lined up his shot, landed on the green, and turned back to the three of them with a natural air of superiority. "I hope you young people were paying attention."

As Noreen set her ball on the tee, Aiden moved closer to the

Colonel. Thirty-five days. There wasn't a lot of time to be subtle, but he couldn't tip his hand either.

"You played some golf when you were oversees," Aiden said.

"Ever see a beaver's dam on the middle of the course?"

"Europeans don't want to hurt any of the little animals. You have to play with all manner of distractions. Totally unacceptable. Now if an Elk wanders on to your course." He paused to study the bull and two cows grazing in the distance. "If an elk wanders on your course I don't care if you shoot it and dress it for dinner or leave it be. But a beaver? Get rid of them. It's not like you'd need one of Wallis's bombs to stop the thing."

The Colonel moved beside Noreen as they walked to the next hole. Aiden forced himself to speak casually as they continued to the ninth. It wasn't easy. He'd found another of the terrorists.

"The Colonel?" Martin asked. "I'm not convinced, Aiden."

"Then why did you send me to play golf with him?"

"Because Coyote needs to believe your cover."

"It's him." Aiden paced back and forth across the meeting room, finally stopping in front of the surveillance team. "Tony, I want a tap in his room today, and I want to know everywhere he's traveled in the last five years. Also run a check on his girlfriend. Her name is Noreen Hunt."

Walking back to Martin, he collapsed into a chair beside his boss' makeshift desk.

"It makes sense. The Colonel was a career military man until they forced him to retire. Supposedly because of an injury during the Gulf War. But play golf with the man—I guarantee you he had no physical reason for retiring. Something happened during his deployment. Something to turn him."

"He wouldn't show up on any of our watch lists," Tony admitted. "He's outside the parameters of our search profile."

Martin held Aiden's gaze for a minute that seemed like much

more. Aiden refused to look away. With a heavy sigh, Martin picked up his phone. "I'm going to need the complete military record for Colonel Peter E. Bishop. Make sure it includes everything, especially anything classified."

He slammed the phone down and stood up, dismissing Aiden with a wave of his hand. "Leave. Go sleep or have a massage or do whatever playboys do when they look like death warmed over. I want you back in the bar tonight, and I want you at the top of your game."

Aiden gave him a mock salute and headed for the door. As he walked out of the room he heard Martin complain to Tony, "Worst game of golf I've ever seen in my life."

It *had* been one of his worse games. The lack of sleep, thoughts of Madison, and suspicions about the Colonel had combined to destroy his ability to focus. Golf was a game of concentration.

Aiden once again resisted the urge to go to his room and phone Madison. He had strict orders to remain undercover, which did not include calling family or friends. After all, he was a self-centered playboy. It would be out of character to call home.

Jacob had assured him she'd made it back to Edgewood with the team.

Aiden should have felt good about identifying the Colonel as one of Yassin's team. He didn't though. All he could think of was the one they hadn't found. The one who could cause the kind of chaos it was his job to stop.

One more man.

Thirty-five days.

The clock continued to tick.

Chapter Forty-Nine

Aiden woke to the incessant ringing of his cell phone. Looking at the clock, he saw it was 4:17, but it took a full ten seconds for him to realize it was 4:17 in the afternoon. Stumbling to the phone he answered it with a growl.

"Lewis."

"Go home." Martin's voice sounded much cheerier than it should have.

"Say again."

"Go home, Lewis."

Aiden walked over to the windows as he waited for an explanation. Pulling the drapes open he saw a flawless fall day in the Canadian Rockies.

"You were right. Colonel Bishop is our man. His military files have significant gaps. Even I couldn't access information on the missing parts." Martin sighed and Aiden heard him lean back in his chair. "The fact I needed a federal court order was suspicious enough, but then we started pulling his visa records. We can pinpoint him in proximity with Yassin on at least three occasions. Furthermore, he has no close family. In many ways, he fits the classic profile."

Aiden allowed himself a moment of satisfaction. It didn't last long.

"Go home. Unless contacted, your involvement with this operation is over."

Aiden's temper exploded. "What do you mean my involvement is over?"

"Sir—"

"What the hell do you mean, Sir? There's still one out there."

"Not your problem."

"But—"

"Look, Lewis. You've done a good job here. Now go home. If we need you, we'll call you."

Martin clicked off, leaving Aiden with an overwhelming urge to put his fist through something, or preferably someone. He took his frustration out on packing instead.

It wasn't until he'd stood under the hot shower a good ten minutes that he began to relax, that he realized he could see Madison. He had no idea how he'd make everything right with her. Flowers wouldn't work, but he vowed to find a way.

Jacob had pulled up to the front drive by the time Aiden made it downstairs. As he was checking out, Caroline walked up.

"Aiden."

"Hello, Caroline."

"You're leaving."

"My golf game's off, so I thought I might as well head home."

He saw the disappointment in her eyes. She was a nice lady, and he hated that he'd raised her hopes with his drunken display. "Listen, I'm sorry about last night."

"It's all right." She raised her chin ever so slightly, regained the teasing look in her eyes, and touched his arm lightly. "Maybe next time."

Aiden smiled, then kissed her on the cheek. He understood she knew there wouldn't be a next time, but she had her pride. He respected her for that.

After he slid into the backseat of the limo and shut the door, Jacob lowered the window.

"Heard you tagged the Colonel. Nice job, Iceman."

"Any other word on Madison?"

Jacob met his gaze in the rearview mirror. "Do I hear the sound of ice cracking?"

Aiden didn't bother to respond.

"She's fine. We don't actually have someone watching her twenty-four seven, but I have a friend in town who confirmed she's at the school teaching today."

Aiden nodded. "Thanks."

"How are you going to make it up to her?"

"I haven't the slightest idea."

"Flowers?"

"Tried that."

"Jewelry?"

"Knowing Madison, she'd throw it back in my face."

"You have a couple hours to think on it. We should be in Edgewood by ten-thirty tonight."

Aiden crossed his arms behind his head and leaned back against the leather seat. He knew he'd done more than disappoint her. He'd betrayed her trust, and there was no chance he could tell her why.

Maybe he could give her Sierras, but where would she put a horse? Did she even know how to ride a horse? He'd think of something. He had to.

He suddenly realized he hadn't ever cared this much for a woman before, and that scared him more than he wanted to admit.

Chapter Fifty

Madison looked at the name that appeared on her cell phone and forced herself not to answer it. The day had been long and exhausting, as only days with one hundred and twenty teenagers could be. She knew she'd have to face Aiden eventually, explain to him why she couldn't deal with this sort of relationship, but she couldn't do it tonight.

She sank down onto her new sectional couch and picked up Nora Roberts' latest, but the words on the page might as well have been hieroglyphics. She didn't regret coming to Montana, but it was lonelier than she'd thought it would be. Starting over was hard. She missed her old things—her ratty couch and her cats. She missed her old life.

A knock on her door pulled her out of her reverie. It couldn't be Aiden, since he'd just called from his house. She didn't know many people well yet and couldn't imagine who would be stopping by her house at nine o'clock on a Wednesday night.

"Open up, Madison. I come bearing gifts."

Madison opened the door to her mentor/friend, holding two Starbucks cups.

"You're bringing me coffee at this hour?"

"It's decaf." Pam said. "Strong, with whipped cream—the way you like it."

Madison retrieved two packages of Girl Scout cookies from the kitchen.

"Thin mints or Somoas?" she asked.

"Both, of course."

Madison dropped the cookies on the giant ottoman that squared out her couch, accepted the cup, and flopped back into a corner. "You're a saint, and I don't deserve you."

"True. But since you have good taste in Girl Scout cookies, I'll be your friend anyway. Now spill. I want to know what happened over the weekend and why you've been moping around all week."

"What makes you think anything happened?" Madison focused on taking the lid off her coffee without spilling it and blowing on the steaming liquid.

"Please. You left acting like a giddy seventeen-year-old and returned looking like the stars had dropped from the sky."

Madison thought about the star that had fallen as she and Aiden were kissing. At the time, she had thought it was a sign. Now she was pretty sure it was a warning.

"Spill it, sweetie. I probably won't have any answers, but it'll help you to share."

"Short version? I had a wonderful time driving up to Missoula."

Pam's precisely arched eyebrow went up a notch, but instead of interrupting, she opened the thin mints, took four, and passed them to Madison.

"Saturday's golf meet went well. The boys were amazing. You should see them when they're on the course, Pam."

"Tell me that part later."

"Right." Madison nibbled on a cookie. "Where was I?"

"Saturday's meet."

"When we got back to the C'mon Inn, Aiden asked me to dinner."

"You stayed at the C'mon?" Pam reached for more cookies, kicked off her shoes, and pulled a blanket over her lap.

Madison nodded and reached for another cookie. "Isn't that where they normally stay?"

"Maybe. It's the most expensive hotel in town. The district would never pay for it, but then Aiden has never been stingy with his money."

"Yeah. It was nice." The memories enfolded her again, and like the countless times before she was powerless to stop them. A starlit night, Aiden's lips on hers...

Then he had left. Again. Like before. Like every other person she had thought she could trust.

Pam stood up, walked into the bathroom, and brought back tissues to wipe the tears she didn't realize she was crying.

"Then you went to dinner?"

"Aiden asked me to dinner in the hotel. The boys ordered pizza by the pool. That's about it."

"It must have been a really bad dinner to make you cry remembering it."

"Ok." Madison sighed. "We made out on the patio. I remember thinking that I like this part. The part before the part where you jump in. The part where you feel dizzy just being near someone."

They sipped coffee and munched on cookies in silence, both lost in memories.

"Then Aiden showed up at my room. It was four in the morning, and he said he had to leave. He said I'd have to bring the boys home by myself."

"He didn't."

"Yup. He did."

"How could he?"

"Actually, he arranged for a driver. Some guy named Samuel."

"Samuel?"

"Right."

"So, Samuel drove you home."

"Nope. I told him we didn't need Samuel."
"Aren't you afraid of driving mountain roads?"
"I told him we could make it fine without him."
"Girlfriend, you rock."
They leaned forward, high-fived, then sank back with their coffee.
"Men suck," Madison said.
"Yeah, sometimes they do."
Madison's cell phone rang again, but she ignored it.
"You going to answer that?"
"Nope."
"You know who it is?"
Madison nodded.
"I guess that means it's Aiden."
"Yeah."
Both women slouched down in the couch, feet up on the ottoman. A few minutes ticked by, neither needing to break the silence. Finally, Pam stood and stretched, took the cookies back to the kitchen, and picked her jacket up from the hook in the front hall.

Madison walked her outside and down to her car.
"Is he a good kisser?"
"Yeah, he's a good kisser."
"You really like him, don't you?"
Madison didn't trust her voice, and she was grateful for the darkness. Tears filled her eyes and threatened to spill over again. She realized she was acting like a teenaged fool. She barely knew the guy. Why did he affect her this way?

"I don't know why Aiden left you, but I do know Aiden. We grew up together here in Edgewood. He might have a reputation as a playboy, but that's not Aiden. He's had a hard time since his parents died."

Madison nodded in the darkness, drew a deep breath, and hugged her arms to herself. "I know all about not having parents."

"Have you had any luck looking for your dad?"

Madison shook her head. She'd confessed to Pam her reason for moving to Edgewood weeks ago. Together they'd spent many an afternoon trying various web searches, but they always ended up where they started—nowhere.

"I'm not telling you to give Aiden another chance. But if he said he had to leave, he did have a good reason. I can't imagine what it would be. Maybe he's a spy or something." Pam unlocked her Volkswagen beetle and slid behind the wheel.

"He does look a little like James Bond."

"And they're both rich."

Madison reached in and hugged her friend. "Thanks for coming by."

"Sure thing. Call me if you want to talk."

Madison watched Pam pull out of the parking lot, then turned and made her way back up the stairs to her apartment. When she reached the top of the stairs she saw a car, idling across the street. It looked like the person was looking her direction, but then they switched their cell phone to their other ear and started hollering.

Not everything was about her.

It took every ounce of energy she had to drag herself back inside. She was fairly sure Pam was right. Aiden no doubt had a good reason.

This wasn't the first time he'd left with no explanation though. Madison might be able to accept he was doing what he had to do, but she couldn't accept that sort of relationship. How would it be any different than the guys back in Dallas? He still wouldn't be there for her. She wouldn't be able to call him when she needed to talk to someone in the middle of the night. She wouldn't be able to count on him to be there when he said he would.

Madison tidied up her living room, turned out all the lights, and walked into her bedroom. As she pulled off her clothes and tugged on a nightshirt, she knew what she had to do. Tomorrow, she'd tell Aiden she valued his friendship, but it couldn't go any further. Somehow she had to forget the way his kisses made her dizzy, how his hands holding hers had the power to burn her flesh. Somehow, she had to give up the childish dream that had sprouted in her heart.

"Face it," she mumbled into her pillow. "He might look like a Prince Charming, and he might even kiss like one. But Prince Charming hung around after he placed the slipper on Cinderella's foot. Therefore Aiden Lewis is no prince."

She punched her pillow since it seemed about to argue with her. As she drifted off to sleep it wasn't Cinderella she was thinking about, it was the shadows on a balcony overlooking the Missoula Valley, and in the distance, streaking across the night sky, were dozens of falling stars.

Chapter Fifty-One

Glancing at his watch, Aiden saw he was late. Nate had picked seven o'clock this morning to show up at his door again, and lecture him on his immaturity—again.

Aiden gunned the Avalanche through the orange light and pulled into the school parking lot.

Madison would already be fifteen minutes into her first-class, but that was too bad. He was going to talk to her. If she wouldn't answer her phone, she'd deal with him in person. He was more charming in person anyway. They were going to settle this now.

He barely nodded at the secretary as he headed through the front hall and toward the old choir room. As he barreled down the back hall, Gabe stepped out from the guy's bathroom.

"Hey, Coach. We took second at the meet."

"Nice job. Sorry I couldn't be there."

"It's all right, Coach. You would have stayed if you could."

Aiden paused in his full court press to Madison's room and considered dragging Gabe down with him so he could repeat that bit of logic. She'd probably ream him out for keeping the kid out of class.

"Aren't you late for somewhere?"

"Ah, Coach, it's Ms. Nickleby. Don't make me go back in there."

Ms. Nickleby had been Aiden's algebra teacher, back when teachers looked and acted old like they were supposed to look and act.

"Go to class." Aiden didn't wait to see if Gabe obeyed. Ms. Nickleby could take care of her own.

By the time he reached Madison's door, students were already scattered around the room, working at various tasks in small groups.

He rapped on the door, then turned the knob. It was locked. Who locked kids in the classroom?

Madison looked up, saw him, and sent a student to the door.

Unfortunately, she'd picked Santiago who had to be the slowest boy on the team. Worse yet, she'd turned her back to him so he didn't have the pleasure of glaring at her.

"Sorry, Mr. Lewis."

Santiago pulled down the window shade.

Aiden stared at a *students testing* sign.

"Open up the door, Santiago."

"Can't Coach. Ms. Hart said to tell you we're testing."

"Santiago, I can see you're not testing. I can *hear* you're not testing. Now open up the door."

"Coach Lewis wants me to open the door, Ms. Hart. You want me to let him in?"

Aiden knocked on the door again, even louder this time. If she wanted a scene, he'd give her a scene, but she was going to talk to him.

Even as he was defending his temper, the door was jerked open and there she stood—prettier than he remembered, though a lot madder than he'd ever seen her.

"Who locks a classroom door?"

"I do."

"Why would you do that?"

"It keeps out people like yourself, Mr. Lewis."

She turned to go back inside, but he reached out and grabbed her arm before she could slip back into the room.

"Look, Maddie. You're going to have to talk to me sometime."

"I am teaching, if you don't mind."

"I do mind. You can step out in this hall or I can pick you up and carry you out here."

A silence had fallen over the room behind them. Madison's face turned a bright red, but she stepped out into the hall. The door closed behind her as he pulled her away from the room. He wanted to drag her into his arms, but he was savvy enough to realize the caveman routine probably wouldn't work at this point.

"This is entirely inappropriate," she said quietly.

"Oh, and making out with me on the balcony was appropriate?"

"Lower your voice. They can hear you."

"I don't care if they can hear me. If you'd picked up your phone last night, we wouldn't be having this conversation this morning."

"We don't have anything to talk about."

"Yes, we do. We can either do it right now, right here, or we can do it tonight."

Madison jumped when they heard a bump against the wall. Taking her key out of her pocket, she unlocked the door in time to see a flurry of students move back toward their work.

"Quiz in 10 minutes."

She slammed the door so hard the *testing* sign rattled.

"Fine. I'll talk to you tonight. Now will you go away?"

"What time?"

"I don't know. Seven. Now go!"

"My place or yours?"

"I'm not going to your place." She looked at him as if he'd lost his mind, and briefly Aiden wondered if he had.

"Fine, yours."

"Fine, mine."

"I'll be there."

"Fine." She turned to jerk the door open. Forgetting it was locked, she nearly pulled the doorknob off. Muttering "stupid cowboys," she pulled the key back out of her pocket, unlocked the door, and disappeared inside.

Aiden didn't wait to hear the students' questions, and he was sure there would be plenty. That wasn't his problem though. Persuading Madison to talk to him was his problem, and he'd solved it.

Now if he could figure out what he was going to say.

Chapter Fifty-Two

Madison checked her reflection in the mirror for the tenth time, scolding herself for caring how she looked. Why had she even agreed to see him?

Flopping down on the couch, she picked up the TV remote and surfed through her eight channels. Without cable there was very little to watch, which she didn't mind because she rarely turned the thing on anyway. Hitting the off button, she dropped the remote and picked up her book instead, but reading also proved impossible.

She nearly threw the book in the air when the knock came. With grim determination she resisted the urge to check her reflection again. She wasn't going on a date for heaven's sake.

Jerking the door open, the sight of Aiden nearly took her breath away. He had on the black Stetson again, and his western shirt fit into his snug jeans just right. Fortunately for her resolve, the wolfish smile on his face ruined the effect.

"Evening, ma'am."

"Don't ma'am me." She stepped out onto the small upstairs landing, forcing him to back up, and slammed the door shut behind her.

"I don't get to come in?"

"No. You don't. Why are your hands behind your back?"

His grin only widened. "Maybe you should guess."

Madison turned to go back inside.

"Okay. Okay. I wanted to give you something special, because you mean a lot to me and your friendship is very important."

Madison rolled her eyes heavenward, praying for patience, then turned back toward him to accept the flowers or balloons or whatever it was he'd brought.

The basket brought her up short.

"Aiden, what's in the basket?"

"Take it and see."

The landing was small, and she had her back against the door. He was already standing too close. The smell of him was permeating her senses, making her dizzy, weakening her resolve. She wanted to flee into the apartment and tell him to call her tomorrow.

But she wanted to see what was in that basket.

It was the old-fashioned wicker kind her mother used to put laundry in, and it was filled with a fluffy beige towel. A ridiculous red bow adorned the top.

"It won't bite. I promise."

She gave him her most skeptical look and wondered how she was going to send him on his way. She had to give the guy points for trying.

"Aiden, I appreciate the thought—whatever the thought is. But seriously, I can't take any more gifts from you."

She paused to think how best to say this. It wasn't like she'd had a lot of experience rejecting millionaires, but she'd had a lot of time to think about her situation. She'd come to Montana for a reason, and it wasn't to meet a cowboy. It sure wasn't to have her heart broken. Better to stop things now.

The towel began to move and a tiny calico kitten stuck its head out.

"Okay. I understand. I'll just take this little guy back."

Aiden turned to start down the stairs, but Madison's squeal stopped him in his tracks.

"Oh my gosh. He's so cute, but...I already have cats. They're in Texas until my friend can drive them up."

"They'll have a new buddy when they get here."

"I'll be the crazy cat lady."

"You could never be that."

She pulled the basket from his hands and sat down on the top step. The kitten reached its nose out toward her, and another piece of her life clicked into place.

Aiden sat down beside her.

"I don't think this step's big enough for all three of us," Madison whispered.

"Feels fine to me."

"You never give up, do you?"

"No, ma'am. I do not."

Reaching into the basket, she pulled out the kitten, a tiny quilt of brown, white, and black patches.

"I've always wanted a calico cat." She placed the kitten gently on top of the towel, but continued stroking behind its ears. The purr coming from it was impossibly loud for such a tiny animal.

"Thank you." She refused to look him in the eyes, didn't want him to see how much his gift meant to her.

"You're welcome."

His voice was so close and tender, and his presence was beginning to make her weak.

He took off the Stetson and turned it in his hands. "Maddie, you have every right to be upset with me. Sweetheart, I wouldn't have left you and the boys if I didn't have to. I can't explain why right now. I hope someday I can. For now though, you're going to have to trust me."

He tilted his head, looked at her, and waited. His eyes on her, even in the near darkness, made her squirm like the kitten in the basket.

"Please." He reached out and touched her hand, caressed her arm.

The birds made their evening noises as the darkness settled around them. The landscape lighting seemed ridiculously intimate. Madison looked out over it all, stared down at the kitten in her lap, and took her time answering. Finally, she scooted down a step, rested her back against the wall, and looked up into those bottomless gray eyes.

"Aiden, I do trust you. And I consider you a good friend."

"Do not give me the friend speech."

His hand reached out and tucked her hair behind her ear, sending a river of shivers straight through her.

"I don't have to know where you go or what you do, if you're my friend. But intimate relationships are a different thing. I need someone who isn't going to disappear every few weeks."

He touched her face, leaned across the basket, and kissed her slowly and softly. When he pulled back, she shook her head.

"Now that's exactly what I mean. You can melt me with a kiss, but what good is it? Tomorrow you might be off on another mystery trip and I won't see you for a week. That's a lot to ask, Aiden."

"I know it is."

"I can't."

"Yes. You can."

"No. I can't."

This time when the tears filled her eyes, she didn't turn away or make any attempt to hide them.

"This move has been hard, harder than I thought it would be. It's only been three months since I lost the one person I loved most in this world. Have you ever watched someone you love die, Aiden?" She looked into his eyes and waited. When he nodded, she went on. "Now I'm starting to care for you, but I never know if you're going to be there when I need you. I feel very vulnerable right now, and I need your friendship. But I don't need this. It's too hard."

Her voice had dropped to a whisper, but she never took her eyes from his face. He had to know she was serious. They had to stop this now, before the pain left scars that wouldn't heal.

"What can I say to change your mind?" he asked.

"Tell me it won't happen again."

"I can't do that."

"Then we don't have anything else to say."

"I know you like being around me."

"I do."

"And when I touch you, I know you feel the same jolt of electricity I feel."

"Yes, I do."

"Then why are you doing this?"

"Because every time you leave you take a small piece of my heart, Aiden. Every time I don't hear from you for a week, I wonder where you are and what has happened."

"You have to trust me."

"I do trust you. But I'm the one still at home. I don't even know where you are, or if you're in danger, or what is going on. Every time the phone rings my heart stops."

"Maddie—"

"I don't know if you'll be gone a day or a week."

"Maddie—"

"And the worst part is I don't know why. I don't know why you're doing this. Maybe if I understood I could stand it, but you can't explain it to me, and I respect that. I respect it, but I can't keep putting myself through weeks like this last one."

He crushed the Stetson in his hands. "I want you. I haven't felt this way in... I don't know if I've ever felt this way."

She shook her head, tears spilling down her cheeks, but she still didn't look away.

"What about the team?" he asked softly.

"We can make it through the rest of the season. Keep it professional. I'll ask for a different assignment next year." She didn't add what she was thinking—*if I'm still here next year.*

Aiden put the Stetson back on. His shoulders slumped and he suddenly looked older than his thirty-two years. She hated what she was doing to them, but she knew it was best. It might hurt now, but it would destroy them both if she waited.

Standing slowly, he made his way down the steps, disappeared into the darkness, and returned moments later with a box of kitty supplies. He carried them back up the stairs and set them on the little landing. As he made his way back down again, he paused at the edge of the light and turned to look up at her.

"Can I at least call you?"

"I'd rather you didn't."

His eyes begged her to reconsider, but he didn't say anything else. As an owl cried out in the night. He turned, then walked off into the darkness. She heard his Avalanche start, saw the taillights as he drove away. It wasn't until he'd pulled out of the parking lot that she let herself wonder if she'd done the right thing. She'd thought he might be the one. It had seemed like a fairytale story come to life.

Only she wasn't Cinderella, and while he looked and acted like Prince Charming, she knew their story wouldn't end happily. She'd only resent him every time he left, and he would hate her resentment.

Stroking the kitten, she let her tears fall freely. She cried for her mother whom she missed so much. She cried for the father she might never know. And finally, she cried for Aiden and what they could have had.

She cried until the kitten began licking her face and meowing. Then she stood up, went inside, and opened the package of cat food that was in the box. As she watched the little calico eat, she convinced herself she'd done the right thing. Now they had to learn to live with it.

Chapter Fifty-Three

Every board he pulled up made an ungodly screeching sound, which was fine with Aiden. Let it suffer like he was. He'd rip the whole structure down board by board if it would alleviate this weight on his chest.

"Are you trying to tear down the entire barn?"

Aiden looked over the edge of the roof into the bewildered face of his brother.

"Morning, Nate."

"Morning, yourself. What are you doing up there?"

"Reroofing the barn. That should be obvious, even to a professional worker like yourself."

Aiden threw another board off the roof missing Nate by a good three feet, but his brother jumped back all the same.

"Come down and have some breakfast." Nate held up a thermos and a Tupperware canister. "Compliments of my lovely wife."

"Can't."

"What do you mean you can't?"

Aiden paused, shrugged out of his coat, picked up the crowbar and pushed it under another rotted board.

"I still have a lot of rotten boards to pull off. Phillip's bringing the new lumber by this morning."

Aiden wasn't surprised to hear grumbling. Five minutes later they were sitting on the northeastern edge of the roof, devouring Janie's rich coffee and fresh muffins while looking out over their northern pasture.

"Why are you doing this?" Nate asked.

"It needs to be done."

"That's what we hire Jimmy for."

"He's checking the fence line along the west side."

"Because you sent him over there."

Aiden drank the last bit of coffee, stood, and pulled his gloves back on. "Thanks for the breakfast."

He picked up the crowbar and continued where he'd left off. He'd managed to complete nearly a third of the roof since sunrise. With any luck at all, he'd be finished pulling off the old boards by the time Phillip arrived with the new lumber.

"Is this about a woman?" Nate asked.

Aiden pushed the crowbar a little harder, causing the rotten wood to splinter and groan.

"Is this about Madison?"

"Who told you about Madison?"

"Nobody did. You did. She's all you've talked about for the last month. Then you disappear again, and now you're reroofing a barn we haven't used in at least ten years."

"It's a good barn. We can store extra feed here."

"You really like this one—the woman, not the barn."

Aiden paused long enough to wipe the sweat out of his eyes, then put his weight into a particularly stubborn board. Nate pulled work gloves out of his back pocket, grabbed one end of the board and pulled as Aiden pushed again with the bar.

They worked in silence for the better part of an hour, then stopped and went down for water. Aiden poured a cup over the back of his neck and finally looked his brother directly in the eye.

"I appreciate the help," Aiden said. "But I'd rather do this alone."

"I know you would."

"So why are you still here?"

"Because I need to know what's wrong."

Aiden put the baseball cap back on his head and guzzled another cup of water.

"Pretty simple. Madison gave me the friend speech."

"A woman turned you down."

"You don't have to look so pleased about it."

"More surprised than pleased. In fact, I don't remember a woman ever turning you down, but then you maintained that farce with Sharon for such a long time they didn't really have a chance."

Aiden walked toward Nate's truck.

"Figured that one out did you?"

"She's been showing up with Bix around town. It's kind of obvious how much they're into each other."

"Sharon's a good friend. Our arrangement worked well for both of us."

"Then Madison came along."

"Yeah, Madison came along."

Nate pulled his keys from his pocket, but he still didn't open the door to the truck. "So why did Madison give you the friend speech?"

"She can't handle my absences. She worries."

"We all worry, Aiden. Why do you do it? Where do you go?" The familiar note of irritation crept into Nate's voice. "I don't understand. You're responsible in every other way."

"I'll tell you what I told Madison. You're going to have to trust me."

Nate shook his head and climbed into the truck. "That's not too much to ask of your family, but it's a lot to ask of a woman."

"I know it is."

"Maybe she's not the one then."

Aiden didn't bother to reply. Instead he turned and walked away, back to the barn. He climbed the ladder slowly as he listened to Nate's truck pull onto the county road. Looking out over their pastures, past them to the mountains rising in the distance, he thought of how he and Nate had grown up on this land. He picked up the crowbar and continued pulling rotten boards in the heat of a Saturday midmorning, rebuilding the playground of their childhood, and wishing he could rebuild his life instead.

Chapter Fifty-Four

Madison arrived early at the café, and requested a table at the back where she could watch the door. Just like she'd been taught in every Nelson DeMille book she'd ever read. You never knew when you were going to be meeting with a perp instead of an informant. For all Madison knew, Sharon Kingsley was a murderer. Okay, that was a stretch even for Madison's imagination.

The email was something of a shocker though and cryptic in typical lawyerly fashion.

> *I propose we meet at Corner House Grille located at 147 Center Avenue, tomorrow (Tuesday) evening at 6:00. Please confirm if this is acceptable.*

Reading over the printed copy, it still didn't make Madison feel warm and fuzzy. Why would Sharon possibly want to meet with her?

Arriving early was a complete waste of time. She didn't feel any more comfortable for sitting there waiting. She obviously hadn't needed to stake out the place.

Sharon walked in at exactly two minutes until 6:00. Dressed in a designer suit with two-inch heels and wearing her signature strand of pearls, she looked as though she were attending a board meeting. Her blonde hair was pulled back severely, as it had been the only other time Madison had seen her.

Somehow, for Sharon, the starkness worked. It highlighted her features, which seemed sculpted by Adonis himself–prominent cheekbones, a nose that would have made a plastic surgeon proud, probably did in fact, and lips that didn't need lipstick though she wore a light shade anyway. Her eyes were accented with a slight amount of liner and there wasn't a doubt they took in everything and everyone.

This was one no-nonsense woman.

Madison briefly considered adopting the look for her classroom. If she could pull it off, which was seriously doubtful, her classes would become a model of perfect behavior.

Sharon raised a perfectly arched eyebrow when the hostess showed her to the back of the restaurant.

"Ms. Hart. You might have enjoyed a table with a view of the mountains more."

"I've probably read too many novels. When in uncertain territory, keep your back to the wall."

"Ah."

Sharon looked toward the kitchen and their waiter appeared as if summoned by the power of her suggestion.

"Charles. I'll have coffee, with a shot of espresso." Sharon looked to Madison, waiting for her to order.

So much for hoping they were going to share a bottle of chardonnay and become bosom buddies.

"Raspberry tea for me."

Charles scurried away, though Madison entertained the thought of asking him to pull up a chair. She suddenly wished she'd picked a table in the middle of the room. This lady was like the ice queen. Madison instantly knew she never wanted to end up in the courtroom on the opposite side of the witness stand from Sharon Kingsley.

"Espresso this late? You don't worry about insomnia?"

"I have to go back to the office."

"Of course."

"Ms. Hart, thank you for seeing me. I'm sure you're wondering why I contacted you."

"I thought maybe you wanted to be gal-pals."

Sharon smiled, but it didn't reach past her lips.

Charles brought their drinks, then asked if they'd like something to eat. Sharon declined, a testament to her size six figure. Madison was instantly tempted to order chicken-fried steak, mashed potatoes with gravy, and dessert to spite the woman. She satisfied herself with adding real sugar to the tea. There were crackers on the table if she began to feel faint.

"I want to talk to you about Aiden."

Madison drew a deep breath. On some level, she had guessed this was coming. Why else would Sharon call? It wasn't like they socialized in the same circles. With a start, Madison realized she didn't socialize in any circle. She needed to start dating, even if it was accepting Bubba's invitations to see those adorable cows.

"Shoot. What do you want to talk about? His money? His golf swing? The way he kisses? Or maybe you'd like to discuss his mysterious absences for days on end."

Sharon silently sipped her coffee, watched, and waited. It was probably an intimidation technique she learned in law school. They probably paid her to teach it to wannabe attorneys—how to make the opposing team sweat into their raspberry tea.

Madison stirred her drink, but she couldn't bring herself to swallow any of it. Suddenly she wanted to be home, with her kitten in her lap, curled up on her couch, and reading a book. She'd take a teeth-jarring Stephen King over a conversation about Aiden.

"I don't know what you want, Sharon. But there's nothing between Aiden and me."

"There was though."

"Yes, there was."

"Until you called it off."

"Did he tell you that?"

"He didn't have to."

"Why am I talking to you about this? I don't even know you." Madison retrieved her purse from the floor, pulled out five dollars, which would surely cover a glass of untouched tea, and placed it on the table.

"I care about Aiden."

It wasn't the words that stopped Madison cold. It was the way she said them. For once the lawyer's voice was gone, replaced by something softer.

"He stood by me when few people in this town would have. He made," her eyes swept around the room, "he made my success possible. Without him my law practice would have suffered a rocky start."

Madison sat back down.

"When I first came to Edgewood, I didn't plan on falling in love with Bix. When I did, I didn't dare tell anyone. It was none of their business. But my parents...well they still had the power to make me feel like a child who couldn't make her own decisions."

Madison thought of her relationship with her mother, how they'd always felt like friends. She'd been lucky.

"At first everyone assumed I didn't date because I was starting my practice. After a year though, people started to gossip. Aiden stopped that talk. He gave people time to get to know who I am, to respect my excellence as an attorney. Now I like to think they see me as a professional and they accept that my personal life is none of their business. Aiden is a very special man, Madison."

"I agree he is a great guy." Madison turned the glass around in her hands. She wished she could sit there, calm and composed like Sharon. She envied her poise. At a time when nothing in Madison's life remained constant from day to day, she could have used even a little of that certainty.

"I don't know what happened between you two, but when you first came to Edgewood, Aiden was happier than I've ever seen him. Happy enough he couldn't maintain our charade any longer."

"He asked to end it?"

"No. He wouldn't have abandoned me. It was plain to see the longing in his eyes the night at the banquet though, and if you could have seen the way he handled my Porsche that evening," Sharon let out a small shudder at the memory. "I suppose on one level I have you to thank for pushing me out of hiding. It really is no one's business if I'm in love with a rocker who wears ragged jeans, sports long hair, and travels over half the year."

This time when she smiled it did go past her lips, and Madison found herself relaxing a little.

"Now Aiden is hurting. His brother Nate is worried. I'm worried. You certainly have every right to make your own decisions, but if there's anything I can say or do—"

It was the first time she didn't finish a sentence, and Madison looked up from her tea to see something akin to pity in her eyes.

"Thank you for offering. I like Aiden, a lot. I'm sorry he's hurting now, but it's for the best that we're not together."

"How can you be sure? If you care for each other, maybe you can work it out."

"Sometimes affection for each other isn't enough. Wouldn't you agree? Sometimes people care, but they keep hurting each other again and again. There's nothing either can do to change."

"Aiden isn't like that."

"I know he doesn't mean to be. Surely, you're aware of his mysterious absences."

Sharon's eyebrows again arched.

"One minute we'll be so close you couldn't slip a piece of paper between us, then he'll receive a phone call, and he's gone. No explanation, no estimated time of return, nothing."

Sharon finished her coffee, then pushed it away.

"I worked a lot of hours while we were seeing each other. To tell you the truth, I didn't really notice his absences. Of course there were times he was gone, but I figured he was seeing women from other towns, trying to keep his private life private."

Madison waited, but Sharon seemed a hundred miles away.

She drummed her fingernails against the table, then reached into her designer bag and pulled out her daytimer, turning it to the month of August. "What day did you come into town?"

Chapter Fifty-Five

"The school banquet was August fifth. I flew in the Monday before."

"The first of August."

"I guess. I really don't see where you're going with this."

Sharon motioned to the waiter, pointed at her cup, and he scampered away to retrieve more espresso.

"Aiden had been out of town all week before the banquet?"

"I don't know. We flew in on a Monday. The weather was terrible. I'd had an incident on the airplane."

"What type of incident?" Sharon asked.

"It was just a headache. I've had migraines for years, but this one was much worse. Apparently I passed out."

"Has that ever happened before?"

Madison shook her head and took a long drink of her tea. Her mind slipped back to that night and curled around something, tried to retrieve an image or voice. "I still can't remember it all. When I came to, Aiden was there kneeling by my seat."

"You were in first-class?"

"No, of course not. I was closer to the back of the plane."

"Aiden always flies first-class. What was he doing at the back of the plane?"

"I don't know."

Charles arrived with Sharon's espresso and a fresh tea for Madison.

"Let's start from the beginning." Sharon pulled a steno pad from her bag and created a crude timeline. "You both boarded the flight from Dallas to Salt Lake on the evening of August first."

Madison nodded, feeling like a character in a John Grisham novel.

"Everything was fine on the plane, but you were experiencing a migraine."

"No. There was a storm, and I'm a little afraid of flying. I don't remember having a headache though."

Sharon set her pen down. "You said you passed out from a migraine."

"Yes. At least when I came to I had one. In fact, I couldn't even stand and the flight attendant had called paramedics. They wanted to take me to the hospital. Aiden offered to help me to the first-class lounge instead. But I don't remember having a migraine before I passed out."

Madison frowned as she pulled the mint out of her tea. "I can't recall anything from that flight. It really bothers me. I've never had a migraine wipe out an entire evening before."

Sharon stared at her a few minutes, then scribbled a few notes. "Aiden walked with you to the lounge."

"Actually, he carried me."

Sharon paused in her writing, glanced up at Madison. "Why would he carry you?"

"I couldn't walk. I couldn't even keep my eyes open. The overhead lights were like long needles piercing my skull. I tried to walk, but barely made it off the plane. Aiden picked me up and carried me." The memory of him slammed into her until she was nearly smothered by it—the strength of his arms, the smell of his shirt, the safety of his presence.

"I've never heard of a migraine with these effects before."

Madison shrugged.

"Had you taken something before you boarded the plane? Any recreational drug use?"

"Absolutely not. I don't use drugs recreationally."

Sharon tapped the pen, finally placed it perfectly perpendicular to her daytimer and turned that steady gaze on Madison. "Have you considered you might have been drugged?"

"What?"

"There's several date rape drugs that might have had this effect."

"Why would anyone drug me?" Madison reached for her necklace and fidgeted with the angel pendant.

"I don't know. Was there anyone else you talked to on the plane?"

The profile of a man darted across her memory for a fleeting second. It was no more than a shadow though, more like an image from a dream. It slipped through her consciousness as quickly as it came.

"No. No one."

"Let's continue. Aiden carried you to the lounge. Later you both boarded the connecting flight to Kalispell. You said goodbye at the airport and didn't see him again until the night of the banquet."

Madison tried not to squirm.

"What am I missing?"

"I have more than a slight fear of flying. The last time I flew was in August of 2005 on a Peruvian airliner. It crashed. I guess you could say I have a phobia of sorts."

"Understandable. How did it affect you the night of August first?"

"I did fine on the first flight, other than the migraine. I didn't realize the second plane would be so small."

"A puddle jumper."

"I might have panicked a little when I saw the plane."

Sharon took another sip of her second espresso.

"Aiden talked me through it. The flight was rather...cozy. I guess you could say we bonded or something."

Sharon pushed the cup away and continued to watch her.

"He was pretty adamant about helping me drive from Kalispell to Edgewood. Then during the flight an attendant told him he had a phone call and that he needed to come to the front."

"The front of the airplane?"

"Yeah. I thought it was strange, but then I figured maybe that was normal for someone as rich as Aiden."

"No, it's not normal. You can't really place a call through to a commercial plane unless there are extenuating circumstances. Even a man with Aiden's connections would have a difficult time with that one."

Madison shrugged. "A few minutes after the phone call, we landed, and he left."

"But he was going to take you to Edgewood."

"Right. After the call, he explained something had come up and he wouldn't be able to." Madison traced the condensation on her glass. "He said he'd call that week, but he never did."

Sharon flipped back through her daytimer. "Because he was gone all week. He was late arriving back for the banquet. In fact," she leaned back in her chair, "when I showed up at his house, he didn't want to attend. I thought it odd at the time, since he was the one who made the reservation."

"It was the first of his disappearances."

"How many others have there been?"

"Three, maybe four."

"Do you remember the dates?"

"No. I might be able to if I looked at my work calendar."

"Would you email them to me?"

"I suppose I could do that."

Sharon closed the daytimer, replaced her notepad in her bag, and placed ten dollars on the table.

"I make it a point not to meddle in other people's business, but I care a lot about Aiden. I think you do too." Without another word Sharon stood and walked out of the restaurant.

Madison grabbed her purse and rushed to catch up. Out on the sidewalk, Sharon pulled a pack of cigarettes from her bag, lit up, then offered Madison one as an afterthought.

"No thanks."

"Nasty habit, but sometimes it helps me to think. Something about this is all wrong. I'm not sure what, but I'll see what I can find out."

Madison realized Sharon would be a terrific investigator. She fleetingly thought about asking her to look for her father, wondered what kind of rates she would charge. She had precious little of the money from her mother's insurance policy left. She'd had no luck snooping around on her own though, not that she'd been able to give it much attention. What with moving, starting the job at Edgewood High, and Aiden Lewis, somehow searching for her father had been pushed to the background.

Sharon stubbed out the cigarette, then placed a hand on Madison's arm. "It's your choice if you want to see Aiden again or not. I don't know what he's involved in, but I'm sure he could use a friend. I know he cares about you. I also know you can trust him. Whatever this is about, it's not about you."

"I'll think about it," Madison said.

Sharon nodded, turned, and walked toward the parking lot. As the sound of her heels on pavement faded into the night, Madison leaned against the light pole.

She wasn't any closer to finding her father than when she'd arrived, now this. Nothing like a little drama to spice things up.

Only Madison didn't want drama.

She wanted peace and quiet.

She wanted family.

And she wanted Aiden.

Chapter Fifty-Six

The phone rang, and Aiden nearly fell off the roof lunging for it.

"Lewis."

"We have a possible tag of the final suspect. Transmitting pictures now. View, confirm, and call me back." Martin clicked off.

The phone's screen immediately filled with pictures of three men. Two of them Aiden had never seen before, but the third was a man he'd seen in the Waldhaus Pub. Aiden returned Martin's call.

"Number three was at the Waldhaus."

"Philip Hansard. He's a nationalized European."

"Connections to Coyote?"

"No, but we can place him in the general vicinity of Abu Yassin at least twice in the last twenty-four months."

"How did we miss him?"

"He doesn't fit the profile. Well educated, a visiting professor on the academic circuit in the states, fairly high profile for someone who is part of a sleeper cell."

"Who's watching him now?"

"Johnson has a team there. Dreiser's part of it."

"Current location?" Aiden had already begun gathering his tools and placing them in the toolbox.

"He's at the Texas-Mexico border in a little town called Providencia and no, you're not going."

"Yes, I am."

"Excuse me?"

"I was there at the beginning of this op, and I'll be there at the end. I'm going to Mexico."

"Last I checked I was still making assignments. When did you start telling me where you're going? I suggest you stand down and wait for further orders."

Aiden looked out across the pasture and somehow quelled the urge to pitch the phone into the field. Taking a deep breath, he sat down on the nearly finished roof of the barn.

"Sorry," Aiden said. "It's just that this has become personal. I'd like to see it through to the end, Sir."

"Johnson is point man on this, Lewis. If I were to send you down there, and I'm not saying I would, you'd only be going as backup."

"I'm good with that."

Martin waited several seconds before mumbling directions to someone in the background.

"It's been years since you've been to the Chihuahuan Desert."

"I trained there in 1998, ran point on the Ramirez bioweapon op in 2000."

"I know your record, Aiden. The situation has deteriorated since you've been that far south. Immigration issues have affected the economies on both sides of the border. The result is the Americans and the Mexicans are more trigger-happy than ever, and along the Rio Grande that's saying a lot. They've never been known for their diplomacy."

"I saw the final target list for Dambusters. Flathead is on there. It could be my town they flood."

Martin uttered a few more oaths, then barked directions to someone in the field office. "Reserve Lewis a flight out of

Kalispell. I want him on a military plane to Providencia in the next three hours."

"Thank you, sir," Aiden said.

"You owe me."

"Right."

"Be careful." Martin's voice sounded tired. "This is the last one. Then we can activate the net. We're down to less than four weeks, and chatter has increased exponentially. We can't lose Hansard."

"We won't."

Aiden clicked off, gathered the rest of his tools, and was on the road back to his house in ten minutes. He'd been itching to do something, anything, all week. The manual labor of the last few days had eased some of his restlessness, but only some.

He'd seen Madison at school twice. Both times during golf practices. Both times she'd been polite but distant, and he didn't blame her. She deserved more than he could offer her right now. All week he'd hammered boards while watching summer turn to autumn. With each blow of the hammer, he wished he could as easily beat the chaff out of his soul. He'd worked until it had been only her face he'd seen, her touch he'd needed.

Somewhere in the building of the roof, he'd made his decision.

A shower, another ten minutes to pack, and one stop in Edgewood.

Chapter Fifty-Seven

As Madison walked across the school parking lot, a new Chevy truck pulled up alongside her. Coach Cole rolled down his window and offered his best I'm-a-good-old-boy-grin. He looked more like a lost pup, but Madison returned the smile anyway. The guy had tried his best all week. No doubt the kids had told him about her breakup with Aiden.

"Madison."

"Coach."

"Need a ride?"

"No, thank you. My car is right there."

George Strait sang about taking someone's bar stool as Coach Cole continued to match her pace.

"Have you been to Dos Amigos yet?"

"I haven't."

"Great Mexican food. How about you and me go there tonight?"

Madison stopped and looked across at the sun beginning to set over the Big Mountain. Taking a deep breath she moved toward the truck, rested her hand against his door, and looked up into Cole's brown eyes and tanned face. He reminded her of a Labrador, and he was a very nice man.

A nice man. That pretty much summed it up. Still, life only gave a girl so many chances.

"Tonight's not good for me, Coach. But would you ask me again?"

A smile broke across his features.

"That's the first time you haven't turned me down."

Madison smiled and looked away. "Next week then?"

"Absolutely. Unless you'd like to do something this weekend. There's this little place—"

They both looked up as Aiden's Avalanche entered the south side of the parking lot and pulled up on the other side of Madison.

Aiden cut his engine and stepped out of the Avalanche.

"Maddie. Cole. How's it going?"

"Great, Aiden. Heard you're redoing the old barn on your northeast pasture."

"Finished it today."

"Remember the time your daddy caught us out there with that keg?"

"I do. I remember the sting of his belt too."

"I decided I'd hike home rather than risk being caught by Aiden's dad. Tripped over my own two feet and went down in the mud."

Madison watched the two as they were caught back in another time. She tried not to compare them, knew it wasn't fair. Cole was a good man in his own right, and he'd tried his best to befriend her. He was also around on a regular basis. So why was it Aiden was the one who made her pulse quicken?

"Maddie, could I talk to you a minute?"

Aiden reached out and touched her arm, sending a shock of electricity through her.

"Sure. I was headed home."

"I'll follow you there."

Cole took in the exchange and apparently decided his friendship with Aiden didn't extend to vying for the new girl in town. "Next week then, Madison."

"All right, Coach."

Cole grinned, tipped his hat, and pulled out of the parking lot.

"Next week?" Aiden scowled as he followed her to the car she'd finally purchased. He opened the door for her.

"It's a long story."

"I'll bet."

Aiden took her laptop bag and set it in the back seat. After she'd buckled up, he squatted beside the car, stared up at her with a look that was more vulnerable than any she'd ever seen. "I've missed you."

She could barely hear him over the hammering of her heart. Not knowing what to say, she merely nodded.

"Can I come to your place? I know you asked me not to call, but I need to talk to you. It will only take a minute."

She couldn't have denied him if she'd wanted to, and she didn't want to. She realized she should, but she'd momentarily lost her resolve. It had been a long five days since she'd seen him. She'd dreamed about him every night, and truth be told, part of her days as well.

She nodded, started her car, and drove out of the lot. He stayed close behind. The image of him squatting beside her car, the way he'd looked at her, melted her heart all the way home.

Chapter Fifty-Eight

Aiden followed her up the stairs. He tried to focus on what he would say, but all he could think about was tunneling his hands through her hair.

He resisted for a full minute, letting her shut the door and set her things on the table. Then he crossed the space between them and pulled her into his arms before she could tell him all the reasons he shouldn't.

Madison was the first to pull away. "You wanted to talk to me about something?"

"Yeah, but maybe we should sit down."

The kitten perched on the arm of the couch, swatting at his hand each time he combed his fingers through her hair.

"Cat's grown."

"Cat's name is Kit."

"Ah. Kit's not a very good guard cat."

"I didn't realize I'd need one."

Madison reached up to touch his face and he took her hand, studied it, and kissed her palm.

A small clock chimed the hour, and he knew he needed to go. Running his hands through his hair he took a deep breath, stood and walked to the kitchen. He rummaged through the cabinet, found a glass and filled it with ice and water. He drank it slowly, giving his pulse time to return to normal, reminding himself why he was there.

Filling another with water, he walked back into the living room. Madison was holding Kit.

"Drink?" he asked.

"Yeah."

Aiden sat on the other side of the L-shaped couch, then moved to the ottoman, where he could hold her hand and look directly into her eyes.

"Maddie, I have to leave." He saw the disappointment surge into her eyes, and his heart tore a little more. "Wait. It's different this time."

She pulled her hand away, crossed her arms, and stared at Kit.

He pulled her hand back. "It's different this time. I've decided this is my last trip."

She pulled the angel pendant out, began fidgeting with it, and he knew she longed to believe him.

"I know you want to know where I go, and I'd like to tell you. But I can't. I can tell you I've decided this is the last time. I can see how it's hurting you, and I can't do that anymore."

Her eyes had grown impossibly large, and he realized she was trying not to cry.

"Sweetheart." He moved beside her on the couch, pulled her into the cradle of his arms, and held her there.

"I don't know what to say. I don't even know what you're giving up for me," she said.

"For us. I'm giving it up for us. I've never cared for anyone this way, Madison. I have to give *us* a chance. I've done what I can for them. I realize now I have to put us first."

Madison snuggled even closer, and Aiden thought he could stay there forever. Except he had a flight to catch. A terrorist to apprehend. A catastrophe to stop. Then he'd be back with her, and he wasn't letting her out of his sight again.

He tried to memorize the smell and feel of her. Struggled to think of how to tell her what she meant to him. He had to settle for the same three words men had been using since time immortal.

"I love you," he said.

She looked up, touched his face, and kissed him softly. "I love you too."

They sat there basking in the knowledge of it. Then the clock chimed again, and he knew he had to leave. Disentangling himself from her, he drew a deep breath, finished the water, and returned both glasses to the kitchen.

When he turned back, Madison stood by the door, the cat sitting on the back of the couch. He wanted to reach out and touch her one more time, but instead, he settled for scratching Kit behind the ear.

"Take care of her, Kit."

The cat began chasing its tail, easing their tension a bit.

"I'll call you as soon as I can."

She nodded and kissed him one last time.

He knew she watched him as he walked down the stairs, unlocked the truck, started it up, and pulled out of the parking lot. When he finally looked in the rearview mirror, she was still standing there at the top of the stairs, holding the scraggly cat in one arm, waving to him with the other.

Iceman.

When he reached Providencia, he'd find a way to don the mask one last time, but as he drove toward Kalispell, he knew the ice had finally melted for good. He would replace it on the outside to survive this mission, but the inside had finally thawed.

Chapter Fifty-Nine

Madison couldn't help grinning at Sharon's obvious discomfort. As usual she was dressed to the nines, this time in a navy suit and matching heels. Did the woman ever wear flats? Maybe some beat-up tennis shoes? Her hair was pulled back in her signature, oversimplified fashion that on Madison would look like she'd thrown it together in five seconds. On Sharon it looked as if she'd paid someone to exquisitely style her hair. Perfectly manicured nails tapped impatiently as Madison finished conferencing with Lucy regarding her essay.

"Do you understand now what you need to do?" Madison asked.

"Sure, Ms. Hart. Thanks. I don't know why I didn't write it that way in the first place. I wasn't thinking I guess."

They both knew the reason Lucy had failed her essay over *The Crucible* was because she'd broken up with Tommy Drake the night before the exam. Although she'd shown up the morning of the essay, she wasn't good for much except using up Madison's box of Kleenex for her supposed cold. That had been a week ago.

Lucy slipped the paper with the "D" across the top into her

backpack and offered a weak smile. Madison walked her across the room, closing the zipper on the pack she had left undone.

"Thanks again, Ms. Hart."

"Are you doing all right? Getting over Tommy?"

"I can't believe I ever thought that dork was special." Madison recognized the bravado for what it was, a way to hide a broken heart. Madison knew all about heartache, especially the high-school variety.

"You're a smart, attractive young lady. There will be other young men. Now rewrite your paper and have it to me next class period."

"Sure thing, Miss." The girl took a couple of steps toward the door, then as an afterthought she turned back and hugged Madison. Without another word she slipped out the door and down the hall.

Madison walked back to her desk, collapsed in the chair, and looked over at Sharon. "Let me guess. High school wasn't a great experience for you."

Sharon pulled herself up straighter, if that was even possible. "Why would you say that? I made wonderful grades in high school."

"I wasn't talking about grades. You seem a little nervous."

Sharon glanced around the room, stared at the reading center, and then looked back to Madison. "I didn't have an English room with a tiki reading lounge, if that's what you mean."

Madison grinned. "Whatever it takes to convince teens reading can be fun rather than a chore."

The silence stretched between them as Madison waited for Sharon to explain the reason for their meeting. She was new at the waiting game though. She gave in first. "I'm guessing you didn't find anything out about Aiden."

"How did you know?"

"When you have something to say, you usually come right out with it."

Sharon pulled a folder from her satchel, shuffled through some papers, and slowly shook her head.

"Something isn't right. Here's a list of his recent charges. See these gaps?"

Madison moved to the desk beside Sharon and looked at the detailed credit-card statement. She didn't want to know how Sharon had managed to access it.

"I'm not really comfortable looking at this. It feels like an invasion of privacy," Madison said.

"Normally I would agree with you, but I'm worried. The dates you gave me when Aiden disappeared show no credit transactions."

"Maybe he used cash."

"Maybe, but I know his accountant. Edward likes for everything to be via credit so there's a paper trail. As you can see, Aiden generally does this. Which makes the gaps very odd."

Madison moved back to her desk, shut down her computer, and shoved it and some papers she needed to grade into her laptop bag.

"What aren't you telling me?" Sharon asked.

Madison smiled and shouldered her bag. "Come on. I'll walk you out."

They were in the parking lot before Madison decided how much she wanted to tell Sharon. "Aiden left two days ago. He came to see me and told me he had to leave—again. He promised this was the last time."

"And you believed him?"

Madison remembered the way he'd held her, the promise in his eyes. "Yes, I did."

"Aren't you worried?"

"No." Madison suddenly remembered asking her mother how she knew her father was still alive. Her mother had said her spirit would know if his spirit had left. At the time Madison had thought it was her medication talking, but suddenly she knew exactly what she meant. She not only knew what she meant, she believed it too. "I know he's all right."

"Did he say anything else?"

"He said he'd given *them* all he could, and now it was time to focus on his own life."

"*Them?*"

"Yeah. I have no idea who he was referring to."

"And you're not the least bit curious?"

"Not really." Madison shifted her bag to the other arm. "I love him, Sharon. And I trust him. I don't know where he is or how long he's going to be gone, but he'll be back as soon as he can. I believe he'll keep his promise."

Sharon gave her that inquisitive lawyer stare. Madison didn't look away.

"You really care for him."

"Yes, I do."

"He's lucky to have you."

"And I'm lucky to have him."

Sharon turned and walked toward her car, then stopped and called out.

"Will you let me know when you hear from him?"

"Of course."

Madison moved off to the little Honda she had finally purchased with her meager funds. Her mood was lighter and happier than since...well since forever.

She knew Aiden would be back soon. She could feel it in her bones. The uncertainty she'd battled since she'd met him had given away to a deep-seated peace. On some instinctual level she knew this was right for them both.

Even the fact she hadn't been able to find her dad didn't detract from her happiness. She'd come to Montana to find John Gibbs, to find the love of a father. Instead she'd found something she wasn't even looking for—the love of a soul mate.

She'd keep looking for her dad, of course. With technology constantly changing, it was amazing the things you could find out about a person—frightening in some ways. But she'd also accepted that perhaps it wasn't meant to be. Her mother used to say some mysteries needed to remain just that, mysteries.

Maybe Sonya Hart had known Madison's destiny was waiting in these mountains, just as hers had been. A very different destiny than either of them could have imagined.

Chapter Sixty

Why Hansard had picked this particular gambling house was a mystery to Aiden, but as he stared through his night goggles, he confirmed the terrorist's identity and waited for Johnson's instructions.

"Confirming Hansard on the second floor at three o'clock," Aiden said.

He wasn't in charge of the op, but he was point man. It was more than he'd expected after the meltdown he'd had with Martin two days ago. The team was in position, and Aiden was fully in his element. He welcomed the icy calm that settled firmly around every inch of his being.

Johnson clicked twice indicating they would wait in the Mexican heat.

It was early yet by Rio Grande time, only one a.m. Within the next few hours some of the remaining caballeros would either stumble away or pass out. As for the men and men working the gambling tables, Aiden could only hope they would stay out of the way.

"I've got a rattler closing in on my position." Dean was three feet east and clearly not amused. "I suppose blowing him away is out of the question."

"Our target looks too occupied to notice, but the cowboy smoking at five o'clock would probably hear." Aiden never took his eyes off Hansard. "Maybe you should try relocating it."

"Relocating a rattler? Not likely."

Aiden heard Dean pull the knife from its sheath. Twice the blade slapped the ground, then Dean was beside him breathing heavily. A quick glance told him his friend was clearly enjoying the mission.

"A souvenir for that girl of yours." He tossed the snake's rattlers on the ground between them, picked up his own night goggles and let out a barely audible groan. "He's a terrible card player. It hurts me to watch this."

"That's why we're paid the big bucks."

"I thought the rattler was why we're paid the big bucks."

The night settled around them while they waited and watched. Located fifteen miles south of the Rio Grande River, Providencia was too small to be considered a village. USCIS had flown in two dozen agents who had taken up positions throughout the desert surrounding the few buildings.

Locating Hansard had taken twenty-four hours, and penetrating the border quietly another twenty-four. Establishing Hansard's exact location hadn't taken ten minutes. Find the only place with women, cards, or liquor. Hansard had a reputation for enjoying all three. Taking him into custody with minimal casualties would be more complicated.

Aiden allowed himself to sink into the desert, literally become one with the night. It was one of the characteristics that had earned him the nickname Iceman. If one of the Mexicans were to stumble within a foot of Aiden, he'd think the agent was another shadow in the desert.

Even on the second of September, in the middle of the night, fall had yet to find this portion of the Chihuahuan Desert. Aiden estimated the temperature to be near 85. Lying on his belly in the dirt, dressed in his government issued flak suit, the sweat poured down his face. He made no move to wipe it away.

His mind was completely on his mission, even while his soul chewed over what had brought him to this place, at this time. He didn't regret what he'd done over the last seven years, but it wouldn't bother him to walk away from it.

Listening to a coyote howl in the brush, having the safety of the best man he knew at his back, knowing he would face death again in the next few hours. It was all part of a job.

But it was only that. A job. It had ceased to be his passion.

He'd joined USCIS so he could become a man. To prove to himself he wasn't a coward, whatever that meant. He was proud of the way he'd served. The missions he'd completed. As proud as you could be of killing other men, of making the world a safer place. Now it was time to move on to other things. Time to move on to Madison. He allowed a part of his mind to linger on her, then pushed the image away. Later. After the mission. After he took care of Hansard.

Watching the terrorist through his night goggles Aiden knew he had let this one become personal. He'd take care of Hansard, then he'd hang up his badge. For him, this was the last one. This one was for his dad.

Johnson's voice pierced his thoughts.

"Our mission has changed from monitor to apprehend. Repeat we are now on apprehend. Take up your positions. We will enter the building in five. Team one will enter through the front. Team two through the back. Team three remain at close perimeter. Team four stay with the choppers."

Then they were moving. Aiden and Dean were set to enter from the front. Johnson and his man from the back—where Hansard was expected to make his escape.

The few remaining sleepy patrons hit the floor as soon as Aiden and Dean crashed through the front door, hoping the noise would send Hansard down the back. The barkeep didn't so much as glance at the shotgun on display behind the counter. Dean was moving up the stairs with his back against the wall and Aiden two steps behind him.

The first sign something was wrong was the closed door of Hansard's room. It should have been flung open. Hansard should have been racing down the back stairs. By the time Dean reached the doorway, bullets had shattered the wood of Door 231.

Dean took more than one hit in the leg, rolled out of the way, and signaled for Aiden to move in without him.

The bullet entered Aiden's arm in an explosion of pain. The thought registered that it didn't matter. It wasn't his shooting arm. It wouldn't slow him down.

He crashed through what remained of the door in time to see Hansard dragging a lovely, teen-aged *senorita* across the bed. With his left arm, he held her in a choke hold and clutched a small remote control. His finger was posed over the button. With his right arm, he pressed the muzzle of a semi-automatic to her temple.

"You are bleeding," Hansard said with a smile.

"Not the first time."

"Do not think I will hesitate to blow her head off."

"Do not think that will stop me." Aiden could hear his voice, but it was as if it came from somewhere else.

"You do not care about the girl. I understand. You do care about your precious American cities though."

Aiden's weapon remained raised. He didn't move any closer. Didn't move away. His gaze remained locked with Hansard's, waiting for the man to blink.

"This trigger works via satellite. It will detonate explosives set at the base of your Dworshak Dam."

The girl sobbed and tried to pull away from the madman in her room. Hansard merely smiled, tightened his hold on her neck, and pushed the muzzle more deeply into her skull.

"You have been to Idaho, yes? A lovely state."

Aiden heard the blood from his left arm dripping on the floor. Johnson and his team were coming up the back stairs. Dean was still down in the hall. He could wait until the cavalry arrived, or he could end this now with a single bullet.

He had a clear shot. He took it.

Chapter Sixty-One

The Mexican girl's screams filled the hotel, but they did nothing to pierce the ice Aiden had encased himself in.

Aiden holstered his weapon immediately. Waited for Johnson to enter. Waited for the questions that invariably came.

The girl ran screaming past Johnson as he entered the room.

"Brewer, we need medics up here. I also want the photographers. No one else is to enter this room."

Johnson looked toward Hansard, then looked away. His hand shook as he holstered his own weapon. "Did he touch the detonator?"

"No."

"You're sure?"

"Yes. Dean?"

"Two leg wounds. Both look like clean exits. How bad is the arm?"

Aiden shrugged. He still hadn't moved, wouldn't move until Johnson gave him permission. As agent in charge he would need to clear the site before anyone entered or left the room. Pictures would need to be taken first. Aiden knew the procedure. He'd been in charge often enough.

He could hear medics in the hall, tending to Dean. Johnson was on the radio, no doubt talking to Martin.

Aiden allowed his eyes to scan the room, see it as Johnson must see it. The place was a mess. Blood plastered the wall behind the wrought iron bed, and Hassard's body lay motionless on the floor.

A photographer bumped into Johnson in his hurry to enter the room, letting out a low whistle.

"I want the photos done in twenty minutes," Johnson said. "We need to have this cleaned and be out of here within the hour. Brewer, get in here and take Lewis's statement now. Aiden, you can at least sit down. Where are the medics?"

Aiden remained standing. In his experience, sitting conveyed weakness. Made agents think you were second guessing yourself. There was no doubt in Aiden's mind he'd made the right call. The good folks in northern Idaho were sleeping peacefully as a result. Madison was safe. His family was safe because of the things they did. No regrets.

All that remained was for him to go home. This mission was the last one. The thought hummed beneath the ice.

Brewer took his statement as the medic cut away his shirt. The bullet had entered and exited the inside of Aiden's arm. He'd been lucky—again.

The medic took out a needle filled with morphine, began tapping it. One look from Aiden had him storing the syringe back in his bag.

Brewer stopped his recording. "No morphine? I'd be asking for double."

"No need for the juice with our medics," Aiden said lightly. "We have the best tailors in the country."

The medic snorted as he sutured both the entry and exit wound. "Agent Lewis has a reputation for turning down our services. You know the routine, Lewis. Keep the wound clean. Report to division when you arrive state-side for X-rays and a more thorough dressing. Don't use the arm to lift anything over a pound for at least six weeks."

They both knew he'd report to division only because he'd have no choice. It was part of debriefing. They also both knew he'd use the arm within the week. Aiden believed it healed faster with use. At least it had before.

Within twenty minutes the medic was finished and Brewer was done taking Aiden's statement.

"Why didn't he run?" Johnson snapped the phone shut. "We were waiting for him at the back stairs."

"I suppose he had his reasons." Aiden watched the cleaning crew as they began their work. Hansard's body was moved into a body bag.

Aiden searched his soul for an ounce of regret for what he'd done, but found none. Instead, he remembered again that Hansard had been willing to sacrifice thousands of innocents for his cause.

Johnson barked a few more orders, then turned back to Aiden. "Maybe he was too drunk to think straight."

"Maybe he was tired of running."

Aiden understood that kind of tired. The Iceman was ready to walk away.

Aiden realized Johnson was staring at him. He turned and looked at the agent. Aiden had always been a fair judge of men, and Johnson was a good one. Young and naïve, but good. What he saw in the man's eyes wasn't condemnation, but a certain amount of curiosity.

Why the ice? That's what he was wondering.

Johnson was probably twenty-five. He might have had three years in the field. A man who hadn't yet seen the things Aiden had. If he was lucky, he never would.

"Am I free to go?"

"Of course."

Aiden turned and walked away. When he descended the stairs and entered the main room, he wasn't surprised to see Dean sitting at the bar. As he walked up to a stool, the barkeep slid a glass of whiskey over to him. He waved Aiden off when he made a move to pay and said in near perfect English, "No one here liked the gringo."

Aiden nodded, accepted the drink.

Dean tapped the glass with his own. The whiskey was warm going down. Not warm enough to penetrate the ice. Warm enough to ease the burn in the arm though. Stir the desire for Madison. Aiden pushed the thought away. He couldn't let his guard down yet. Not until he was back in Edgewood.

"How's the leg?"

Dean shrugged. "They wanted me to ride a medic flight. Can you believe that?"

Aiden swallowed the rest of the whiskey. "Yeah. I believe it."

Dean put money on the counter and signaled for one more.

"How's the arm?"

"I'll live."

They sat that way for a while, neither needing to talk. Liking the fact that neither needed to talk.

"Kids," Dean said. "You take a shot, they want to put you on inactive."

"I'm not inactive, Dean. I'm out."

Aiden had to give Dean credit. He didn't look surprised.

"It's the girl."

"Yeah. It is."

Dean was a good enough friend that he didn't try to talk him out of it.

They finished the second drink, then headed out to the choppers, walking slowly to accommodate Dean's crutches. As they closed in on the rendezvous point, chopper blades and landing lights filling the night, Dean pulled him back into the shadows.

"I'll always have your back, Iceman."

"And I'll have yours."

They left it at that. It wasn't as if they needed to voice their feelings.

They climbed into the chopper. Lifted out of the Chihuahuan Desert. Left behind the dust and dirt and remnants of Dambusters.

The net was activated. The other perps from Dambusters were being brought in even as they flew toward headquarters.

On the outside, Aiden's face remained completely impassive, but inside he savored the fact that his last mission was over. Rolled it over in his mind like you work a piece of ice around in your mouth.

He hoped his dad had been watching. Hoped he was proud.

It wasn't a bear, and it didn't make up for the shot he didn't take so many years ago when he was only a boy, but it wasn't bad.

Chapter Sixty-Two

Aiden stopped at the security counter leading to the east wing of the Pentagon. When the guard nodded for him to do so, he placed his palm against the scanner. The computer verified his prints, and the guard signaled for him to pass through. As Aiden walked toward Martin's office, he was surprised to realize he wouldn't miss it.

"Hello, Agent Lewis." Carol smiled pleasantly.

She had always reminded Aiden of his own mother, and he realized with a jolt that he would miss her.

"Carol."

"Would you like some coffee while you wait?"

"No. Thank you."

"How's the arm?"

"Good. I expect to be rounding up cattle by the end of the week."

"That's not what the medics recommended."

She had the same way of frowning at him like his mother did.

"I suppose I forgot you transcribe those reports."

She gave him the look that said she didn't approve but adored him anyway, then answered her phone. Setting it back in the cradle, she nodded to him. "Commander Martin will see you now."

Aiden stood, straightened his dress uniform, touched his pocket to make sure the envelope was still there. That was stupid, since he'd put it there just twenty minutes ago. Still it wasn't every day you quit your job. He supposed he could cut himself some slack and allow for a little nervousness.

"Agent Lewis." Martin's grasp was as firm as ever, his eyes clear and blue. There was nothing about the man to indicate his seventy years of age or his near fifty years of service.

"Thank you for seeing me, sir."

"Not a problem. You did a good job out there."

"I owe you an apology for my outburst on the phone."

"Apology accepted."

"And I wanted to thank you for allowing me on the mission."

"There's a commendation in your file for your service in Providencia."

"I only did what any other man would have done in my position."

Martin walked to his window and looked out. Aiden knew it meant he was supposed to wait, so he waited.

"You might think so Aiden, but it's not true. Most agents would have hesitated. The smallest hesitation could have meant people in Idaho would have died. The remote was real. We located the explosives at Dworshak—enough to blow the entire dam. Because you acted first and thought about it later no one in Idaho died." Martin sat back down. "You're one of the best agents we have."

"Thank you, sir." Aiden swallowed the lump in his throat. Thought of his father and of Madison. Resisted the urge to touch the envelope in his pocket.

"Unofficially, we have apprehended the other nine operatives. Operation Dambusters is terminated. I think you've earned the right to know that. Of course, there are other threats."

Martin's face aged a few degrees, and Aiden realized there were things he didn't know. Things he didn't want to know.

"But this threat is past," Aiden said. "What about Coyote?"

Martin shook his head. "Run to ground. We'll catch him, eventually, if we decide we want to. For now, he's probably more good to us out there."

Martin glanced at the clock on the corner of his desk. "You asked to see me?"

"Yes, sir." Aiden pulled out the envelope, slid it across the table. "I'm officially resigning my post as of today, sir."

Martin looked at the envelope, but didn't touch it. He raised his eyes to meet Aiden's, and in that moment, briefly, Aiden didn't see his commander's eyes. Instead, he saw the eyes of his father before he'd left him in the cave...before he'd died.

"I'm not going to look at what's in that envelope, son. In fact, I'm going to pretend you didn't even put it on my desk. You've been through quite a lot the last six months. Since you've been with us the last seven years, you've been on twenty-three missions, which is more than we'd normally let an agent participate in, but you insisted. I knew you had something you were trying to prove."

Martin stood, so Aiden stood. It was engrained in him. He was a well-trained soldier.

"Now you go on home. You're off active duty for three months. I've been telling you to take some leave. Now you're going to. You come back here in three months and we'll talk. If you want to hand me that envelope then, I'll consider it."

He held out his hand, and Aiden shook it. Martin dismissed him without another word.

Aiden picked up the envelope and left the room. As he walked through the outer office, Carol smiled at him. He knew Carol didn't listen in on Martin's meetings, but he was willing to bet she had government issued ESP. Her understanding smile said as much.

He'd go home, spend time with Madison, reclaim his life. And in three months he'd come back and give the same envelope to Martin. Dambusters was over, the threat was past, and he was through being an agent.

Chapter Sixty-Three

Aiden had no desire to open the door. He preferred to stand there and drink in the sight of her for a few more hours, maybe a few more years. Then the janitor rounded the corner of the hall, and he figured he'd better go on in before there were three of them in the room. He wanted those first moments alone. Needed her in his arms.

The sound of the sweeper making its way closer covered him opening the door, slipping into the room. He let the door shut behind him, leaned against the wall, placed the flowers he'd brought on the tardy, sign-in table.

"Do I have to sign in here if I brought you flowers?"

Her head snapped up and then she was flying across the room and into his arms, like he'd imagined while he'd crouched in the desert sand. She was softer than she'd been in his dreams, smelled impossibly sweeter. He buried his face in her hair, lost himself in the feel of her arms around this neck.

Then his lips were claiming hers, and he forgot about the missions and the school and the sweeper in the hall.

"I can't believe you're back." She was laughing and pulling away at the same time, dragging him to the ridiculous tiki reading corner. "Have you been home? Why didn't you call? I've missed you so much."

She tugged him down on the floor pillows, covered him with a kiss of her own before he could answer any of her questions. He attempted to pull her back, but she laughed and scooted out of his reach.

"Watch it, cowboy. You might be on the school board, but that doesn't mean you can do whatever you want in the tiki lounge."

"You're okay, Maddie? I missed you."

"I'm fine. Of course, I'm fine. Aiden, I was so worried. What about you?" She reached out to run a hand up and down his arm, and he instinctively jerked away.

"What?"

"It's nothing."

"But—"

"Let's talk about it later. Are you almost done here? I thought maybe I'd take you to dinner."

And then her eyes were searching his, looking deep into his soul, and suddenly, he was tired. Too weary to keep up the mask. He jumped to his feet and walked around the room, picking up books and setting them down again.

"I could come back, if you need to stay. Or I could help. You know. I could help you do things."

Aiden turned to look when she still hadn't said anything, and found Madison had walked up behind him. She took those hands, the hands that could melt him with a touch, and placed them on both sides of his face. Kissed him ever so gently.

"Let's go to my place, cowboy. I'll make you some steak and eggs."

"Steak and eggs?"

"What? You don't eat breakfast for dinner here in Montana?"

Aiden knew she'd seen the hurt, knew the bantering was for his benefit, and he loved her all the more for it.

"Well, now I do remember my mama cooking steak and eggs

up for my daddy every now and then after a hard day on the range."

"You don't say?"

"Course afterwards they started smooching, and we weren't allowed anywhere near their side of the house."

Madison walked around the room, turning off lamps, then crossed to her desk and began packing things into her laptop bag.

"Aiden Lewis, you are making that up."

"No, ma'am. I'm sure steak and eggs were always followed by our being told to go to bed early." He watched her in the half-glow from the hallway's fluorescent lights, thought he could drink in the sight of her forever.

"Remind me again how long your mother and daddy had been married at the time?"

"Oh, a long time."

"And we are not. So, I'm afraid you'll only be having breakfast tonight."

Madison walked past him with her chin high, but made the mistake of passing within his reach. He grabbed her with his good arm and pulled her close, nuzzling her neck until he was sure her heart was beating as fast as his own.

"What were you arguing with me about?" he asked.

"Can't remember."

"Just like a woman."

"Um-hm."

"I like my eggs over easy."

"Got it. Over easy."

"And I like my women sassy."

"Which explains why you're nuzzling my neck."

"I missed you, Madison."

Instantly, they were serious again, and both seemed to know instinctively how close they'd come to never sharing this moment. They held each other. Held on to the moment and the knowledge of the chance they'd been given, until the janitor came in, flipping on the light and apologizing profusely.

Madison pretended to check a few things around the room, but Aiden saw her wipe the tears from her eyes.

He was lucky to be home, lucky to have her. And he wouldn't leave again. Not for USCIS or for anyone else. It was time to settle down. As Aiden walked Madison into the parking lot, he knew—without a doubt—he'd finally found the reason that made settling down the one thing on this earth worth doing.

He knew if Dean could see him now, he'd raise a toast to that.

Chapter Sixty-Four

Madison set the coffee to percolate, removed the steaks from the microwave where they'd been defrosting, set them in the pan, and nearly jumped out of her skin when Aiden pulled her into an embrace.

"I cannot cook with you in here."

"We don't need to eat."

"Correction. You most certainly do need to eat. When was the last meal you had?"

"Hmm. Sweetheart, I'm satisfied feasting my eyes on you."

He began to nibble on the back of her neck, and Kit picked the same moment to yowl.

"Cat food is under the sink."

"Domestic duties." Aiden gave her neck one last nuzzle, then turned to retrieve the kitty food. "One bowl of cat food coming up, Sir Kit."

Aiden fed the cat, then relaxed on the bar stool watching Madison cook.

"You might as well take your jacket off. I'm going to see whatever's wrong with your arm eventually."

Madison resisted the urge to turn around, forced herself to focus on browning the steaks, pulling eggs, butter, and fruit from the refrigerator. She could practically hear him sorting through his options, which were precious few.

Finally, she adjusted the stove's burner to low, picked up her glass of water, took a long drink to settle herself, then turned to face him. As she suspected, he was still wearing the brown leather bomber jacket.

"Obviously, you aren't ready to talk about it," she said.

"It's not something I can really explain."

"Fair enough."

"If you were to ask questions I'd have to lie."

"Then I won't ask."

She met his gaze. The twelve days he'd been away had given her plenty of hours to think, enough time to realize when he came back—if he came back—she was going to give this relationship all she had. She didn't have to know where he went or what he did. All she had to know was it was over. She didn't have to know what the scars were from. She only had to know there would be no new ones.

Walking around the bar, she moved behind him and pulled the jacket slowly from his shoulders. She sat down on the bar stool next to him, let her fingers lightly touch the bandages covering his muscles. Her heart raced as her mind calculated the short distance from his arm to his heart, and in that moment, she breathed a prayer of thankfulness for those inches. When she'd settled her emotions, she finally looked up and met his eyes.

"You said you liked those eggs over easy?"

"Over easy will be fine."

Her fingers were still lightly resting on his arm, but now she moved both hands gently up his shoulders, then to his face. She kissed him. Let her hands trail back down his arms, stopping again above the elbows, stopping where the bandages ended.

She let her forehead rest against his. Breathed in the smell of him, the miracle of him. He was here, this night, and she wouldn't waste that gift.

"You might want to wash up," she whispered. "Dinner's nearly ready."

She walked back into the kitchen. Heard him go into the bathroom, listened to the faucet run.

She wouldn't ask. She wiped the tears away quickly. She didn't need to know. Had no desire to hear the details. He was here now, and he wasn't leaving again. It was enough.

That's what she'd learned in the last twelve days. She'd discovered who she was and that just possibly Aiden Lewis was the man who could complete her, patch the holes in her life. He had a past. So did she. They'd work through that in time. As she moved the steak and eggs to the plates, she knew it was worth working through.

Madison forced herself to focus on the meal. She continued to glance at his arm when she thought he wasn't looking. As far as the meal, she'd yet to take a bite.

"You going to eat that steak or fork it to death?"

"I'm eating." Her chin came up in what she hoped was a *don't mess with me* gesture.

As if in proof, she popped a piece of steak into her mouth, but then her eyes slid from his eyes down his arm to the bandage and the chewing stop. She set the fork down, tried to swallow, failed, tried again.

He handed her the glass of water.

"It's okay, Madison. It might take a while to accept the idea you have an injured man."

"You're my man, are you?" She spoke around the bite of steak she was still trying to chew. "Think you could fix a few things around here?"

"Of course, I could. What kind of things?"

She cleared her throat and glanced around, her mind suddenly blank. Then she spied the list on the refrigerator, hopped up, retrieved it, and handed it to him. "I've been meaning to give this to management, but I don't really like the idea of a stranger being in my apartment. It's all small stuff, and I feel silly even bringing it up now."

"Are you kidding? I got my man card taking care of stuff like this."

"You? You're...rich, right? So you probably hire someone to do these things."

"Ha! Not the Lewis way."

"Well, it's nothing big—leaking faucet, door hinge that squeaks, toilet that runs all night."

"I've got this. I'll stop by tomorrow and take care of it while you're at school."

He stuffed the list in his pocket and squeezed her hand. It felt good to talk about normal things, everyday things.

"Didn't realize you Texas girls knew how to cook like this."

"Excuse me? I come from the land of steak and taters."

"How did you manage to fight those Texas cowboys off?"

"What makes you think I did?"

Aiden started laughing hard enough that Kit joined them to find out what the commotion was about. By the time dinner was over, some of the tension had eased. Aiden had even managed to prod her into talking about her classes.

"School's going well. I love the kids. They're even enjoying *The Crucible*."

"Tell me you are not making them read that book."

"I don't pick the readings. The state does. You should know that. You're on the school board."

"I try to skim curriculum issues and stick with sports and facilities. I remember junior English though. I hated *The Crucible*."

"Are you kidding? All that passion and romance and illicit love?"

"Are we talking about the same *Crucible*?"

"There's only one I know of. Unless you're confusing English with Chemistry. We're reading the one by Arthur Miller. You know, the one where they burned the witches."

"Maybe. I think I only read the *Cliffs Notes*."

"Typical boy."

Aiden swiped her with his dishrag, which sent Madison around the corner into the living room, flopping down on the couch.

"Other than the grading, which is always a pain, and the problems with my laptop, everything is going great."

"Why is grading a problem?" Aiden asked.

"Too much of it. All those essays take time."

"You really read those things? I figured teachers just stuck a grade on top."

Madison hung her head back, petitioning heaven for patience.

"And the laptop?"

She sat up immediately, looking perplexed. "It's the strangest thing. My laptop works fine at school, but when I'm home it acts bizarre."

"Bizarre how?"

"As if someone else is controlling it, but I know that's impossible."

Chapter Sixty-Five

Aiden tried not to overreact to what she was saying, but a sense of dread turned his stomach to lead. Keeping his voice light, he asked, "Sure it's not the operator?"

Aiden moved over beside her on the couch, put her legs on his lap and began massaging her feet. Her groans told him he was touching the right spots.

"Nope. I'm actually very good on computers. It might be my wireless router. I guess I should take it in, but I haven't had time."

"Are you receiving an intermittent signal?"

"No. Strong, steady light. Strange, right?"

Aiden continued massaging her feet.

Madison's hands moved to her pendant, began worrying the angel. "The mouse starts moving on its own. Opening files, things like that. Sometimes I won't even be sitting there. Maybe I've watched too many Bourne movies. I've started to wonder if someone is remotely manipulating my files. But who would be interested in an English teacher's files?"

Aiden was way ahead of her. Files could be manipulated remotely. Any mid-level techie could hack into a wireless router. Or she could be remembering wrong. "Sweetheart, maybe you're working too much."

"Seriously though, it's strange. I'll walk out of the room for a drink, or to check on Kit, and when I come back something is open I know I wasn't working on."

"What else?"

"Files will begin opening all over my computer. Sometimes my emails will open on their own. I think my computer has gone schizophrenic. Then I'll go into work, and it seems to act fine. So, I think it might be my wireless box here. I need to take it in and have it checked. Or maybe I should buy a new one."

"I could look at it for you. I'm pretty good with computers, you know."

She nodded, grew suddenly quiet. When she glanced again at his arm, he noticed tears in her eyes.

"Don't cry, Maddie."

She nodded as if she agreed with him, but then she was in his arms sobbing.

"Hey. Hey. What is this about?"

But it was as if all the fears she'd held inside had finally broken free. She cried until his shirt was wet and she'd begun to hiccup. Then she sat up and scrubbed away her tears, smearing her makeup in the process.

"I was scared you wouldn't be back, and you are. I was afraid we'd never..."

"You don't have to worry about that now. You never have to worry about that again."

She nodded, believing him, and he understood that her love for him was deep enough to bridge the past, the secrets, the things which he could never tell her.

They sat there until Kit was fast asleep and the clock told him he should go.

"When will I see you again?" she asked.

"Tomorrow if you're not tired of me."

"Of course, I'm not."

Aiden's fingers practically twitched to check her computer. It took all his effort to resist the urge to sweep her apartment from top to bottom.

"I could take it home with me."

"Take what?"

"Your computer."

"Why would you do that?"

"Sometimes I have trouble sleeping is all."

"You have to be exhausted."

"I'm just saying I could take a look at it."

She chewed on her thumbnail and finally nodded. "Okay, I guess. But don't...you know...make yourself stay awake to do it. Anything wrong with it can wait until the weekend."

"Sure. Okay." He accepted the laptop and carried it to the door.

Leaning in to kiss her once more, he said goodnight, promised he'd see her in the morning, and walked to his vehicle.

He wouldn't risk frightening her.

He wouldn't even suggest she was being watched.

First he'd look for proof.

But if it was there, he would figure out who had invaded her space and why.

Chapter Sixty-Six

"It's fixed?" Madison accepted the coffee and scone first, then the laptop. She was already at her car on the way to school by the time he arrived.

"Sure is."

"Oh. I guess it wasn't as bad as I thought then."

Instead of answering, Aiden closed her car door, leaned in to kiss her, and said, "I'll fix dinner tonight."

"After you take care of that to do list?" She pulled an extra apartment key from her purse and handed it to him. "I like you being home."

"I'm glad."

She kissed him again and offered a backward wave as she drove away.

Now as he stood drinking his own coffee and thanking heaven he'd asked for the extra shot of espresso, he pulled out his cell phone and punched in Dean's number.

"Iceman. What's up?"

"I need you to run an IP address. I'm transmitting it to you now."

"Got it."

"I want most recent physical location as well as when it last received transmissions from the computer address I'm keying in now."

"Copy that."

Dean clicked off, leaving Aiden staring at Madison's apartment. He wanted to believe the laptop had been bugged in August when she'd first come to Edgewood. He desperately hoped the laptop was the only thing tagged, but his instincts told him otherwise.

Slowly and methodically he began taking the apartment apart.

Five hours later Aiden looked at the pile of hardware on Madison's table, listened to Dean's voice, and fought an overwhelming urge to put his fist through a wall. Any wall would do.

If he hadn't been on an open frequency with most of the central USCIS office he would have at least let loose with a string of profanity. As it was he had to satisfy himself with imagining what he would do to the person who'd bugged Madison's apartment when he caught him, and he would catch him.

"Could you have made an error?" he asked.

"Negative," Dean said. "Checked it twice."

"Well this is one messed up situation then. I'm looking at a dining room table full of surveillance equipment I've pulled from virtually every room in Madison's apartment. Now you're telling me someone in Montreal has been receiving data from her laptop as recently as last night?"

"Roger that. 2:45-4:06 a.m."

"Which was exactly the time I was on-line tracing the IP address."

Aiden collapsed onto the couch, the same couch someone had been watching him and Madison on last night. The thought made him want to draw his weapon and start shooting. Since he couldn't, or shouldn't, he did the next best thing. He went ice cold with anger.

"I assume we've already sent agents to the address," he said.

"Aiden, this is Martin. Agents Johnson and Trent were already in Montreal. They went to the address two hours ago and found a vacated apartment. We swept it for prints, but so far haven't found any. Canvassing the neighborhood and interviewing the apartment super hasn't netted us anything either. The place was rented online to a corporation, paid six months in advance. Corporation is a dead end. No activity reported in the apartment since we pulled the net on Dambusters eleven days ago."

"Maybe the monitoring software was set on autopilot," Dean said. "Whoever was watching Madison, whoever was watching you, was caught in the net."

"Who cleaned the apartment then?" Martin asked.

"Coyote," Aiden said it quietly.

"All right," Martin agreed. "That's a possibility. He's highest on our list of *Most Wanted*. Let's assume this was a cleanup operation. We'll comb Montreal, but I suspect he's gone to ground. I'm putting another agent in Edgewood to watch Madison."

"I want Dean."

"Agreed."

"I'm leaving now," Dean said.

"I'll meet you at the Kalispell Airport."

"Watch your back, Aiden." Martin's voice suggested something more than concern.

"Yes, sir." Aiden clicked off and looked at the clock. He needed to load the table full of spyware into a duffle bag. He needed to complete her list, which shouldn't take an hour, and he needed to explain why he wouldn't be home when she got there.

He fixed everything but the leaking faucet, which required a part he didn't have. So he scribbled a note telling her he'd left to get the part and that he'd pick her up for dinner later. He carted his toolbox down to the Avalanche, along with the menagerie of spyware, and headed to the ranch.

Chapter Sixty-Seven

Dean was the last man off the plane. They exchanged only a nod, waiting until they were beside the Avalanche to speak.

"You swept it?" Dean asked.

"Twice."

As Aiden started the engine, Dean reached into his backpack, pulled out what looked like a snow globe and placed it on the dashboard.

"New toy from the guys in ops—a magnetic array displacer. Should hurt their ears if they managed to slip anything inside while my plane landed." Dean buckled up, pulled a larger box out of his duffel and placed it on the seat. Then he set a smaller gift-wrapped one next to it. "The big one's for your mansion, the gift wrapped one's for the lady."

Zipping up his pack, he turned to look at his friend. "You look terrible."

Aiden accelerated onto the blacktop, taking his frustration out on the road. "Madison told me her computer was acting strangely, so I thought Coyote might have slipped something on there. I had no idea--"

"Yeah."

They drove in silence awhile, each gearing up for whatever lay ahead.

"I'd rather move Madison to the ranch," Aiden said.

"I gather she doesn't know about your alter ego yet."

"We're not quite to that point of disclosure in our relationship."

"Ah."

"And she's a little old-fashioned."

"So staying at her place isn't an option," Dean said.

"No. It's not."

"Gotcha."

The sun slipped behind the mountains as Kalispell fell behind them.

"Aiden, we both know Coyote has probably run down a foxhole and any surveillance was left behind from a previous op."

"I read the briefs."

Dean nodded.

"It's not what my gut is saying," Aiden said.

"Mine either."

They rode another twenty minutes in silence.

Ten miles outside of Edgewood, Aiden pulled into the parking lot of a motel and parked next to a somewhat battered Ford Explorer.

"Your room is 356 on the corner. Good view of the parking lot and Main Street."

Dean nodded, accepted the room key and car key Aiden offered.

"There are three thermoses of coffee, some sandwiches, and a C.J. Box novel in the passenger seat. Also a burner phone I bought today preprogrammed with the number to my burner phone. No one else has it. Standard equipment in the back seat—night vision goggles, rifle with a scope, a knife, and a Kevlar vest. The car's equipped with satellite, GPS, and radio with local police channels. Our sheriff's name is Bonner. He hasn't been briefed yet. He will be if and when he needs to be. I'll relieve you at three.

There's a map under the driver's seat marking your rotation points."

Dean offered a grin, then pulled his hat down low. "To old times, man," and then he was gone.

On the drive back to Madison's, Aiden attempted to calm his emotions. He didn't want to frighten her. He didn't know how much he should tell her, if anything.

Madison opened the door as he was about to knock. "Now this is a service I wasn't expecting."

"It's not flowers, but—"

"It's better."

Madison accepted the sack of take-out and turned toward the dining area.

"Wait," Aiden said.

"Wait?"

"I, um, forgot to give you this the other night." He held out the gift-wrapped box, feeling more than a little foolish.

"More presents." She walked back to the front door, apparently unable to resist the allure of wrapping paper. "You shouldn't have."

They both looked in surprise at the snow scene of Glacier National Park.

"Aiden. It's precious."

She leaned forward, gave him a kiss that had him wanting to skip dinner and pull her into his arms. If that's what a snow globe earned him—correction—if that's what a magnetic array displacer earned him, imagine what she'd do with a piece of jewelry.

Chapter Sixty-Eight

"This feels personal." Aiden threw the printouts on the table and reached for the cold coffee.

Dean checked his weapon, holstered it, then shrugged into his jacket. "Martin says it's either kids playing a prank or animals setting off the perimeter sensors. There's nothing to indicate you've been tagged or are being watched."

Aiden tapped the printouts and the map of his property, "Someone's trying to find a weak spot in the perimeter security system. They're doing it at random locations and times to make it look haphazard. Did you upload these results to central?"

"Yeah. He says it's a hunch and with the G8 in two weeks, we don't have men to spare on anyone's gut feeling."

"Someone's watching her, Dean. I know it. And now they're trying to connect her to me."

"So what are we going to do about it, boss?"

"We're going to catch him. I want you stationed in here. I'll weaken the perimeter sensors where he can break through. When he comes in, I want you to stun him."

"And you will be?"

"Stationed outside."

"In case he's not alone."

"Once we've confirmed he is alone, we'll bring him around, extract the information we need from him. Then you can transport him to Martin."

"Who will not be happy to see him. What about Madison?"

"I'll ask Sharon to babysit."

"Sharon? Isn't she the lawyer you used to date?"

"Yeah, she's an expert marksman and won't hesitate to shoot if she has to."

"Sounds like a plan, Iceman. When?"

"It'll take me two days to set the trap. Saturday night?"

"I'll be here. Until then I'll continue with the rotations. Edgewood is a pretty quiet town. I'm going to need another novel."

"Living room, left bookcase, bottom shelf."

"See you at three."

Aiden rolled up the plans, stored them in his study, and set his alarm for noon. He needed to see Sharon before golf practice with the team at two thirty, then dinner with Madison at six, and then relieve Dean at three in the morning.

His last thought before dreams claimed him was that for a retired millionaire, he sure wasn't getting enough sleep.

Sharon looked up in surprise to see Aiden leaning against the open door of her office.

"Afternoon, beautiful."

Moving across the room, she pulled him into her office without a word, only stopping to leave directions with the secretary in the outer office.

"Brad, hold my calls while I'm with Mr. Lewis."

"What about your one o'clock?"

"Put Ms. Tramsley in the conference room, give her coffee and pastries, and have John start going over the depositions. I'll join them as soon as I can."

She shut the door before he could ask anything else.

Aiden flopped into an armchair and gave her his best cowboy smile. "How are you, sweetheart? I haven't seen you in ages. You have a new secretary, and he's more handsome than me."

"Save the charm, Aiden. It won't work. I'm not interested. Besides, I've been worried. What is this about you being shot? And why haven't you called? I don't want to sound like Nate, but you're making me feel like a nag. If it weren't for Madison, I wouldn't even know you were back in town."

Sharon sat back in the two-thousand-dollar leather chair and let its comfort, well, comfort her. Aiden was happy to see her doing so well professionally, and he was sorry to have worried her, not that he could do anything about it.

"You look terrible. Madison said you look great. Is she stupid or so in love she's blind?"

"Ouch. Thank you for the compliments and the concern." Aiden sank lower in the chair, dropped the charm and the fake energy. "Madison is why I'm here, Sharon. I need a favor."

Sharon waited, one eyebrow raised.

"I need you to babysit her on Saturday for me."

"Babysit?"

"Yes, and don't tell her I asked you to do it. Take her to some place public, or to your place. I don't care where. But she can't go back to her apartment until you receive a call from me. It might be late."

"I don't suppose I should ask why."

"It would be better if you didn't, then I wouldn't have to lie to you."

Sharon steepled her fingers. "All right, Aiden. Anything else?"

"There is one other thing." He stood, stretched, walked around to her side of the desk. When he squatted down in front of her, he knew he had her full attention. "You still have your handgun?"

"Of course."

"Be sure you keep it close."

Chapter Sixty-Nine

"You don't think it's odd she would call?" Madison asked, pausing to look through her binoculars.

"Now why would I think it's odd?" Aiden stopped beside her, thought of looking through his own binoculars, but decided he preferred the view of her to whatever she might be looking at.

"Sharon never calls me."

"Maybe Bix is out of town."

"That's what Sharon said, but she doesn't seem like the girlfriend type. What did you say you had to do tonight?"

"Nothing really, sweetheart. But you two go ahead and have fun. I'll stay home and watch some golf film, prepare for the boys' next meet."

"Did you make that up, or is there really such a thing as golf film?" Madison turned to look at him.

"I made it up," he admitted.

Madison nodded and raised her binoculars again.

"Aiden, is that an elk over there?"

"Probably, or it could be a deer, dear."

She punched him in the arm, his good arm, then reached for her water.

"I love hiking."

"I do too. I especially love that you drove up here this time."

Madison made a face, screwed the top back on her water, and resumed walking. "I still had a few queasy moments though."

"But you kept driving, and you almost reached the speed limit." Aiden stopped and looked out over Edgewood. From the slopes of Big Mountain, it looked like a quaint little village. "I think the traffic jam has actually started to unwind."

She threw herself on him with enough force to land him in the leaves on his backside.

"If it weren't for Old Man Jackson, I'd say we stay here and smooch a bit."

"Oh, you would?" She tilted her head, a mischievous look in her eyes he'd seen before. "I thought Jackson passed us twenty minutes ago."

While he was trying to remember if she was right, Madison jumped up and danced ahead of him on the trail. "Or maybe you're too old for hiking and you're looking for an excuse. Maybe the cowboy isn't up to it anymore."

When he took off after her, she moved even more quickly around the bend. He had to push to catch up with her, which was a testament to how much she had acclimated to the altitude, and how little time he had spent in the gym.

He caught her near a boulder by the trail, tackled her gently, and kissed her.

"Are you going to behave now?" he asked.

"Maybe."

"Are you going to quit running ahead?"

"Uh-huh."

"Tell me why."

"Oh, Aiden."

"Tell me the rules," he nibbled on her neck, making her squeal. "Tell me."

"Hikers should always stay in sight of each other."

"Tell me the other rule. The most important one."

She was gasping now, trying to squirm out of his grasp. "Which one is that?"

"Tell me."

"How does it start?"

"You know."

"Never—"

"Never what?"

"Never hike alone."

And then she melted out of his grasp like butter. But once out, she only turned, reached for his hand, and held it as they ascended the last of the trail.

"Hike down or ride the gondola?" he asked, looking out at the sunset. It had been a perfect Saturday.

"Gondola."

"Gondola it is, then."

Riding down the mountain, Aiden couldn't help wondering what he'd find that night. Clouds were moving in from the west, promising rain before nightfall. From the looks of it, they were in for a good storm. Reaching for Madison's hand, he entwined his fingers with hers.

"Promise me you girls will be careful."

"Sure. But seriously, how dangerous can Edgewood be?"

Chapter Seventy

"Movement at three o'clock."

"Copy that. I'll circle round." Aiden crept through the southern portion of his property silently, more fleeting than a shadow. The evening was pitch black with no moon at all, the cloud cover blocking out what little light the stars would have provided. The absence of wind made the slightest sound echo into the darkness, which didn't matter since he made no sound.

He edged across the property he knew as well as his own bedroom. He'd lived here for fifteen years now, but more than that he'd walked the property nearly every day. It was more than a place to lay his hat. It was his home. The fact that someone was violating it made him want to put the gun away and pummel the man with his fists.

Instead he inched forward and reported back to Dean who was waiting in the first-floor study. "He's disabled the remote perimeter cameras and is moving toward you now."

"Copy. I'm in position and waiting."

Aiden pushed thoughts of Madison from his mind. He needed the ice now. He needed to maintain his cool. Capturing this intruder was secondary, although it would no doubt go a long way toward making Madison safer. In the long run though, he needed to find out who he was reporting back to. There were two ways to do that. Send him back to Martin, who would take several days to process and interrogate him. Or capture him and make him talk tonight.

If everything went as planned, he'd have answers in the next hour.

"I have a visual now. He's entering through the back terrace." Dean clicked off.

Aiden could make out Dean and the intruder through his night-vision goggles. Dean had his stun gun raised and was ready to take the shot when a car pulled into the front drive, setting off the motion sensors and lights.

"Drop back," Aiden said, and Dean faded into the night.

Nate walked through the front door, turning on more lights and calling out.

Aiden was in the house in seconds, but not before Nate had entered the study, not in time to warn him. The intruder had his weapon pointed at Nate by the time Aiden burst into the room.

"Drop your weapon, Mr. Lewis." the man said, "Or I shoot your brother."

"I don't think so." Dean stepped out from behind the curtains, his weapon inches from the intruder's head. "You drop it."

"I will kill him." The intruder's eyes were locked with Aiden's. "Do not test me on this, Mr. Lewis. Instruct your man to back down. Tell your brother to keep his hands up high, and drop your weapon."

"Aiden?" Nate's hands were shaking, but he held them high, just as the man said.

"That's good, Nate. Dean, you back away like the man said. Just like in Mexico."

And then Aiden took the shot. He didn't wait, didn't think. He just took the shot.

Nate looked at the dead man on the floor, at Aiden, then at

his hands which were now splattered with blood. As understanding dawned, he turned and vomited in the trash can by the desk.

Dean knelt by the body and immediately searched the man's pockets, while Aiden walked to his phone and punched in Martin's number.

"No papers. There's a cell, but it's clean." Dean threw him the phone.

"Check the screens. See if anyone else is out there."

Dean nodded, sent a questioning look in the direction of Aiden's brother who had yet to move, then walked to the computer and began tapping keys to display monitor feedback fields.

"Screens show no activity."

"You shot him." Nate continued to stare at his hands. "You killed a man."

"I need to talk to Commander Martin. This is Lewis."

"This isn't Iraq. We're in Montana, and this is your house." Nate looked over at the body, then sat on the couch and leaned forward, arms propped on his knees, lungs working to draw in deep breaths of air.

"Do *not* hyperventilate," Aiden said, then turned back toward the phone. "I need to talk to him now. Yes, I'll hold."

"You have a man's brains on your wall." Nate looked up to confirm his own words, began to turn green again, and turned his gaze back down at the carpet.

"Lewis here. I have a package to pick up, sir." Aiden held the phone a little away from his ear. "Yes, sir. I understand."

Aiden paced the floor, stepping around the body and his brother. "No papers, and a clean phone. No, sir. He was not on our watch list. It appears he was working alone."

There was another pause as Aiden again held the phone a bit from his ear.

"Dean and my brother Nate. Yes, sir. I'll put you on speaker now."

"This is Commander Patrick Martin with the United States Citizenship and Immigration Services. I need everyone in the room to identify themselves for the record."

"Agent Dean Dreiser." Dean never glanced up from the computer monitors.

"Agent Aiden Lewis." Aiden looked at his brother and nodded.

"Nate Lewis."

"Is there anyone else in the room?"

"Only the deceased, sir." Aiden sat down across from his brother and locked eyes with him.

"Nate, as Commander, a representative of the U.S. government, and officer in charge of this operation, it is my duty to inform you this is a covert operation. As a covert operation, all parties involved, including yourself, are under direct orders from the President of the United States to limit any intelligence gathering or dissemination to other sanctioned members of this operation previously approved by myself or the President."

Martin paused. Aiden watched Nate as the words sank in, saw his gaze move to the dead man, slide off to the white carpet that had turned crimson, then move back to the man on the floor and remain there.

"I'm sorry you had to see the death of this man, Mr. Lewis. It's very important you tell no one about what happened tonight. Your brother is involved in an ongoing operation of extreme importance to national security, and you stepped in the middle of it. You're going to have to deal with that, and you're going to have to deal with it alone for now. Am I clear?"

"Yes, sir."

"Should I receive any indication you have discussed the events of tonight with anyone—including your wife, your priest, or the guys you see at the coffee shop—-you will be arrested and kept in a government facility until such time this operation is no longer active and pertinent to national security. Is that clear?"

"Yes." His voice shook, but he was nodding his head nervously up and down. "Yes, sir."

"Aiden, take me off speakerphone."

Aiden reached across the desk, picked up the phone, and spoke with Martin another fifteen seconds. When he disconnected the call, he turned and spoke to Dean first. "We're authorized to run prints on him and put it through the database. A team will be here within two hours. There's a field kit in the bottom drawer."

Dean nodded and set to work.

Aiden pulled a still stunned Nate to his feet, "Come on, bro. Let's get you some coffee."

Chapter Seventy-One

Nate visibly calmed down once they were in the living room, though he was still a little unsteady on his feet.

"Sit down for a minute." Aiden made coffee from the high- end espresso machine on his bar and handed it to Nate. "Drink this. It'll help some."

Nate looked as if he was going to argue, then seemed to reconsider. With a shake of his head, he accepted the tiny cup and swallowed the scalding espresso.

"Better?" Aiden asked.

"I guess."

Aiden sat down across from Nate and looked directly at his brother.

"I work for USCIS—a branch of the US government. I've been an agent there for seven years now. Mostly on domestic missions. Sometimes overseas."

"That's why you disappear for weeks at a time."

"Yeah."

Aiden stood, walked to the windows, and stared out at the darkness. Wondered what he could tell Nate. What he should tell him. "I've wanted to explain for a long time, but I didn't want you to worry. And they prefer we inform as few people as possible."

"So you're an undercover agent?"

"Something like that. We mostly monitor terrorists, run-up leads, track suspects. Sometimes we're on more active missions."

"I guess you'd call tonight an active mission."

"Tonight wasn't supposed to happen." Aiden walked back to the chair across from his brother and forced himself to sit down, though sitting was the last thing he wanted to do right now.

"So who was this guy? And why was he in Edgewood?"

"I believe we'll find he's a part of Dambusters."

"Dambusters?"

"An international operation that was stopped two weeks ago. Details of the operation were supposed to be leaked to the media tomorrow. It's been in the works for over a year. It became an active mission in August when it was confirmed simultaneous operations were planned to blow ten dams in the US and Canada. We stopped all those ops two weeks ago. Caught all ten operatives, but the mastermind slipped through our net."

"He was the mastermind?" Nate turned and stared back toward the study.

"No." Aiden sat down and ran his hands through his hair. "We don't know who he was or why he was breaking in here."

"You lost me." Nate picked up his cup, realized it was empty and set it back down.

"The mastermind is a man named Coyote. I tagged him on a flight from Dallas to Salt Lake."

"The same flight where you met Madison?"

"The same flight. He used Madison for cover on that flight. Drugged her. Maybe he hurt her. She doesn't remember."

"She doesn't remember? You mean she doesn't know? And you haven't told her?"

"No, I haven't. And don't think that hasn't torn me up. I keep thinking it will come back to her, but so far it hasn't. And then—"

"Then you fell in love with her."

"Yeah." Aiden allowed his head to drop between his hands and his shoulders to slump, allowed the weariness to creep in for a moment. "I didn't plan that."

Nate reached over and rubbed his brother's neck. "You killed that guy in the other room."

"Agents do that sometimes."

"You couldn't just hit him with something?"

Aiden looked up, thought of all the men he had killed in the last seven years—five men total. Not that many in USCIS tallies, but the way he'd killed them, nearly all eye to eye, had earned him his title of Iceman. And truth be known, he didn't really dream about them at night. No, his nightmares were still reserved for the one man who mattered most.

"You're not forgetting he was holding a gun to your head, are you? He would have killed you, Nate. I know his kind. They don't hesitate. The only solution is to kill them first."

Nate paled, then swallowed hard. "Guess I owe you one."

"No. You don't owe me. You're forgetting I owe you. I'll always owe you." Aiden stood and paced back to the window.

"What are you talking about?"

"I'm talking about Dad, Nate. I'm talking about the bear. If I hadn't hesitated, he'd still be here. I'm the reason he died."

Suddenly, Nate was beside him, turning him, looking in his eyes.

"You are not the reason Dad died, Aiden. The bear is the reason Dad died. A bullet would not have stopped a nine-hundred-pound grizzly. We're lucky she didn't kill you too."

Then Nate's arms were around him, and they were embracing in a way they hadn't in years. The weight of the guilt he'd been carrying lifted off him as the tears clogged his throat.

"Don't mean to break up a family moment, but I think I found something," Dean drawled.

Aiden and Nate pulled apart, made man noises as they dried their eyes, and slapped each other on the back. They followed

Dean into the study, careful to walk around the body, and stopped in front of the computer.

"Ran the prints. Looks like we have Coyote's brother."

"Coyote. Isn't he the mastermind you were looking for?" Nate looked from the monitor to the body and then back toward the monitor again.

"Yeah. The question is why did he send his younger brother here?" Aiden rubbed his eyes as he punched in Martin's number. When the line connected, he relayed the information, listened for less than a minute, then disconnected.

"Martin confirmed. Last known alias is Donato Mancini, Coyote's brother. Hasn't been spotted in the last three years."

"Why was he here in Edgewood?" Nate asked.

"Apparently Coyote has connected Madison to me."

"But you said the operation was over, shut down, everyone's been captured, or nabbed, or whatever you spy guys do to them. So what's the point?"

"Dambusters is over," Dean agreed. "Standard operating procedure would be to move on to his backup plan."

"Or begin working his next mission," Aiden said.

Dean closed down the computer, stopped, and looked at Aiden with the same puzzled look Nate wore. "Why would he risk sending family to come back here?"

"The same reason that has inspired men since the battle of Troy," Aiden said.

"I don't follow, boss." Dean sank onto the couch, staring out at the rain that had begun to fall. "If it's not on the Comedy Channel, I'm afraid I haven't seen it."

"Revenge," Nate said softly.

"Exactly." Aiden looked out at the storm and wondered if Coyote was crouched in the darkness watching him. "I ruined his plans, or at least I'm the one he can easily blame."

"So now it's personal?" Dean asked.

"Right," Aiden said.

They all walked to the front of the house. Aiden opened the

door, and they stepped out onto the front porch into a Montana night that was cold and rainy. The wind had picked up and threw the cold drops back at them. By morning it would begin to freeze. Fall had arrived and winter would follow closely on its heels.

Dean moved toward his vehicle after a brief "I'm back on patrol if you need me."

Nate and Aiden stood alone, looking out at the rain.

"Martin was serious about what he said back there. Don't mention this to anyone. Not even Janie."

"Bro, if I told my wife about this she'd come out here and kick your butt for allowing me to walk into the middle of danger with a capital *D*—though we both know I managed that just fine all on my own. After she kicked your backside into next week, she'd kiss you for saving my life, and round it all out by insisting you move in with us so she could watch over you. Trust me. I will not tell Janie."

Aiden smiled in the darkness. Janie was the mother hen of the family all right.

"Where's Madison?" Nate asked.

"She's with Sharon," Aiden said.

"Want me to call her?"

"Yes. Check on them. I'll clean up here. Dean's headed to Maddie's place, but I'd rather she not sleep there tonight."

"Done. I know I'm not trained like you are, but I can shoot, and you can trust me, Aiden. I'm family. I've got your back. You call me if you need anything. And we'll take care of Madison."

"Thank you."

They shook hands in the way of brothers, and what had been between them since that night when their father had died was gone. The very last remnants of ice around Aiden's heart cracked and fell away as he watched Nate walk into the night.

He went back into the house to wait on the USCIS team. He would have to give his statement as he had so many other times. How many more nights like this were in his future?

But he had resigned.

He'd told Madison he was done, and he thought he was. This time though, they had come looking for him. This time they'd crossed a line, trespassing onto his land, coming into his home. A man had to protect what was his. Had to keep his own family safe.

Dawn was nearly breaking when the debriefing was finished and evidence had been washed away, though the crimson stain in the study would remain. Aiden reset the security system and crawled into bed for a few hours' sleep. He wanted to call Madison, longed to hear her voice, but he wouldn't risk waking her. It would have been a selfish thing to do. He satisfied himself with closing his eyes, picturing the way her brown eyes looked when she smiled up at him.

He'd fix this. Somehow, he'd make it right.

Chapter Seventy-Two

Sergio stared through his binoculars. Watched them climb into the truck. Studied the domestic scene and planned when he would strike.

"Tonight?"

"No," Sergio said. "Not tonight."

"But—"

"I will tell you when. It is not for you to know the time and place."

"Of course."

Sergio seethed as the Avalanche continued down the road, turned at the light, and drove toward Nate's house.

He had planned the exact moment when he would exact his revenge. The infidel would be made to pay, but first he would know what his sins had cost not just him and his family, but the American people. Aiden Lewis would suffer even as Sergio had suffered.

Donato had made the ultimate sacrifice. Sergio was proud his brother had given his life for their cause. He had died a hero.

Soon Mr. Lewis would sacrifice his family as well, but he would not have the satisfaction of knowing they had died for a higher purpose.

The prospect excited him. USCIS agents thought they were so intelligent, and yet they knew so little. They had only found what he wanted them to discover.

Chapter Seventy-Three

"How many hours is this trip?" Madison forced herself to smile, but she wasn't ready to climb into the van.

"You have a book, don't you?" Aiden asked. "We'll be there before you know it, sweetie, but you have to get in the van."

"Yeah, Ms. Hart," Melvin piped in. "This trip is going to rock."

Chants of *We Will Rock You* filled the afternoon air, causing Madison to look back toward her car with something close to longing.

"Don't even think about it." Aiden slid his hand to her back and nudged her toward the open van door.

"I could follow in my car."

"For six hours? On mountain roads? Are you forgetting that you're afraid to drive on those steep roads?"

"Exactly. It would be good practice for me."

"Forget about it. You're a flatlander, and I'm driving. Now climb in." He squeezed her hand, waited until she'd buckled up, then shut the door and walked around the van.

A small group had assembled to see the golf team off. Colorful banners proclaimed, "Edgewood Huskies Putt Perfect" and "Bring Home the Gold." The principal, a few parents, and several of the players' girlfriends waved as they pulled out of the drive.

"With any luck, we'll make Banff by six tonight," Aiden said.

"Just in time for a swim," Jason bellowed.

"Forget the swim. I'm hungry already," Santiago grumbled.

"Santiago, you just ate," Madison looked at him in disbelief.

"I think I'm growing again. Anyone have a sandwich?"

Madison shook her head, opened her book, and cornered herself into her seat.

"You going to read the whole way?" Aiden asked.

"Did you have something else in mind?"

"You could sing with the choir."

We Will Rock You had been exchanged for the theme song for Oscar-Meyer wieners. All it had taken was the mention of food.

"I think I'll pass. You mind if we listen to the music on my cell phone?"

"I'll do you one better." Aiden turned on the satellite radio and cranked it up to seven. Soon the sounds of George Straight overpowered the great Oscar-Meyer wiener.

"You're my hero."

"And I'll let you prove that to me in six hours and thirty minutes."

The next afternoon, Madison sank into the bubble bath and thought about staying there. Then she remembered Aiden's note, and she poked one painted toenail out of the bubbles. She was suddenly glad she'd splurged on a pedicure. You definitely didn't want to meet Prince Charming for a late-night rendezvous with chipped toenails.

Looking at the clock above the marble tub, she saw she had plenty of time to enjoy both the bath and the exquisite champagne he'd sent to her suite.

"I could enjoy being spoiled," she murmured, sinking down into the cloud of bubbles.

Twenty more minutes, then she'd towel off and dress for the evening. After spending all day on the golf course, she deserved the extra rest. Plus, it wasn't every day you took a luxurious bath in a marble tub.

Dinner at six, an eight o'clock meeting with the team, then Aiden had asked her to meet him in the hotel's lobby at nine. She hadn't had this much fun in high school or college. She sank into the bubbles trying to imagine what Aiden had been like in high school.

It wasn't until the water grew cold enough to cause her to shiver that she realized her twenty minutes were up. Dragging herself out of the tub, she wrapped herself in the giant red towel and padded across the room.

The nine o'clock date had lasted until eleven. They'd talked about their families, their dreams, even their most embarrassing moments. Hers had been when she'd fallen down the stairs in high school. His had been when he'd fallen asleep in English class and the teacher had scared the living daylights out of him by blowing a whistle in his ear.

He'd waited until they were back in her suite to get down on his knee and hand her the velvet box. Though she'd been expecting it, hoping, she still couldn't stop the tears.

"Will you marry me Madison Hart?"

She didn't say anything clever, but when she threw herself into his arms that seemed to be all the answer that Aiden needed. They'd laughed and cried and kissed and then Aiden had insisted she get some sleep.

When she walked him to the door, he'd turned and asked if he could pick her up at five in the morning.

"Five?"

"There's something I want to show you."

Aiden knocked on her door at five sharp, carrying a covered basket.

"A picnic? At this hour?"

"I can take it back."

"What's in there?" She poked around even though he tried to hold it out of her reach.

"Hang on, Snoopy. I wanted to take you to a special spot."

He led her out onto the golf course where they could see moonlight bouncing off the greens, elk grazing beneath the stars, and the best part was they had it all to themselves.

Aiden unpacked a blanket, a thermos of coffee, and a plate of still warm scones.

They'd polished off the sweets and were pouring a second mug of coffee when his cell rang.

"I better get that." He kissed her quickly, then reached for his phone, stood up, and walked a few feet away.

"Lewis." His voice was crisp, solid, sure. Exactly like the man she had come to love.

She smiled in the darkness and stretched. Madison looked around as she pulled the blanket snugly around her shoulders. Dating a millionaire sure had its perks. Correction—marrying a millionaire.

She held her hand up in the semi-darkness, saw the sparkle from the diamond, and sighed in contentment. Could life be any more like a fairytale?

She looked around her. She wouldn't mind moving into this place, especially if Aiden was included in the package. She turned to look at her fiancé, and that was when she noticed his posture had gone rigid.

"How many casualties? Repeat that number." His voice was

cold and clipped, all business now that he was fully awake. "Where is he now?"

He moved closer to her and began collecting their picnic things. "That's an unacceptable solution."

He reached for her phone and pulled up a twenty-four-hour cable news site.

"I understand, but—-yes sir. Copy that."

Madison barely noticed him disconnect the call. It took all her concentration to comprehend the images of carnage and destruction displaying across the screen of her phone.

Chapter Seventy-Four

"To recap, we're on the scene here in Bath County, Virginia where the dam has apparently exploded. Authorities have not yet confirmed reports this was a terrorist attack, but we have been told by several inside sources that the President will speak shortly."

Aiden reached for Madison's hand.

"What we do know is that most of the towns of Covington and Clifton Forge have been wiped out and at least thirty thousand people drowned as they slept. There was simply no time to evacuate. The water from this dam continues to move downstream, following the path of the Jackson River. Towns along this route, which are to the south and east, are currently being evacuated by the National Guard. Bringing you that report is..."

Aiden finished packing up their supplies, pulled his service revolver from the bottom of the picnic basket, and holstered it, all the time keeping an eye on the phone and Madison.

She still hadn't said a word, simply sat staring at the emergency news program in disbelief, holding the cell phone in her hand as if she could somehow turn back time, reclaim the lives that had been lost.

Aiden pulled the phone from her hand, clicked off the site,

and waited for her to raise her eyes to his. When she finally did he sat back down beside her on the blanket.

"Madison, I need you to listen to me."

"Are they all dead?"

"Many are."

"But they were just sleeping. Like we were. How—"

"Sweetheart. I can't explain it to you now. But we need to collect the boys, and we need to stay together."

"I don't understand. The dam." She looked out across the golf green, as if she were still seeing the destruction in Virginia. "The dam is in Virginia. What does it have to do with the boys?"

"Look at me, Maddie. I need you to look at me." He took her hand in his. "The dam that exploded was in Virginia, but we're in danger here. I can't explain it all now. We need to bring the boys together. We're supposed to wait here, and someone will come to escort us to a safe place."

"Is there a dam here?"

"No. It's not about a dam. Maddie, you're going to have to trust me. Can you do that?"

He held her face in his hands. Pressed her forehead to his, the way she did when she needed to touch him. It always seemed to Aiden it was a physical way for their souls to touch. He prayed this time it would be enough to reach through to her. He knew from Martin's call that he didn't have much time. He needed her to trust him. Coyote was close. They were going to have to move quickly.

Madison sensed Aiden's desperation and something more. This wasn't Aiden the millionaire or even Aiden the golf instructor. She'd learned to trust both of those sides of the man.

Then she realized who it was holding her. This was the man she'd met in the airport. The man who had carried her through the terminal. The mysterious man Aiden Lewis hadn't been able to let her see. Suddenly, she knew the man holding her face in his hands was the man who disappeared for weeks without calling.

But he wouldn't disappear this time. He was here to keep her safe. Protect her and the boys.

She knew without a doubt she had to put their lives in his hands.

Somehow this morning was about that part of his life he hadn't been able to talk to her about yet. And the tragedy still playing out in Virginia. And her. And the boys back in the hotel.

Inexplicably, all the pieces of Aiden's life had come crashing together at five o'clock on a golf green in Banff, Canada.

Madison didn't yet know the details. She couldn't see the way the pieces fit together. But what she had, what she knew, caused her heart to thunder with more fear than she'd ever thought possible—more fear than she'd even known as she'd watched her mother die in their little house in Dallas, Texas. What she finally had was all the pieces of the man she loved in one place. All the bits of Aiden Lewis finally gathered together into a whole.

She would trust him. He was broken in pieces before her. He was the one who was strong, but he needed her. He needed her to believe in him.

"Can you trust me, Maddie?"

"Yes. Of course, I can. I will." She wiped at the tears she didn't realize were falling. Silently willed them to stop. "What do you need me to do?"

"That's my girl."

Aiden rubbed the remaining wetness away with his thumbs, took the time to kiss her once more, gently and quickly, then he stood and hurried them back toward her suite.

"Should I pack?"

"Yes. I'll bring the boys here. We'll have their things sent to Edgewood later. Don't open the door to anyone but me."

They were nearly to her room, his hand on the doorknob, when Madison's cell buzzed.

Chapter Seventy-Five

Aiden opened the door to her room as she stared down at her phone.

"It's a text message," she said.

"Who is it from?"

"I don't know."

She looked up at him, eyes wide and afraid, and he cursed himself for involving her in this.

"Let me see it." Aiden took the phone from her, a glittery pink thing, as she looked over his shoulder.

> Ice. Unit compromised. Servensky is mole and coming for you now. Move. Bring Maddie & boys bck. Meet u n Glcr s lot. Dn.

Aiden thumbed backed through the message. Read it again.

"Aiden, who sent that? What does it mean?"

"Dean sent it. The one person inside the agency I can trust."

"Agency? What agency?"

"I can't explain right now, Maddie. We have to go."

"But why did he send it to my phone?"

"Because mine has been compromised." He clicked off the message and handed the phone back to her. "Okay. Forget packing. We have to leave here now. You're coming with me to get the boys."

He was reaching for her purse when there was a knock on the door, followed by a maid's voice.

"Room service."

Aiden pulled the Glock from his holster, put his fingers to his lips when Madison's eyes went wide.

Neither of them had ordered breakfast.

Moving to the door, he looked through the peephole. A girl of about seventeen stood in the hall with a tray of food.

He couldn't see anyone else, which meant nothing.

He had to open the door sometime if they were going to access the boys' rooms. Maybe if he played along...

He walked back across the room to Madison, whispered into her ear. "I want you to open the door wide enough so you can see if anyone else is in the hall. Have the girl set the food just inside the room. Clear?"

She nodded and looked at the gun in his hand, her eyes as big as silver dollars.

"You can do this." He rubbed a thumb down her cheek.

"Room service." The knock came again, louder this time.

Madison nodded...attempted a smile. She pushed her phone into her jeans pocket while Aiden moved behind the door, gun positioned. When he signaled he was ready, Madison opened the door.

"You ordered room service?" The girl asked, tray raised high, a smile upon her lips.

She didn't look dangerous to Madison, but at five in the morning in the Banff Springs, Canada resort, what did dangerous look like? A seventeen-year-old in a maid's uniform? Maybe.

"Yes, I guess we did."

Madison opened the door wide, exactly as Aiden had

instructed her. Glanced down the hall to her left, nearly collapsing with relief when she saw no one there. For the entire length of the hall there were only closed doors with newspapers set neatly on the floor in front of them.

When the maid cleared her voice, Madison realized she still hadn't looked down the hall the other way, and that Aiden was still standing behind the door with a gun drawn and ready.

"Where would you like me to set this, Miss?"

"Right inside the door is fine."

"Here? I can take it to the table, or by the windows perhaps. The sunrise from this room is quite nice."

"No. Thank you. Here is fine."

"Yes, ma'am."

The maid placed the tray table down just inside the door. As she went about positioning the tray on top of it, Madison took a quick look down the hall in the other direction, somehow resisting the urge to sing and dance when she saw it too was empty of bad guys with Uzis.

"Thank you." She signed the receipt quickly, tipping way too much, and nearly pushed the maid out of the suite in her rush to free Aiden from behind the door.

Aiden holstered the Glock.

"Good girl," he whispered in her ear. "Hall was clear?"

She nodded.

"Make sure you have your passport. I'll check the suite and make sure there's nothing we need to take. Do not touch the food."

As if she would think of eating at a time like this.

Chapter Seventy-Six

Aiden swept the room one last time, then hurried to Madison's side. He touched her back to steady her, steady himself. He'd been on many missions, but never with the woman he planned to make his wife and twelve teens.

He whispered in her ear, "Stay close."

She slipped her hand into his.

He squeezed it quickly, then released it to draw his gun. With his other hand he opened the door, still holding his gun ready. The hall appeared empty, but he knew that meant nothing. An empty corridor did little to calm his nerves.

There was a mole in his agency.

He didn't need lab work to tell him the food the maid had brought was drugged.

He had to escort Madison and the boys back to the States.

He slid down the hall, back against the wall, pulling Madison in his wake.

Three doors down he came to Justin's room. He'd had enough foresight to have his card keyed to all of the boys' rooms. He tapped lightly then let himself in.

A video game flashed silently on the screen, but no one manned the controls. Four boys in different stages of undress were passed out around the room. The bed and tabletops were littered with pizza boxes and soda cans.

Aiden moved to the windows, checked the balcony and curtains, then moved on to the bathroom. He returned to the main room and holstered his weapon.

"It's clear. Help me wake them up."

Madison started shaking the two younger boys, who had actually managed to crash on the bed even though they hadn't made it under the covers.

Aiden pulled Justin and Kevin to the side of the room, whispered something to them. Within two minutes they were dressed and helping Madison with Matt and Melvin. Four minutes after entering the room, they were ready to leave.

Aiden paused at the door and turned to look at them all. Madison knew he wanted to draw his weapon, but resisted so he wouldn't scare the younger boys.

"Chase's room next," Aiden said. "We all leave together, and we all stay together. If anyone comes down the hall, don't look at them and don't talk to them. Understood?"

The boys nodded. Matt and Melvin still not quite awake, Justin and Kevin understanding the gravity of the situation even if they didn't understand the details.

Silently they walked four more doors down.

Aiden again tapped on the door and entered his key, and they all piled through the door.

Only this time the room was empty.

Everyone began talking at once.

"Their stuff is here," Justin said.

Kevin picked up a Huskies jacket. "This has to be the right room."

"Maybe they were kidnapped," Matt suggested.

"Where are they, Coach?" Melvin looked scared and moved a little closer to Madison.

"We should call the police," Matt said.

"If they're not kidnapped, they are so busted," Melvin added.

Aiden squeezed Madison's arm and nodded toward the patio where the curtains blew in the predawn breeze. Someone had left the sliding glass doors open.

Aiden walked to the curtains and drew back the fabric.

He slid the patio door open enough to slip through it, then looked back across the room to see if the boys were watching. Melvin and Matt were preoccupied discussing the future grounding of their teammates. Justin had his eyes on Aiden, and quickly caught Kevin's attention when he saw Aiden pull his weapon.

They all grew silent when Aiden stepped out onto the patio.

Madison started across the room after him, but Justin stopped her.

"Don't go out there, Miss. Give him a minute."

Madison gulped. Nodded. Sat down on the bed before her legs gave out.

Aiden was back in the room in less than a minute.

"Nothing," he mouthed silently.

He heard Justin and Kevin let out the breath they'd been holding.

"Who saw Chase, Santiago, Gabe, or Isaac last?" Aiden asked.

"They were with us until around midnight." Justin brushed his fingers through his hair, which was already standing on end. "I swear, Coach. They said they were going straight to their room. We'd been playing video games, and then we heard you and Miss Hart coming down the hall. So we waited until the coast was clear, and all four of them took off from our room. I watched them come in here."

"Maybe they're with Marcos. They could have decided they were bored. Or homesick." Madison stood up, began pacing. "Maybe after you saw them walk in here, they went down to Marcos's room."

"The patio door was open though, so they must have been in here at some point. They wouldn't have—-" Aiden turned back toward the patio, and this time they all followed.

"Yeah, they would have." Justin walked out onto the patio. "Hang on. Chase always carries a flashlight in his bag. He reads after lights out."

He was back with the light, shining it across the balcony, revealing a two by eight board propped against the adjacent balcony.

"Tell me they did not walk across that," Madison said.

"Apparently they did." Aiden's voice was grim. "Let's go."

"We're five floors up. They could have been killed. Where did they even find a board that long?"

"Top of the closets," Aiden said. "We'll ground them later. Let's find them first."

Even Melvin and Matt were wide-awake now, either by the thought of their teammates being eternally grounded or by the sheer act of shuffling from room to room and their coach carrying a gun.

Aiden knew Justin and Kevin had figured out this wasn't a standard evacuation. They weren't asking questions yet, but they had definitely clued into the fact something big was going down. The mood had moved away from confused chaos and closer to raw fear.

"Remember. We all stay together, and don't speak to anyone."

Everyone nodded their understanding. It sounded so simple, and it would have been, only this time when they stepped out in the hall, it wasn't empty.

Aiden recognized the three men immediately—Servensky, Jackson, and Jones. Aiden's finger itched on the trigger of his weapon. He couldn't afford an open confrontation at this moment, and he couldn't stand the thought of letting this mole in their organization go.

He had served with all three men before. Each of them on previous missions, some as far back as five years ago.

"Sir, we're here to escort you to your room." Jackson stepped forward. "Our orders are to remain with you until transportation arrives."

Aiden shifted his weapon to his other hand, grateful he could shoot as well with his left, aware Servensky knew it too. He shook hands with each of them, the ice now firmly in place.

Servensky might not be the only traitor. He searched each man's eyes. If the others were moles, they were good ones. Not that Aiden believed you could see into a man's soul through his eyes. He knew too well how you could limit what you showed a person.

"I was gathering the last of the boys together. Let's convene in my suite in fifteen minutes. Two of you proceed to my room. One monitor from the balcony, the other remain on the inside. We'll need someone else at the end of the hall in the stairwell."

Aiden turned to go, expecting his orders would be followed.

"Negative, sir." Jackson's voice was firm but quiet.

"Excuse me?" Aiden allowed a bit of the ice back into his voice.

Servensky stepped up to rescue Jackson. Servensky had served with Aiden the longest, knew his reputation and his temper. Or perhaps he was simply forcing the altercation.

"Easy, Aiden. We've been given orders to stay in visual contact with you. It's not Jackson's fault."

"Who gave you those orders?"

"Straight from Martin."

"Did Martin happen to mention who was the agent in charge?"

"Yeah, he said you were. But he also said we were to remain in visual contact."

"And I'm changing those orders as your agent in charge. You have a problem with that Servensky?"

Neither man blinked for a full ten seconds.

"You have fifteen minutes, then we come after you. Something happens, I won't be the one slung out to dry over a bunch of kids."

"Secure the suite while I gather the boys."

"Jones, take the back stairs," Servensky ordered. "Jackson, I want you on the patio."

Aiden allowed Servensky to take charge of the other agents, hoping the illusion of control would satisfy him for the moment, but knowing that moment wouldn't last long. At the most he had half the time he'd demanded, but he only needed enough to reach the last room.

Servensky couldn't leave it alone though.

"Fifteen minutes, Lewis."

"Servensky, do you have a problem with this mission?"

"Let's say I'd rather be catching the whoever is responsible for the disaster in Virginia than babysitting a golf team here in Canada."

"Focus on your mission, agent." Aiden stepped in closer and lowered his voice enough to add a degree of danger. "If anything happens to these boys or to Miss Hart, I'll personally see you transferred to Louisiana where your missions are spent belly down in a bayou and the alligators are a much bigger threat than the terrorists. Is that clear, agent?"

"Yes, Sir." Servensky practically spit the words.

Aiden took a step back, and the man turned and stormed down the hall. No doubt he would call reinforcements.

The boys stood staring at Aiden, mouths slightly open, eyes wide.

"Let's get the rest of our team," he said, but he waited until the corridor was clear before he tapped on Marcos's door.

Chapter Seventy-Seven

When they stepped inside, Madison nearly collapsed in relief to see eight boys passed out around the room. She counted heads twice before she drew a deep breath.

The air was returning to her oxygen-deprived brain when Aiden pulled her into the suite's walk-in closet.

"We need to leave here fast. When we don't show up, those agents will come looking for us."

"We're not going back there?"

"No, we're not."

"But they were on our side. Weren't they?"

"Maddie. You trust me, right? We need to go, and we need to do it now."

"Where?"

"Home, baby. We're going home."

Then his hands were holding her face, his thumbs running the length of her jaw. Before she could say another word, he'd pulled her into his arms.

"Yuck. That's disgusting." Jack declared.

"Exactly the reason you should knock first," Aiden said.

"Knock on a closet door?"

"Knock on any door. Now get dressed."

Aiden turned him around and marched him into the main room. As the three entered, the room grew silent.

"I know you boys have a lot of questions, and to be honest I don't have many answers. Most of the ones I do have I can't tell you right now. I can tell you we need to leave, and you need to trust me."

Twelve pairs of eyes locked with his.

As Madison watched she was reminded of something she had heard in her education classes in college—that it only took one good relationship with an adult to turn a teenager around.

She didn't know what they were involved in, what this day would entail, but she did know that in Aiden Lewis these boys had a good relationship. The way they looked at him and the obvious respect they had for their coach showed in their eyes. They immediately threw on their clothes.

Not a single one asked questions. They simply put their lives in his hands. They trusted him. If a group of teenage boys could do that, Madison figured she could as well.

"Everyone have their passports?"

Thirteen people patted their back pockets, nodded.

"Phones?"

Again, a search of pockets. Again affirmative nods.

"Let's go then. We'll use the stairs instead of the elevators."

Twelve minutes later, they were making their way across the parking lot. As they climbed into the school van and pulled out of the Banff Springs Resort, the sun broke over the horizon promising a gorgeous day.

"Check your phone. See if Dean has sent any other messages."

Madison pulled out the phone, fumbling through the menu. "No. Nothing."

Chase watched them closely, his head stuck forward between the front seats. "Has anyone told you two you're very strange?"

"No one's told me that," Aiden said.

"Me either," said Madison. "I thought we were normal."

"Funny. Very funny. Wake me if we stop at a McDonalds." Chase flopped back into the second seat.

"Chase?"

"Yeah, Coach."

"One more thing."

"Sure, Coach."

"I need you to gather up all the cell phones. Give them to Miss Hart."

Chase was suddenly back up front, head stuck between the two front seats.

"You want to say that one more time?"

"I need you to pick up all the cell phones. And make sure no one has two."

"Who would have two?"

"Just make sure."

Chase tugged his ball cap lower. "Right."

Madison waited until Chase had moved away from the front of the van.

"Why do we need their cell phones?"

"9-11 legislation. All cell phones are now listening devices. As long as they're turned on, they can be monitored by government satellites."

"Huh?"

Aiden checked his rearview mirror, then shifted his gaze to the side mirror. He moved his right hand to his gun, but the car that had been following them passed and turned left at the light.

Aiden put both hands back on the wheel. "What were we talking about?"

"Cell phones."

"After 9-11 the government claimed they needed the ability to listen in on conversations, which they did in certain situations. Most people leave their cell phones on all the time."

"But it's not really on," Madison objected.

"Right. Before you can talk you have to hit the talk button, which is how you request permission to connect to a cell tower.

That can be done remotely. The phone company can turn on the microphone without your knowing it."

"Tell me you're kidding."

"Not at all. Could be useful in a bank robbery turned hostage situation. The Hostage Rescue Team blocks all incoming traffic to the cell tower and turns on all the landline phones and cell phones responding to that specific tower. Then they're able to listen in and cut out phones, plotting them as they go on a map of the building, until they know where the criminals are and who is saying what to whom."

"So who would want to listen in on our phones?"

"Whoever has the ability to infiltrate USCIS would be able to obtain that sort of permission. If they could listen in, they'd find out where we are, where we're going."

"Why us?" she asked softly.

"It's a long story. One I will tell you." Aiden glanced in the rear view mirror at the boys. "Soon."

Chase returned with a ball cap full of cell phones.

"Here you go, Coach."

"That's all of them?" Aiden asked.

"That's it. Scout's honor."

"You're not a scout, Chase."

"Right. Golfer's honor, Coach."

"Good enough."

Madison took the cap, held it in her lap and stared down at the conglomeration of cell phones. Tried to make sense of what Aiden had said. Attempted to wrap her mind around it.

"Miss Hart? Could I have the cap back?"

"Sure. Yeah."

She looked over at Aiden.

"Try the glove compartment."

Opening it, she saw it was empty except for a road map and flashlight. Plenty of room for twelve cell phones. Perhaps if she put them in there, shut them away, they would once again be safe.

"Double check they're all turned off and remove the batteries if you can. Put yours and mine in as well."

Madison dumped the phones in, checking them as she did so, then handed the cap back to Chase. When she was finished, she looked over at Aiden.

"It's a long trip, and the boys are going to be hungry," she said. "We need to stop for food if we can."

"And gas," Aiden agreed.

They had driven through most of Banff, leaving the tourist shops behind them.

"There's a twenty-four-hour gas station on the edge of town," Aiden said. "We'll stop there."

"Will they be watching?"

Aiden stared out the front window as he drove.

"Aiden?" Madison reached over and rubbed his arm.

"I don't know." He looked over at her, ran his hand over his face. "But we need gas. This will be our only stop. From here we'll push straight through. We'll have to hope whoever is tracking us doesn't expect us to stop this soon."

Chapter Seventy-Eight

Aiden knew they needed to stop, and he knew it was dangerous. Once they were on the road, they had a good chance of making it to the border. Stopping was taking a big risk, but they had to have gas.

"Justin and Chase, can you come up here?"

The boys unbuckled and moved to the front of the van.

"We're going to stop once to buy gas and food. We can't all go in. It would look too obvious. I want the two of you to go in. Ms. Hart will stay in the van with the rest of the team. You'll only have a few minutes. Purchase as much food and drinks as you can. Stay away from the junk. If something happens we might need enough to last us a couple days."

The boys exchanged looks.

"Sure thing, Coach."

"You want us to use your credit card or cash?"

Aiden reached for his wallet.

"Behind my license are some twenties. Take five of them. Check out separately. Try to act like you're not together, though it's going to be pretty obvious you are."

"What kind of drinks?" Justin asked.

"Only water and sports drinks."

"Got it, Coach."

"One more thing."

"Yeah, Coach?" Chase tugged on his cap.

"Explain to the team I want them to lie down before we pull in. I need them to stay down until we're back on the road."

Justin and Chase exchanged looks of disbelief.

"Did you say lie down, Coach?" Justin asked.

"It's better if the people who might be looking for us aren't sure we're all together. The more we can do to confuse them the better. Let's assume someone is watching. When whoever is following us interrogates the clerk, it would be help if that person didn't look out the window and see a van full of kids."

"OK, Coach," Chase said. "You want them to lie down, they'll lie down." Then he turned around and addressed his team.

Chase had been team captain for two years, and the boys admired him almost as much as they admired Aiden. He was the perfect older brother. He was also graduating this year, with plans to attend college in Missoula. No one wanted to talk about what the team would be like without him. Yesterday it had seemed like their biggest problem. Strange how a few hours could change things so drastically.

"Listen up, guys." Chase tugged the cap lower as he squatted between the front seats, facing toward the back of the van. "As you all have guessed we have something of a situation here. Now Coach can't exactly explain it to us right now, but you know we left all our things back in our hotel rooms. Don't worry about your stuff. They'll ship it back home, so you'll still have a chance to wash your dirty socks."

Aiden was splitting his attention between the road and the boys. Chase was doing a good job. He'd earned a few snickers from Gabriel and Isaac, who were known to wear the same pair of socks for most of a trip.

"Here's the thing. We're about to stop for gas. Me and Justin are going in to grab some grub."

Jack bounced up at once. "I want to go in too."

"Nah, Jack. You go in and next thing we know you'd be chatting up the clerk. She'd remember your face for sure, and what we don't want is to be remembered. Ugly guys like me and Justin, folks tend to forget us as soon as we walk out the door."

Justin seemed to realize Chase was trying to put the team at ease. Determined to do his part, Justin reached over and punched Chase in the arm.

"What we really need you all to do is play a little game of hide and seek. Problem is you have to hide here in the van, and we don't know who's doing the seeking."

"Almost there, Chase," Aiden said.

"So I'm counting to ten, and I don't want to see a single Husky from the time I reach ten until this van is back on the blacktop."

Aiden had to hand it to his team captain. What sounded pretty goofy actually worked. When he stepped out to fill the tank up with gas, he didn't see a single Husky cap or Husky face. All he saw was two scruffy teens walking toward the convenience store and one beautiful lady staring out her window as if this were any other day and they were about to embark on another normal trip through Waterton-Glacier International Peace Park.

Chapter Seventy-Nine

Madison thought they were actually going to make it. No sounds were coming from the back of the van. She wouldn't have bet the change in the bottom of her purse ten boys could be so quiet.

She heard the gas pump click off and relaxed a fraction, knowing Aiden had finished filling the gas tank. Then as he was replacing the pump handle, Justin exploded from the convenience store. Chase hurried after him, carrying two bags of groceries.

"I want my cell phone, Coach."

"Get in the van, Justin."

"I'm not getting in the van until you give me the cell phone."

"I need you to lower your voice and get in the van."

"I saw what happened. When were you going to tell us? I saw it on the TV. I want my cell phone, and I want it now."

Justin moved around the van, closer to Madison's door.

"I tried to stop him, Coach." Chase had caught up and was standing resolutely in front of Madison's door. "We saw about the dam on the TV when we were checking out."

Chase's voice cracked when he mentioned the dam, but he held firm in front of Madison's door as if protecting the cell phones in the glove compartment from Justin's rampage.

"You're on his side, Chase? Well I don't care about whatever is going on here. I'm calling home." Justin moved to the side door.

Madison had seen angry teens before, but Justin was more than mad. He was desperate, and he was scared. From where she sat inside the van, she could see his eyes were darting from place to place, looking for something to settle on.

"I have family there, Coach. Do you think you can stop me from calling my family? Now give me my phone."

Justin again lunged for the door. Aiden grabbed his arms and pinned him against the side of the van.

"Justin, I need you to calm down."

"Did you see what happened to those people? My brother lives there, Coach. Are you telling me to forget about my brother?"

Tears were streaming down Justin's face now.

"I'm sorry about your brother, Justin. Maybe he's all right. Maybe he's not." Aiden turned the boy around, though he still held his arms pinned down. "Look at me, Justin. Calling him won't change the odds of his being alive, but calling him could kill every person in this van."

Madison knew the moment realization hit Justin. He literally collapsed in Aiden's arms. Aiden's hold turned into a hug.

Chase stood watching, shifting his weight from one foot to the other, still holding the two bags of groceries. Madison noticed the clerk had come to the window and was watching the entire scene play out.

"It's okay, big guy. Let's walk."

And then they were moving away from the van.

When Chase tapped on her window, Madison nearly jumped out of her skin.

"Sorry, Ms. Hart."

Madison unlocked and opened the door. Chase moved into the van, stowing the groceries between the front seats. They both watched as Aiden and Justin stopped a few feet from the van, spoke for another minute. Justin wiped his eyes on his sleeves and stuck his hands in his pockets. And then they were walking back.

Justin moved into the back seat, sitting with his head between his hands. Chase placed an arm across his back.

When the tires of the van hit the blacktop, ten more Huskies rose out of various hiding places, and grub was passed out. No one mentioned Justin's meltdown, and no questions were asked about the Virginia devastation. It sat there in their van though, more proof that their world had changed forever.

Chapter Eighty

As they neared the checkpoint, Aiden reached over for Madison's hand.

"I don't know how this is going to play out. If they take me into custody, I want you to insist you won't go anywhere or speak to anyone until the boys' parents are contacted and you're in the presence of a representative of the American Consulate."

"Do you think that will happen?"

Madison's hand went cold in his grasp. He rubbed her fingers, tried to fill her with the courage and strength she might need.

"I don't know. It will depend if my commander has been compromised. If he hasn't, then he'll assume I had a good reason for going dark. If he has, well do what I said. You'll be fine."

"What about you?"

He heard the fear in her voice, recognized it was for him, and loved her even more for it.

"I'll be all right, Madison. I'll meet you back in Edgewood."

"You promise?"

When he turned to look at her, he saw it there in her eyes. Their future, the possibility of all they could have. It occurred to him he had always been carrying a weight, since he'd been a teenage boy facing down a silvertip bear. Suddenly, he knew it was a weight worth carrying though, the weight of love was always worth what it cost to shoulder.

He wanted their future.

Wanted it more than he'd ever wanted anything.

More than he wanted the past back so he could change it, correct it.

And he knew wanting the future more than the past meant he'd finally turned a bend in the road.

Even though he was tired all the way through to his bones, his love for her and her love for him gave him a jolt of energy that penetrated to the core of his soul. He knew he'd make it through this. He'd make it for her and for the boys in the back. He'd make it for her and for him.

"Yeah, I promise."

Then he was pulling up to the international border. He handed his identification papers to the agent, and the guard spoke the words he had known he would hear.

"Mr. Lewis, I'm going to have to ask you to step out of the vehicle and keep your hands in the air."

Madison watched as they frisked Aiden, removed his weapon, and walked him over to the office between two agents.

"Wow. I didn't know Coach carries a gun to golf meets," Matt said.

"I don't think he did last year," Gabe said.

"I've never even seen a gun like that," Santiago offered.

"I have," Marcos said. "In the last James Bond movie."

Chase tried to distract the boys by making everyone hold up their passports for the fourth time.

"When can we get out of the van?" Isaac asked.

"As soon as the guys with the guns say we can." Chase proceeded to try and interest them in a game of golf trivia, something they did not fall for but pretended to be interested in for his sake.

Justin hadn't said a word for the last five hours. Madison unbuckled and moved beside him.

"You okay?"

"No." He continued staring out the window.

"I watched a little of the news this morning. I don't think I know much more than you do though."

"How is Coach involved in this?"

"I don't know, Justin. I do know he's a good man, and he's trying to get us home."

Justin nodded without much conviction.

When he finally turned to look at Madison, she wanted to reach out and wipe the lost look from his eyes. She wished she knew how.

"Why would anyone destroy entire towns?"

"I don't know the answer to that. I know on September 11 a lot of us were in shock, trying to figure out how anyone could do such a thing."

"But this is worse. Isn't this worse?"

"Yeah. I guess it is."

"We really are at war. Aren't we?"

"Yeah, Justin. We are."

"I've been hearing that since I was a boy. But I didn't believe it. Every now and then someone would enlist, deploy overseas, but not very often. The battles were always fought somewhere else, so it never really felt like we were at war. Until now."

Madison was trying to think of how to answer him, listening to the boys in the back. Chase was still attempting to distract the team. Matt and Melvin were rummaging through the snack bags. Gabe was telling Jack he'd seen a bear in the woods. Someone had to go to the bathroom.

A sudden silence fell over the van as Aiden came out of the building, followed by two guards. One of the guards was shouting, and Aiden had his hands raised over his head.

When one of the border agents pulled his weapon and aimed it at Aiden, two other agents looked up from the vehicles they were processing.

The next few seconds were a blur. Someone hit an emergency button and gates came down across the border, ensuring no vehicles crossed. Every agent pulled his weapon, although most seemed confused as to where the threat was coming from.

Madison watched in horror as two more guards assumed combat position and aimed their weapons straight at Aiden.

Chapter Eighty-One

Aiden continued to hold both hands in the air, but he didn't back down or break eye contact with the man in charge.

"Tell your men to stand down, Agent Dobbs."

"Face on the ground, hands behind your back."

"Stand down," Aiden repeated.

"Face on the ground!" Dobbs screamed.

Aiden could see the other agents waver. He'd been through this checkpoint a hundred times. They knew him by face as well as name. They'd obviously recognized him the minute he'd stepped out of the van, and at this point he was more coherent than their commanding officer.

Furthermore he was calm and in control.

Dobbs was not.

His uniform was rumpled, and he looked as if he had slept in it, or rather as if he hadn't. From the duty board inside, Aiden had gathered he'd been in charge for over forty-eight hours. Dobbs was long overdue for a break. Relief was late, and Dobbs wasn't the type to leave his post unmanned. So he'd pushed through.

Now he was running on too much caffeine and too little

sleep. He kept blinking his eyes, darting his glance back and forth as if he might miss something.

The man did not instill confidence.

Aiden watched Dobbs's finger twitch on the trigger of the assault rifle. Sweat trickled down his face and the middle of his back.

"I said on the ground, Lewis."

"Tell your men to stand down. We'll go inside and contact Martin. Let him make the call."

"Get on the ground."

"Call Martin, Dobbs. I'll wait right here. Surely six of your men can handle me. I'm not even armed. You took my weapon, remember? Go call Martin."

The two agents standing closest to Aiden remained at alert, but lowered their weapons almost imperceptibly. When they did, Aiden knew he had won. He lowered his hands, but kept them in the open and took a step back.

Dobbs's face turned an even deeper shade of red. He strode to the command terminal and punched in the command to release the gates.

"Process these vehicles," he snarled.

Turning to the agent closest to Aiden, he added, "I want you to escort Mr. Lewis back into my office. If he so much as coughs, you have my permission to shoot him."

The agent exchanged a worried look with Aiden, but escorted him in as commanded.

Once they were inside, he looked to make sure Dobbs was still outside, then turned to Aiden.

"He's been this way the last few hours. We think his wife is in Virginia. A couple of the men suggested he step down, but he flat out refused. Said he was going to catch the men who did this."

Dobbs entered at that moment, slammed the door, and strode over to the phone.

"My orders are to hold you, contact central, and wait for someone to arrive and pick you up. My orders are not to contact

Martin." He picked up the phone and shoved it across the desk. "You want to contact him? Fine. It's your freedom on the line, and sounds like you're in plenty of trouble as it is."

Aiden hit the speakerphone button and punched in Martin's direct line.

"Martin here."

"This is Lewis."

There was a slight pause on the other end as Martin picked up the handset, taking the call off speaker.

"Aiden, where are you?"

"Sir, this is Lieutenant Commander Dobbs at the Glacier Border Crossing. We apprehended Lewis per your instructions and are holding him here. Agent Lewis insisted on contacting you directly."

"Lewis, take us off speaker."

Aiden picked up the handset, even though he knew, and Martin knew, that an operator was recording every word they said.

"Sir."

"What are you doing?"

"What I have to, Sir."

"Why did you go dark?"

"We've been compromised."

"Explain."

"I can't do that, Sir."

"I'm assuming our mole was one of the men I sent for you."

There was silence over the line as Aiden waited for his boss to make the decision of whether to arrest him or trust him.

"That would be a good reason for not waiting in your hotel room like I ordered. I know you're trying to take those boys home. Whatever else you're dealing with, there's some nasty weather headed your way. A norther pushing down should arrive in the next hour. Chances are they'll close Going to the Sun Road, which won't be a problem for you since you're not going that way."

Aiden coughed, and Martin paused in his update.

"What does that mean, Lewis?"

"I can't say, Sir."

"This is a secure line. Of course, you can say."

"No. I can't."

"If you have some idea about crossing into the middle of Glacier, don't. This weather system is bringing a record setting snowstorm. Stay on 89 and head straight home."

Aiden remained silent.

"It's that bad then?"

There was a pause as Martin was interrupted with updates from Virginia.

"I'm spread thin here. The casualty numbers in Virginia are higher than we predicted. I don't know how this one got through. They had eleven planned—not ten. Aiden, I can't send anyone to you, and if what you say is true I wouldn't know who to send anyway. Give me twelve hours, and I will figure the identity of our mole. Until then watch your back and contact me when you're in the clear."

"Affirmative."

"Put me back on speaker."

Aiden punched the button and set the phone back on the cradle.

"Dobbs?"

"Sir?"

"You will allow Agent Lewis and anyone with him to pass. Also, if there are any supplies he needs you will provide those. Am I being clear?"

"Yes, Sir."

Martin ended the connection, effectively cutting off any questions Dobbs might have.

Dobbs threw Aiden's passport onto the desk, then addressed the guard still standing at the door.

"Show Lewis our supply locker. I have more important things to do than babysit every agent who decides to wander through my checkpoint. We're at war for God's sake."

He stormed out of the office and was gone.

Aiden followed the guard to the supply locker, picked up supplies he prayed he wouldn't need—snowshoes, backpacks, water, emergency medical kits, extra jackets, and additional ammunition. Ten minutes later he climbed back into the van.

After a quick restroom break for the rest of his group, they were on the road.

Unfortunately, Martin's forecast was accurate. It was only twenty-three miles later, as he was turning off Highway 89 west onto Going to the Sun Road, that the snow started to fall in big fat, wet flakes.

Aiden drove as fast as he dared, but the wind had picked up considerably, pushing the van around the bends in the road. With one eye on the temperature gauge and one on the icing road, Aiden prayed they would make it to the Continental Divide alone and before the roads froze.

Chapter Eighty-Two

Madison tried to take deep breaths as they neared Going to the Summit Gorge.

"She doesn't look so good, Coach." Chase pushed his cap back to take a better look. "Yeah. I'd say she's going to hurl."

"Cool," Jack piped up.

"We can't see," Matt and Melvin proclaimed at the same time.

"When you're a junior, you can sit up front and see the cool things like teachers hurling," Daniel said. "For now, you have to stay in the back and watch the snowstorm."

"It's boring," Matt said.

"It all looks the same," Melvin agreed.

"Except for the white car following us." Matt turned in his seat to point at the car. "Every now and then he comes close enough that I can almost see the three men, but then he backs off again."

Madison paled as the last bit of blood drained from her face. "What did he say?"

"I've been watching it for the last twenty minutes. They never close in more than a quarter mile." Aiden reached over and patted her hand.

"Here they come again," Matt shouted.

"Chase, would you make sure everyone's buckled up for me? The roads are starting to ice."

"Sure, Coach."

As Chase made his way toward the back of the van, the white car came into view again, steadily closing the gap.

"Uh Coach, I don't think they're stopping this time."

As Madison turned toward Chase, the car rammed them. It was probably a good thing she was looking toward Chase. If she'd been looking in the direction the curve they were pushed toward, she might have died of a heart attack right then.

Chase had been crouched in front of Melvin, checking his seat belt. The impact knocked him sideways into the window. Madison turned toward Aiden in time to see him turning the wheel in circles to the left, then back to the right. Neither seemed to have much effect on the direction of the van.

For a brief, insane moment it reminded Madison of ice skating.

Then the wheels of the van met pavement, and they skidded back across the median and into their lane. They careened around the corner, the white car momentarily out of sight, and everyone began talking at once.

"What was that?"

"What happened, Coach?"

"Did you see him hit us?"

"Chase, are you okay? I think you dented the window, man."

"Everyone, quiet down." Aiden kept his voice calm but commanding, his eyes on his rearview mirror. "Is anyone hurt?"

Twelve "No sirs" filled the van.

"Chase, how bad is your head?" Madison asked.

"I'm fine. It's only a little bump."

"All right. I want everyone buckled, facing the front." Aiden's voice was grim. "If it happens again, it's better for you to be facing the front on impact."

There was complete silence for a good five seconds.

Finally, Kevin pushed up his glasses and asked, "Why would it happen again, Coach?"

Before Aiden could answer, the white car appeared in his rearview mirror.

"Everyone hold on."

Madison could never have imagined going through such a thing once. The fact it was happening twice sent her mind reeling into shock even as their van leapt forward. This time she saw the cliff that dropped in front of them. Saw the ledge they would go over if Aiden hadn't managed to find pavement for the tires at the last possible moment. How he did so while the white car was ramming them, backing off, then ramming them again, was nothing short of a miracle.

The van was filled with an eerie silence. Madison's head seemed stuffed with cotton. A kind of white noise prevented her from screaming. She wondered if this was what insanity sounded like, but then she chanced a look at the boys behind her and realized it wasn't madness. It was cold white anger.

They went around another curve, and the white car again backed off.

"What are they doing, Aiden? They could kill us." Madison unbuckled her seatbelt, moved toward the back, and began checking on the boys.

"I think that might be their point, sweetheart." Aiden accelerated around the next curve, causing the tires to scream on the icy pavement. "Justin, can you come up here?"

"Uh, sure, Coach."

Justin unbuckled and moved into Madison's seat.

"Do you know these roads?"

"Course I do. My dad and I come up here all the time." The newest danger seemed to have knocked him straight out of his lethargy. If he was still in shock over the devastation in Virginia, he managed to put it behind him for the moment.

"There's an old park map in the glove compartment. Pull it out and open it up."

Justin fumbled in the glove compartment as they careened around another curve.

"Coach, uh, the speed limit sign said twenty and you're doing like thirty-five in a snowstorm."

"Yeah, but they're having trouble keeping up." Aiden punched the accelerator again as they came out of another curve. "You find the map?"

"This ancient one? Yeah. It's right here."

"I think there's an old logger road at Hidden Lake Nature Trail. It runs parallel to the Garden Wall. You see it?"

"Yeah, I see it, Coach. But you can't take that road. It's been closed for years."

"Which is exactly why we're taking it. We can lose the three amigos behind us. We should be able to cut back to the main road at Triple Arches."

By this time Chase had moved up and was looking over Justin's shoulder. His baseball cap was pulled up high, and he was holding a cold soda can to the lump forming on his head.

"Demon car is still back there," Matt reported from the second row. "He can't keep up with you though, Coach."

Chase bent even closer to examine the old map. "So we take the logger road. He'll be waiting for us when we come out at Triple Arches. What good does that accomplish?"

"He won't go as far as Triple Arches. When he comes out of this curve," Aiden leaned over and pointed to a spot on the map. "When he doesn't see us here, he'll realize we ditched him. He'll backtrack and find us on the logger road."

"You lost me, Coach." Justin removed his cap and scratched his head. "If he finds us on the logger road..."

"We'd gain twenty minutes on them," Chase said. "Is that the point?"

"You're letting me out of the van when we access the logger road. Justin, you'll drive the team back to Edgewood. Chase, you'll help Ms. Hart navigate. With any luck at all, the guys following us will pick up my trail and follow me up the mountain.

Right now, I need you two to go in the back. Pack me a full outfit of hiking supplies, including snowshoes, night goggles, and an emergency first-aid kit. Don't forget some food rations."

Justin set the map aside. "So you'll lead them on a goose chase, but where to, Coach?"

"There's a ranger station at the top of Mt. Gould. I should have a twenty-minute head start, and I know the area better. By the time they catch me, if they catch me, we'll be waiting for them."

"We?" Justin asked.

"Coach, you don't even know if the ranger station's manned," Chase said.

"You're going to hike in this?" Justin asked. "You can't hike the mountain alone in this storm with those madmen behind you."

"He's not hiking alone," Madison said. "I'm going with him."

Chapter Eighty-Three

"No. You're not," Aiden said.

"Number one rule of hiking—never hike alone." Madison nudged Justin out of her seat. "Make that two outfits of hiking supplies, boys, and hurry."

Justin looked from Madison to Aiden, braced himself between the seats as they careened around another corner, and then moved toward the back of the van. "I'll bring up enough for two, but I'm not endorsing this plan."

"Madison, you are not going with me."

"Yes, I am, Aiden. You're not going alone, and you're sure not taking one of these boys. I checked everyone. Miraculously they're fine, but it really infuriates me that those men would hurt children because of...why? I don't even know why they're following you. These are children, Aiden. Yeah, I'm going with you."

"I can do this alone."

"Why would you do that? We're a team, remember? Teams depend on each other. I might not be an agent, but I know how to hike. We pack out of here together while the boys drive into Edgewood. I can read a trail map as well as you can. I'll lead while you watch the rear."

Aiden ran a hand over the top of his head.

"What she says makes sense, Coach."

"Thank you, Kevin."

"Not a problem." Kevin pushed up his glasses and held on to the chicken strap as they took another corner too fast.

Aiden jerked the wheel in time to avoid another collision. The white car spun into a pull-off area, but quickly recovered. "Listen up, Huskies." Aiden checked the rearview mirror and made sure he had every boy's attention. "We're heading into two S curves, and then we're making a hard-right turn. Everyone hold on."

Then they were spinning in a world of white, and Aiden only thought of force and acceleration and distance. He didn't allow himself to think of the thirteen lives in the van or what they had come to mean to him. Instead he focused on the mission, on the objective, broke it down into executable tasks until he was taking the exit to Hidden Lake Nature Trail on two wheels. He maneuvered past the barricades and on to the old logger road.

Twenty minutes later the van came to a stop. He fought the urge to pull up the emergency break and count heads, as if a Husky might have fallen out on one of the curves. But he didn't have the luxury of time. Outside the van, the world was blanketed in undisturbed white—the first true snow of winter.

He was out of the van before Madison had unbuckled. "Hand me the supplies, Chase. Justin, follow this road until it intersects with the main one. Keep driving south until you reach Lake McDonald. Dean Dreiser will be waiting for you in the south lot. He's five feet eleven, one-hundred-eighty pounds, and I've trusted him with my life many times." He stopped and settled his gaze on Justin. "I'm trusting him with all of yours."

He slapped the side of the van and whispered "Godspeed" as he looked at the forlorn faces pressed to the van's windows. He picked up his pack with one hand, reached out for Madison with the other. Together they walked toward the trail and turned for one look back at the van.

"I love those boys," Madison said.

Aiden squeezed her hand, then they turned toward the mountain rising over 9,000 feet above them. It wasn't a particularly tall peak, but in the waning light and with virtually no foot traffic, it loomed ominously.

At the trailhead, they stopped to take all of the trail maps from the box, put them into their packs, then started up the mountain.

Despite the snowfall, the trail was still discernable. Madison led the way. Aiden didn't bother to cover their tracks. It would be evident the van had stopped in the lot, and they wanted the men to follow them up the mountain. Aiden's fervent prayer was they could outclimb them, and when they reached the top they would find help at the ranger station.

They'd climbed for twenty minutes when they heard a car engine. Stopping on a switchback, they stepped back into the shadow of a boulder, pulled out their binoculars, and focused them on the parking lot below. The white car had pulled up, and two of the men had stepped out.

A tall man gestured toward the trail, talking rapidly and pointing upward. His shorter companion was just as adamantly pointing in the direction of the van tracks. The argument continued for a few more minutes, with neither man persuading the other.

Finally, a third man exited the vehicle. When he did, the first two quit speaking. The third man walked around the car, looked after the tracks of the van, and shook his head. Then he turned and looked up the trail. He seemed to look up at the very spot where Aiden and Madison stood.

He only had to glance toward them for Aiden to recognize the face. Coyote.

Aiden heard Madison suck in her breath. He wondered if she remembered him, if some part of her subconscious struggled to recall the incident on the plane.

Or perhaps her reaction was a normal one to Coyote's expression of naked hatred. It was as if he bore a personal vengeance for them, and Aiden was reminded again that Coyote's brother had died on the floor of his home in Edgewood from a bullet he had shot through his head. Not only had he lost his family, his work—his mission for many years—had been destroyed largely because of Aiden's mission with USCIS.

Were it not for Aiden and men like him, the ten other plans conceived and set into motion by Dambusters would have succeeded. Ten other towns like those in Virginia would be struggling to retrieve their dead this morning.

Aiden understood why the man's face filled with a pure hatred, a personal vengeance that would stop at nothing.

Coyote turned back to his two companions, made the decision for them quickly. With a small movement of his wrist, they opened the trunk of the car.

Aiden wasn't surprised to see the semi-automatic rifles they pulled out. He had expected as much. He was a little more discouraged to see the winter parkas, snowshoes, and fully equipped hiking packs.

"At least we know the boys are safe," Aiden said.

Madison nodded.

It was a large comfort to them as they hiked up into the afternoon cold. If they were to die this evening, at least they would die together, knowing they had saved twelve Huskies. Many agents had been killed for less.

Chapter Eighty-Four

Madison had no trouble following the trail markers. She was grateful for the weekends she had spent hiking in the western portion of the park. Mt. Gould was more exposed than what she was used to, and they certainly weren't hiking in ideal conditions. Nonetheless, she found her pace easily and didn't struggle with the steep trail. The snow was firmly packed at this point, not yet slippery. She forced herself to focus on her footing instead of the men with guns following them.

The Huskies were safely on their way home. She repeated the words to herself like a mantra. She was so focused, when Aiden tugged on her arm, she nearly toppled over in surprise.

"Hold up."

"Need a break, cowboy?"

He held a bottle of water out to her, insisting she take a long drink. After he'd recapped it and placed it back in the pack, he pointed off the trail to the north.

"We're going this way."

"The trail doesn't go that way."

"Exactly."

"Exactly what?"

"We can't maintain this pace in the dark. We need a place to hold up and rest."

Madison looked doubtfully in the direction he'd pointed.

"What's over there?"

"I thought you were going to trust me."

"Uh-huh."

"I want to tie a lead rope on just in case." He took a rope out of his pack, fastened it around her waist, let out three feet, then fastened it to his waist. The remaining amount he placed back in his pack. "I'll lead."

"In case what?" Madison asked, but he was already disappearing into the dusk. When the rope became taut she looked down at it, grimaced, and followed. "I feel like a two-year-old on a leash."

"I heard that."

"Maybe you should make this leash a little longer."

"There are bears out here you know."

"Maybe you should make this leash a little shorter."

"That's my girl."

"Tell me there's another resort over here," she pleaded.

"There's another resort over here."

"With hot chocolate and warm blankets." She had caught up and was now following so close her voice was only a whisper.

"Hot chocolate with marshmallows and toasty blankets," Aiden agreed.

He stopped and turned to look at her in the closing darkness. Put his hands on her shoulders, his nose to her nose. She could feel his breath on her, the heat from his hands even through the cold, even through the layers of their clothing. She shivered from the closeness of him, from the intensity of his gaze.

"Keep your eyes on me. Don't look down."

"It's never good when someone says not to look down."

"You'll do it though?"

"Sure."

He turned and led her around a ledge.

She had no trouble keeping her promise. If she looked down she would freeze to the path, and stopping wouldn't help her team one bit. So she trained her eyes on Aiden and put one foot in front of the other. When they reached the other side, he circled his arms around her.

"Nice going, Maddie."

"Really?" She wanted to sound courageous, but her teeth had started to chatter.

"Really. Now I'm going to untie us for a minute, and I want you to sit right here with the rope. You think about what you're going to order for dinner when we're home in Edgewood. By the time you have the meal ordered, I'll be back."

"How many courses?"

He kissed her forehead, put the rope he had untied in her hands. "As many as you want."

And then he was gone, disappearing into the twilight, back the way they had come.

She started with an appetizer. Worked her way through soup, salad, seafood and steak, with three side dishes. She was deciding on dessert with coffee and an after-dinner cordial when he returned.

"A real coyote couldn't find our trail now. Let's go." Instead of tying on to her, he took her hand in his and led her a few more yards into the woods. When she began to think they were going to spend the night in a tree, he turned again.

"Put your other hand out to your side. Feel the rock? That's the south side of Mount Gould. Most people never see this side of her. They all climb the northern slope, take their pictures, and hurry on home. They don't stop to know her."

Madison let her hand trail along the rock face. Some heat remained there from the sun that had already set. She wondered if they would rest here beside it, huddle up next to the rock that had existed longer than man. Let its warmth seep into them.

Aiden squeezed her hand and pulled her farther down a trail

she couldn't see. When they stopped, darkness had enveloped them.

"Squat down," Aiden whispered.

So she did.

"Stay down for a count of ten. This low entrance is the only reason bears don't use this cave."

Her heart pounded to the count of ten. She stood when he did, found her hand squeezing his in a death grip as the blackness grew impossibly darker still. She hadn't realized there was light outside until they'd stepped into the complete absence of light inside the cave.

"Let's see what she looks like," Aiden turned on his headlamp.

The dimensions of the room were nearly the same size of Madison's bedroom–probably fourteen-by-fourteen feet. It was surprisingly dry. Other than some old graffiti on one wall, there was no sign any other person had ever been there.

Chapter Eighty-Five

Aiden turned her around, unzipped her pack, and pulled out her headlamp. Maybe if he gave her some light of her own the scared rabbit look would go away. If he had to stare into her vulnerability much longer, he would fall apart from it rather than his own fatigue.

He was careful to turn his own lamp toward the ceiling before he turned her back around. Then he pushed her hood back and pulled the elastic strap over her head.

"The on switch is at the top."

She reached up, but he stilled her hand.

"Don't turn it on when it's positioned straight at someone. You'll blind them." He pushed it up toward the ceiling like his. "Now turn it on."

She did, and a smile as big as Christmas covered her face.

"Never night hiked before?"

"Nope. I've seen these though—on the Discovery Channel. Always wanted one."

She walked around the cave, playing with the light. Aiden spread what would have to pass for dinner on top of a thin blanket then positioned the entire thing near one of the cave walls.

"Madam. Our finest table is ready."

When she turned, she ignored the food and walked straight into his arms.

"Hang on a minute." He unzipped his coat, then unzipped hers and pulled her to him. He wanted her to feel his heartbeat, his warmth. "We're going to make it, Maddie. You'll see."

She nodded as she huddled against him. Inside his coat she seemed incredibly small and defenseless, but he knew she wasn't. She'd proven her strength this afternoon. Actually she'd proven it a dozen times since that rainy night in Dallas. She was the toughest woman he'd ever met. But even tough women needed time to pull themselves together when terrorists with semi-automatics were chasing them up a snow-covered mountain in the dark.

After a minute, she pulled away and swiped at her nose. "I dripped snot on your shirt."

"One of the downfalls of being a maître d'."

"Right," she tried to laugh, but only managed to gulp back a few more tears. "What kind of food do you serve at this restaurant?"

"Only the best. We have energy bars, water, and, well, more energy bars."

"Exactly what I was daydreaming of."

Madison sat on the blanket, reached for a bar, and leaned back against the wall.

"How did you know about this cave?"

"I used to hike this mountain with my dad." Aiden tried to push the memory away, but he was tired of avoiding it, weary from fighting the guilt. "We hiked nearly all of Glacier as I was growing up, but this side was our favorite."

Aiden chose a bar, forced himself to chew, and swallowed.

"Why was it your favorite?"

"More rugged, less tourists. Also, more dangerous. Twenty years ago, the trails weren't as well-defined. Once you did achieve the summits though, the glaciers were an amazing sight to behold, and the wildlife was something else—moose, elk, bear of course. Always the bear.

Aiden picked up a bottle of water, then handed it to Madison. Chose another bottle for himself. Every move caused their lights to create patterns on the ceiling. As Aiden gazed up, it reminded him of the dance of life. Suddenly, sitting there with Madison, he sensed his father's presence. The guilt slid away and the lights hinted at the celebrations of life still to come.

For the first time in a long time, and against the odds he would give them, the lights seemed to promise hope and a future. Isn't that what his mother had talked about, even after the accident? Some verse out of the Old Testament about God promising a hope and a future. He shook his head, but the words remained lodged firmly in his heart.

"What is it, Aiden?" Madison moved closer to him on the blanket so her thigh pressed against his, her head rested against his shoulder. "Are you thinking about the men following us?"

Aiden leaned his head back, pulling her even closer as he slipped his arm around her. "Not really. I was remembering something my mom used to say to me. Can I tell you a story, Maddie?"

"Is it a bedtime story?" she asked sleepily.

"That might depend on whether you like the regular fairy tales or the Grimm Fairy Tales."

Madison circled her arm around his waist. "You're talking to an English teacher. Any story that captures the imagination is a good story, and I love a good story after an excellent meal."

"I was fifteen the last time I climbed this mountain with my dad. We were in the woods you and I just passed through. It was late afternoon, and we were planning on making it to a cave to camp when we came upon a mother bear and her cub—a silvertip grizzly. We'd seen bears before, but never that close. We both knew what to do. You don't make eye contact, try not to threaten the bear in any way, especially when there's a cub involved. Just quietly back away, which we were doing when my dad stepped on a twig."

Aiden paused. His heart rate accelerated as he remembered that day, the bear, and how quickly life is taken.

"She was on him in an instant. I tried to draw my rifle, but it hung up in my pack. By the time I pulled it out, she had collected her cub and was gone. My dad, he was hurt real bad. He could talk, barely, and he had me pull him into this cave." Aiden stopped as he realized Madison was shivering. He rubbed his hands up and down her arms, warming her and warming himself, then continued because he needed to.

"So I did. I made a gurney of sorts. I was such a kid. I knew first aid, or thought I did. But it was my dad. At that age, you think your old man is indestructible, but mine bleeding to death before my eyes. I tried to bandage him, stop the hemorrhaging. I wanted to pull him down the mountain on the gurney, but he insisted I climb up to the ranger station for help."

Madison reached up and wiped away the tears he hadn't realized were falling.

"It was night by then. The bear might have still been out there. I half hoped she was. Wished she would kill me like I knew she had killed him. But she didn't. So I stumbled on to the ranger station. Got help. By the time we made it back, it was the next morning. It was too late."

He paused and took a deep breath. It was the first time he'd talked of that night so many years ago.

"Aiden, I am so sorry. What a terrible thing for a boy to go through."

"I've spent the last seventeen years trying to make up for what happened that night. I know now it wasn't my fault. There was nothing I could have done. A bullet wouldn't have stopped that bear, wouldn't have saved my father's life. But it's taken me a long time to see it."

"So you've been trying to make up for your father's death?"

"I've been running from ghosts." Aiden looked around at the shadows of life dancing on the roof of their cave. "There are no ghosts here, and I'm through running. I'm through running from life. Have I told you I love you?"

She reached up and kissed him tenderly, but he wasn't through confessing. If something happened to him in the morning, and he knew there was at least a fifty-fifty chance something would, she deserved to know the truth about him.

"I wanted to join the military when I graduated from college, but by then my mom was sick. When she died, I thought I was too old. I joined USCIS instead. We're a branch of the US government that tracks international and domestic terrorists."

"You're a spy?"

"Sort of."

"Wait a minute. Is that what you were doing on the plane to Salt Lake?"

"Yeah. I was tracking the man who is chasing us tonight. His name is Coyote, and he's a leader of a group of terrorists. Their current operation is called Dambusters. He's responsible for what happened in Virginia."

Madison scooted a little away from Aiden where she could look directly at him. "Back up a little. When I saw the man step out of the car today, I thought I recognized him. He was on the plane to Salt Lake?"

Aiden nodded and waited for her to remember.

Chapter Eighty-Six

Madison reached for the water bottle and took a long drink. There was something she remembered about that trip. It seemed so long ago. What was lurking at the edge of her memory?

"He sat beside me in the plane."

"Yes. He did."

Madison looked at him curiously. "Why would he do that?"

"We don't know why he sat by you. Terrorists have to sit by someone. Our best guess is you looked innocent. Maybe you were distracted because of your move and the recent death of your mother, so you didn't pay as close attention to the people around you."

"I remember the handle had broken on my suitcase. I was ready to throw the stupid thing when he offered to help me with it. I thought he was such a gentleman."

Madison fiddled with the label on her water bottle. There was something else, beyond the corner of her consciousness, like the tickling of a feather.

"Wasn't there a big storm that night?" she asked.

"Yes."

"And I'm still so afraid of flying after Peru."

Aiden nodded.

"He agreed to change seats so I could be near the aisle. Mancini. His name was Sergio Mancini." She looked at Aiden. "That's not his name though, is it?"

"He goes by many names. Sergio Mancini is one."

"He was such a gentleman. But then he changed. He found something. I don't remember."

Madison stood up and began pacing around the cave.

"He found a button thing on my sweatshirt, and then he turned into this madman."

"The button was a listening device I put on your sweatshirt, Madison. We had to know if he was going to hurt you in any way."

Madison stopped and stared at him. "You what?"

"If we had arrested him then, we would have lost our best contact for the plan to detonate dams in ten American cities. We couldn't risk that happening. We also couldn't let him hurt you. So we had to place a listening device on you to gather information and be sure he didn't plan on hurting you in any way."

Madison walked across the cave and sat cross-legged in front of Aiden. Her voice was barely a whisper as the memories came flooding back.

"He threatened me, then took me in the bathroom and searched me. He said he would kill me, slowly, if I called for help. He said he would blow up the plane. I tried to pull away, but he forced me to take a pill. I don't remember anything until I woke up with this terrible headache and saw—"

"You saw me. I suspected he had drugged you with Mexican Valium. I wanted to kill him with my bare hands, and I still do. Maybe tomorrow I'll have my chance."

"I remember you carrying me through the airport."

"I wouldn't have left you, Madison. Please believe me."

"And then you stayed with me until we reached Kalispell."

She ran out of words as the flood of memories stopped. The

tickle gnawing at the back of her head all day had eased. It was a relief to finally remember.

"I'm sorry I couldn't tell you, sweetheart. In most cases of amnesia, it's better to wait until the person remembers."

She didn't say anything, but continued to stare at him.

"I hope you can forgive me," Aiden said.

She stood and walked back across the cave, thinking of all they'd been through in such a short time. She looked down at the ring on her hand. Finally, she walked back to Aiden and knelt down in front of him.

She placed her hands on his face, pulled his forehead to hers, and whispered, "You are my guardian angel, Aiden Lewis. You've been watching over me since the moment we first met. I want you to catch Coyote or Sergio Mancini or whatever his name is tomorrow. I want you to end what began in Dallas. Then I want us to continue the life we were meant to have together."

She let him hold her then, and there was nothing between them. Their lives had come together completely and although there was still fear there was also the knowledge that they would face whatever the next day brought together. Somehow, it was enough.

Chapter Eighty-Seven

Aiden shook her awake when his watch beeped at 4:00 a.m. "We need to go."

It took her a moment to wipe away the cobwebs. She sat there with a befuddled look as he gave her water and a breakfast bar.

"Sure you can do this?"

A trace of defiance came back into those lovely brown eyes. "Don't even think about leaving me in this cave, cowboy. It's cozy, but it's not that cozy."

Then he had to take a moment and pull her into his arms, feel the warmth and strength of her. "You're an amazing woman, Maddie."

"Maybe that's why I dig amazing men."

Hand in hand they stepped out into the darkness.

Aiden estimated the temperatures to be in the twenties. When they left the warmth of the cave, the first breath of the night air was a painful one. Looking up at the moonless, star-filled sky, it was nearly worth the danger and the cold.

"You don't see those stars in Dallas," Madison whispered as Aiden checked the rope one last time.

"The final ascent will take about two hours. The snowpack is going to be tricky with the temps this low. I assume you've never climbed in ice?"

"I've never climbed."

"I've rigged you a harness, and you're tied to me. You can't fall. Step in my step. Coyote will be expecting us to approach from the north. This will be harder, but we'll have the element of surprise. Unfortunately, we'll have to do it in the dark. We'll use our lamps until we reach the top. I think by then there'll be enough light to switch them off."

Madison nodded. When he looked in her eyes, he saw only trust.

"What's the smile for, cowboy?"

"You're my best girl. What else?"

And then they were climbing into the night. Madison learned quickly how to clip on to his holds and pull up behind him. They climbed close together in the darkness. Aiden decided the lack of light was probably for the best. He was thankful Madison couldn't see the sheer drops beneath them. He remembered them well enough from his childhood. It surprised him how it all came back with such clarity.

His hands found crevices that were still there. His feet reached for footholds that had held hundreds of climbers and would hold hundreds more.

These weren't the trails for tourists or the climbs most guides would take paying customers on. These were the paths locals used, had used for years, and would continue to use. One day Aiden would bring his own son here. The thought caused the breath to catch in his chest as he reached up to find the next hold, and instead his fingers found the ledge. Rather than pulling over the top, he lowered down to Madison.

"What's wrong?" she whispered.

"We're at the top. I want you to switch off your lamp and wait here while I take a look."

Aiden looked down the two-thousand-foot slope they had climbed since yesterday. In the gradual morning light, he could barely make out the Continental Divide and the Many Glacier area. He wanted to tell Madison to turn and look, wanted her to feast on this vision before them.

He didn't want her fainting on the rope though. She had done an amazing thing climbing this in the dark. Where had she found the courage? Maybe there were guardian angels after all. He sure wasn't one, but maybe they did exist.

"Don't look down," he whispered.

Madison didn't need two warnings. She nodded, eyes as big as silver dollars, swinging in her harness and clutching her rope with both hands.

He climbed back up, skimming the top with his night-vision binoculars, looking for a good two minutes more even after he was sure no one was there, then climbing back down to her.

"Looks clear. When you scale the top, I want you to lie down flat while I unclip us. When I tell you to go, run in a low crouch to a cluster of boulders to the west. Clear?"

"Which way is west?"

"To your left." Aiden tried not to smile.

"You are not laughing at me."

"There's an orienteering class in your future, sweetheart."

"I can guess who the instructor is going to be."

"You've got that right." He reached out and touched her face, tucked a strand of hair behind her ear. "Can you do this in the dark? All you have to do is turn left and run. It's a clear field. There's enough starlight for you to see by."

"I'll be fine," she said softly, reaching out to kiss him gently.

Then they were climbing up. He pushed her over the top, prayed the sound of bullets would not pierce the morning air. When he'd joined her he said softly, "Go."

They both ran left, just shadows in the darkness before dawn. No one could have seen them, unless they were watching with night scopes. The cold morning air pierced their lungs, and the sounds of their packs rattling and feet slapping the earth rang out across the top of Mt. Gould.

Aiden pulled her down between two of the rocks.

"Now you can look at the view."

Aiden turned her back toward the direction they had come. The night sky spilled out before them where thousands upon thousands of stars stretched out and fell into an endless chasm.

"We climbed out of that?"

"Yes, we did. I guess you're over your fear of heights."

"It's a little easier when you can't see the fall that will kill you."

"Roger that."

"It's magnificent, Aiden."

He nodded. "It is. The ranger station is half a mile from here. Easy hike."

"No rope necessary?"

"No rope."

They set out at a brisk pace. Ten minutes later the outline of the station rose out of the darkness. Aiden's heart sank as soon as he saw it. No smoke came from the chimney. There wasn't a single light visible from the windows. Quite obviously, no one was home.

Chapter Eighty-Eight

They stopped twenty feet shy of the ranger station in a grove of trees.
"I'm guessing the ranger isn't home."
"Good guess, sweetheart. Luckily, I have a key."
Aiden dropped his pack to the ground, shuffled through it, and removed a set of picks. Then he pulled out a rifle, chambered a round, made sure the safety was off, and handed it to Madison.
"Watch through the night scope. If you see anyone approaching, you shoot. Brace yourself against this rock, steady your arm with your left hand. This is a semi-automatic so it will continue firing as long as you keep pulling the trigger. You have plenty of rounds. Don't worry about running out. You keep shooting until they go down or take cover."
Madison nodded, scared but determined. The rifle felt heavy in her hands, deadly. She remembered the way Coyote had touched her. The memories had been coming back to her all night, all through the climb, and she knew without a doubt she could kill him.
From her stand in the trees, she watched Aiden walk to the back door of the ranger station, drop to his knees, and begin to pick the lock. He'd been there less than fifteen seconds, had

opened the door, and was motioning for her to follow when a tall figure stepped out of the woods behind him.

She stared at the figure approaching Aiden. He had his weapon drawn and was saying something. She watched the scene play out as if it were a video set on slow motion. She couldn't make out the man's words, didn't need to know exactly what he was saying. It didn't really matter. She knew she couldn't shoot this man.

Aiden raised his hands, never glanced her way, no doubt hoped she would shoot or run or hide.

Madison knew she couldn't do any of those things. She'd recognized this man the moment he'd stepped into the crosshairs of her scope. He looked so much like the pictures she'd seen. There wasn't a doubt in her mind.

Even in the darkness of this night, she knew that after all her searching, she'd finally found what she'd come to Montana looking for.

She was looking at John Gibbs.

The man holding a gun on Aiden was her father.

Aiden watched the man in the ranger uniform and prayed Madison wouldn't shoot.

"There's a woman in the woods with a rifle pointed at you. She's scared and tired and might shoot. Lower your weapon before she does something we'll all regret."

The ranger never took his eyes off Aiden.

"I'm afraid I can't do that. Ever think of knocking before you break into a ranger station?"

Sweat trickled down Aiden's back. The man was wisely standing too far back for Aiden to lunge at him. Madison would probably miss if she shot, but the sound would alert Coyote and his men. He'd rather not have a shootout until they had a chance to set up their positions.

"I'm a USCIS agent, and there are terrorists somewhere on the northern slope."

"There are three men camped half a mile below," the ranger confirmed.

"We need to set up a defensive position, and we need to do it quickly. I'm going to turn around and call my girlfriend from the woods."

"No need," Madison said.

Aiden turned in surprise as Madison walked out of the darkness into the light of the ranger's headlamp. She was holding the rifle in her right hand, pointed at the ground. The look on her face was unreadable, and Aiden found himself wondering if the ordeal of the climb and last night's revelations had been too much for her. Perhaps shock had finally set in.

She stopped when she reached his side, never taking her eyes off the ranger.

"Ma'am, I'm going to have to ask you to drop your weapon."

She finally turned to look uncertainly at Aiden. He nodded.

"Go ahead. We need to move inside, so I can show him identification. He can call in and confirm what I'm telling him."

"Won't be calling anyone. Someone cut all our communication and power lines last night, which is why I slipped out early this morning." The ranger moved over to Madison, picked up the rifle she had placed on the ground, and motioned for her to move closer to Aiden. "When I spied your friends on the north slope, I came back. Figured they'd make their way here sooner or later. Why don't we go inside and straighten this out? Both of you do me the favor of keeping your hands in the air until I can confirm you are who you say you are. Ladies first."

Madison walked into the ranger station. Aiden followed, wondering how long they had before Coyote and his men made their move. If they began hiking up the switchbacks at first light, they'd be at their doorstep in another forty-five minutes.

Chapter Eighty-Nine

Madison watched as her father removed all of Aiden's weapons and set them on the desk. He also placed their packs well out of reach.

"Quite an assortment of guns you have here."

"We should be preparing for an attack. Coyote is an international terrorist who is responsible for the devastation that occurred in Virginia."

"Is that so? Now what would he be doing climbing a mountain in Glacier?"

The ranger seemed unfazed as he accepted Aiden's identification and examined it closely.

"I'm an agent for USCIS."

"I believe you said as much outside."

"I've been following Coyote for two years and was involved with dissolving his plan to blow up ten other North American dams."

"Anyone would know that from reading the papers."

"Would anyone know they were also planning to attack the G8 Summit two weeks ago? That plan was stopped by my unit. Yesterday we learned he had eleven ops planned not ten; the eleventh was Virginia. Now he's cleaning up, and that means he's after me, which is why he's on your mountain. You should have received a special bulletin putting the US-Canadian border on its highest alert level from Commander Martin."

The ranger handed Aiden his identification back. "Thank you, Mr. Lewis. No, I suppose only agents and border crossing guards would have that information. Please keep your hands up in the air for me."

Madison choked back the hysteria building in her throat, in her heart, as her father frisked her for weapons.

When she pulled out her driver's license and handed it to him, he looked at the name, paused, and looked at her face. "Knew a Hart once. Sonya Hart from down in Texas. Don't suppose you know her."

"Sonya Hart was my mother."

It was the ranger's turn to look surprised, confused even. "Well now. It's a real small world, isn't it? Sonya Hart is a very special lady. Many times I've wondered what happened to her. We used to write, but she stopped about six months ago."

"Mother died last summer."

"I'm sorry to hear that, real sorry."

The ranger cleared his throat and turned to Aiden.

"I obviously have no way to check out your story. You're asking me to take a defensible position, and I assume, kill a group of climbers who are camped out on my mountain, all on your word. You're asking a lot, son. I want to believe you, I do. But I can't go out there with guns blazing because you tell me to. I would be hard pressed to put my neck on the line for a local boy, let alone one of you federal boys."

Aiden had been staring in frustration out the front window of the ranger station where the sky was beginning to lighten. His head shot up at the words local boy.

"You must not go into town much. I'm from Edgewood."

"Well now, I know there are some Lewis boys from Edgewood."

"Nate is my brother."

The ranger's frown deepened. "Never got to know the boys myself. I did happen to know their father."

"Gus Lewis was my dad. If you knew my dad, then you know he died on this mountain." Aiden walked across the room, hands lowered now. He stopped in front of the ranger. "Most people around here know Gus Lewis died on this mountain—a story that was in all the papers. But the papers never reported the whole story, because I never told it. Only the rangers and my family knew a female grizzly killed him, and I pulled him into a cave on Mt. Gould. Then I climbed up to this ranger station. By the time we got back down to my dad, he had died."

"No. No one else would know those details." The ranger paused, searched his eyes a moment longer, then held out his hand. "Name's Tom Gibbs. Always wanted to meet the young man who was brave enough to climb this mountain in the dark at the age of fifteen. I guess now I have."

Madison watched confusion play across Aiden's face as her father introduced himself. She didn't understand either. The name might be slightly different, but there was no doubt in her mind. The man standing before her was her father. When Aiden raised his eyes to hers, she nodded slowly.

"I guess we should prepare for a shootout at the O.K. Corral if what you say is true." Gibbs moved to his weapons' cabinet, unlocked it, and began removing gear.

"There are three men," Aiden said. "They are heavily armed. What's their exact location?"

Gibbs walked over to a map on the wall. "They were camped out here. Still there thirty minutes ago. If they had left as soon as I did, which I doubt, it would still take them forty-five minutes to come up the face. They don't know this mountain. It'll take them at least an hour."

Aiden looked around the room. "We have a fairly defensible position. Maddie, I want you on the south side, behind the counter. You'll be protected there, but still able to shoot."

"Does she have any experience?"

"No, but she climbed Gould in the dark. She can shoot a terrorist if she has to."

They proceeded to lay out their ammunition and weapons. Twenty minutes later, the shooting began.

Chapter Ninety

When the first bullet penetrated glass, Aiden realized the enormity of their situation. He fully expected to marry Madison when he got off this mountain, which meant the ranger firing beside him would be his father-in-law. The word stuck in his mind.

Father.

He had never thought he'd have one again. Hadn't thought he deserved one. He was not going to lose another on this mountain.

So he sought the ice that had served him well on every other mission. And he couldn't find a single shard of it.

In the freezing cold of this mountain morning, at nearly 10,000-feet elevation, high above Going to the Sun Road, he could no longer hide behind the wall of ice he'd often encased himself in. The dreams had become too real, the emotions too raw. Life in all its pulsing reality was filling the room around him, and there was no blocking it out.

Another window shattered.

"Bad guy at two o'clock," Gibbs muttered.

"I see him. Maddie, keep your head down over there. I don't want you shooting unless one walks right in front of your scope."

Madison let out a squeal when glass near her shattered, then let go with enough semi-automatic fire to send anyone or anything on her side of the building with a lick of sense dodging for cover.

"Think you might have problems teaching that one to listen," Gibbs said.

"So I'm learning."

Aiden stood straight up from his defensible position. He'd seen one of Coyote's men streak west and was betting he'd reappear in his line of sight.

He took the shot as soon as the man appeared, aimed to kill. The way the body kicked, then dropped, told him he succeeded.

"Nice shot," Gibbs said quietly.

"Two more," Aiden replied. He'd turned to reload the rifle when Coyote appeared at the window, much closer than he should be. "Tom, look out."

But it was too late. Coyote took the shot, and Madison's father fell. Blood stained his shirt, seeping onto the floor. Coyote jerked at the same time. Aiden saw him grab his arm, then turn to run.

Aiden knew he had a choice—look after Tom or go for Coyote. His training took over. He exploded out the door of the station, hit the ground rolling, aimed at the feet he saw running, and took the man down in a shower of semi-automatic fire.

He stood in time to see the final man running for the front slope. Aiden trained his rifle on him, took his time with the shot, correcting for speed and the slight morning breeze.

He could hear his father telling him, "Aim high, the bullet will drop a little." Always his father's words in his ear.

"This one's for you, Dad."

Suddenly, he didn't mind feeling again. Even as he saw the man drop and accepted the pain of ending another life, knowing it had to end. Even then, he knew it was better to feel, to hurt, to experience pain and sorrow along with the joy, than to be numb in the cube of ice he had built around himself.

The bullet had found its mark. The man's body lifted slightly, then fell. Aiden walked around to each body, checked for a pulse, assured himself it was over. Only then did he stumble back into the station, where he found Madison kneeling over her father.

"Step back, Maddie. Just a little, sweetie. How is he?" Aiden moved her ever so gently. If the man didn't die from the gunshot wound, he'd die from lack of air.

"How do you feel, Tom?" Aiden was relieved to see an exit wound in the man's shoulder. "Maddie, I need you to bring me the first-aid kit out of my pack."

She nodded and ran for the pack.

"She tells me I'm her daddy," Gibbs said.

"Yes, Sir. I sort of suspected as much. She's been looking for you since she arrived here in August."

"Feels different. Being a dad. I think I kind of like it."

"Guess we better stop this bleeding so you can live long enough to get used to the idea."

"I was shot once before," he confessed. "Gulf War. Didn't feel great then either."

Madison appeared with the first-aid kit.

"Sweetie, I want you over here. Can you help me? We need to cut away this material and stop the bleeding."

"Ok. Yeah. I can help." Her hands were shaking, but she was holding together. Sweet Maddie, always holding herself together.

Tom looked at her, tears standing in his eyes, but not from the pain of the bullet. "Sonya never told me. I feel like such a fool. I should have been there all these years. For you and for her. Not hiding out on this mountain."

"Please don't talk." Madison's tears fell freely as she wiped away his sweat and tears. "Just rest."

"I've been resting all my life. Resting and waiting. Ever since I came back from the Gulf. I should have gone to her then, but I thought she deserved better. Will you forgive me?"

"Of course. Of course, I do." Madison stroked his hand as Aiden continued to lay out what he would need from the kit.

Tom nodded, squeezed her hand, then turned to Aiden. "I

don't hear any more shooting, so I suppose you killed the rest of those men."

"Yes, Sir. Your front yard is strewn with bodies."

"Cecil will be surprised when he comes to relieve me."

Madison and Aiden exchanged glances as Aiden administered a dose of morphine. They proceeded to clean and dress the wound.

"When is Cecil supposed to be here?"

"Cecil? Well, let's see. He should be here any time I guess. Wednesday. He comes on Wednesday. Wow. I had forgotten how great morphine is. They had that in the Gulf too."

"Try to rest now." Aiden looked across at Madison. "I don't want to move him. Find a pillow and a couple of blankets."

They made him as comfortable as possible. Unfortunately, the room was freezing. Coyote had managed to cut the power as well as the communications.

Chapter Ninety-One

Aiden went out to check the backup generator, came back, and reported it had been destroyed in the gunfight. He brought several loads of firewood inside the station. By the time he had a roaring fire going, Madison had pulled out more food rations and water for them. The morphine had done its job, and Gibbs was sleeping.

"What are we going to do?" Madison asked. "It's only Monday. Do we wait for them to notice he hasn't called in?"

"The wound's clean, but he's lost a lot of blood. It could take twenty-four hours for the authorities to figure out he's in trouble up here. It's not unusual for the power to go out because of storms. They won't assume he needs help."

"What about the boys? They'll have told the authorities we started up the mountains."

"True, but honey we could have gone any direction. They'll be searching, but again it'll take time."

"You think we should go for help?"

"I think I should go for help."

"I think you should both go for help."

They both turned to look at Madison's father.

"If you think I can't take care of myself for twenty-four hours, you don't know how tough old rangers can be."

"I hate to leave you here alone, Sir."

"You know the number one rule of hiking."

"No one hikes alone," Aiden and Madison said in unison, then smiled at each other. It was a smile tinged with sadness. They had won this morning, but it had come with a price.

"If you leave now, you can hike down this mountain before dark. Storm's moved on out. They can call a helicopter up here now. You're sure those terrorists didn't have anyone else with them?"

"We didn't see anyone else. The car tailing us only had those three, but we don't know that more weren't behind them."

"Good enough. Leave my weapon within reach. Move me over to the couch where I can watch outside."

"I'll need to cover these windows with plastic," Aiden said. Every window had been shot out, and although the fire was crackling it was still quite cold.

"No time for that," Tom said.

"You're going to be fading in and out, Sir. There is some danger."

"Life is full of danger. I suppose you know that already. Have known since you were fifteen."

"Yes, Sir."

"Let's get on with it then."

They moved him as carefully as possible. Set water and rations near him. Covered him with blankets, and put his weapon and ammunition within reach in case he needed it.

After they had put on their coats and set their packs by the door, Aiden walked over and shook his hand.

"Take care of Maddie. Take care of my daughter. You hear, Agent Lewis?"

"Yes, Sir. I will."

"I'll see you in a few hours." He turned to Maddie then, and she came to him, kneeling beside the couch. "I'm not going to die while you're gone. You mean too much to me. I have a lot to make up for, Madison."

He reached out and touched her face. "You look a lot like Sonya. Your mother would be proud of you."

"I tried so hard to find you." She forced the tears back. If she started crying again she might not stop this time. "I was looking for John Gibbs."

Her father smiled, a genuine smile that suggested better days might be ahead of them. "Guess I didn't introduce myself properly. My full name is Jonathon Thomas Gibbs. When I came back from the war...well, I saw some difficult things there. Did some difficult things."

"I know about the Purple Heart."

"There was that. But there were also Senate hearings, reporters, things I couldn't deal with at the time. I took this job, hid out on this mountain, dropped my first name, and tried to forget all of that. I kept one post office box open in St. Mary's under John Gibbs so I could correspond with your mother. I didn't think anyone else would ever need to find me. I didn't know about you."

Madison nodded and kissed his hand. The important thing was they had found each other. Somehow and against all odds. She wanted to stay right here beside him, but one look at Aiden waiting impatiently near the door and she knew she couldn't. They still had one more job to do.

Chapter Ninety-Two

Then they were gone, hiking down the front of Mt. Gould. It wasn't such a hard hike, nothing requiring a technical knowledge of climbing.

As they worked their way down, Madison couldn't help comparing it to their hike up in the darkness. That had required her to completely put her trust in Aiden. The total darkness had been like her life before she had met him.

As she looked out now, she could see her way, see the trail in front of them. She didn't know exactly what lay ahead, but she knew she could trust the man by her side. He had proven she could believe in him.

She knew, without a doubt, Aiden and her father both loved her very much.

Enough to die for her.

And enough to live for her.

A girl couldn't ask for more. Such was the weight of love. The depth of their feelings reminded her of Mama's quilt on a cool Texas night. She knew then that love was a precious thing, a thing not to be taken lightly. It was a weight worth carrying, up and down a mountain. Up and down the hills of life.

The last three months had taught her to believe in destiny, then to throw herself toward her dreams with everything she had. Once she got off Mt. Gould with Aiden and her father, that was exactly what she planned to do.

Epilogue

Aiden glanced out over the group of friends and family. His brother Nate gave him a thumbs up. Sharon had her arm through Bix's, looking quite pleased with herself. Apparently her parents had grown accustomed to the idea of their daughter dating a renegade musician, or perhaps after the tragedy in Virginia they'd all learned the value of family, of love, of letting the unimportant things go.

Everyone on the golf team was wearing a suit, something Aiden thought he'd never see. They stood together as a group. The trip through Glacier had bonded them into something strong, something that would probably last through the years and the life changes to come.

"Ready?" Martin asked. Who would have thought that his commander had his license to perform weddings. But there it was. Life continued to be full of surprises.

Aiden couldn't have personally ordered a more perfect day—trees budding, a slight breeze cooling the sweat on his neck, sunshine peeking through the surrounding forest. He'd thought Madison might pick a more traditional venue, but it was her idea to hold the wedding on the grounds of his home.

The violinist began to play, Martin stood up even straighter, and Aiden looked up to see Madison appear at the back of the gardens, her arm tucked through her father's, and she looked...she looked resplendent.

She glanced up and the smile didn't settle across her lips until she'd found him, until he'd given her a smile and a nod, assurance that he was all right, that he was waiting at the end of the aisle.

"I'm not sure what she sees in you," Dean murmured.

"That makes two of us."

"But I'm glad you found each other." The teasing left Dean's voice as he suddenly grew serious. "You deserve each other, after what we've all been through."

The country was pulling itself back together.

Aiden had reconsidered his decision to retire.

There was still work to be done, still threats to their national security, but it wasn't work he had to do today.

Today his only job was to begin the rest of his life...with Madison by his side.

The End

Thank you for reading **Coyote's Revenge**. I hope you enjoyed the story. If you did, please consider rating the book or leaving a review at Amazon, Bookbub, or Goodreads.

Continue the Defending America Series with **Roswell's Secret**, Book 2...

National security comes at a price. Dean Dreiser learned that lesson long ago. Now, domestic terrorists are testing a biological weapon in southern New Mexico, and Dean is assigned a new partner—Dr. Lucinda Brown.

Lucy is the leading expert in molecular biology, but she has no field experience. The terrorists are willing to kill thousands in order to trigger the fall of the two-party system and usher in a new political dawn. Lucy tracks the genetic print of the weapon while Dean hunts the insurgents. Separately, they don't stand a change against the terrible secret that dominates the night skies of Roswell, New Mexico. Together, they can do more than survive. They can combat and conquer this frightening threat.

This fast-paced romantic thriller combines a twisting plot, believable characters, and fascinating details about military ops, bio-agents, terrorists, and forensics—all set against the backdrop of the dusty desert land of the Southwest. Be prepared for a read that will keep you up well into the night and an ending that will leave you questioning the true nature of Roswell's Secret.

Keep reading for a preview of book 2, **Roswell's Secret**.

An Excerpt From

Roswell's Secret
Book 2
Defending America Series

Dean Dreiser did not want to start his day viewing a biologically hot, still decomposing body. He preferred stiffs with bullet holes.

He shuffled out of the central command trailer, convinced the biohazard suit he wore had been designed to amplify the desert's heat. It occurred to him he should have taken his dad's offer to help with the family's Brazos River guide business. Why did he think he needed to be a government agent?

If he weren't an agent, he wouldn't be working for U.S. Citizenship and Immigration Services. If he didn't work for USCIS, he wouldn't be in New Mexico at White Sands Missile Range. At forty miles wide and one hundred miles long, it seemed to Dean that God had forsaken this land long before the U.S. government arrived. "This way, Agent Dreiser." The lab doctor took off on a southeast heading, assuming Dean would follow.

The man had to be at least seventy and looked as if he'd been in the desert most of those years. His skin had wrinkled up so that he resembled a prune more than a person. By Dean's calculations, the old guy didn't weigh enough to keep his biohazard suit from floating off the desert floor.

Ten yards away, the good doctor noticed Dean had stopped. He turned with the impatient expression of someone who had important lab experiments to run and demanded, "Is there a problem, Agent?"

They could communicate through a universal intercom system within their suits, a fact that had Dean at a distinct disadvantage. He knew the doc's security clearance, but he did not know the clearance level of every man on this frequency. He'd learned last year what a single security breach could do, and he wouldn't risk it again.

That security breach had come in the form of an agent Dean had met only once—Keith Servensky. A mole inside USCIS, Servensky had nearly killed Dean's best friend and one of their best agents. If someone had checked Servensky's security clearance at every point in the mission, he would have been stopped before he'd done any harm. Instead, he'd pushed his way into operational maneuvers above his level. In the confusion of the moment no one had stopped him. As a result, he was complicit in Operation Dambusters and the killing of thousands in Bath County, Virginia.

Dean wanted his weapon, and he didn't want to state why on an open frequency.

Doctor Kowlson—Dean could see his name sewn on his BHZ suit now that he'd stomped back to join him—raised his left hand, pointed at the blue intercom button, and pushed it. "This opens a direct channel between the two of us. Now, is there a problem, Agent?"

"The problem is my weapon is still in the trailer, and even if I had it, I couldn't very well use it while I'm in this suit."

Doc Kowlson held his gaze for a count of five, then glanced toward heaven as if to pray for mercy. Finally he held up his hands, as if in surrender. He looked to Dean like the Pillsbury Doughboy, hands waving in the morning heat.

AN EXCERPT FROM

Kowlson used his white gloved fingers to enumerate each point, as if the visual would lend credence. "One. You're surrounded by armed military personnel, so one less weapon shouldn't concern you. Two. The threat we face is biological and therefore microscopic. You can't shoot it. Three. It's ninety-eight degrees and rising, and I'd like to finish before it reaches one-hundred-and-ten. If you don't mind."

Without waiting for an answer, the good doctor shuffled off. Dean had never been put in his place by a Doughboy, and he still wanted his Glock on his person where it belonged. But ten years in active operations had taught him some battles cost more than their net worth. The New Mexico sun combined with the two dozen guards holding a ready military stance—and no biohazard suit—confirmed this would be one of them.

Dean took off after the doc. For a little old guy he moved with amazing speed.

They reached the front of the site in ten minutes. The biohazard dome stretched roughly the size of half a professional football stadium and rose out of the desert like some freakish giant jelly fish. All to cover the location of one deceased?

Another twenty military personnel surrounded the side they approached from, including guards posted at the single entrance. Anyone going in passed through an ocular scan first. Dean started to remove his helmet, but the guard stopped him. The lieutenant, a young man who couldn't have seen thirty, placed the scanner over Dean's helmet and waited for the light to blink green.

The site resembled a NASA moon outpost he'd seen in some old science fiction movie. It was easy to forget Albuquerque lay just seventy-five miles to the northwest. Once the scanner confirmed his identity, the guard allowed him to pass. Dean stepped inside the dome, thinking the inside could not be more surprising than the outside. He was wrong. The facility glowed with enough computer and satellite equipment to run a very large, very advanced op.

As if in answer to his unspoken question, Doc Kowlson said,

"All computers respond to voice prompts, since typing in these suits is quite cumbersome. Of course, each computer has to be synced to the operator's vocal nuances. The victim's body is over here."

A smaller tent, approximately twenty feet by twenty feet, sat off to one side. A separate air supply ran from this structure into a filtration system and out of the bigger dome to an area Dean couldn't see.

"Still a hot zone?" Dean asked.

"Yes, and it will remain contaminated for some time. Possibly years."

They stopped outside the smaller tent's entrance, where yet another armed guard stood at attention. This one recognized Kowlson and stepped aside when he approached. Instead of entering, the doctor turned to Dean, held out a hand to prevent him from going any further.

"Do you have any firsthand experience with victims of biological attacks, Agent Dreiser?"

"I've seen plenty of vics, Doc."

Kowlson paused, then nodded. "I'm sure you have. Biological weapons have a way of degrading the body, as you've been taught. It can be disorienting when you witness this. The body has a natural reaction, wants to reject what it sees—often by vomiting. You must fight this response since you're in a biohazard suit. Under no circumstance should you attempt to pull off your hood, or one of the men inside will shoot you with a tranquilizer."

"I appreciate the lecture." Dean shifted in his suit, but never broke eye contact with the doc. "I have a terrorist to catch, so can we get on with this?"

He saw something less cynical appear in Kowlson's eyes, then it vanished like a fleeing shadow. It wasn't a look of doubt—regret maybe. Before he could figure out why the man might have misgivings, they entered the hot zone.

"Push your yellow com button. All communication within this zone must be recorded."

AN EXCERPT FROM

Dean pushed the button. Let the shirts in Langley review his every word from their safe distance. If he did his job well, they'd have that luxury. If he didn't, no doubt Virginia would be on the target list.

Four additional guards stood watch over the victim inside the tent. They stood at rigid attention—their weapons at the ready. Their eyes never met Dean's. They reminded him of the sentries posted at the unknown soldier's grave in Washington D.C.

Even through his suit, he noticed a marked drop in the temperature.

"The colder temperature maintains the integrity of the body," Dr. Kowlson said.

The young woman, if she could still be called that, lay on the floor in the middle of the area. She wore hiking clothes—khaki shorts, a t-shirt, and sturdy boots. The shirt had been sheared up the middle for the preliminary autopsy.

Dean's first sight of the victim told him why Kowlson had felt the need to issue his warning. He'd seen many victims in various stages of dismemberment, but he'd never seen one with most of their skin dissolved.

He swallowed the bile that rose in his throat, kept his hands still at his side. Some lab technician outside would be reading his heart rate. Dean didn't care about that. Anyone who could look at this poor girl and not register an increased heart rate wasn't human.

"Estimated time of death?" Dean forced his voice to sound normal.

"Less than twelve hours ago."

"How is that possible?"

"This agent works quickly, as weaponized forms usually do. I would like to say her death was painless, but my medical opinion is, it was not."

Dean glanced up as new guards replaced the men who had been standing there.

"We rotate guards every seven minutes. We're fully protected

in our suits, of course, but it makes everyone feel better—psychologically—if we rotate the personnel."
"Who found her?"
"Two hikers who were, let's say, lost."
"What will happen to them?"
"That is not my problem, or yours."
Dean willed his feet to step closer to the girl. His skin began to tingle and burn, but he recognized it as a psychosomatic response to what he was seeing. He wanted the expression of horror on her face engraved on his memory. The more he understood of what she had endured, the better chance he had of catching those responsible. And he would catch them.
"Why is only the hair from the front half of her scalp gone?"
"A good question. When she inhaled the bio-agent, it went to work immediately, dissolving the skin around her face. The hair at the front of her scalp lost purchase and fell out. The agent then travelled down the bronchial tube toward her lungs, which is why you see the burn marks down her throat."
"She didn't grab her neck?" Dean squatted beside the body.
"She didn't have time. That would have been a natural reaction to a tickle along the throat. But at the same time her esophagus began to burn, the bio-agent paralyzed all the neurons in her brain. Although she wanted to grasp her neck, her fingers had forgotten how."
"She would have collapsed then."
"Yes, but she wouldn't have been able to crawl or move." The doctor now spoke in a clinical, detached tone.
"She would have been conscious?"
"So our preliminary results indicate."
"For how long?"
"Perhaps ten minutes. No longer. Much of her skin dissolved causing her to sustain a great amount of blood loss. She bled out. That, technically, would be the cause of death. It would have been a very agonizing ten minutes."
Dean had all the information he came for, but he stayed a

AN EXCERPT FROM

moment longer and stared into pale blue eyes that would never again see a New Mexico sunrise.

"Approximate age?" he asked softly.

"Early twenties."

Dean stood and made eye contact with Kowlson who nodded toward the opposite end of the tent.

They exited out a different door, where they passed through three different showers. Dean would have stood through a dozen had he been ordered to—anything to mitigate the burning and itching that had begun in his throat but now had spread to every inch of his body. Then he stripped and stood under two additional showers, dressed, and again submitted to the ocular scan. Stepping into the desert sun, he took a deep, steadying gulp of fresh air.

As an afterthought, he turned back to the guard. "We're being extra careful that the same folks who go in, come out."

The lieutenant—this one a woman and no older than the one at the entrance—didn't bother to reply.

Dr. Kowlson joined him, and they made their way back toward Dean's once red Jeep. A layer of dirt made it nearly indistinguishable from the surrounding desert. Anyone watching would be hard pressed to name the color, or year, for that matter. The Jeep had seen better days, as had Dean.

He could have been imagining it, but the old guy seemed less annoyed.

"You handled yourself well in there," Kowlson said.

"It's my job, sir." Dean held out his hand, shook the doc's, then climbed into his Jeep. "What kind of group creates something able to do that?"

"The worst kind. Ones we haven't had on our soil before."

Dean stared out through his windshield, but made no move to drive away.

"We're sending you the best person we have in bioterrorism," Kowlson said. "She's a genius in the area of bioweaponized agents, and she completed field ops training last month. Her name is Dr. Lucinda Brown. She's better than whoever did this."

"She'll have to be."

Kowlson nodded and stepped back. They both recognized the task facing them was daunting, had both received the same encrypted message from headquarters three hours earlier:

Terror alert critical.
Attack imminent.
Message received and confirmed—
What you will find in the desert is only a taste.
You cannot stop the justice you deserve.
We will strike where you will suffer the most.
We will strike swiftly.
We will strike soon.

While the terrorists hadn't made any demands, they had made themselves clear. According to government analysts, the attack would occur in ten to fourteen days, and the weapon would be dispersed over a minimum of six major metropolitan areas.

No why.

No terms of negotiation.

Only the threat and the proof they could do what they claimed.

Dean started the engine and drove through the makeshift military facility that had been set up around the victim's body—a body found in the middle of a government base. As he drove the sun continued its daily climb, oblivious to the plans of men.

Why New Mexico, why now, and why on his shift? Why had the terrorists even bothered sending the message? It had told them nothing, but had managed to put them on alert. Why would they want to do that? Commander Martin had relayed nothing else. More data would come from the body of the girl. Bodies always gave up their secrets—eventually.

Dean pulled to the side of the road in time to vomit up the

AN EXCERPT FROM

little he'd eaten for breakfast. He grabbed a bottle of water from behind his seat to wash the taste of sour coffee out of his mouth. They'd never shown him corpses with no skin in ops training. He'd battled many terrorists in his ten years, but he'd never dealt with one his trusty Glock couldn't kill.

Leaning against the door, he gazed out over the barren landscape.

Dr. Brown better be as good as her reputation.

USCIS had staked all their lives on it.

Roswell's Secret is available for purchase from Amazon.

Also by Vannetta Chapman

Defending America Series
Coyote's Revenge (Book 1)
Roswell's Secret (Book 2)

Kessler Effect Series
Veil of Mystery (Prequel)
Veil of Anarchy (Book 1)
Veil of Confusion (Book 2)
Veil of Destruction (Book 3)

Allison Quinn Series
Her Solemn Oath
Support and Defend

Standalone Novel
Security Breach

For a Complete List of my Books, visit my
Complete Book List

Contact the Author

Share Your Thoughts With the author:
Your comments will be forwarded to the author when you send them to
vannettachapman@gmail.com.

Submit your review of this book to:
vannettachapman@gmail.com or via the connect/contact button on the author's website at:
VannettaChapman.com.

Sign up for the author's newsletter at:
VannettaChapman.com.

Made in the USA
Las Vegas, NV
10 December 2023